The Belly Dancer

The Belly Dancer

DeAnna Cameron

BERKLEY BOOKS, NEW YORK

THE BERKLEY PUBLISHING GROUP
Published by the Penguin Group
Penguin Group (USA) Inc.
375 Hudson Street, New York, New York 10014, USA
Penguin Group (Canada), 90 Eglinton Avenue East, Suite 700, Toronto, Ontario M4P 2Y3, Canada
(a division of Pearson Penguin Canada Inc.)
Penguin Books Ltd., 80 Strand, London WC2R 0RL, England
Penguin Group Ireland, 25 St. Stephen's Green, Dublin 2, Ireland (a division of Penguin Books Ltd.)
Penguin Group (Australia), 250 Camberwell Road, Camberwell, Victoria 3124, Australia
(a division of Pearson Australia Group Pty. Ltd.)
Penguin Books India Pvt. Ltd., 11 Community Centre, Panchsheel Park, New Delhi—110 017, India
Penguin Group (NZ), 67 Apollo Drive, Rosedale, North Shore 0632, New Zealand
(a division of Pearson New Zealand Ltd.)
Penguin Books (South Africa) (Pty.) Ltd., 24 Sturdee Avenue, Rosebank, Johannesburg 2196,
South Africa

Penguin Books Ltd., Registered Offices: 80 Strand, London WC2R 0RL, England

This is an original publication of The Berkley Publishing Group.

This is a work of fiction. Names, characters, places, and incidents either are the product of the author's imagination or are used fictitiously, and any resemblance to actual persons, living or dead, business establishments, events, or locales is entirely coincidental. The publisher does not have any control over and does not assume any responsibility for author or third-party websites or their content.

PRINTING HISTORY
Berkley trade paperback edition / July 2009

Library of Congress Cataloging-in-Publication Data

Cameron, DeAnna.
    The belly dancer / DeAnna Cameron.—Berkley trade pbk. ed.
        p. cm.
    ISBN 978-0-425-22778-7
    1. World's Columbian Exposition (1893 : Chicago, Ill.)—Fiction.   2. Belly dance—Fiction.
3. Belly dancers—Fiction.   4. Young women—Fiction.   5. Upper class—Fiction.   6. Family
secrets—Fiction.   7. Self-actualization (Psychology)—Fiction.   I. Title.
    PS3603.A4495B45 2009
    813'.6—dc22

                                                                                        2009010395

PRINTED IN THE UNITED STATES OF AMERICA

10   9   8   7   6   5   4   3   2   1

This book is dedicated to women
who love to belly dance,
whether it's on a stage, in a classroom,
or alone in a room with the curtains pulled closed

One

CHICAGO, 1893

Dora Chambers entered the Egyptian Theatre behind the crowd of gritty laborers and pale office clerks, the older gentlemen and boys barely of an age to shave. The masculine scents of their hair pomade and Ivory-soaped skin mingled with the fragrance of the tendrils of smoke curling from brass burners set along the stage. She raised her handkerchief to her nose.

"Are you sure you're up to this, dear?" Agnes Richmond placed a grandmotherly hand on Dora's shoulder and leaned closer to be heard over the high-pitched whine of a horn.

"Of course she's up to it," muttered Geraldine Forrest as the three settled along the back of the standing room gallery behind the rows of filled seats. She brushed at the sleeves of her tailored wool jacket and, for the third time since they'd arrived, adjusted the wide-brimmed hat sitting atop her sweep of golden hair. "I'm sure she'd do anything to keep her new husband happy."

"Yes, of course," the older woman said. "You must have felt exactly the same about Mr. Forrest, God rest his soul." She took

Dora's gloved hands in her own. "It doesn't appear those women intend to follow through with their threat after all. It's quite a relief, really. I understand their concern, but frankly, the Columbian Exposition hardly needs the trouble."

A commotion at the entrance interrupted her, and the shoulder-to-shoulder crowd in the cavernous hall pressed back, nearly sweeping Dora off her feet. When she righted herself, a stream of women in black wool frocks and simple hats had cleaved its way down the main aisle and toward the stage. Each held a sign in her grip with letters still dripping with wet paint: "Send the foreign filth home," "Propriety before profits," and "Close the belly dance theater now." Their shouting drowned out the music until it stopped altogether.

"Move back, dear, out of the way now." Mrs. Richmond urged Dora toward the rear of the gallery, though everyone around them pushed toward the door.

Dora followed instructions, and huddled with Mrs. Richmond and Mrs. Forrest at the back of the emptying theater. Perspiration dampened Dora's forehead and two droplets slid down the crevice of her back where the corset was pulled the tightest. She dabbed at the trickle but couldn't reach it through the layers of linen and whalebone, cotton and wool.

On the stage, she saw several dancers huddled together as well.

"That's enough, that's enough now. Clear out." A uniformed man pushed his way inside and was waving his hands over his head in a call for order. Behind him stood another dozen uniformed men, poised to act.

"We won't leave until this den of vice is closed down," cried a dour, elderly woman who emerged from the pack to stare down the officer. "We will not allow it to defile our city any longer!"

"You've been warned, madam. We'll arrest anyone who disrupts this theater's lawful operation."

"Is it lawful for these women to flaunt themselves in this vulgar manner? Is it lawful for these men to witness this obscene display?" The woman adjusted the glasses on her nose in a way that made her look down on the officer though he towered over her.

"Not for me to say, ma'am. Grievances should be taken up with the Fair directors. Now, you and your sisters here have two minutes to disperse." He made a show of pulling out his pocket watch and checking its face.

The grim-faced woman turned to the stage, where the dancers still stood against the back wall. "You have not heard the last of this," she hollered. "We will rid this Fair of your filth." Then she turned and with a swipe of her hand signaled her fellow protesters to follow her out.

The officers followed behind, leaving only the performers, Dora, Mrs. Richmond, and Mrs. Forrest.

"That was the Society for the Suppression of Vice?" Dora asked, tucking a stray strand of her black hair behind her ear beneath her straw boater and gripping her parasol more tightly, still unaccustomed to its constant presence. "It's just a group of ladies. What harm could they possibly do?"

"Never underestimate a group of ladies, my dear," Mrs. Richmond admonished. "Take our Board of Lady Managers. The directors themselves put their trust in us to sort out this mess, and I for one am proud to say it is our Lady Managers' privilege to contribute to the Fair's success. Remember, if this World's Fair succeeds, Chicago succeeds. The opportunities will be endless."

"Chicago is full of opportunities, isn't it?" Dora liked the sound of it. It's what Charles had said on their wedding day two months ago in New Orleans, when she'd packed her dresses and twenty years of memories into a steamer trunk, ready to start a new life eight hundred miles away. "The past is irrelevant in Chicago," he'd whispered in her ear as they stood at the steamship bow, waving to strangers and feeling the rumble of the engine choke smoke into the sky as it prepared to leave the only home she'd ever known.

Mrs. Forrest craned her neck to see out the open door. "I'm sure I just saw Mrs. Sheffield and Mrs. Loomis."

"Where, dear?" Mrs. Richmond searched in the same direction. "I should say hello."

"I'm sure that isn't necessary." Mrs. Forrest smiled demurely. "Let me convey your tidings for you. You and Mrs. Chambers don't really require my assistance here, do you?"

"Of course not. I'm sure Mrs. Chambers and I can manage; there's no reason we all must endure this dreadful business."

"I knew you'd understand." The woman air-kissed Mrs. Richmond, ignored Dora, and made her way down the crowded aisle.

Dora noted the snub as she watched the woman leave. She leaned in to Mrs. Richmond. "Have I offended her?"

"Don't mind Mrs. Forrest. It takes her a while to warm up to new people. I was surprised she asked to join us. It really isn't like her." She pulled up the timepiece that hung from a chain around her neck. "The next performance will be getting under way soon, but I want to have a few words with the Egyptians first." She looked around the theater. "That must be the manager," she said, pointing to a man walking toward them from the door.

He was tall, with broad shoulders, a lean waist, and blue-black hair that fell in thick waves to his shoulders like a soft shroud against the hard angles of his cheeks. Dora guessed he was Egyptian, for he wore the typical white tunic over narrow pants and had the same bronze skin as the performers on the stage. He regarded her with eyes like polished obsidian stones.

"You must be Mr. Hossam Farouk, the man in charge here?" Mrs. Richmond stiffly extended her hand in greeting and introduced herself, emphasizing her title as vice president of the Board of Lady Managers.

"I am Hossam Farouk," he replied. He took the proffered hand and lifted it to his lips. "But I would hesitate to say I am in charge." His accent made the words sound like a song.

"Surely you're being modest. Mr. Sol Bloom himself has told me you're the man to see. I'm sure you're familiar with Mr. Bloom?"

"By reputation." He crossed his strong arms over his chest and stretched his six-foot frame to its full height.

Who in Chicago didn't know Sol Bloom by reputation? Even Dora had read stories of the young entrepreneur from San Francisco. He'd been recruited by the Fair's directors to turn the Midway Plaisance from what had been conceived as a collection of anthropological exhibits into a carnival of profitable amusements to help recoup the Fair's staggering building costs. The games, the rides, the animals, the alehouses, even the dancers were added largely by his orchestration. Some claimed he even coined the name "belly dancers" to titillate the public and sell more tickets.

"In light of today's events, we were hoping we might have a word with the dancers, if that's convenient," Mrs. Richmond said.

He bowed. "We are always willing to accommodate Lady Managers." His chin lifted to a proud angle. "Please, excuse me, and I will see what I can do."

He went to the stage and the dancers, who had been watching the conference, and they quickly gathered around him. They exchanged words and flashed quick glances at Dora and Mrs. Richmond. The one who had been performing just before the interruption took a step back and folded her arms over her chest. She was the smallest of the troupe, but carried herself with a confidence that contradicted her size. She shook her head and the other dancers did the same. The man rubbed his face with his palm, shot another glance at Dora and Mrs. Richmond, and continued his speech.

"I'd say Mr. Farouk might be right; that little one looks like the boss around here," Mrs. Richmond said under her breath. "A spitfire, for sure."

The small dancer inclined her head and relaxed her stance. She turned to the others, said something, and they all nodded. Then all those dark eyes turned toward Dora and Mrs. Richmond.

When they neared, it was the little dancer who spoke first. "You have something to say to us?"

These performers were known by so many names: belly dancers, muscle dancers, posture dancers, dancing girls. Dora had seen them in newspaper etchings alongside stories about the shows, but the images hardly captured the exotic women in front of her. The one who spoke—she couldn't have been any older than Dora's own twenty years—was outfitted in a short crimson vest that stretched taut across her bosom and left her abdomen uncovered, except by a blouse that fit snug as a stocking and exposed her collarbone and too much of her upper limbs. She clearly wore no corset, which alone could cause a scandal. Her skirt lacked proper length, revealing far more of her bow-tipped slippers than the rules of modesty should allow. The other adornments—a belt of tassel-tipped ribbons dangling to her knees, a profusion of beads and stringed coins roped about her chest, coils of metal bracelets wrapped around her wrists, even the loose dark hair hanging down her back—hardly concealed any more of her form. The other dancers wore similar costumes of varying colors—cobalt, marigold, persimmon, and plum.

And like Mr. Farouk, this little dancer spoke English with an accent that gave her speech a rhythm nearly as exotic as their desert music.

Mrs. Richmond jutted her chin. "If it is convenient."

The dancer shrugged.

Dora gaped. These dancers surely had no idea who the Lady Managers were.

"We won't keep you long, Miss . . . " Mrs. Richmond said. A swollen blood vessel cut an angry path along her temple.

"My name is Amina Mahomet," the dancer replied. "Shall we sit?"

Mrs. Richmond scanned the uneven rows of empty wooden chairs. In the haste to leave, the audience had left behind discarded tickets, crumpled programs, and stray kernels of molasses-covered popcorn that no one seemed inclined to retrieve. "This will not take long."

The dancer went to a chair she turned to face Mrs. Richmond, stepped out of her low-heeled slippers, and sat. A handful of the others did the same; the rest moved to stand behind them. Mr. Farouk receded to the background, watching but no longer taking part. He stood by, more like a guard than a manager.

Dora couldn't help but stare at him—and when she noticed that he was watching her, she glanced away and forced herself not to look in his direction again.

Mrs. Richmond, however, paid no attention to the man. She focused on the unladylike display in front of her. The seated women hunched forward or propped their feet on adjacent chairs. Those who stood thrust out their hips to the side or leaned on the backs of chairs.

"It pains me to be the bearer of bad news," Mrs. Richmond said at last, when it was clear no one else would begin the conversation, "but the Fair directors have requested the Lady Managers' assistance with this matter of the protesters. They find it quite disturbing."

Amina pulled a foot up to her lap and massaged the arch.

"When you arrived," Mrs. Richmond continued, "we discussed expectations. Do you recall that conversation?"

Nothing but blank stares on the dancers' faces.

"Any of you?" The strain in Mrs. Richmond's voice raised it an octave, maybe two.

"The others speak almost no English," Amina said. "You may direct your questions to me."

"Then do you recall that conversation?"

Amina lifted her shoulders in assent.

Mrs. Richmond touched the bulging blood vessel at her temple. Her lips twitched. "We discussed proper conduct and attire. So I am disappointed to learn our guidelines have been ignored." She met Amina's gaze squarely. "This cannot continue. The directors have instructed us to resolve the situation, as we are best suited to deal with such sensitive, feminine issues."

"What of the other dancers?" Amina took one of the ribbons hanging from her waist and ran her finger down its length. "There are many along the Midway: the handkerchief dancers at the Algerian Theatre, the Jerusalem woman who dances with a dagger in the Moorish Palace, the Ouled Nail women in all their veils and silver jewelry who stand and tremble on the Turkish Village stage."

A new bloom of rage spread over Mrs. Richmond's face. "The protesters cite the Egyptian dancers as their concern."

Amina crossed her arms.

"It is my hope," Mrs. Richmond continued, "and I hope it is yours as well, that we can remedy this situation ourselves. If we cannot, I will be forced to tell the directors you will not cooperate."

Amina's glance slid from Mrs. Richmond to Dora, and made Dora shift uneasily.

"I do not presume to know the directors' minds," Mrs. Richmond added, "but I would expect the consequences to be severe. Perhaps a fine, but I'm sure a complete forfeiture of the troupe's wages might also be considered."

Amina's jaw twitched. She studied the floor beneath her as if reading a secret language in the swirls and knots of the wood's grain. "At our last meeting, you said we should not allow our virtue to be compromised. I can assure you, we have not."

Mrs. Richmond's fists clenched at her sides. Dora studied a bare wall.

"Then you deny the existence of any impropriety?" The older woman's voice sounded shrill and thin.

"What impropriety could there be? It is only a dance."

"It is a matter of common decency," Mrs. Richmond stammered.

"Are you referring to your decency or mine?"

Mrs. Richmond ignored the challenge. "As you do not even see fit to wear proper undergarments, I must insist that you choose your outer clothing more wisely."

Amina glanced down at her stomach and to the folds of her crimson skirt. "Now you want to punish us because we do not wear corsets?"

Mrs. Richmond pressed her temple again. "Young lady, please consider this a warning. From this point forward, you and the other dancers must cover yourselves more appropriately. Veils and something more substantial than what you are wearing today would be a good start. Lewd and salacious movements also will constitute a breach. And to be sure these rules are enforced, Mrs. Chambers"—she glanced at Dora—"is, as of this moment, appointed board liaison to this establishment. If there are any violations, she will report them directly to me."

Dora stared in horror at Amina and the other dancers. A liaison? She couldn't return to this wretched theater. It was no place for a proper lady, and especially not one trying to establish her place on the Board of Lady Managers. Her cheeks burned and her heart raced.

"Mrs. Chambers?" Mrs. Richmond turned to her, a pleading look in her eyes. "You can begin your duties promptly?"

Dora choked out a "Yes, of course."

Mrs. Richmond turned a steely gaze on Amina. "Please be sure to share with your colleagues what we have discussed and what has been agreed. And just so we are clear, the Board of Lady Managers has assured the Fair directors that this nonsense will stop. One way or another." Then, in a swish of skirts and petticoats, she turned and marched toward the door.

Dora stood paralyzed. This wasn't happening. Surely there must be someone else for the job. And why was this little dancer looking at her that way?

Amina had risen when Mrs. Richmond departed and was now staring at Dora. She cocked her head to the side. "You're not like the other Lady Manager, are you?" Her voice was calm, far too calm for someone who had just argued with one of the most powerful women in Chicago.

Dora clutched the lace at her throat. "I am a Lady Manager," she stammered, and hurried to the door.

*   *   *

*O*utside, the afternoon sun hit Dora's eyes like a blinding light. She opened her parasol to shade herself against the burning rays, and searched the busy, brick-paved square for Mrs. Richmond. She scanned the faces of the passersby, a tapestry of derbies, bowlers, and feathered hats on the visitors, and the turbans and shawl-covered heads on the umber-colored Egyptians brought to live in this Middle Eastern quarter as if it were a living, breathing village, not just a facsimile re-created for the Fair.

"Hello, Mrs. Chambers. Yoo-hoo, over here."

Dora followed the direction of the voice and found Mrs. Richmond standing in the shade of the theater's western wall, a few paces from the line of men queued for the next performance.

"What an ordeal," Mrs. Richmond said when Dora joined her. She smoothed her wide leg-of-mutton sleeves and adjusted the flounces of her bustle. "I'm sorry you had to see me lose my temper in there, but that girl, oh, that girl was exasperating to say the least." She shot a glance at Dora. "I hope you aren't worried about the liaison assignment, dear. I didn't think such a measure would be necessary, but you saw for yourself how difficult they were."

Dora planted her parasol on its tip in front of her. This was her chance. "I'm honored you've entrusted me with such an important task, I'm just not sure—"

"I know what you're going to say." Mrs. Richmond gave her a sheepish smile. "You're new to our board and you think you haven't yet earned the right for such a significant assignment? Hogwash, I say. This is the perfect opportunity to show everyone what I already know: You are clearly Lady Manager material."

Dora let the rest of her argument die on her tongue.

"You needn't worry about a thing, dear. I'll make sure you have a partner. We'll make the arrangements at our next board meeting. I already have someone in mind."

Dora thought of Mrs. Forrest. To be matched with a woman like that, to be her equal? The prospect thrilled her.

Mrs. Richmond ran her fingertips along the brim of her hat and straightened. "I really should be getting back to the house, though, to see about dinner before Archibald gets home. Shall we go?" She hooked her arm through Dora's and set off for the gate.

Behind her, the mournful sound of that strange horn rose over the din of voices and clopping hooves in the square, signaling the start of the belly dancers' next performance. Dora rested her parasol on her shoulder and fell into step beside Mrs. Richmond.

They found the carriage where they'd left it outside the Cairo Street gate, the horse hitched to a post along the street.

Soon they reached the Tudor-style mansion Dora now called home. When the carriage turned the corner, she could see it set back from the street by its ribbon of green lawn, flanked by an Edwardian-style manor on one side and a red-brick estate on the other. She still wanted to pinch herself each time she saw it. When Charles told her the neighborhood was called the Gold Coast, she'd expected it to be nice, respectable. It was so much more. The neighborhood earned its name after local real-estate baron Potter Palmer built a castle of a home for his family on Lake Shore Drive. With the soot and noise of the railroads and the expanding vice district encroaching on the affluent residences along Prairie Avenue, other wealthy families soon followed.

Charles's father had the wisdom to be one of the first to join the migration. He built a house that was not the largest or the grandest, but it wasn't the smallest, either. And it was completely and utterly a home. Never again would she have to tiptoe through the corridors like she had in New Orleans so she didn't disturb lodgers or give up her place in the sitting room when the seats filled up.

Mrs. Richmond jerked the reins and brought the horse to a stop at the home's front walk. "You've been so quiet, dear. I hope you aren't worrying about that Egyptian Theatre business."

The belly dancers. They'd slipped her mind completely.

"You'll be fine. We'll talk more of it soon."

"I'm sure you're right," she said, and lowered herself to the ground, "and I'm happy to do whatever I can to help." She tried to mean it.

Mrs. Richmond snapped the reins. The horse whinnied and lurched forward. "Farewell; please give Mr. Chambers my regards."

Dora waved and watched the carriage disappear down the street.

Her first day as a Lady Manager and she'd performed pretty well. She walked up the dirt ruts that the carriage wheels had carved into the grass alongside the house and stopped at the bougainvillea she'd planted against the northern wall. The purple-leaf bushes grew like weeds around the courtyard of Mama's hotel, and when it came time to leave, she'd wrapped seeds in a towel and stowed them in her luggage. The first time Dora saw that sad and empty brick wall, she knew it would be the perfect backdrop for those bright and happy petals. It had taken a month for shoots to break through the soil, and now two had grown a few inches and had the beginnings of a dozen tiny leaves. She gathered her skirts and bent to check the shoots' strength.

"A fellow green thumb, I see."

Dora shot up and nearly toppled over.

The man grabbed her arm to steady her. "I didn't mean

to startle you, Mrs. Chambers. Thought you might need some assistance."

"Dr. Bostwick. How nice to see you." She brushed a tendril of hair off her cheek.

"Nice of you to say so after I gave you such a scare," he said. "I was just looking in on my roses, you see"—he shot a glance at the row of white rosebushes along the front of his house—"and I thought I'd be neighborly."

"I was tending. Two nice bougainvillea sprouts, wouldn't you agree?"

He adjusted the wire-rimmed glasses resting on his nose. "Bougainvillea? I'm not familiar with the species. Is it foreign?

She stared at her sprouts. "I don't think so. It flourishes in New Orleans."

"I'm sure it'll be fine," he added quickly. "If you have any trouble, I'm always happy to do what I can to help, so don't hesitate to ask."

Dora thanked him, bade him a good afternoon, and patted the earth around her sprouts a final time before going to the back door that opened onto the kitchen. She knew Bonmarie would be there. She breathed in the warm onion and garlic smell of a hen simmering on the stove. At the counter, Bonmarie sliced a carrot into coins.

"Look who it is. Little Miss Lady Manager. Don't those fancy ladies tell you back doors are for common folks?" Bonmarie's low rumble of a laugh reminded Dora of being in Mama's kitchen. Bonmarie was always laughing about something, sending ripples through her chocolate-colored flesh until it jostled like a choppy sea.

"Doors are doors. Why should it matter which I use?" Dora nabbed a piece of carrot from the pile and tossed it into her mouth.

"Well, that is the truth, *ma chere*. Did those rich ladies have anything—" Her gaze locked on Dora's face. "Isadora Bernice, what have you been doing? Come over here."

Reluctantly, Dora obeyed. What had she done?

Bonmarie grabbed her and pulled her close, took a small towel, dabbed it with her tongue and swiped at Dora's cheek. "Black smudges all over yourself." She took Dora's hands and shook her head. "Look at this. Goodness gracious, take those gloves off and leave them for washing."

Dora cringed. She'd forgotten to remove her gloves before tending to the bougainvillea. How ridiculous she must've looked to Dr. Bostwick.

"That man of yours will have a conniption if he sees you like this, so clean up good."

She removed the gloves and washed her hands, then checked her blouse and her skirt. The skirt had a spot at her knee. "Charles won't see anything; he's not even home yet."

"Oh, he's home. Been home nearly an hour."

Dora's heart jumped into her throat.

"He's in the study," Bonmarie said. "If you ask me, it's not right to coop yourself up like he does in that study. Not enough fresh air, that's his problem." She paused and her lips pursed like they did when she wanted to say something Dora wouldn't want to hear.

"I should go see him," Dora said before Bonmarie could speak. She leaned over the counter, snatched another piece of carrot, and went to the door.

"You know you should be more careful when you go out," Bonmarie called after Dora. "This isn't New Orleans."

Dora ignored her and walked into the hall.

* * *

*T*hat girl. Lord, what was she going to do with that girl? Bonmarie took three more carrots from the bunch, ripped off their greens, and lined them up nicely on the cutting board, straight and narrow like three skinny little soldiers. When was Dora going to realize this was a different world? Everything was different here, but still she traipsed around like she was safe behind the walls of her mama's hotel. She never did appreciate how good she had it, always thinking she was above the guest business, even when she was little. But that was her mama's fault, wasn't it? Charlotte Devereaux should have known better than to put those ideas into the girl's head.

This man of hers was trouble, too. She knew it the moment she laid eyes on that Mister High-and-Mighty Charles Chambers. Refused to eat her food that first night. Too spicy, he'd complained. Instead, he'd gorged himself on plain bread and butter. Mrs. Devereaux had charmed a promise out of him to give them another chance and then begged Bonmarie to prepare his meals separate, without any seasoning. Imagine, food with no peppers, no salt? But she'd given in and that was her mistake. She should have dumped every spice in her cupboard into that meal and been rid of him long ago.

It still bothered her that she hadn't seen his marriage proposal coming. He'd visited the Devereaux Hotel a few times a year for three years and never paid Dora any mind. She was still in short dresses in the beginning, but she'd grown into a striking young lady right before his eyes. Yet even when Mrs. Devereaux tried to push them together, he'd dodged her matchmaking games like someone with other intentions. He was well past the age most men settled into family life, but he never acted like any of the other bachelors who visited the hotel.

Maybe she was too suspicious for her own good, but it seemed strange that it all dawned on him that last time he'd come to the hotel. Couldn't take his eyes off Dora, refused to leave her side even for a minute. After just two days of courting he'd asked her mama's permission to marry her, as if those three years of nothing never even happened.

Mrs. Devereaux called it the answer to her prayers. Maybe it was. In New Orleans, the past never lets go and it never lets you forget. She'd wanted so badly to get Dora away from New Orleans, where it wouldn't matter what the girl overheard on the street or what she saw in the faces of her neighbors. And Dora had started to ask questions.

Then came Chicago and all the promises. Now Dora thought this fancy new husband of hers was the answer to everything, him and those fancy ladies with their fancy titles and uppity ways. Bonmarie held her soldiers with one hand and forced the knife through them with the other.

Why did that girl have to aim so high? These people were different. They liked their own kind. She saw the way they looked Dora over with shadows of doubt in their eyes. They just better be good to her little girl.

She tossed the carrot coins into the bowl and grabbed another handful from the bunch.

*D*ora paused when she reached the hall. Why did Bonmarie have to start harping on her, too? It was just a little dirt. She wore the dresses Charles wanted her to wear, and did her hair the way he said she should. She used her best manners when she went out. She was doing everything the way the fashionable ladies did, just the way he wanted.

But maybe Bonmarie was right. Charles would be angry if he saw her like this. "A lady should always look like a lady," he'd say. She made sure a fold hid the spot on her dress, but maybe she should run upstairs and change, just to be safe.

"Dora, are you there?" Charles's voice sounded hollow through the walls. "Come in here, please."

She sighed; she couldn't put him off now. She checked the fold again and went to the closed door. She opened it and leaned in. "I didn't expect you home so early."

"Come in and close the door, please." He was sitting behind the mahogany desk that filled most of the wood-paneled room, leaning back in his oxblood leather chair with the evening *Tribune* spread before him. He was still dressed in the twill coat he'd worn when he left for his office at the bank, and a stiff white shirt with a tall collar. His dark beard was spotted with gray and dropped like fuzzy pork chops over his jaw. The black ends of his bow tie lay loose around his neck.

She entered the room just enough to close the door behind her.

His hazel eyes pinned her like a bug on a board. "Where did you go?" His voice was low and measured, the tone he used when he was particularly upset and didn't want the servants to overhear. He lifted a cigar smoldering in a crystal ashtray at his elbow and rested it on his lips.

Her pulse throbbed in her ears. What had she done this time? "Mrs. Richmond sent a messenger this morning after you left. She wanted me to join her at the fairgrounds."

His frown deepened; she moved to the news that would cheer

him. "The Lady Managers gave me an assignment. Aren't you pleased?"

"Is it too much to ask that you be here when I return in the evenings?" He tapped the cigar's ash into the ashtray. "Isn't that what wives are supposed to do?"

"I intended to be. It's just that I didn't know you'd be home early. You should've said something."

His eyes snapped up. "So I'm at fault?"

Why was he angry when he should be pleased? The Lady Managers had been his idea; he wanted her to make the right friends. How many times had he said a woman's place in society must match her husband's place in business? She wanted to remind him of that now, but instead she forced a smile and walked around to the back of his chair. She placed a gentle hand on his shoulder. "I know you want me to be home when you're here, dear. I only thought it would be what you wanted, to win Mrs. Richmond's favor."

She could feel him soften beneath her fingers as she stared down on the thin spot in his hair. "What sort of wife to a future bank president would I be if I don't do my best to fit in?"

He covered her hand at his shoulder with his own. "Bank president, well, that might be overreaching a bit. Vice president, that would be respectable enough." His voice was calmer. "But I also want you home when a woman should be home. Otherwise people might get the impression you've tired of your old husband already." He mustered a sheepish grin that made him look almost boyish.

"Forty is hardly old." She ran her fingers lightly along the sweep of his slicked hair and kissed his cheek. "A man comes into his prime when he's forty." The anger was draining from him; she could feel it. "You must be hungry. Shall I check on dinner?"

Charles's glance lingered on her, then he turned back to his newspaper. "Yes, see what your cook is up to, and tell her no more of those damned peppers. I want to be able to digest my food tonight. Tell her if she ruins my meal one more time, I'm sending her back to your mother."

Dora gave his shoulder a squeeze and pulled away. "Yes, dear, I'll tell her."

She left his study but she had no intention of going to the kitchen. She wouldn't pass along his threat because he would never send Bonmarie back to New Orleans. Dora's heart had broken when the woman told her she wouldn't join her in Chicago. It was the only part of leaving home that had made her cry. Thank goodness she'd changed her mind. On the day they were to leave, a few hours after the wedding ceremony in the hotel's courtyard, she and Charles were saying their good-byes and Bonmarie had appeared with a carpetbag and her one and only hat, a small black thing with a veil that sat crooked on her head. She never told Dora why she'd changed her mind, and Dora was too grateful to ask.

Going up the stairs to her room, Dora wondered again what could have made Bonmarie reverse course so suddenly that day. But she didn't want to think about the past. It didn't matter anymore. Everything was better now. For the first time she was happy, too happy to worry about belly dancers and scandals, or even Lady Managers.

Two

Charles pushed back his dinner plate, the lamb shank, braised carrots, and potatoes hardly touched, and folded his napkin into a perfect square beside it. "You won't mind if I don't join you in the drawing room this evening, will you? I have work to finish in the study."

He rose and patted Dora's shoulder as he passed. When he paused to align one of the dozen high-back chairs set around the rosewood table that filled the length of the room, she considered protesting. He'd eaten in silence, and now she faced an evening with only her embroidery and women's magazines for company. She bit back the complaint. Saying anything would only trigger another lecture on how hard a man must work to provide the luxuries women take for granted.

"Of course, dear," she said. She poked at the last bites on her plate and consoled herself with the certainty that invitations would come soon enough. Charles had assured her that Lady Managers attend the best dinner parties and salons, music recitals and balls, she just had to be patient.

If only patience required less effort. The visit to the Fair and the ordeal at the Egyptian Theatre had left her weary. Playing the part of a Lady Manager could be so exhausting: The constant thinking of the right thing to say (clear "yes" and "no," not "uh-huh" and "uh-uh") and the right thing to do (never scratch beneath your corset no matter how terrible the itch). The right way to hold one's hands (palms always down), and the right way to nod (slowly so you don't loosen your hat or the pinned-up curls). All so draining.

But she played the part well enough. No one could guess she wasn't born to this life. And in Chicago she'd never hear the whispers that followed her in the French Quarter. *That poor Devereaux girl. Such a shame. Not a surprise her mother hides her away.*

Mama told her to ignore the things people say, that she did her schooling at home because she refused to lose anyone else to yellow fever. The disease had taken Mama's parents and her sisters, and the lives of so many others in New Orleans during the steamy summer of 1878.

Mama said that was the reason she didn't allow Dora to leave the house, except to accompany Bonmarie to the market now and then. But even on those rare occasions, Dora had heard enough whispers to learn a few things Mama hadn't told her. Things like how Mama's father lost the family fortune when a trading ship sank in the Mediterranean Sea. And why Dora had no father: John Devereaux had captained that ill-fated ship and lost his life when it went down. But Mama never talked about him, not ever.

Dora had heard other stories, too, about how Mama had eloped against her family's wishes and gone to live with John Devereaux in Baton Rouge. When the family reconciled and he went off to captain her father's ship, Charlotte Benoit returned to her ancestral home as Charlotte Devereaux with a young daughter on her hip.

When he didn't return and her parents and sisters perished, people wondered if Charlotte could cope. But something changed in her, they said, the day she stood on the veranda, watching creditors cart off everything they could sell. By the end of it, Charlotte had only her daughter and that empty mansion with black lacquer shutters and fluted columns on the Esplanade. What else could explain how she could look at those bare rooms and still see hope?

Soon after the creditors left—Bonmarie had told Dora this part—Mama struck a bargain with the household servants. She couldn't afford to pay wages, but she told them if they stayed and helped her run the mansion as a hotel, she would share the profits. They all agreed to do so, and the hotel prospered.

The Devereaux Hotel had always prospered. Well-to-do travelers from the north were charmed by its grand facade and the lingering sheen of the family's former affluence, and they spread the word among their friends.

Dora couldn't remember a time when strangers didn't fill her home, or when Mama didn't treat it like Dora's private finishing school. From the time she could walk, Mama told her to pay attention to how the fancy ladies carried themselves and how they talked, how they chatted about the weather or fashion, and how they always acted entitled to the best of everything. "That is the life you want, Isadora," Mama would whisper when the fancy ladies walked away. "You won't have to pay for my mistakes. I promise."

Mama had kept her promise by making sure Dora was nearby whenever rich, unmarried men stayed at the hotel. That's how it had started with Charles. When he came on business trips, Mama insisted Dora deliver his meals or be the one at the door to take his coat.

And Mama had been right. Dora looked around the dining room, with its finely carved furniture and crystal chandelier, the velvety green wallpaper and silver tea service. Her life was better here, just as Mama said it would be. Dora rose from the table, her porcelain china plate picked clean of food, and fought the inclination to gather both plates and take them to the kitchen for washing. She shook her head. How long would it be until she acted like the lady of the house without effort?

In her room, she watched the lamplighter amble down the sidewalk, lighting the street lanterns with his long pole torch. When he was out of sight, she pulled the blue brocade curtains across the window and sat at her dressing table, took the pins from her hair, and let it fall in thick, dark waves around her shoulders.

If only Charles hadn't been so ill-tempered these past few days. Married life took some adjustment, she understood that, and he was certainly still mourning the loss of his parents. But what if it was something else?

"Stop it," she said to the mirror. Nothing useful came from doubt. She wrapped a lavender ribbon around her hair, pulling it back from her face, and went to the washbasin in the corner of her room. She poured the warm milk Bonmarie had placed there in a pitcher and submerged her hands to the elbows, letting her skin drink in its whiteness. Every night the ritual washed away a little more of New Orleans's tropical stain; she could feel it. With cupped hands, she lifted the milk to her face and let it drench her eyes, her cheeks, her lips, soaking in the alabaster color, making it part of her. One day she would be as white as the fairest Lady Manager.

A tap sounded at her bedroom door. "Dora, are you awake?" Charles was almost whispering.

"Yes." She hadn't heard his footsteps. She wiped the milk from her face and hands with a water-dampened cloth and dried herself before slipping into the chair at her dressing table.

Charles entered like someone testing bathwater. His eyes roamed the chamber, lingering on the canopied bed, and the settee and upholstered chair beside the brazier that flickered with smoldering coal. "I can't get over how different the room is. Mother, God rest her soul, would be quite surprised to see how modern her old bedroom looks."

"I hope you like the wallpaper. A workman gouged the plaster below the lamp when he installed it. But the paper covers the mark well, don't you agree?"

Charles ran his palm across the paisley pattern beneath the sconce, and a finger found the groove of the slender gash. "You were right about the electric light. It does brighten the room better than the gas sconces. Perhaps I'll have one installed in my study." He moved behind her and laid his hands on her shoulders.

"I told you you'd like the lamps." Through the mirror she could see his gaze survey her dressing table, evaluating the glass perfume bottles and pewter-handled brushes, the wooden jewelry box and pin holder, making sure everything was in its proper place.

"Have you thought any more about the bicycles?" she asked, hoping to distract him before he found something to correct. She went to the stack of magazines on her bedside table, took them in her arms, and handed them to him.

She'd spent the last few nights poring through the copies of *Collier's Weekly* and *Harper's Weekly* she'd taken from the sitting room and dog-eared each advertisement and illustration depicting ladies—stylish, respectable ladies—riding the new two-wheel "safety" bicycles. It was a risk bringing up the topic again, but eventually he had to see there was nothing wrong with it. She pointed to the page he was perusing. "See, even Lillian Russell rides one. One of her admirers had one fashioned from gold and mother-of-pearl. Of course, I wouldn't require anything so elaborate."

"I should hope not," he said, flipping to another marked page. He set the magazine aside and flipped through the next one in the stack and the next one after that.

Dora dug her teeth into her lip to keep quiet. He had to see for himself.

He worked his way through four magazines before setting the stack on the dressing table. "I'll give it more thought. But I want to hear about your day with Mrs. Richmond."

The comment came so casually Dora knew it was the reason he had ventured to her room. "It was lovely." She picked up a hairbrush and ran it through her hair.

"What will this assignment you mentioned involve, exactly?"

She told him Mrs. Richmond's instructions. "It's my duty to ensure the belly dancers don't make a spectacle of themselves, I suppose."

His brows pinched. "I'm not sure I approve of my wife loitering about that kind of place. Perhaps I'll have a word with Mr. Richmond about this."

She stopped the brush. "Please don't. I'm sure it will be fine. Mrs. Richmond has a partner in mind for me. Please don't make a fuss." As much as she didn't want to return to that theater, it was more horrifying to think of her husband complaining to Mr. Richmond after the man had been kind enough to intercede and get her on the board.

Charles rubbed the whiskers on his jaw. "Even if you have a partner, that theater isn't fit for ladies."

"But we're Lady Managers, so it isn't the same thing at all."

"One can never be too careful." His gaze softened and he ran his finger over the hair around her face. "You look so beautiful when your hair is down like this. Let me brush it for you."

The request surprised her; he'd never asked before. She handed him the instrument and felt him sweep it through her long strands.

"How did Mrs. Richmond treat you?"

The words hardly registered; her thoughts were floating on a cloud of sensation. The tickle of the bristles pressing against her hairline; the long, slow pull through her curls; the anticipation that it all would happen again.

"Dora?"

How quickly his temper flared, as if it always lurked just beneath the surface. "We got on well. She was quite pleasant."

He ran the brush through her hair more briskly. "She must be taking a liking to you. I knew she would." His gaze grew distant. "Do you remember when I found you in your mother's parlor discussing Parisian fashion with the Baroness De Roquefort over afternoon tea? She was convinced you were an English duchess visiting on holiday."

The memory gave him a chuckle, but it made her cringe. She remembered the baroness. She hadn't intended to deceive the woman; she'd only wanted to practice bits of a conversation she'd overheard, to try on the words like a fine silk dress. The exchange had begun so naturally that by the time Dora realized the woman had made the wrong assumption, it was too late to correct. What a thrill it had been to have the attention of that grand lady, but once she'd learned Dora's true station, she never spoke to her again.

Charles seemed to read her thoughts. "Isn't it good to know all that is behind you? Here you can be the woman we both know you can be."

For a long moment neither spoke. Through the mirror, she watched a smile play on his lips, as if he were thinking something wonderful to himself that he didn't share. She wanted to be everything he wanted her to be. To enter any room with her head high and proud, never again to feel ashamed of what people said in secret. When he had proposed, it had seemed so possible. But now that she was here, she wasn't so sure. She could mirror these Lady Managers, but was it enough? These northern women were so pale. What did they make of the raven hair shrouding her shoulders, the brown eyes, and olive skin that tinted too easily in the sun? Such appearance was common enough in even the finest salons of New Orleans, but here it was so rare. She couldn't help but doubt.

"Charles?" She caught his glance in the glass. "May I ask you something?" The words came before she had thought them through. Already she wanted to take them back.

"Of course you can."

The question ached within her.

Charles was watching her, waiting. He set the brush down and put both hands on her bare arms, near the soft curve of her shoulders. She could feel the heat of his skin.

"What is it?"

With his eyes on her, her courage melted. She couldn't do it. "Do you think I'm beautiful?" she offered instead, hoping it sounded sincere.

"How can you ask such a thing?" He dropped to his knees and his lips neared her throat, exhaling hot breath as he said the words and making her neck come alive with feeling. "You are a beautiful, tropical flower. Anyone can see that."

A warm sensation started in her fingers, traveled up her arms, and through her body. Of course he loved her, yet it was wonderful to hear, and to feel his lips against her skin so tenderly. When their bodies were close, there was no room for doubts. To feel him near would be enough.

She turned and his warmth embraced her like fingers around a glass. He took her hand in his and kissed her palm gently. There was no reason to worry. He loved her; that's all that mattered. They were man and wife; she had no reason to hold back. There was no more reason for Mama's warnings.

She'd let those words ruin her wedding night. She'd wanted so badly to please, but when the moment came, when she'd joined her husband in bed that first time, she could think of nothing but Mama's words. *A woman can give up her bed secrets only once. Keep yours safe for your husband, Isadora.*

She had kept her bed secrets easily enough, but now that she could share them, she didn't know how. When Charles had come to her on their wedding night, in that tiny cabin on the steamship, she'd turned out every light and buried herself under the sheets. He'd tried to be gentle, to calm her with his words and his touch, but nothing put her at ease. Their coupling had been quick and painful, and she'd been glad when he'd returned to his own room when it was done. He hadn't tried to initiate the act again.

She knew he was waiting for her to go to him. She lowered her lips to the curve of his neck, and whispered, "Shall I sleep in my husband's bed tonight?"

His lips met hers and pressed hard. His breath quickened, and she could feel his heartbeat against her chest. His hands roamed over her back and down her thighs, searching for the hem of her chemise.

She wanted to return his fervor, but the tingling inside frightened her. Her body pressed against his as if of its own volition, and she moved in ways she couldn't control. She ached for his hand to reach up under her chemise, but she dreaded it, too. When his fingertips reached her hip, the fire between her legs made her gasp and jerk back. A seam ripped and the sound of tearing made them both stop short.

He pulled away. "I'm sorry, I've pushed too hard." He stared into the carpet and she could hear the disappointment in his voice.

"No, it's fine. I'm fine." The words sounded false even to her ears.

His face flickered with confusion, then a scowl. "Perhaps another night."

Dread swelled within her. Again she had ruined everything. Why must she be so clumsy when it came to bedroom matters?

"Besides, it's not a good time for me," he added. "I must get an early start tomorrow, and if I don't get a full night's rest, I won't be any good at the office. This is an important time for me. For us."

Dora turned her mouth to his and kissed him, once gently on the lips and then on the cheek. "Of course. Another night, then."

His desire had drained away; she could see it in the way he settled on the edge of her bed, his fingers raking the top of his head. "Mr. Richmond asked me to clear my appointments tomorrow. I told him of my proposal to partner with the Fair's popular foreign exhibitors, to import their goods after the Exposition closes. I think he's interested." That faraway look returned, the one he always got when he talked about business. "I think there's a chance he might take it up with the bank's directors. He must know if we don't seize this opportunity, someone else will. People love what they're seeing at the Fair: the French perfume, the Swiss clocks, the Japanese teapots, all of it. There will be a market for that merchandise, you can bet on that. They say this Fair is about Columbus's discovery of America, but what's really happening is America is finally discovering the rest of the world."

Dora smiled and nodded and tried to look interested, as if she hadn't heard his refrain so many times before. "Is that why you've been working so hard?"

He paused and she could see his passion rising again, though a passion of another sort. "If Mr. Richmond supports me on this, coupled with your place with the Lady Managers, I know the directors will consider me for the vice president position. They'd be fools not to." He shook his finger at her, but his eyes grew more glazed. Then his attention came back to her. "I know this is difficult for you." He put his hand on her knee. "A new city, new people, new expectations. It will all be worth it, though, you'll see. My only regret is that my father didn't live to see my success."

Dora squeezed his hand. *Please let that be his only regret.*

*C*harles dipped the head of his wooden toothbrush in the water in the porcelain basin beside his bed and scooped a spoonful of the powdered soap from the tin canister on the ledge. He tilted the pewter utensil over the bristles and tapped the side, preparing the brush for the evening ritual, the final act before he could crawl into bed and forget the miserable day.

What was wrong with that girl? Frustration roiled like a bad piece of mutton in the pit of his stomach. She was his wife, yet she treated him like an unworthy suitor. She was young, he realized that. But it had been two months and still she recoiled. The problem wasn't him, it couldn't be. Geraldine Forrest could have had any man she pleased, yet she had turned those beautiful, tender blue eyes to him.

He worked the brush vigorously over his teeth. He couldn't think of Geraldine now. All that was done. The bank directors had made sure of it. He owed Mr. Richmond a great debt for telling him that when his name was mentioned as a successor for Mr. Forrest's place on the board, several had refused to consider him because they'd heard rumors of his affair with Mr. Forrest's widow.

Charles had expressed shock, and Mr. Richmond had conveniently interpreted it to mean the allegations were false.

He took a sip of water, swirled it in his mouth, spit into the basin, and patted his mouth dry with his cloth. He took up his comb and pulled it through his hair. The unfortunate incident had at least revealed how to get what he wanted. He'd broken it off with Geraldine, headed down to New Orleans, and made himself a married man by the next board meeting. It was easy enough to convince his colleagues of his devotion to Dora; she was perfect: beautiful, mannered, and nothing in her appearance reminded him of Geraldine. The shortcomings in her lineage? Safely buried beneath his name. She was Mrs. Charles Chambers, nothing less.

The girl was also smart, smart enough to know he'd rescued her from the dismal life of operating a hotel, and she'd been only too happy to join the Board of Lady Managers. In so many ways she wanted to please him, but how long would it be before she satisfied him the way a man needs to be satisfied by a woman?

The waiting was difficult, and Geraldine wasn't making it any easier. If only she would stop finding reasons to drop by the bank. A certain number of visits were to be expected, as she was one of the bank's major investors. But some visits he suspected were simply made to flaunt herself in front of him, to remind him of what he could no longer have. Today was one of those visits. She'd wanted to check her account balances for no reason in particular. Of course, that's not what she'd said. She'd said she wanted to be sure the investments the advisors had suggested were paying off. She hadn't spoken to him, but she'd lingered in front of the door to his office when she was talking with Mr. Richmond. She'd glanced his way more than a few times, and she'd worn that amber wool coat, the one she'd worn that evening they'd strolled after the Richmonds' dinner party and kissed on a Japanese moon bridge. It couldn't have been a coincidence.

He went to his wardrobe to pull out his bedclothes, and he couldn't resist slipping his fingers into the inside pocket of an old jacket pushed far to the back. He felt around until he found what he wanted. He pulled out the oval picture frame he'd hidden there, so small it fit neatly in his palm. He opened it to reveal the delicately painted image of Geraldine Forrest, a gift she'd given him one night after they'd made love. She must have known how he would cherish it. Even now he couldn't bear to throw it away. He followed the upward sweep of her blond hair with his finger, touched the delicate pink of her lips. How beautiful she was, and oh, how she could make love. He thought of her hands. Their likeness wasn't in the picture, but he could see them in his mind. Fingers so soft and smooth, but still so strong when they wrapped around his neck and squeezed into his back. The way she touched him made him groan with pleasure and he groaned a little now. He clasped the picture frame closed and put it back in its hiding place. He would have that pleasure from a woman again. Someday.

Three

*D*ora lifted the bedcovers to her cheeks and hid from the soft gray light seeping into the room from the edges of the drapery. In the distance, she heard cupboards slam and walls rattle. What on earth was Bonmarie doing downstairs?

She thought about heading down to investigate, but it was still too early. Hazel would be lurking about somewhere in the house. That white-haired woman with the spider fingers usually didn't devise a reason to go into town until midmorning, either to pick up cleaning supplies or hire a new laundry girl or whatever other task she made up for herself. Dora never questioned her; she was too glad to see her go.

Unless it was absolutely necessary, Hazel wouldn't speak to Dora, not since Charles allowed Bonmarie to take over the cooking. Hazel hadn't liked the change; she considered herself above the other household chores. If Dora walked by as she was polishing a banister or folding linens, she mumbled about the superior way Charles's mother had run the house. Dora found it best to avoid her.

She pulled the sheet more tightly around herself, feeling its soft warmth against her bare skin. All those times she had complained about morning chores at the hotel—peeling potatoes for Bonmarie or hanging the laundry to dry—she never imagined she could miss them. Other than wash and dress, what were ladies supposed to do at this time of day?

She'd already learned not to take breakfast too early. The long hours after the meal was cleared, when it was still too soon to visit the lake or downtown, could be torture. The first few days she had walked the halls, looking into rooms, poking into closets and drawers, examining the crystal sets and linens, exploring every corner of her new home. But that thrill had waned. The aimless wandering made her feel empty, more like a ghost haunting the world, but not a living part of it. Maybe that's why apparitions spooked; they were just bored.

She preferred to stay in her cocoon of bedcoverings and dream. Dreams weren't like the real world. She could be whomever she wanted to be and do anything she pleased. She might be the belle of a society ball, or even something more remarkable, like a bird swooping through a meadow or over the cresting seas, feeling the spray of the waves splash across her cheek. Sometimes she dreamed about her father.

She'd been thinking about him more since the wedding. It had been a traditional service, except Mama had walked her down the little aisle. She'd said it didn't matter, but all the old questions came back and still Mama refused to add anything new to the story. "John Devereaux was French," she would say. He was tall and strong, and he had the same thick black hair that Dora had, and his eyes were dark like Mississippi mud on a moonless night.

That was all Mama would say. Nothing about what he liked to do, what food he ate, who his friends were. That hadn't stopped

Dora from conjuring a vision of him in her dreams. Sometimes she dreamt of him walking in the hotel's front door to surprise her and Mama, or that she was standing with him at the ship's helm, helping him guide the vessel through a treacherous storm. Those dreams made him feel alive to her, and she tried to slip into one of them now. She could see him, but the image sat motionless. She couldn't make it move. She couldn't make it real.

"Ma chere?" Bonmarie's husky whisper barely reached her ears through the closed door.

Dora pulled up her blankets.

Bonmarie entered, her white apron streaked with strawberry preserves. "You'd better get yourself up if you expect my help getting you dressed for that Lady Manager meeting."

Bonmarie pulled back the drapes and the morning light burst into the room. Dora tugged a pillow over her head, but not before she breathed in the aroma of the French toast and melting butter, and the chicory coffee delivered special from New Orleans.

Her mouth watered but she wasn't ready to give up her cocoon. Not yet.

"If you aren't up by the time I get back, I'm going to dump that coffee on your head," Bonmarie growled.

Dora yanked away her pillow. "All right, all right."

Bonmarie left the room, and Dora sat up, holding the bedcovers around her bare skin. She couldn't bring herself to wear nightclothes, even here where the nights got so cold. She had tried wearing a chemise to bed on her first nights in the house but had awakened each time with the muslin twisted so tightly around herself she feared she'd never get free. An extra coverlet proved a much better solution.

Today she hardly noticed the cold, because today would be her first Lady Managers meeting. She rose with her sheet wrapped around her and went to the tray by the fire. Dora sank into the settee's soft velvet cushion and took the gold-rimmed porcelain cup in both hands. The sheet encircling her drooped to her waist. She could wear the pale blue dress with the bustle or the charcoal one with the slimmer, more modern skirt. Probably the charcoal, so the Lady Managers would see she kept up with the latest Parisian styles.

The coffee's steam filled her nostrils and warmed her cheeks as she drank. Nothing tasted better in the morning than Bonmarie's chicory brew. She pulled the cup to her chest to let it warm her skin, misjudged the tilt, and sent a splash down her stomach. She jerked the cup and sent more of the burning liquid splattering onto the white sheet around her and the rug below.

Dora set down the cup and hurried to the hall cabinet where the extra linens were kept. She rummaged for a towel. Then Bonmarie's heavy footsteps were on the stairs.

"Have you no shame?" Bonmarie's voice boomed.

Dora turned. She'd forgotten her sheet on the floor.

"I know your mama taught you better than that. Get back in that room and put on some clothes before anyone sees you."

Dora pulled a folded sheet from the cabinet and tugged it around her naked body. She tucked a towel under her arm and went back to her room. Fuming, she knelt at the spill and dabbed at the rug. Bonmarie couldn't talk to her that way. She wasn't a child. This wasn't Mama's house, and Charles was right: Bonmarie needed to learn her place. She watched the woman pour warm water into the washbasin. "So what if anyone does see me? It's only skin." There, let the woman stew on that.

It wasn't an argument she necessarily believed, but she wasn't about to let Bonmarie make the rules. And come to think of it, maybe she did believe it. "The Fair's Palace of Fine Art is filled with hundreds, maybe thousands of pictures of nude women. Nobody finds that shameful. Nobody calls them indecent."

Bonmarie tilted up the pitcher and wiped her finger beneath the spout's lip. The lines of her mouth cut deep into her cheeks. "If some harlot wants to toss off her knickers so a dirty old man can leer at her unmentionables, other people can call that art. I call it a disgrace, an abomination, and an insult to God's creation. If the child I raised thinks she is going to traipse around this house in her bare skin like she was the Devil's daughter, she is mistaken. Sadly mistaken."

Dora's courage melted. When Bonmarie threw God and the Devil into an argument, there was no way to win. Nothing meant more to Bonmarie than being a good Catholic. What the Bible says, what the priests say, it was God's word and no one could dispute it. Original sin, cardinal sin, mortal sin, she believed it all.

Dora didn't see the world that way. God was too big to fit in a church, and certainly too big for a book. But this was no time to debate. "Maybe you're right. Maybe naked bodies are art and maybe they're not; at least I'm willing to consider it a possibility." She went to her wardrobe and pulled out a fresh chemise, dragged it over her head, and let it fall to her knees.

Bonmarie glared for a moment, then her fleshy features softened. "Possibilities?" She shook her head. "One of these days, you'll see this world has fewer possibilities than you ever dreamed."

Bonmarie moved toward her. She took the towel Dora had tossed on the bed and bent to the floor. She poured the last of the water from the pitcher onto the coffee stain and rubbed. When only a wet spot remained, she rose to leave.

Dora stepped in front of her, blocking her path to the door. She threw her arms around the woman's wide shoulders and squeezed.

"I know you're only looking out for me, and I love you, you know." When she pulled away, Bonmarie's eyes glistened.

She patted Dora's shoulder, smoothed her hair, and went to the door. "Be a good girl. Wash up and pick out what you want to wear to that meeting. I'll fix your hair when I'm done with the preserves." Then she was gone, the staircase rattling as she went.

The polished oak door of the Richmond mansion opened before Dora could knock. Inside stood a butler in a stiff black morning coat with tails, his face turned up, his eyes cast down. He greeted her coolly.

She entered and took in the staggering grandness of the foyer with a sweeping glance. A mirror in a gilt frame rose nearly to the second-story ceiling, and in front of her a curved staircase descended to the middle of a white marble floor streaked with gray veins. Above, a chandelier held a dozen tiny brass cups for the candles and crystal teardrops that swayed and jingled from the cool breeze before the door closed behind her. Dora swallowed hard and felt moisture gather in her palms beneath her white lace gloves.

The butler helped her remove her cape, and a door slid open in the shadow of the staircase across the hall. The din of party chatter and strains of a violin drifted out. The door slid closed again, and a woman's heels clicked sharply against the floor.

"Mrs. Charles Chambers has arrived, madam." The words poured from the man like molasses.

The sight of Mrs. Richmond's cheery yellow dress with a white frill around her bustled chiffon skirt made Dora's charcoal wool feel like a bruise against her skin. She longed for the frothy pale blue dress she'd left hanging at home.

"Good afternoon, Mrs. Chambers." Mrs. Richmond gestured to a set of double doors on the far side of the foyer. "The Managers are gathered in the gallery."

The door chimed and Mrs. Richmond stopped. The butler moved to get it.

Mrs. Richmond stood riveted, her ears perked.

"Good afternoon, Mrs. Forrest," the man intoned, a little louder than was necessary.

Mrs. Richmond turned to Dora, a look of panic etched in her face. She patted Dora's arm as if in consolation, and left her. "Mrs. Forrest, hello, my dear, it is so good of you to come. Here, let me help you with that gorgeous wrap."

Mrs. Forrest crossed the threshold and slipped off a white knit shawl with long sweeps of feathery fringe. Beneath she wore a dress of pure white with a bustle even larger than the one trailing Mrs. Richmond. A black ribbon tied around her throat held a cameo, and more black ribbon wove through the white feathers atop her hat. When she moved, she glided like a swan moving effortlessly across a pond, so elegant, so assured.

"Mrs. Sheffield, it is a pleasure to see you as well."

Mrs. Richmond was speaking to Mrs. Forrest's companion, a woman who stood not much taller than she was wide. She wore a lilac wool dress with matching velvet trim, but it was the blue jay ornament on her hat that caught Dora's eye. The bird looked so real, as if it had just touched down on the platform of flowers and feathers atop the woman's head and at any moment might fly away again.

"Thank you, Agnes," Mrs. Forrest said, relinquishing her mantle to Mrs. Richmond. "You are too kind—" Her smile vanished when she saw Dora in the hall.

Mrs. Richmond stepped in front of Mrs. Forrest to block her

view. "Cecil, will you escort Mrs. Chambers to the gallery? I'll be happy to see to Mrs. Forrest."

"As you wish, madam." He snapped his heels on the marble floor, turned from the door, and sliced his way through the tension in the room. With a nod, he indicated to Dora that she should follow.

She obliged reluctantly. Mrs. Forrest had been cold at the Egyptian Theatre; here she was openly rude. Dora lifted her head and pulled back her shoulders. She would project the appearance of pride, even if she couldn't rally any at the moment.

She followed the butler and listened hard to the whispers behind her. She could make out the aggrieved tone, but not the words. When the butler reached the double doors, he slid one into its pocket in the wall, stepped aside, and swept his hand for her to enter.

The scene inside made Dora forget her irritation. The gallery was larger than any drawing room she'd ever seen—as if it belonged in a museum, not a home. She noticed the paintings first, dozens of them encased in golden frames and stacked three or four high along the walls. And then there were the women. So many filled the space, standing in groups, sitting on settees, gathered around a table of chafing dishes and platters and teapots. In the back a man in a mocha-colored waistcoat held a violin beneath his chin. His bow rose and dipped, and his happy tune filled the air.

Dora noticed all the dresses. Such beautiful pastel hues: lavender, pale pink, robin's-egg blue. She tightened her arms across herself, regretting even more her dress's sooty color. She scanned the room. Everyone was immersed in some conversation and no one looked her way. They all belonged, they all had their place.

She went to the long table, set with porcelain plates heaped with scones and petit fours, biscuits and puddings. She passed them and went to the silver teapots, picked up a cup and saucer, and poured the Darjeeling.

As she blew on her tea to cool it, Mrs. Richmond entered with Mrs. Forrest and Mrs. Sheffield. Mrs. Richmond approached Dora; the other two joined a group of women across the room.

"We'll be getting started in a moment," Mrs. Richmond said, threading an arm around Dora's waist and moving her toward the middle of the room. "Are you enjoying yourself?"

Before Dora could answer, they had reached a clearing and the crowd fell silent. Faces turned and Dora felt their gazes like lead weights. She squared her shoulders and met the looks with all the confidence she could muster.

Mrs. Richmond motioned to the violinist to rest his bow. "Ladies, allow me to introduce Mrs. Charles Chambers." The woman paused for the reticent applause. "Mrs. Chambers is new to Chicago, by way of New Orleans. Isn't that right, dear?"

Dora nodded and, unable to stop the nervous wobbling of her cup, deposited it and the saucer on the closest available table. In front of her a woman with an enormous peach bow on her hat leaned in to whisper something in her neighbor's ear.

"And as our newest member, she has already earned our gratitude by volunteering to be our liaison to the Egyptian Theatre, a sorely needed enterprise now that the Society for the Suppression of Vice has involved itself. At least they have promised to end their silly protests, and seem to have moved their efforts to the local newspapers."

A round of murmurs spread through the room.

"Ladies, please." Mrs. Richmond tamped the air for quiet. "With a little oversight, I'm sure the theater can be brought into compliance. And that reminds me." She searched the faces in the crowd and settled on one. "Mrs. Tillday?"

The sea of eyes turned to the back of the room and landed on a woman sitting alone in a corner, staring into her lap. She could not have looked more oblivious to the proceedings, as if she were alone in a park and not on that burgundy chaise examining the cup and saucer in her lap. Her head shot up at the sound of her name, exposing wide pale eyes beneath curled ginger bangs. Something like fear and embarrassment mingled on her face.

"I am hoping that you, Mrs. Tillday, will take Mrs. Chambers under your wing and help her along." More murmurs passed through the crowd. "Unless you have any objection?"

The waifish woman shifted under the weight of the roomful of stares. "Yes, of course. I mean, no, I have no objection."

The meekness of the voice fit the woman. From the plain high-collared blouse to her black wool skirt, Mrs. Tillday looked as out of place among the pastel ruffles and high bustles as Dora felt.

She swallowed hard to hide her disappointment. Anyone else in the room would have been a welcome match.

Dora tried to concentrate on what Mrs. Richmond was saying.

"Mrs. Palmer sends her regrets; the Fair directors required her attention so she could not join us. But she asked me to let you know that we will be staging a luncheon to honor Miss Susan B. Anthony, who has played such a supportive role with the Fair's Women's Department."

The women muttered their agreement. Mrs. Richmond continued: "We'll be forming a committee of volunteers, and let me add that I'm sure Mrs. Palmer will be paying close attention to how well these duties are carried out. A good job is sure to earn her notice. May I see a show of hands?"

Gloved palms shot into the air. But not every palm, and not any from Mrs. Forrest's corner.

Mrs. Richmond called out names. "Mrs. Loomis, Mrs. Charleston, Mrs. Rupert, and, yes, you, Mrs. Gilmore."

Dora drifted to the knickknacks arranged on the giant fireplace mantel behind her, wishing herself invisible until the selection was finished. She studied the Chinese vases and jade figurines and tried to ignore the popularity contest taking place around her.

Then she felt a tap on her shoulder. It was Mrs. Tillday, a shy smile playing on her lips.

"Mrs. Tillday, hello," Dora said. The woman might not be the partner she would choose, but she was her partner nonetheless. "I'm Mrs. Charles Chambers."

Mrs. Tillday's glance remained on the floor. "Yes, I know."

Dora shifted uneasily. "Of course. Mrs. Richmond's introduction."

Mrs. Tillday's gaze shot up. "No, long before that. Everyone knows who you are." Her hand flew to her mouth. "Oh dear. I've said the wrong thing, haven't I? I'm always saying the wrong thing. Please forgive . . . I mean, I didn't—"

"Don't be silly," Dora stammered. But what exactly did everyone know, she wanted to add, though she didn't. She couldn't. And she didn't want the woman to see the tremble it sent through her.

"I've made you uncomfortable. I can see it." Mrs. Tillday's shoulders sank as if she would coil into herself and disappear altogether.

Dora calmed herself. She'd misunderstood. That's all. "Please, let's forget it. I just had no idea. I didn't realize . . ." Why were words so difficult?

Thank goodness, Mrs. Richmond was heading toward her.

"Mrs. Chambers, if I could borrow you for a moment." The

woman looked almost giddy. "Mrs. Forrest has asked for a word with you, if it's all right. I think she'd like to welcome you aboard. Won't you excuse us, Mrs. Tillday?"

Mrs. Richmond tugged Dora by the elbow without waiting for a response. Over her shoulder, Dora watched Mrs. Tillday retreat back to the settee and resume her staring match with her cup and saucer.

It was probably wrong to feel so relieved, but the guilt lasted only until they reached Mrs. Forrest. The woman was striking in her brilliant white dress, so radiant with her blond curls piled high on her head.

"It's so nice of you to join us, Mrs. Chambers," Mrs. Forrest said. "I know we're practically strangers, but I feel as though I already know you so well. Charles has told me so much about you."

Was that a giggle from Mrs. Sheffield, huddled with the others behind Mrs. Forrest?

Dora struggled for a return pleasantry, but it didn't matter because Mrs. Forrest didn't pause. "Agnes, dear, a servant was searching for you a moment ago. The poor girl looked frantic."

Mrs. Richmond touched her brow. "New help. They require so much hand-holding, you know." She excused herself and hurried toward the foyer door.

Mrs. Forrest turned to the women behind her. "Go, mingle. You don't want to be called snobs, do you?"

The women snickered as if this were a private joke and moved themselves a little farther away, though still, Dora noted, within earshot.

"Charles tells me you met in New Orleans."

Charles again? Wouldn't Mr. Chambers be the appropriate way to address someone's husband?

"So it must have been his business with the bank that brought you together."

Dora shifted, feeling her toes pinch in her new boots. "Yes, I suppose it was."

"I can't say I'm familiar with New Orleans. What sort of business is your family in?"

"Importing spices and textiles mostly, but business never interested me much." It was her practiced reply. And it *had* been her family's business. Once. Dora met Mrs. Forrest's glare and froze the muscles in her face into the semblance of a smile.

"Importing can be so lucrative. Your family must have its own ships. I've heard you must have your own ships if you are to make any respectable profit at all."

Dora turned to admire a vase of red roses on a table beside her. "What beautiful blooms. I wonder if they're from Mrs. Richmond's garden. Look, they're even bigger than my fist." She clenched her hand next to one of the flowers. It was a ridiculous thing to do, but the only thing she could think of to get the conversation on another track.

Mrs. Forrest ignored the flowers. "My friends tell me one must have at least three ships to make the venture worthwhile. What do you say?"

Dora kept her eyes on the rose petals and felt sweat gathering in her palms. "I really don't pay attention to that sort of thing." The last words cracked; her throat was dry.

"I see." Mrs. Forrest crossed her arms and tapped one of her elbows. "How long has your family been in the merchant trading business exactly?"

"I really couldn't say," Dora said, staring hard at the blooms.

"Even one who has no head for business should take some

interest in the family means. It's really quite remarkable that you've been kept so sheltered from any details whatsoever."

Dora stole a glance at Mrs. Forrest. The woman's eyes narrowed with suspicion. She sensed the truth; Dora was sure of it. Of course Dora should know the details of her family's fortune; it was her pedigree. She stalled, ran a finger around the rose petals, as if engrossed in their beauty, looking only at the flower, ignoring the woman's stare, pretending to be oblivious to anything amiss. "How do you know my husband, Mrs. Forrest?"

"My goodness, hasn't he mentioned me? I wonder why that is?" Mrs. Forrest's voice trailed off as if she knew very well the reason but would not speak it. "Everyone knows we have been close friends for ages." The way she emphasized "close" made Dora's stomach tighten.

"I'm sure he has not mentioned you."

"He and my late husband were friends, like brothers really. He was such a comfort to me when Randolph passed away last year. You really don't find compassion like that in a man these days. He was so consoling. But you see, he had just lost his parents; we understood each other's pain." The woman sighed. "He is quite a catch, your Charles. Did you know he was one of our most popular bachelors?"

"No, I didn't know." Charles consoling? Compassionate? Dora faked another smile.

"Some of his friends wondered why he would roam so far to find a wife. So many ladies here adore him. He really could have had his pick. To be honest, quite a few were terribly upset to hear of his hasty marriage. But sometimes there's no accounting for a man's whims."

As Dora looked into those icy blue eyes, she realized the venom in the words was no accident. She could see it in the rise of that single blond eyebrow and the way the lips twitched after each malicious word. But she would not let the woman see her pain. She would deny her at least that satisfaction.

Mrs. Forrest glanced away, hardly hiding a smirk, already sensing Dora's distress. A glimmer of triumph twinkled in her eyes.

Dora tried to mask her outrage with a smile. She knew she should say something demure, something complimentary to push the conversation back onto civilized terms. But Mrs. Forrest was grinning so broadly that Dora thought she could count each one of her wicked teeth. She imagined them falling out, one by one, hitting the polished wood floor with a *tink, tink, tink.*

Mrs. Forrest prepared another strike. "Women in our circle take such care not to expose themselves to the sun, but I see that concern doesn't burden you. Or have your circumstances merely left you no choice?"

The insult left Dora speechless. A refined lady would return with a perfect, dispassionate retort, but Dora wanted only to kick this woman's shin. Rage seethed through her clenched teeth. She looked squarely at Mrs. Forrest, and when she had recovered herself, she spoke. "If every woman in Chicago is as hateful as you, I don't wonder at all why Mr. Chambers looked elsewhere for a wife. And if you really think Mr. Chambers is your friend, you should know this: Never in the years—yes, Mrs. Forrest, years; there was nothing hasty about our courtship—never has he mentioned you. Not once." She had known Charles for years. Maybe it wasn't all courtship, but Mrs. Forrest couldn't know that. "I would say he doesn't hold you in the high regard you think he does. In fact, I'm sure he'll be interested to learn what sort of friend you really are."

Mrs. Forrest's lips tilted into an awkward smile, and she

leaned toward Dora. "I would be careful about stirring up trouble if I were you, especially if I were married to a man who couldn't afford to alienate certain people."

The way she said "certain" made it clear she meant "powerful," and that she included herself in the category.

For a moment, Mrs. Forrest's sneer could have been every sneer ever turned Dora's way. Children taunting her on the street, young men who looked her over then looked away, every hotel guest who ordered her about like she was nothing but hired help. All these collided in her mind, crystallizing into the porcelain perfect face of Geraldine Forrest.

"You are a vile woman. I am Charles's wife, and as long as I am mistress of his home, you will never be welcome in it." She hoped the hatred burning inside her spilled into her words. Perhaps it had, for Mrs. Forrest was shooting glances around the room to see who might have overheard.

Dora saw several heads turn their way, including Mrs. Forrest's friends. Standing there facing a mute Geraldine Forrest, remorse settled on her: She'd given in to her temper and what had it won for her exactly? Her pride? An enemy?

Mrs. Forrest leaned closer and whispered: "You may be a pretty thing, but you have much to learn about proper behavior." Her face was so placid that even the nearest bystander wouldn't believe the cruelty harbored inside that golden beauty. "And I won't worry about keeping Charles off my visiting list. From what I've seen, you won't be the mistress of his house for long."

Mrs. Sheffield, with a sideways smile and a lopsided gait, appeared at Mrs. Forrest's side. "You must come and hear Mrs. Loomis's story." It was clear the request was intended for Mrs. Forrest alone. "A friend of hers stopped in to see that belly dance show, on a lark, you know. They were practically shedding their clothes right there on the stage." The shock in her voice hardly disguised her delight in the gossip. "Come, you must hear about it for yourself." Mrs. Forrest said nothing, but Dora knew something unspoken passed between the women, the twist of a smile, a tilt of the head. The sign language of conspirators.

Mrs. Forrest lifted a thin smile to Dora. "Yes, I would like to hear that. Dora and I are finished here, aren't we? It really has been a pleasure getting better acquainted. I'm sure we'll be seeing a lot of each other." Mrs. Forrest turned as if she would follow her friend, then turned back. "Please do give my regards to Charles."

Dora watched the woman glide away, as if she moved without bending a fold of her skirt or a drape of her sleeves. Dora fought the lump in her throat and felt the room close around her, each wall feeling so near that it blocked the air she struggled to breathe. She watched the two women join a growing circle as others gravitated to hear the story about the belly dancers.

Leave. She should just leave and never return. She knew it was her temper. She knew she would regret these hasty words. She tried to be calm, to think rationally. Was the damage so severe? She searched for Mrs. Richmond but the woman was nowhere to be seen. Etiquette required she thank her hostess before a departure.

But what good were manners now? She had been tried, and the verdict was in. She could feel it as not one set of eyes turned her way. She was no one in this room, and no one noticed her slip out the door.

She collected the carriage, climbed onto the seat with an attendant's help, and maneuvered Delilah down the street. Only when she'd turned the corner did Dora let the tears flow. They started as a trickle but soon grew into streams coursing down her face. She brushed them away with quick swipes of her gloves.

Her ears throbbed with each sob, and her crying was the only sound she could hear over Delilah's clopping and the scrape of metal wheels.

By the time she reached the house, the emotion was spent. Her breath was calm and the tears dried. Only numbness remained. Her swollen eyelids drooped, making the house blur in a dream-like image.

It was still too early for Charles to be home; his questions still hours away. There was time enough to rest, to compose herself, to prepare again for the role of a good wife. A nap was what she needed, a little sleep to feel restored.

She guided Delilah into the stable behind the house and handed the reins to Harold, the groundsman who fed and cared for the mare. He greeted her with a nod and a dip of the corn-cob pipe dangling from his lips, and his Irish green eyes lingered on her. He never bothered to hide his distaste for women getting around without the aid of a proper driver. "Didn't expect you back so early, Mrs. Chambers."

"The meeting ended earlier than I expected." Why was she explaining herself to him?

"I see." Harold didn't look up, but she could see a smirk twisting his cheek.

She brushed past him, trying to get out of the stable before the tears returned. Her feet felt as heavy as flour sacks, and it took all her strength to get to the back door. Just a few more steps, she told herself. A few more steps until she reached her bed, her sanctuary. Inside the house lay quiet. No kitchen sounds, no cleaning sounds, no Hazel sounds or Bonmarie sounds at all. The stairs. She trudged up the stairs.

She landed on her bed with Mama's words echoing through her. "You're as good as they are, any of them." What a farce. She pulled the quilts up to her chin. Nothing felt as good as fresh bed linens and quilts. Thick, soft, and new. Nothing like the worn, hand-me-down blankets she had to use at the hotel. She'd sleep just a little while, just enough to get back on her feet. A brief retreat from the world while there was still time.

*M*orning sunshine filled the room when Dora awoke, the feeling of Bonmarie's warm hand on her brow.

"Well, there you are. You gave Mr. Chambers quite a scare." Bonmarie felt around her head. "Temperature seems fine. Let me see your tongue."

"Why?" She ran her hand over her face, trying to wipe the sleep from her eyes.

Bonmarie cocked her head. Dora complied.

While Bonmarie peered at her, Dora realized it wasn't morning at all. The light wasn't pouring in from the windows; it came from the lamps. And Charles was standing at the foot of the bed. It was late. "I'm feeling all right," Dora stammered. "I just lay down for a nap before dinner. What time is it?"

"Eight. Mr. Chambers tried to wake you to get you to eat some supper, but you would not—"

"Dora, are you sure you're feeling all right?" Charles came up beside her. His hands balled at his sides as if they didn't know what to do. "I was sitting right where Bonmarie is now. I tried to wake you, but you didn't stir, not in the slightest. I thought maybe . . ."

But he didn't finish.

She couldn't remember the last time Charles had shown such concern. Compassion. Been consoling. Geraldine Forrest's words came back to her and she cringed. "I feel fine. Just tired . . ." She couldn't finish the sentence; she'd been dreaming. She could remember dancing on a stage in Egyptian garments. She could feel her body moving, every part of her alive. What a strange dream it had been.

"You have no fever, far as I can tell," Bonmarie said. "I told him you've always been a heavy sleeper." Bonmarie shot an irritated glance at Charles, then patted Dora's hand and rose from the bed.

"I just wanted to be sure everything was all right," he said. "Are you sure you don't need a doctor?"

The memory of the afternoon came back to her. "Don't be silly. Bonmarie's right. I am a heavy sleeper. It's at least one thing I'm good at." She realized she was cuing him to disagree. He didn't, and her heart sank a little. She asked Bonmarie, "Could you bring up my dinner?"

The woman nodded and went to the door. Charles smoothed his vest with his palms as if he, too, were preparing to leave.

"Wait, Charles. Keep me company?" She purred the words.

His face softened, and he lowered himself to a place at the edge of her bed. "Of course." He took her hand in his. "That must have been quite a meeting today to tire you so."

There it was; there would be no reprieve. The questions would come next and she would have to tell him how stupid she'd been. No, she didn't have to tell him. Not yet, anyway. She didn't have to let Geraldine Forrest take this moment from her. She played her role. "You know how women are. Gossip, mostly. I'm sure your day was more interesting."

With no more prodding, he launched into the details of Mr. Richmond's enthusiasm for his plan to form trade partnerships with some of the Exposition's foreign vendors. He was well into his story when Bonmarie returned. She placed the tray across Dora's lap and interrupted him midsentence.

"You let me know if you want more. There's plenty on the stove."

Dora thanked her. Bonmarie patted her on the shoulder and left, closing the door behind her.

Dora could see Charles grimace. "Don't be angry," she said. "It's just her way."

"She antagonizes me on purpose. She's a servant, for God's sake. She should act like one."

When had Bonmarie ever acted like a servant? "I'll talk to her, dear. Don't be upset. You were telling me about Mr. Richmond." She took up the knife and fork and positioned them on the ham steak.

Charles touched her hand. "You aren't feeling well. Let me do this for you." He took the utensils and cut the meat. "What was I saying?" Before her first bite, he was immersed in his story again, and the worried crease across his forehead faded. When he told her Mr. Richmond had invited them to dinner, he looked truly happy.

Dora laughed when Charles did and nodded at intervals, but the words passed over her like so much air. She watched how his smooth fingers wrapped around the fork and how his eyes narrowed on the plate as he scooped a small cut of ham, then three peas, and topped them with a smidgeon of mashed potatoes. Each forkful exactly the same. So precise and predictable. So like him.

Still, for all his fussy habits, he could be pleasing. He wasn't exactly handsome, but he had a nice look. Not exceptionally tall or muscular, and maybe a bit too thin, yet he had a pleasant face, and when he smiled, a glimmer shone through of the lighthearted young man he must have been years ago. And he was always a gentleman.

It still amazed her that he was hers, that all of this—the house,

the servants, the status—was hers. He had seemed so ambiva-
lent for so long, friendly but detached. And it could be embarrassing how Mama pressed him with her meddling. That's what
men needed, she'd say, a little nudge in the right direction, especially the ones like Charles, who'd been bachelors for so long. He
acquiesced to evenings in the hotel courtyard after dinner and the
walks to the riverfront, but he had always seemed distracted, as if
his mind roamed elsewhere. Perhaps he really had disguised the
feelings he'd harbored from the start, like he'd said when his woo-
ing began in earnest. She wanted to believe that. And when he'd
arrived in April and confessed his intention to make her his wife,
everything about him changed. His usual mild manner turned
forthright, decisive, even a bit impatient. It was as if once he'd
made up his mind, he couldn't make the wedding happen quickly
enough.

She was sure it stemmed from the loss of his parents. He had
told her they expected him to follow in his father's footsteps,
and they hadn't been silent about their disappointment that he
spent most of his working life at the menial chore of checking on
loan-seeking merchants' collateral for the thrill of traveling to port
cities. In their view, that time would have been better spent lob-
bying for a place in the boardroom.

Then his father had died last year, believing his only son had
squandered a promising career. At his father's bedside, he'd vowed
to be a better provider for his mother. She'd lasted only half a year
after her husband's death, but Charles's pledge put him on a new
course. He had arrived at the Devereaux Hotel just a few weeks
after his mother's passing, and that was when Dora noticed the
change. Questions were asked, expectations were discussed, and
the offer of marriage was made—not a romantic proposal, but
Dora was glad for it just the same.

She wondered how many others he had turned away for her. Mrs. Forrest had said there were many. Dora hadn't made any such sacrifice for him. She watched a smile tug at his eyes as she accepted another bite. Mama's strict ways kept Dora at the hotel much of the time, so there wasn't the opportunity to meet many potential suitors. The only men she met were either servants or guests at the hotel. She thought of the handsome young man who'd been hired to deliver groceries, but he wasn't the sort of suitor a girl should encourage. No ambition, no future. Certainly no means of giving her the life she craved.

Charles Chambers was a gift. She couldn't forget that. He loved her; she could see it in his face even now. Mrs. Forrest was a liar, and he would forgive Dora for her impetuous words today. She just had to be the wife he wanted, smile when he smiled, go where he wanted her to go, and be home when he told her to be home.

She couldn't undo the afternoon's events, but maybe they could move somewhere new and make a fresh start. New York or San Francisco. Anywhere. She would be perfect; she would never lose her temper. Anyone could say anything, and she would keep her composure. Banks were everywhere. Charles could find another, maybe one where he could be a vice president. He would do it for her, wouldn't he?

But might it all just turn out the same? Perhaps there was truth to what Mrs. Forrest had said.

That bitter, terrible question was back, the one that made her stomach churn and the air dissolve in her lungs. And then it was out, like her last breath, as if a stranger had uttered it. She heard herself say: "Darling, do you think I'm too dark?"

She wanted to take it back, but it was too late. She studied his expression, knowing the answer might lie in a muscle twitch or a drawn-out pause.

His eyebrows pinched into a crooked line above his nose. "What do you mean? Dark and mysterious? Or gloomy?"

Did his voice break just then? Did he glance away?

"My skin." There it was, that horrible thought. Her insides ached. Every muscle tensed.

Charles laughed. "You're making a joke, right? What has gotten into that little head of yours?"

It was too late to back out now. She had to know. "The women here are so pale, so white. I don't look like they do." She lifted her arms, their creamy mocha color as plain to her eyes as the azure of the drapes and the dusky rose of the quilt. "In New Orleans, it's not unusual, but it is here. Might others get the wrong idea? Will they think I look common?" She caged the other fear, the other interpretation. The one that could never, ever be mentioned aloud.

Charles set the fork down on the tray. He took her hands and cupped them in his. "You are beautiful, my dear. I don't think I could stand it if you looked like all the other women here." He moved one hand to her face and ran a finger across the arch of her brow. "Has someone said something?"

She pushed Mrs. Forrest from her thoughts. "No. It's just something I've been thinking."

"You are an exotic, mysterious, wonderful New Orleans flower. You are perfect exactly as you are, and I wouldn't change a thing about you, my sweet girl." He lifted the tray and set it on the floor, then took her hands and kissed her fingers. He laid her hands against his chest and looked into her eyes, holding her gaze, watching her. He leaned close and his lips found hers. The kiss was not the sweet peck he usually bestowed. This was a long, lingering kiss, a forceful, eager kiss that pressed against her. He slid down beside her on the bed and wrapped her in both arms, maneuvering himself against her. She could feel the heat of him, and it frightened her. She couldn't move. His hands roamed across her back and his lips dipped down along her neck, and she couldn't move. She couldn't breathe. She had no idea what she was supposed to do.

When a knock on the front door rattled through the house, she pulled back, happy for the distraction. "Who can it be?"

Charles closed his eyes.

In the quiet they could hear the door open and Bonmarie greet the caller. There was mumbling and then the door closed. The staircase groaned with Bonmarie's heavy footsteps.

"She's coming," Dora whispered, pulling farther away from Charles. When he didn't move, except to roll onto his back, she rose from the bed and sat at her dressing table.

A quiet rap sounded on the bedchamber door.

"Yes, Bonmarie, what is it?" Charles's voice sounded gruffer than usual.

The door cracked open and Bonmarie peeked in.

"A letter came for you, sir."

"From whom?"

"Just said it was urgent." She entered the room and offered him the white envelope.

He rose and took it. For a long moment he stared at the inscription of his name on the front and turned it over as if examining it for other clues. Finally he opened it and read the brief message written inside. When he finished, he folded the paper again and tapped it against his palm.

"Who's it from?" Dora asked. "Who would send a note at this hour?"

"It's business, I'm afraid." He started toward the door.

"Can't it wait until morning?"

He seemed to contemplate the question. "I don't think so." He clenched the message in his hand and she heard it crumple.

"Is something wrong?"

He was already out the door, but he paused and turned back. "No, everything's going to be fine. You should rest. Do you have plans for tomorrow?"

"Nothing really. Maybe write to Mama." Though what she really had in mind was to sulk, sleep, maybe scheme up a way to make him leave this city and make a fresh start.

"Good. You should rest so you're fresh for Sunday's visit with the Richmonds. I'll be home soon." He tapped the door frame twice before disappearing down the hall.

Dora went to the door and listened to him descend the stairs, gather his hat and coat from the rack, and walk out the front door. She closed her chamber door and went to her window, where she saw him emerge from the side of the house with Delilah and the carriage. She watched until he vanished down the street.

She tugged off her rumpled day dress and laid it over her dressing table chair, then crawled under the covers of her bed. Charles was gone, but his disappointment seemed to still linger in the room. She shouldn't have pulled away. He was her husband; he was entitled to that affection. So why did it make her so uncomfortable? Next time she would be better. She had to force herself to be better.

*T*he note had come as a surprise. Perhaps it shouldn't have, but it did. What was Geraldine thinking to be so bold? A shiver ran through him, though the night was not particularly cold. Charles took the reins in one hand and hiked the collar of his tweed coat up around his ears with the other. He'd told her it was over before he'd left for New Orleans, and now he was a married man. If he was smart, he would throw the letter away and forget it. But when had he ever been smart when it came to Geraldine?

The note said simply that she needed financial guidance on an inheritance matter. She was still in negotiations with Randolph's creditors, so the request wasn't out of the ordinary. The timing, however, was.

With a tug, he guided the mare around a corner to a street where the mansions gave way to more modest homes and then to shops. It was late, but a good number of carriages were still out and couples strolled the sidewalks. It was a nice night for a stroll. The afternoon's clouds had parted and the quarter moon sat bright and clear in the sky. Perhaps tomorrow he'd take Dora out; maybe that would relax her. The girl was too tense, at least whenever he tried to get near her. And what had been that nonsense about being dark? She'd looked close to tears. Maybe it was natural for her to feel different. But it was precisely because she didn't look like those women that she had attracted him. How could he look on a porcelain face and not think of Geraldine? How could he run his fingers through blond hair and not wish it was hers? Dora's looks were so opposite, but just as beautiful, and that was the only hope for him. She never reminded him of Geraldine.

Yet there was one way he wouldn't mind Dora being more like Geraldine. A man wanted his wife to be pure and virtuous, but he also had his needs. He wouldn't press the matter, not after that ordeal on their wedding night, with the sobbing and her insistence on scrubbing the blood from the sheets before the housekeeping staff could find them. For weeks he'd been patient, but there was a limit to how long a man could wait.

And now there was Geraldine's letter. How cruel that woman could be. Did she know how much he ached to feel her soft, translucent skin? Or to taste the sweetness of her lips?

He stiffened at the thought of her, as if his body had intentions of its own. But that wasn't why he'd left his wife's bed, or why he was urging the mare toward the brick mansion just around the bend. He was not going to give in to her. He could rise above his urges because he must. Being a good husband to Dora would show the bank's directors there was no truth to the rumors he was carrying on with Geraldine Forrest, and that he was the logical, no, the inevitable choice for the position of vice president.

He just needed to tell Geraldine it was over one last time.

Four

*D*ora heard the sitting room door creak open. She turned from where she stared out the window at the elm trees along the street, watching them glisten under the midmorning light.

Bonmarie stood in the doorway, rubbing a silver serving spoon with a kitchen rag. "Are you going to mope around all day, or are you going to do something productive?"

Dora turned back to the window. She didn't want to speak to Bonmarie. She didn't want to speak to anybody.

"It's not like you to sulk," Bonmarie said.

"I think I'm coming down with something." She kept staring. Three boys in short pants ran down the street, screaming and batting at a ball with brooms, the sunlight bleaching the tops of their heads into halos.

"I know when you're ill, and you're not ill."

"You don't know everything."

"I know you."

Something moved in the reflection. Dora watched the woman walk up behind her.

"What's so interesting out there?"

A brown finch flew up to the windowpane, perched on the sill, and chirped. In an instant it flew back to a tree branch. Even a bird wanted nothing to do with her. "I'm thinking."

"Nobody said things would be easy here, *ma chere*."

Dora fixed on the reflected image of the white scarf tied around Bonmarie's head.

"What happened to the girl who couldn't wait to get out of her mama's house because she was so sure something better waited for her?"

Dora shrugged.

"Seems to me that girl found a better place."

Dora swiveled the chair to face Bonmarie; the woman was still rubbing tarnish from the spoon. "But it's not how it was supposed to be."

"You have a fine husband. You're sitting in a fine house. You're wearing a fine new dress, and you have fine places to go if you'd get up out of that chair." Bonmarie breathed on the spoon and rubbed harder. "Doesn't seem like anything's ruined to me. Maybe you're just looking at it wrong."

"I've ruined everything." She'd never be able to face the Lady Managers again, especially not Mrs. Richmond. Last night she'd tricked herself into thinking she could persuade Charles to leave Chicago and start again somewhere new. But now, in the clear light of day, she knew he would never leave. Not for her, not for anyone. Chicago was his home. It would be easier for him to send her back to New Orleans, just like he threatened to do to Bonmarie. That was the terrible truth she'd been turning over in her mind all morning.

"I've seen you get yourself out of bad situations before."

"Not like this."

"I don't know about that. There was the time you skipped Sunday school." Bonmarie's chest bounced with a low, rumbling chuckle. "I've never seen someone get herself out of trouble like that."

"I wasn't skipping. The class was walking to the riverfront. I got lost."

"So that's how you ended up at Congo Square, clear on the other side of town? I think you just wanted to see what all the ruckus was about."

*I*t was the fourth day of May, and the first heat wave of the year held the city in a sweaty grip. The morning started in the restless way that follows a night that's been too hot to sleep, too humid to move, and too uncomfortable to sit still. Dora passed the hours with her covers kicked off and her nightclothes stripped away, staring at the ceiling and filling the empty time the way she usually did: imagining the privileged life of the families who stayed at Mama's hotel. She was just six years old, but she knew that was the life she wanted, and it would be hers someday; she could feel it like she could feel her fingers and her toes. Mama called it destiny.

Dora rose with the first light of day, too jumpy to stay in bed. In the moist heat it took all her energy to dress and head down for Bonmarie's pre-church breakfast of biscuits, sausage, white gravy, and grits. At the kitchen table, she drifted into daydreams, and Mama hollered at her twice to hurry or they'd be late for Mass.

Outside, as she and Mama walked along Rue Royale toward St. Louis Cathedral, the air felt like soup and dripped with the scents of magnolia blossoms. Dora heard that familiar drumbeat, the one she always heard on Sundays, coming from the open field just beyond the French Quarter called Congo Square, where black people gathered to play their African music. People said they danced, too, but she'd never seen it. She asked Bonmarie if it was true, but the woman wouldn't say. She talked about a lot of things, but never Congo Square.

When she and Mama reached Rue Dumaine, the thumping increased, rolling over the shops and the lush ferns that hung from the ironwork balconies of the Creole town houses, over the shotgun houses and walled-off mansions and carriage houses they passed. It grew even louder when they neared the cathedral.

By the time she and Mama reached St. Louis's wrought-iron gate, Dora hardly saw the street in front of her, lost instead in a vision of those people dancing in the field. She didn't notice the children loitering about while the other parishioners filed inside, not until Sister Bernadette approached Mama.

"I'm taking the children to the river for today's lesson," the young nun said after greeting her mother. "It would be cruel to force them to sit inside. May Isadora join us?"

Mama assented, ignoring Dora's anguished looks. She hadn't attended catechism class in weeks, not since the plantation girls started pointing out the flaws in what she wore. Then she'd passed three of them in the corridor, and they bent their heads together and laughed. She overheard one say "her father," and they burst into another peal of giggles.

Mama didn't know anything about the girls and offered no reprieve with Sister Bernadette. Forced to join the outing, Dora kept to the back, as far as possible from the plantation girls and their new dresses, shiny boots, and perfectly curled hair. She was last in the line Sister Bernadette marched down the alley. When they turned at Rue Chartres, a pebble slipped into a worn spot in Dora's boot and she sat to fish it out. When she rose again, she saw her classmates passing the courthouse next to the cathedral and rounding the corner of Jackson Square.

No one noticed her missing. And then another thought took hold: Maybe she didn't have to go to the river and face the plantation girls after all. Maybe she wouldn't have to sit through another boring Mass, either, because she could go anywhere.

Anywhere.

Over the tolling church bells, she heard the drumming from Congo Square, and the sound beckoned her.

She rounded the courthouse and turned up Rue St. Anne, holding herself close to the building to stay out of sight of Sister Bernadette and the others. She passed Rue Bourbon, Dauphine, Burgundy. The drumming grew louder with each step. When she emerged from the narrow street to face the open field, she stopped. Even with the sun still low in the morning sky, hundreds of black faces filled the space, most of them gathered in a circle beneath an ancient magnolia tree budding with giant white blooms. The women wore dresses, some in tatters, some in finely tailored percale and silk. Many wrapped their hair in scarves wound high upon their heads, others pulled it into tight knots at their necks. The men wore britches to the knee or long pants; some wore shirts, while others bared their dark chests. And what ornaments they wore! Long fringes and ribbons dangled from their arms and legs, bouncing and flapping like streamers as the dancers rocked and stamped their feet to the music. Some wore feathers and shells and raccoon tails.

The road that separated her from the field was deserted except for the festivities on the other side. A carriage in the distance rolled toward them but turned before reaching the square.

Dora crossed over and the music filled her. It was so loud now, and there weren't just drums. There were banjos and quill pipes, fiddles and tambourines. A woman clanked the inside edges of a metal triangle with a baton. Dora edged closer to the circle, eager to see more.

"Let the little girl get by," a woman beside Dora hollered to her neighbor. Both wore blue muslin dresses like the maids in the better homes. The one who hollered smiled down on Dora.

Dora backed away.

"You go on in there if you want to." The woman turned to her friend. "You should have seen her back there, bouncing her head and wiggling back and forth. Never seen a white girl dance before." She laughed a deep, hearty laugh.

Dora pretended she didn't hear. She wasn't bouncing or wiggling or anything of the sort. She moved to the inner rim of the circle, until she had a good view of the dancers in the middle. They were shaking and throwing up their hands. Women hiked up one side of their full skirts to keep them out of the way or tied them up in knots as they stomped to the beat. Their whole bodies moved, gyrating and undulating and spinning around and around.

Dora couldn't resist stepping in. The stomping came first. She mimicked the steps of a woman who looked to be in the throes of a trance. Dora threw her head forward and back, tentatively at first, and then the music took hold. It swept her to a place that felt so alive, she never wanted to leave. It lifted her up and up, until she soared. And then she literally *was* soaring, her feet lifting from the ground. She was free.

But she wasn't; she was in Bonmarie's arms. The woman held her tight and was shaking a fat sausage finger in her face. She was yelling. Had Dora been in that circle a minute? An hour? She felt dizzy. She couldn't make out what Bonmarie said, but she knew what that grimace meant. Bonmarie was angry.

The woman held Dora in her arms and marched her halfway home like that, until the weight of her was too much. She set her down on the street and dragged her by the elbow the rest of the way.

Mama was already home when they arrived, her forehead wrinkled with worry. "Thank Jesus you're all right," she said when they came through the back door. The tone changed when Bonmarie explained where she had been found.

"What in the world were you doing in Congo Square?"

Dora waited for Bonmarie to tell Mama the details, but the woman remained mute. Dora turned back to her mother. "I got lost," she stammered. Mama's frown deepened. Dora knew she'd have to do better than that. She looked to Bonmarie again, but the woman turned and went into the kitchen. "It's those girls," Dora blurted. "The girls laugh at me and now they're laughing about my father."

The look on Mama's face changed into something Dora had never seen. Anger? Surprise? Fear? After a long pause, she said, "Your father?"

Dora nodded.

"Go upstairs and wash," Mama said. She turned from Dora and went to the kitchen window. She put her hands on the counter as if to steady herself. When Dora didn't move, her mother turned back. "Now, Isadora. Go upstairs now."

Dora did what she was told, but it worried her the way Mama had stood there. She went to her room and was halfway out of her Sunday dress when Mama came to the door.

She came in and closed the door. Dora expected she would still be mad, but instead, her mother came up beside her, laid a hand on Dora's cheek, and said, "You'll never be teased by those awful girls again, sweetheart."

She was right. Mama never forced Dora to go to church again, and she never had to go to the schoolhouse, either. The next day Mama told the schoolmistress that because Dora was ill, she was going to hire a home tutor. That's how Dora had finished her lessons, and that's when Mama had decided Dora should stay close to home. There was too much danger and disease in the streets, she'd say, and Dora needed to be protected. She never said anything about Dora slipping away from her catechism class, and she never again mentioned Congo Square.

*D*ora fidgeted with the crocheted doily on the chair's armrest. "But I did get lost that day." Dora glanced up at Bonmarie. "I just didn't try to get found."

"You must've convinced your mama of that. I wouldn't have thought it possible, but you did."

"She never let me go anywhere after that."

"That was for your own good. Yellow fever, typhoid, not to mention scoundrels."

Dora shrugged. It was true. She had gotten off easy.

"Why don't you take the carriage down to the lake? Get some fresh air." Bonmarie held up the spoon for a final check, and tucked the rag under her apron strings.

"Maybe I will. Or maybe I'll see if Mrs. Tillday wants to go to the Fair."

"Take a shawl," Bonmarie said, going to the door. "If you're catching a cold, you should stay warm."

"Don't be fussy. I feel fine."

"That's what I thought." Bonmarie left the room, but kept the door open wide behind her.

Dora went to her writing desk in the sitting room, pulled out two sheets of stationery, and loaded the fountain pen. She wrote the first note quickly, an invitation to Mrs. Tillday to accompany her to the Midway Plaisance to begin their work at the Egyptian Theatre. It wasn't her first choice for a Saturday afternoon outing, but she had to do something if she wanted to remain a Lady Manager. When she finished, she sealed the envelope and called to Bonmarie to have Harold deliver it and wait for a reply. While she waited for his return, she worked on the more important letter: her apology to Mrs. Richmond. What must the woman think? Across the top of the page she wrote "Dear Mrs. Richmond" and paused. How would she explain herself? She thought of Mrs. Forrest and those hurtful words. She couldn't repeat any of that. Even if Mrs. Richmond believed her, it would create many more problems than it solved. She tapped the pen again. Then it came to her. She dipped the pen in the inkwell and wrote:

> *I hope this note finds you well. I wanted to write to explain why I left so mysteriously yesterday and to allay any concerns you might have about my sudden departure. I did the clumsiest thing, you see. I was wearing a new pair of boots and I caught the heel on the edge of a rug when I was trying to get one of your lovely scones. I nearly twisted my heel right off. The pain was unimaginable, and I was so afraid I might cry or make a nuisance of myself at your gathering. It seemed best to leave quietly. I hope you will accept my sincere apology for not taking a proper leave.*

She read it over again. The lie gave her a sick feeling, but there was no other way. She signed her name, sealed it in an envelope, took it to the foyer, and set it on the silver tray to wait for Harold's return.

Back upstairs, she changed into a town dress. She was tucking the last pins into her hat when she heard the carriage turn up the driveway and then a second carriage stop in front of the house. She peeked through the side of the curtain sheers and saw Mrs. Tillday stepping down from the second carriage's driver's seat and Harold trotting up to help her. Dora checked herself in the mirror and was on the stairs when Harold opened the door and ushered in her guest.

"I was so happy to hear from you," Mrs. Tillday said. "I decided to come straightaway. I hope that's all right."

"Absolutely," she said. To Harold, who stood beside the door with his hat in his hands, she added, "I have another letter for you to deliver." She handed him the note from the silver tray. "For Mrs. Richmond. You know the place?"

He nodded, slid the envelope into his coat pocket, and slipped away.

"Have you been to the Egyptian Theatre yet, Mrs. Tillday?" she asked as she pulled her parasol from the rack.

"Henry wouldn't allow it." The woman grinned bashfully. "Dreadful place, he said. But he's glad enough to have me do Lady Manager business."

"Funny, Mr. Chambers feels exactly the same way."

"You must think me a complete fool for my behavior at the meeting," Mrs. Tillday said, guiding the carriage past one Gold Coast mansion after another.

No one had ever worried what she thought before. "I don't think anything of the sort," she said.

"Really?" Mrs. Tillday smiled shyly. "I wanted to invite you out today, but you left in such a hurry yesterday. I thought I must have offended you."

"That wasn't it, not at all." It was Dora's turn to feel sheepish. "I just couldn't stay any longer. I had to get home."

"Yes, of course," her partner said.

Mrs. Tillday guided her silver-haired horse around a bend onto a newer street of grand mansions with wide swaths of manicured lawns. In the French Quarter, the best houses kept their gardens hidden behind courtyard walls, but not here. Lush, green grass and shrubbery surrounded the homes, and the bigger the house, the more exquisite the garden. Across the front of one Federal-style estate with white shutters were carefully tended tulips and gladiolus. "Look at that one," Dora said. "That might be the grandest house I've ever seen."

"Mrs. Forrest would be glad to hear you say so," Mrs. Tillday said.

"She lives there?" The words sounded so feeble.

Mrs. Tillday nodded.

A sick feeling came over her. The sound of the clopping and the exhalations from the horse, and the wheels grinding against the hard earth reverberated in her ears.

"She's not home if you're worried about seeing her," Mrs. Tillday said.

"Why would you say that?" Dora tried to sound casual.

Mrs. Tillday kept her gaze on the road ahead of her. "Just a guess. I'm sure she's at the train station, though. I heard her talking to Mrs. Sheffield after the meeting."

"She's leaving?" Dora's heart lightened.

"Mrs. Sheffield is. I heard Mrs. Forrest say she'd accompany her at noon, so I'm sure that's where she'd be now. The train station is on the other side of town."

Dora fidgeted with a fold of her skirt. "It's a pity Mrs. Sheffield will miss the Fair. She and Mrs. Forrest seem terribly close friends."

"Terribly close, yes," Mrs. Tillday said with a smirk. "But I wouldn't say Mrs. Forrest has any particularly close friends."

"It didn't appear that way at the meeting."

"Most people think she's vile."

"Then why do they tolerate her?"

"Her money, of course. She has loads of it." Mrs. Tillday snapped the reins. "No one would dare say a word against her or they'd be left off the guest list to her dinner parties and afternoon teas. People fear her."

When Dora didn't say anything, Mrs. Tillday continued. "You know, I've been introduced to her at least a dozen times, and every time she looks at me like she has no idea who I am."

"You should consider yourself lucky," Dora muttered, and adjusted her parasol to block the sunlight warming her cheek.

"I hadn't thought of it that way. Perhaps I should," Mrs. Tillday said, then laughed.

Dora laughed, too. For the rest of the ride they talked of amiable things: the weather, dressmakers, husbands. Dora wondered how it was that this woman sitting beside her and talking so freely could be the same one who could barely lift her gaze from the floor in Mrs. Richmond's gallery.

The closer they came to the fairgrounds, the more crowded the streets became with carriages and pedestrians on their way to the Exposition. Soon they could see the Ferris wheel and the captive hot air balloon swaying over the trees, and the dozens of flags and spires and domes that rose from the tops of the buildings that made up the architectural wonderland that was called the White City, those beautiful alabaster palaces with their grand columns and statues. "Have you seen the Court of Honor yet?" Dora asked.

"Henry brought me on opening day, but there were so many people it was difficult to see much of anything."

Charles had refused to come to the May 1 opening because of the crowds. The newspapers predicted a strong showing for President Grover Cleveland's speech at the Administration Building, and the reporting later told of the legions that had poured into the Court of Honor for the ceremony. When the president pressed the button that turned on the Fair's lights and set its motors in motion, it triggered a frenzy. The mob surged and several ladies caught in the crush fainted; children were separated from their families; and thieves picked pockets and stole purses. Charles said they were missing nothing but grief by delaying their visit until the next day, and Dora had to agree.

"How brave you were to persevere," Dora said. "The newspapers said it was awful."

"The papers exaggerated. It wasn't nearly as bad as what I read the next day. I suppose you can't believe everything you read."

Mrs. Tillday brought the carriage to a stop where other carriages had congregated between the Illinois Central Railroad line and the Transportation Building. Gunshots rang out when they climbed down; Dora ducked beside the carriage in fright.

Mrs. Tillday came around beside her, smiling. "Don't mind that. It's Buffalo Bill's Wild West show." She pointed across the street to a giant tent that housed the traveling show of cowboys, militiamen, American Indians, and Annie Oakley, a sharpshooter who people said could split a playing card in two with one bullet and riddle it with another few holes before it reached the ground.

Dora straightened and smoothed her skirts and sleeves. "Of course. I don't know what I was thinking." She tried to hide her embarrassment by hurrying toward the entrance, where a line had formed in front of a ticket seller collecting the fifty-cent admission charge. Dora and Mrs. Tillday walked to the front of the queue, where they announced to the young man behind the counter that they were Lady Managers. He waved them through before moving on to the next in line.

Dora guided her partner to the Exposition's Court of Honor, the ring of brilliant white palaces—the Agriculture Building, Machinery Hall, the Mines and Mining Building, the Electricity Building, the Administration Building, the Manufacturers and Liberal Arts Building. She relished the sight of all the spires and domes, pillars and arches, the rolling arcades and carved columns, and the pantheon of gods and goddesses carved in relief or rising from the rooftops, entreating the men and women below to raise their ambitions, to strive for greatness. It didn't matter that the White City buildings were crafted of mere plaster made to look like marble. When sunlight struck those white exteriors, it alchemized them into gleaming diamonds that radiated greatness. The whole place was like a crucible that could transmute something ordinary into something profound, and it whispered to Dora of possibilities.

Dora took a deep breath. She'd know where she was even if the White City wasn't laid out before her. The sweet molasses-covered popcorn, the savory chili con carne, the roasted corn on the cob, the beer—all the smells of the dining rooms, snack counters, and vendor carts blended into a single scent that belonged only to the Fair.

Her stomach rumbled; she hadn't eaten since breakfast.

She spotted a cart selling nickel scoops of ice cream. "Have you tried these yet?"

Mrs. Tillday shook her head.

"Two, please. Vanilla." The attendant handed her two heaping scoops on cones and she handed one to Mrs. Tillday. "It's sweet and creamy and cold and delicious, all at the same time."

Mrs. Tillday accepted the confection but looked at it as if she didn't know what to do with it.

"Like this." Dora planted her lips on the scoop and worked off a small bite.

Mrs. Tillday tried, tentatively at first, but quickly became adept.

With their cones in hand, they joined the throng of bodies parading through the Court of Honor, the ring of neoclassical buildings extolling the highest ideals of Western progress and achievement. At the center of it all was the great basin, a man-made lagoon in the shape of a ship's hull, a tribute to Christopher Columbus's celebrated vessels: the *Pinta*, the *Niña*, and the *Santa Maria*. On the lagoon's near end stood the Columbus Fountain, with robed figures frozen in the act of rowing the great explorer's ship toward the horizon over Lake Michigan.

But it was what stood at the far end that most excited Dora: the golden figure called the Statue of the Republic, rising sixty-five feet with a laurel wreath set upon its head, holding a spear in one hand and an eagle perched atop a globe in the other. The classical figure embodied the fulfillment of the New World's promise, a stunning vision of a robust America confidently greeting its prosperous and optimistic future.

"Isn't it wonderful that the Statue of the Republic is a woman?"

"I hadn't thought about it before," Mrs. Tillday said after swallowing a bite of ice cream.

"It might have made more sense to be a man. A man discovered America, men built it, and men run it. But things are changing."

"I suppose you're right."

"I think even the Board of Lady Managers is proof of it. Charles says the Fair's directors didn't realize what a monster they were creating when they formed the board, but look at how much these women have accomplished."

Originally, the Lady Managers had been charged with decorating the Women's Building and selecting jurors for the female art competitions. But with the leadership of Bertha Honoré Palmer, a woman admired for her intelligence and accomplishments long before she married Potter Palmer, the board gained influence. It didn't take long for the Lady Managers to begin advising the Commission on nearly every facet of the Fair. They fought unsuccessfully for limits on alcohol sales and Sunday closure, but everyone knew the group's counsel was always sought and usually abided by.

"We should probably get to the Egyptian Theatre," Mrs. Tillday said.

Dora finished the last of the ice cream and wiped her fingers with her handkerchief. Mrs. Tillday did the same, then they set off toward the Midway Plaisance. They passed the Transportation Building, where every day visitors arrived by the thousands by rail. They followed the Lagoon and its Wooded Island, where the peaks of the Japanese teahouse poked above a leafy canopy, passed the Horticulture Building, and then the Women's Building.

The mile-long Midway Plaisance jutted off behind the Women's Building toward Washington Park, clinging to the main fairgrounds like a scruffy little sister clutching to the backside of a sophisticated lady. It wasn't formally part of the Fair, but its exhibits—most offered for an additional fee—were helping the Commission recoup the Fair's building costs.

Though the Exposition and the Midway sat side by side, they shared little more than visitors. The Exposition's buildings and grounds reflected the genius of the country's best architects, luminaries like Daniel Hudson Burnham, Richard Morris Hunt, and Charles McKim, along with the landscape artistry of Frederick Law Olmsted, designer of New York's Central Park. It was his skill that turned what had been marshland along the banks of Lake Michigan into this network of ponds, canals, islands, and parkland that more than a hundred thousand visitors descended upon each day.

The Midway Plaisance, on the other hand, looked like what it was—a set of slapped-together concessions united by a single common goal: to part people from their money. Here, the power of green—or silver or copper, depending on what was in your pocket—trumped the White City's lofty ideals. There were beer gardens, dancing halls, snack shops, and souvenir stalls; if people would pay for it, it could likely be found somewhere along the Midway.

When Dora and Mrs. Tillday passed underneath the Illinois Central Railroad viaduct separating the Midway Plaisance from the fairgrounds, Dora kept her eyes on the Ferris wheel, its giant iron beam spokes rotating like a monumental bicycle wheel.

And it *was* a monument, built for the sole purpose of outshining the Eiffel Tower, the architectural crown jewel the Parisians debuted at their Exposition Universelle four years earlier. In sheer size, the Great Wheel didn't awe its visitors as the Eiffel Tower did. It stood 264 feet tall, roughly a fourth of the height of the Eiffel's spire, though it still dwarfed the Cairo Street and Moorish minarets, the German Village's spire, and even the flags waving atop the tallest White City buildings on the Exposition's main fairgrounds. Yet it was like nothing anyone had ever seen, nothing anyone thought possible—because it *moved*.

American engineering made it possible for passengers who

paid the fifty-cent toll to board one of the wheel's thirty-six wood-veneered carriages, each so large it could carry sixty people for a two-revolution ride, and see not only the rooftops of the Midway and Exposition halls, but miles of the Chicago landscape: the factory smokestacks and tenements, the railroad tracks and stockyards, the banks and churches, even the blue expanse of Lake Michigan stretching along the horizon. It was a feat without equal.

From the ground, it also served as the Midway's central marker, standing conveniently, Dora thought, at the entrance to Cairo Street. Today she followed it like a beacon.

When they neared the entrance to the medieval Irish Village, with its makeshift castle that looked like a displaced battle fort, Dora fought the urge to linger near the trio singing a tune in their native Gaelic. At the Hagenbeck Animal Show building, she tugged at Mrs. Tillday's sleeve when her partner stopped to watch a short, pudgy man with a limp as he yelled in German and chased a pink poodle through the back door.

"Couldn't we stop in to see the animals?" Mrs. Tillday asked, pulling Dora toward the wide, red double doors. "They have a tiger who balances on a ball, and parrots! I've never seen a parrot."

Dora pulled back. "We'll hardly make the next show as it is."

Mrs. Tillday's shoulders slumped. "I don't see why you're in such a hurry. I've heard the shows are just dreadful."

"It's what Mrs. Richmond wants," Dora countered. "We can't disappoint her."

Grudgingly, Mrs. Tillday acquiesced and they headed onward along the broad thoroughfare, between the long houses perched on stilts of the Javanese Settlement and the thatched roof huts of the Samoan Islanders, past the timber framed German Village buildings and the domed ones in the Turkish Village. At each camp, recommenders stood out front, clamoring for attention, hollering about the souvenir shops or a performance or some other not-to-be-missed and never-to-be-seen-again attraction inside. A dizzying array of smells wafted from the food carts, some sweet, some savory, and the hungry hordes queued for a taste.

Finally they reached Cairo Street, sometimes called the Street in Cairo or simply the Street. A line of men snaked its way through the theater's arched doorway.

Dora and Mrs. Tillday went to the ticket seller, told him they were Lady Managers, and entered without charge.

Inside, Dora brushed by the men who stood in the back. The theater was more crowded than she remembered it being last time. She could hardly breathe, let alone see the stage. Mrs. Tillday was looking around as though she were lost. "Should we stand back here or try to find a space closer to the stage?" Dora asked.

Mrs. Tillday made a face. "Are those our only choices?"

Dora teetered on her tiptoes, looking for seats, but could see none. A musician began a slow melody. In one corner, she could see a turbaned man on a bench hunched over a long, slender horn, his bronze fingers tripping along his instrument's spine. Then another musician wrapped his arms around a bulbous mandolin and joined the tune, and a third balancing a chalice-shaped drum over his lap added percussion. From the whistles and catcalls, the dancers also must have come onto the stage. She tapped Mrs. Tillday on the shoulder and motioned for her to follow.

Dora worked her way deeper into the crowd, passing more men until the sight of one made her stop. Mr. Farouk. He stood with his back against the wall at the rear corner. A long black tunic over narrow pants and that black hair that brushed the tops of his shoulders made him look like a shadow. His arms rested across his chest. She would've turned back, but he'd already seen her.

Beneath the drift of hair that crossed his brow, she could see he watched her.

She lifted her palm in a tentative wave and tried to smile. How inadequate she felt. His expression didn't change, but he moved toward her.

"Another visit from Lady Managers," he said, breaking into a smile only when he approached.

"Yes, hello," Dora stammered, hoping she would be heard over the rising music. "You do remember our arrangement, I hope." Dora felt Mrs. Tillday tap her on the back. "Yes, oh, Mrs. Tillday, may I introduce Mr. Farouk. He is the manager here."

Mr. Farouk nodded solemnly at Mrs. Tillday. "Welcome to our theater, Mrs. Tillday."

"I don't know if you remember me, but I'm Mrs. Chambers. Mrs. Richmond—"

He raised his palm and closed his eyes. Dora noticed how long his eyelashes were, longer than her own. Longer than any she'd ever seen.

"I remember," he said when he opened his eyes again. "Mrs. Chambers, it is a pleasure to see you again, and we have been expecting your return. I wish I could offer you better viewing, but our theater is quite full. However, if you'll permit me, I think I can be of some service." Without waiting for an answer, he tapped the shoulder of the man in front of him. When the gentleman turned around, Mr. Farouk leaned into his ear and whispered something. The listener shot a look at Mrs. Tillday and Dora, leaned in to say something in the ear of the man in front of him, and then stepped aside. The man in front of him did the same and soon there was a pathway to the edge of the standing room. Mr. Farouk slipped through, leaned down to the ears of two men sitting in the last row of seats, pulled something from his pockets that looked like dollar bills, and handed one to each of the men. The men rose, shook Mr. Farouk's hand, and took places in the standing room gallery. He gestured for Dora and Mrs. Tillday to take the seats.

"Thank you," Dora said, a blush coming over her. "You really didn't have to do that."

Mr. Farouk smiled at her. "Ladies should not have to stand. Next time, consider arriving earlier, or send word and we will reserve seats for you."

Mrs. Tillday thanked him and then he left, disappearing into the crowd. She leaned over to Dora, and whispered, "Who did you say that was?"

"Mr. Hossam Farouk," she said, feeling the weight of each vowel and consonant linger on her tongue.

She turned her attention to the stage. With her unobstructed view, she saw three musicians sitting on one of the long benches at the back of the stage and several dancers sitting on the other. Between the benches stood a potted ficus tree and across the wall behind hung two framed mirrors, a portrait of a man—an Egyptian leader, by the formal look of it—and framed Arabic writing. A woman danced at the center of the stage, and she and the others sitting along the back wore the same costumes they'd worn on Mrs. Richmond's visit. They did not wear veils or anything that suggested they had made any change at all. Dora rubbed her temples.

"What are we supposed to do?" Mrs. Tillday whispered.

Dora searched the faces of the men behind her, and the rows of men's heads in front of her. "I'm not sure exactly."

Just then the dancer, a woman who might've been Dora's mother's age, sashayed closer to the musicians. Two of them stopped their playing and only the drummer continued. Using both palms and a good number of his fingers, the drummer created his own symphony of percussion. Each pulse pushed the woman's hips in a different direction. They bounced and thrust and wiggled. She moved them in a way that made her look like she was walking, though she didn't move her feet. Then more of her body was moving. Her arms glided through the air with flourishing flips of her wrists. Then she stomped, making every part of herself tremble and shake. The audience erupted with roars of cheers.

In front of her, Dora saw a man elbow his neighbor. When the dancer kicked out her leg, exposing her skin-tone stockings almost to the knee, Dora didn't need to hear the whistles to know it wasn't appropriate. By taking stock of the audience's responses, Dora compiled a mental checklist of what the dancers would have to change.

A few minutes into her performance, moving from center stage, then over to the musicians, and back, the dancer worked her way to the other women, who sat watching her or dazing off in distraction. When she neared, one rose from the bench and mimicked the dancer's movements. They danced together, facing each other for a moment and then turned away from each other. The new dancer then made her way to the center of the stage and the first one took her seat. It was a rotation that continued down the line, with each woman taking a turn on the stage.

When the last one rose to begin her dance, Dora recognized it was Amina Mahomet. Today she wore a blue skirt and vest over a white gauzy shirt, and the same ribbon belt and ropes of beads and coins she'd worn before.

The music's tempo slowed and the woman's movements seemed to stretch and crawl. In her dance there was a subtlety the others didn't have, as if the roll of hips and the arc of her arms told a story one movement at a time. The drummer remained quiet, and the horn and a mandolin-like instrument accompanied her with a quiet, mournful melody. She swayed back, leaning until she was nearly parallel to the floor, and then scooped herself up again in a wavelike motion.

Dora watched the woman's shoulders sweep through undulations, and then the movement flowed into her hips and they rolled and churned in a mesmerizing way. When the woman arched her back and lifted and rotated her chest, Dora realized what image the dance brought to mind, and a heat flushed her cheeks. She looked away and studied the men.

Each stared forward, engrossed, drinking in the dancer as if she were water to drench their parched lips. The gentleman sitting beside her rested his hands on his knees but she could see how they clenched, his fingers gripping into the wool of his trousers and his flesh. His breath quickened. The dancer was showing more of herself and the secrets of a feminine body than any proper lady would betray even in her husband's bed.

A woman such as this would never disappoint a man as Dora had with Charles. She knew she was a failure in that realm. The truth of it gnawed at her, but what did he expect? He demanded she be a proper lady, yet when she behaved properly when he made his advances, he turned away in frustration. She disappointed him either way.

Dora's glance darted between the men and the dancer, watching the effect of each dip and sway and wiggle. Even as the men's fever increased, the dancer remained serene. How easily she corrupted them, how easily she led them.

"No wonder so many people want to shut this place down," Mrs. Tillday said, her eyes narrowed on the stage. "It's beyond indecent."

The music's tempo quickened and Amina Mahomet finished her dance with a sweep of her hand above her head, striking a pose on the last beat. The men jumped to their feet in a roar of cheers.

"What should we do now?" Mrs. Tillday looked around, almost fearful.

While the men filed out around them, Dora and Mrs. Tillday did nothing. Dora composed herself; they had a mission. The Lady Managers expected results. When the theater was nearly empty, she stood. "We must speak to them."

Mrs. Tillday hesitated, then rose. "If we must."

They approached the lip of the stage, where the dancers and musicians sat on the benches and pillows on the floor. The men were silent, as if biding time until the next performance. The women chatted and giggled, some braided other women's hair. Amina Mahomet watched Dora and Mrs. Tillday.

"Hello again, Mrs. Chambers. How did you like the performance?" Amina asked when they approached. "I hope we did not break any of your Lady Manager rules." She turned to her companions and added something in Arabic that made them giggle.

Dora gritted her teeth. "It was a lovely performance. It is remarkable how you are able to move with so much . . . " She stopped and tried again. "I'm sure you are aware that yesterday's *Tribune* was filled with letters to the editor from the Society for the Suppression of Vice calling for your removal, and I know you must be as eager as we are to remedy this situation."

Amina's expression hardened.

Dora took note of all those vacant stares. Perhaps they didn't know much English, but they knew some. "On our last visit, Mrs. Richmond made suggestions for improvement—"

"Improvement?" Amina's lips tilted into a sneer.

"She requested changes, and I assure you it is critical those changes be implemented."

"I don't recall that request," Amina said. "Would you refresh my memory?"

Mrs. Tillday offered no help at all. The woman was gazing around as if counting the stripes on the wallpaper. Dora forced a smile. "Of course I can." She reiterated Mrs. Richmond's comments about proper conduct and more modest costumes. "If you change these things, perhaps the Fair's directors will allow you to keep your wages."

Amina stood, defiant. "We have earned our wages. They cannot take them."

"Mrs. Richmond seemed to be under a different impression." Dora caught Mrs. Tillday's eye. With a tilt of her head she motioned her to follow her to the door. Mrs. Tillday obeyed.

"What do you propose?" Amina called after them.

Dora paused before turning back. "Small things. The kicks, for instance. You must notice how the men react to them." She scanned the dancers' faces, letting them know she included all of them in the directive. "American ladies never expose this part of their anatomy. It's unchaste. Must that particular maneuver be part of the act?"

Amina spoke in lowered Arabic to the others. Some nodded, some shook their heads. One dancer, a feather of a girl with a gap between her front teeth, turned away from Amina and crossed her arms in a huff. To Dora, Amina said, "This can be accommodated."

Dora continued through her checklist. The hip thrusts, the shoulder shimmies that made their bosoms sway, the eye contact. In some ways it was the eye contact that seemed the most intimate breach of all. "Do you have anything to add?" she asked Mrs. Tillday.

Mrs. Tillday shook her head. "Are we finished?"

"Almost. There is still the matter of the veils."

While none of the other requests were met with whole-hearted assent, none received outright rejection, either. But this one caused a stir. Arms crossed over chests, heads turned away. Amina rubbed her eyes.

Dora felt her edge slipping. "Could you give them a try? It would show the Lady Managers good faith."

Amina spoke to the others in Arabic. There were many harsh words and head shakes. Finally, Amina turned back to Dora. "May we speak in private?" A few of the other dancers whispered harshly between themselves. Amina shushed them over her shoulder. "Just for a moment?"

Dora didn't know what to say. "Do you mind?" she asked her partner.

"Is it necessary? What shall I do?" Mrs. Tillday's face registered confusion, distrust, then worry.

"I apologize if the request appears rude," Amina answered. "It's just that there is a sensitive matter I'd like to discuss with Mrs. Chambers. I would prefer not to discuss it openly."

Dora knew she couldn't refuse. Already she was failing Charles; she couldn't fail here as well, not when she was so close. And she was close, she could see it in Amina's eyes. With a pleading look she beseeched Mrs. Tillday to allow it.

Mrs. Tillday fumed. Her lips pressed into a straight line and she looked everywhere but at the dancers. "I'll wait outside. Please don't make me wait long." Mrs. Tillday gripped the sides of her skirts and went to the door, punishing the wooden floor with each step.

Dora watched her go. She wouldn't have guessed her partner could show such anger.

"Will you come with me, Mrs. Chambers?"

The decision was already made, and there was no turning back.

*A*mina Mahomet stepped out of her slippers and reclined on a nest of tangerine, emerald, and turquoise cushions. Her silky indigo skirt spread out like a fan around her. "We sit on the floor cushions, but you might be more comfortable on the divan," the belly dancer said to Dora, motioning to a bench along the wall.

Along with the bench, the room, tucked behind a door marked "Performers Only" beside the stage, contained a scattering of large pillows, three small tables arranged haphazardly around the room, and Oriental rugs overlapping the floor.

Dora set her parasol and purse on the bench and lowered herself onto a set of cushions across from the dancer. When she bent, a stay point in her corset jabbed her and made her straighten. She tugged at her corset's bottom edge through the loose fabric of her blouse and tried again with the same result. She gave up and sat on the bench.

The dancer watched Dora but said nothing of her difficulty. "So what is the sensitive matter?" Dora asked.

Amina reached around the table beside her and retrieved a long, skinny vase with two long tubes protruding from its side. "Do you smoke, Mrs. Chambers?"

Dora shook her head and watched the dancer fit one of the tubes between her lips, light a match from a nearby tin, and hold it to a tiny metal bowl atop the vase. When she breathed in, a brownish resin in the bowl glowed orange and bubbles formed in the water inside the vase. The dancer held a deep breath, then slowly let the wisps of smoke escape her lips. She tilted the vase toward Dora in offering. Again Dora declined. The dancer took another long, slow inhalation.

"Is this why you brought me here?"

Amina exhaled and set the contraption aside. "No. It is our custom to offer something before asking for something from another. This is what I have."

"I'm sorry, I didn't—"

"Do not apologize. I am still learning everyone here is in a hurry."

"It's just that my partner is waiting."

"Yes, the woman who wears her disgust for us like her pretty pink dress. She would never help us. We are no better than animals to her, are we not?" Amina paused. "Do not answer. I see something different on your face; that is why I am asking for your help."

"I'm a Lady Manager just like Mrs. Tillday."

Amina acted as if she didn't hear. "One of our dancers is sick. A fever."

"Have you summoned a doctor?"

"Hossam asked the Fair men to send one, but they will not."

"Did he explain it was serious?"

"He asked them to see for themselves. They would not even do that."

"So you want me to ask them for you?"

"No, we do not want their help. We can help her ourselves. We have American money."

"Then why do you need me?"

"We need to find a doctor."

"I hardly know anyone."

"I trust no one else," Amina said. She leaned forward, her face solemn, her voice low. "Already everyone here has lied. You are the only person who does not look at us like we are the same as the camels and the donkeys. You are kind. I see it in your face."

The words stabbed at Dora. She wasn't kind and she couldn't do it. She shouldn't even be in this room.

"Our friend will die if she does not get help," Amina said.

Die? "There's no one else you can ask?"

Amina shook her head.

She couldn't let a woman die. "I'll try to find someone for you. It just might take some time."

Amina rose from her pillows and came toward Dora. Dora rose, too. "You do us a great service." She threw her arms around Dora and kissed both cheeks.

Dora stumbled backward.

"In return, we will do what you ask. Everything. No kicking, no flirting, even the veils."

It was more than she could have hoped. "Thank you," she whispered, taking Amina's hand in her own and squeezing it gently before letting it go. She could already see Mrs. Richmond's pleased face when she reported the success; she could see the pride in Charles's eyes. "Thank you," she said again.

Outside the theater, Dora found Mrs. Tillday huddled in the shadows, watching a middle-aged man atop an empty vegetable crate address a group gathered around him. He grabbed the lapels of his tweed jacket and puffed out his chest. "Ladies and gents," he called out in a thick Irish brogue. "Gather round to witness an astonishing feat of athletic skill. The Club Swingers of Persia have traveled across land and sea to share with you a most ancient rite, a revered exercise, an awesome demonstration of masculine strength and precision."

She sidled up to Mrs. Tillday as two bare-chested men in turbans and breeches, holding fat wooden clubs in each hand, emerged through the wall of people standing around the barker. They took places like sentinels at his side.

"So what was so secret?" Mrs. Tillday asked curtly.

"As you probably suspected, there was no secret. She wanted to save face in front of the others. Appearances, you know." Dora studied Mrs. Tillday's expression, hoping it was the answer the woman wanted.

"Imagine that, an Egyptian trying to save face." Mrs. Tillday shrugged, her look of indifference unchanged.

Dora's mind raced as she watched the Club Swingers twirl their heavy clubs, whipping them overhead and flinging them from side to side in furious figure eights. The crowd gasped, but Mrs. Tillday stood stone-faced.

"Shall we shop for souvenirs before heading back?" Dora asked. "I've been considering a Persian rug for the foyer. Wouldn't that be lovely? Something colorful and—"

Mrs. Tillday slanted a glance at the rug shop on the far side of the square with its carpets rolled into tall tubes that lined the inside walls. "I'd hardly trust their craftsmanship. Marshall Field's would have much better quality."

Dora tapped her lip. "I suppose you're right. Perhaps a turn on the Ferris wheel, then?"

"It's awful. Henry forced me onto the thing last week; I nearly fainted." Mrs. Tillday's tone softened. "There is someplace I'd like to visit if you don't mind. I mean, if we have time . . . "

"I'd love to. Whatever you like."

"The Zoopraxographical Hall, then? It's just around the corner there." She pointed away from Cairo Street to the main Midway avenue.

"The Zoo-what?"

"Come with me. It's easier to show you." Mrs. Tillday grabbed her hand and pulled her past the Street's entrance toward a squat red-brick building that looked more like a bank. She dragged Dora up the steps and doled out the twenty-five-cent admission for them both. When they entered, Mrs. Tillday paused. "Just look at them," she said breathlessly.

Photographs covered every gallery wall, all of them grouped in long rows or clusters of rows. Dora stepped up to the closest series. The first photograph depicted a man crouched as if ready to jump. In the next frame, the same man extended his legs just a bit, in the next he extended them a bit more, and so on, so that each frame captured a progressive stage of the man's leap. When aligned together, they created a graceful arc. In the adjacent series, a woman twirled, making her diaphanous dress spin away from her. In another, the frames held frozen moments of a horse's run.

"It's all movement, you see." Mrs. Tillday stood beside her. "Each frame a precise flicker of time, and when they're strung together, it's as if you can see the subject moving right before your eyes."

"I've never seen anything like it," Dora said, moving down the wall to a sequence of a man walking and holding a large stone on his shoulder.

She stopped when a British man with a long white beard stepped onto a platform on the other side of the gallery and cleared his throat. On the table beside him sat a wood and metal contraption.

Mrs. Tillday grabbed Dora's arm, and whispered, "Oh, this is going to be marvelous. You're going to love this."

Dora smiled, delighted by the giddiness in her partner's voice.

There seemed nothing left of the ill feelings about the Egyptian Theatre when Mrs. Tillday tugged Dora toward the crowd pressing toward the lecturer.

When they left the hall afterward, Mrs. Tillday looked almost smug.

Dora threaded her arm through her partner's. "What are you so happy about?"

"I can't wait to tell Henry how wrong he is. He calls it poppycock, all these photographs of men and women and animals. But you saw for yourself that they're more than pretty pictures."

When the white-bearded lecturer, who introduced himself to the crowd as Eadweard Muybridge, the photographer of the images on the walls, had cranked a gear on the contraption he called a zoopraxiscope, it turned a disk emblazoned with a series of horse images and cast a moving picture onto the white screen behind him. Dora had gasped with the others when it looked as if the horse would run right off the stage.

"Henry says the zoopraxiscope is nothing but an imitation of the kinetoscope Thomas Edison demonstrated in New York a couple of years ago, but it's a ridiculous claim. Edison hasn't even perfected his machine well enough to display it here at the Fair. Besides, even when it's ready, the moving picture can be seen by only one viewer at a time because it runs inside a box. The zoopraxiscope projects the image for anyone to see. It's by far the superior invention. The British can be very clever, even if Henry refuses to acknowledge that an Englishman could ever outdo an American."

Dora nodded as though she agreed, but she was too happy to be back in Mrs. Tillday's good graces to care about inventions.

When they approached the carriage, Mrs. Tillday turned, and said, "The belly dancer, you say she's agreed to the changes?"

"Absolutely," she replied, alarmed by the turn in the conversation.

"I'm surprised they didn't give us more trouble than that," Mrs. Tillday continued, unwrapping the horse's reins from the hitching post.

"She was quite rational about it, actually," she said, yet immediately wished she hadn't.

"You are joking, aren't you? They're Egyptians." The way she drew out the syllables of the word made it sound like a disease, or worse.

"Of course, you're right," Dora said quickly, and hoisted herself up onto the carriage's passenger side. The last thing she wanted to do was argue about the Egyptians, but there was still that troubling matter of her bargain. It gave her an idea. Perhaps she could change the subject and get the answer she needed at the same time. "Do you know any doctors you could recommend?" she said as casually as she could manage.

Mrs. Tillday's eyebrows twisted. "Are you feeling ill?" She reached over from her side of the carriage bench and took Dora's arm.

"No, I'm fine," she said, pulling back. "I just thought of it. I mean, I've been meaning to ask. It's Bonmarie. My maid hasn't been feeling well."

"The poor dear. I do know a doctor, a splendid one actually. Dr. Cheswick. Highly recommended."

Maybe this was all going to work out easily after all. "How might I find him?"

"He's coming by the house tonight for dinner. I can say something to him, if you'd like."

Dora's smile faded. "You know him quite well?"

"We've been seeing him for years. He's become one of Mr. Tillday's closest friends."

"Don't say anything yet." Dora paused. Her mind raced. "Sometimes Bonmarie exaggerates to get attention. You know how the help can be." She forced a laugh. "Let me just be sure, and then I'll make the arrangements."

"If that's what you prefer," Mrs. Tillday said, giving the rein a snap to set the horse in motion.

What she preferred, indeed. Dora took refuge under her parasol, as much to hide her disappointment as to protect the bit of cheek her hat brim didn't shade. What she preferred was to be done with this business, but like everything else in Chicago, it couldn't be easy. How could she find a doctor without the Lady Managers or Charles finding out?

Mrs. Tillday cast a sidelong glance in Dora's direction and twitched the rein to one side to signal the horse to turn at the corner. "I think this place is taking a toll on you," she said when they rounded the bend.

Dora looked back over her shoulder at the Cairo Street minaret and the Ferris wheel and all the rest of the Midway diminishing in the distance, and thought she couldn't agree more.

Five

*D*ora was coming down the stairs in her ruffled tea gown for Bonmarie's Sunday breakfast of biscuits and sausage gravy with chicory coffee when Charles poked his head out of his study.

"Dora, may I see you, please?"

She flinched. Had she done something wrong again? "Good morning, dear. You're up early."

"Nine is hardly early. I've been waiting for you."

"You should've told me. I've been writing to my mother." In truth she'd crawled out of bed only moments before, but there was no reason to tell him that, not if he was already angry.

"Come with me." He guided her by the shoulder down the hallway.

"How mysterious you are." Dora caught a funny look on Bonmarie's face when they walked through the kitchen.

Charles said nothing until he opened the door and ushered her through it. She followed his gaze to the back wall of the house.

Her hands flew to her mouth. "Oh, Charles!" She rushed to the white two-wheelers leaning there. She went to the ladies' model with the basket in front. "Is it really for me?"

Charles came up beside her and chuckled. "I brought them home last night, but I wanted you to see them in the daylight. Are you pleased?"

"What changed your mind?"

"I just felt it was time."

All those magazines had done it, all those flagged advertisements. But he'd said nothing of it. She'd nearly given up.

"I do have conditions."

She hardly heard him; she was already imagining herself whipping along the lakefront, the wind against her cheeks.

"Tell me when you'll be out and promise to wear riding boots."

"Yes, dear, absolutely." Bicycling boots rose to the knee and had a reputation for being more than a little uncomfortable. But it was a small price to pay.

"I know how men leer at women's ankles when they're on the street, and I won't have my wife subjected to that."

"May we get the boots today?" It was all she could do to resist jumping into the seat right that moment and taking a turn around the grounds.

"No need. Bonmarie will already have delivered a pair to your room. I hope you approve."

"I'm sure I will. Can we go for a ride now? I can change quickly."

Bonmarie came to the door then, her shawl wrapped around her shoulders. "I'll be off to Mass now, but you'll find your breakfast on the table. Hazel will clear the dishes when you're finished." She stepped delicately around Charles.

"But the boots?" Dora asked.

Bonmarie patted her shoulder. "Your boots are in your room."

"Thank you." Dora leaned in and gave Bonmarie a kiss on her cheek.

"Dora, please!" Charles said through clenched teeth. "She's a servant."

Dora pulled away from Bonmarie and the woman patted her arm again. "He's right, *ma chere*." She tapped Dora's cheek and walked off down the path.

"Come inside." He tugged her back through the door. "Really, Dora, is this how you think the lady of the house should behave?"

"She may be a servant, but she's Bonmarie. I love her."

Charles's face bloomed red with rage. "Never say that again in this house. You are a lady and she is a servant. Is that clear? I did not marry beneath myself so you could bring me down; I rather thought it possible to raise you up. Was I wrong on this account?"

She could feel the venom from his words. She shook her head.

"Good," he said, the fury draining from him. "I've got work to do in the study. I'd like to leave for the Richmonds' at seven. Please make yourself ready by then."

She nodded and he walked back inside. She watched him close the door.

Not once did he look back.

She returned to her room to find the boots beside her bed. Brown leather lace-ups. She went to try them on and check the fit, but she couldn't touch them. She couldn't even look at them. Not now. Maybe never. She'd wanted that bicycle so badly, she'd imagined gliding through the streets, but now it was the last thing she wanted.

She pulled out a dress to wear to the Richmonds. The silk peacock blue skirt and matching bodice that shimmered in the candlelight. It was Charles's favorite. She fitted it over her dressmaker form and draped it with rose petal sachets to scent it for the evening. If she looked exceptionally beautiful tonight, maybe Charles would forgive her. She swiped her palm along the bodice to smooth the wrinkles. She was doing everything he wanted, everything he asked. She swiped the wrinkles again and swatted away tears forming in the corners of her eyes. She was trying. Didn't he know that? She swiped again at the bodice and then at her eyes. The swiping wasn't working; the wrinkles weren't smoothing. She pressed harder at the creases. She should've set the dress out the night before. Now she'd have to heat an iron and risk damaging the delicate fabric. She fought the tears and swiped again. It was no use. The dress was a disaster. She shoved the form away from her and sent it tumbling to the floor. The skirt billowed like a sheet on the drying line before coming to rest in a heap. She dropped to her knees, her head in her hands, and sobbed.

She was the disaster. She couldn't even prepare herself properly. She'd vowed to Charles she could be the wife he wanted, and she was failing at every turn. She pressed her fists to her eyes. Where was Mama's calm reassurance now? Where was Bonmarie's soft shoulder? If she could just hear the woman's velvety voice tell her it was all going to be all right . . .

But those days were over, weren't they? She wasn't Dora Devereaux anymore; she was Mrs. Charles Chambers. And she was running out of chances. She needed to pull herself together and be the woman Charles wanted her to be.

It would be difficult to treat Bonmarie differently, but the alternative was worse. Bonmarie would understand. She'd speak to her tonight. She'd explain it so the woman knew it was for the best.

Dora wiped away the last of the tears and pulled herself up from the floor. She was Mrs. Charles Chambers, and she needed to behave accordingly. This was all part of her new life.

She checked herself in her wardrobe mirror and straightened the few wandering stands of hair that had worked their way loose from the knot on her head. She lifted the dressmaker form and smoothed the persistent wrinkles a last time. She'd ask Bonmarie to take an iron to it before their departure. No, she'd tell Bonmarie to do it. The sooner she started acting like the lady of the house, the better.

No one said it was going to be easy.

When she went back downstairs, Charles was in his study. She poked her head in the dining room and saw he had already eaten his fill. Hazel was clearing the remainder away.

The narrow-faced woman saw Dora as she lifted the bacon platter. She stopped midair, frowned, and nudged the platter in Dora's direction.

Dora shook her head. She had no appetite.

Hazel set the platter on the others she held in the crook of her other arm and resumed her task.

Dora went into the sitting room and picked up a *Collier's* magazine from the table, flipped through a few pages, and set it down again. She straightened the edge of a crocheted doily spread across the back of an upholstered chair. She went to the window. White puffy clouds scattered across the blue sky and the midmorning sun gave the trees, the lawn, even the street a golden glow. She thought of her bougainvillea.

She closed the front door quietly behind her so she wouldn't disturb Charles and went around the side of the house. There it was, still just a few leaves, but the small green nubs along the branches showed more were on the way. She checked the soil around the base. Too dry, perhaps? She went to the back shed where the gardening tools were kept and saw Harold wheeling one of the bicycles toward the horse stable.

"Did you mean to use this?" he called to her.

She bristled at the sight of it. "Not just now," she replied. Maybe never. "Is the watering can in the shed?"

"Should be. But I can look after that plant, if you like. I'm sure Mr. Chambers would want it that way."

"Thank you, but I prefer to do it."

Harold shrugged as if to say it was all the same to him and continued rolling the bicycle toward the stable's open door.

She found the tin watering can with the giant pour spout and took it to the stable's pump. She filled it halfway and needed both hands to lug it back to the nascent bush. Carefully she positioned the spout over the plant and tipped. Water rained out and soaked the ground. She pulled her feet back so she didn't wet her boots in the process. When the soil drank in all the water, she tipped the can again. The tiny bush needed all the help it could get.

"You might want to be stingier with your watering, Mrs. Chambers."

She turned to find Dr. Bostwick, in his gardening overalls and a straw hat, walking toward her.

"You'll drown the roots if you aren't careful."

She tilted the can up. "I just want to be sure there's enough."

"Doesn't take much. A light sprinkling every other day or so until her leaves all come in, then she'll be able to take what she needs from the soil."

Dora brushed her hand across the top tier of leaves. "Have you ever seen a bougainvillea in bloom, Dr. Bostwick? There's so much color; more color than you've ever seen. I can't wait for it to cover this entire dreary brick wall."

"You are going to have to wait, though. You can't make it grow faster by drowning it." He chuckled and shoved his hands into his pockets. "I sometimes think plants are a lot like my patients. When my patients are sick, I might wish I could fill them up with medicine to make them better, but giving them too much too fast will only make them worse. Bodies can only absorb so much of a good thing. We have to accept that things work on their own time, not ours. But I'm sure a lecture was the last thing you wanted on a beautiful morning like this."

"I'm happy to have the benefit of your wisdom." But she wasn't thinking of the bougainvillea anymore. Her mind raced with thoughts of her promise to the belly dancers. She set down the watering can. "You're so helpful, Dr. Bostwick, I wonder if I might impose on your help with another matter." She could see she had his attention. "I have a friend, an acquaintance really, who's fallen quite ill but isn't in a position to seek medical attention for herself. I have offered to do it on her behalf, but I admit I'm at a loss as to how to go about it."

He rubbed his chin. "Doesn't this lass have family? Medical matters are often better handled by family."

"No, she's quite alone."

His face softened. He drew closer to her and lowered his voice. "My dear, if there's something you would like to share with me in confidence, I assure you—"

"I'm not speaking about myself." Her hands rose defensively. "Perhaps I should be more candid, but"—she wanted to be sure Harold was out of earshot—"I must ask that this remain between the two of us."

He hesitated, then nodded.

"I find myself in a peculiar position with the Fair's Egyptian belly dancers." She watched a look of surprise flicker across his face. She continued, "They have confided in me that one has fallen ill. Bedridden with fever, I'm told, though I haven't seen her myself. They sought medical attention through the Fair's officials, but those requests have been ignored. They've turned to me for help, and frankly I don't know what to do."

"I see," he said, running his thumb over the gray whiskers of his mustache. "Why wouldn't the Lady Managers get involved? It would seem their influence could have some sway."

"This is my dilemma. I cannot turn to the board because I fear they'd consider my efforts improper for a Lady Manager. Yet I cannot in good conscience allow this poor woman to suffer."

"Quite a dilemma," he said. "What if I looked in on the lass myself, and then no one else need be involved?"

"You wouldn't mind? I don't want to put you to any trouble. I could pay—"

"Please, Mrs. Chambers, I wouldn't dream of charging for such a thing. I'd be happy to be of service to you. I've been meaning to get back to the Fair anyway."

"Really? Are you sure? I know they would be so grateful. *I* would be so grateful."

"Then it's settled." He smiled and his eyes twinkled. "So if I make my way to the Egyptian Theatre, how would I find this woman?"

"Ask for Amina Mahomet at the door. She's one of the dancers. If you tell her I've sent you, she'll take care of it. Dr. Bostwick"—she reached out and took his hand—"I don't know how to thank you."

*D*ora was sitting at her dressing table and pinning curls for the Richmonds' dinner when Bonmarie opened her chamber door.

"Thank goodness, you're here," Dora said. "I can never get my hair to behave the way you can. Will you?" She lifted a hairpin.

Bonmarie shuffled in and took the pin. "Are you sure that man of yours isn't going to throw a hissy fit if I do?"

It had been hours since Charles's outburst but they hadn't talked about it. When Bonmarie returned home from Mass, she'd kept to the kitchen and avoided Dora. Dora had done her part to stay out of Bonmarie's way, too.

"You shouldn't blame him," Dora said. She heard a grumble behind her as Bonmarie reached for another hairpin and slid it into a coil of hair she'd twisted at the back of Dora's head. "Really, it's my fault." Silence, just a tugging on her scalp as Bonmarie worked the hair. In the mirror she could see Bonmarie's frown deepen. "It's because I give him too many reasons to doubt that I'm the kind of wife he thought I would be."

"Don't you say that," Bonmarie admonished. "There's nothing wrong with you. You're too good for a mean old man like that, if you ask me."

Dora smiled weakly. "I wish that were true. But I know he's right. Chicago is so different from New Orleans. And it's not just that. Before the wedding, he'd only seen my front room manners, my best behavior. He wanted the drawing room Dora to be his wife, not the girl who spent most of her time in the kitchen. I thought it would be easy to change, but it's more difficult than I thought. Was I wrong to ask you to come here? I just couldn't bear—"

"Hush now," Bonmarie said. "Don't you ever think you should've left me behind." She dropped the section of hair she was holding and put both hands on Dora's shoulders. Their eyes met in the mirror. "My place is with you, and that's how it is. It doesn't matter what that man says, or how you have to treat me when he's around. You do what you have to do, but you know I love you."

Dora had to swallow hard before she could speak. She could see the watery glisten of her own eyes and the shimmer in Bonmarie's. "I love you, too," she whispered.

"You stop that sniffling now. Ladies don't let themselves get all worked up like that." Bonmarie took the brush and whipped it through Dora's hair.

In the mirror, Dora could see she was smiling.

*S*hortly before seven o'clock, Dora emerged from her room. Charles was already in the hall, pulling on his overcoat and putting on his bowler. "Good, I was just going to call up for you."

"How do I look?" She spread out her arms and pirouetted.

He looked her up and down. "Don't you think you're a little overdressed? It's dinner, not the opera."

Her shoulders sank. "I thought you liked this dress."

"It's a bit much, don't you think?" The grandfather clock at the top of the stairs chimed the hour. "Never mind, we'll be late if you go up to change now." He pulled her shawl from the rack, held it open, and waited for her to come close so he could wrap it around her. Then he opened the door and ushered her outside.

The carriage was already at the front. Charles helped her up, then took the driver's seat himself. Several minutes later, they pulled up to the Richmonds' ivy-covered stone mansion. Golden light shone through the lace curtains of the front windows.

Charles tied up the horse and helped her down. Side by side, they walked to the door. He knocked and the butler greeted them and showed them into the gallery. Mr. Richmond rose from his seat beside the fireplace.

"Come in, come in," he said. He grabbed Charles's hand in a hearty shake. "So good of you to come. And so good to see you again, Mrs. Chambers." He took her hand and brushed it with a kiss, then ran his fingers over the sparse wisps of white hair lying across the crown of his head. "You look exquisite. What a stunning shade of blue! What do you call it?"

"Peacock, sir." She beamed at the attention.

"A beautiful shade, for a beautiful young lady. It suits her indeed, don't you agree?"

"Yes, sir," Charles said. "And the Lady Managers are taking to her marvelously."

"Charles, please." Dora hid her face behind her hand, trying to hide her embarrassment.

"I don't doubt it for a moment," Mr. Richmond said. "Charlie, you've done quite well for yourself. It's good to see you're settling in to married life. It's long overdue."

Charles coughed and motioned to the crystal decanter on the table beside Mr. Richmond.

"Why is that?" Dora inquired, but Charles cut in with another cough.

Mr. Richmond pretended not to hear and went to the decanter, poured a glass, and handed it to Charles. He picked up his own glass, clinked it with Charles's, and they both sipped.

"Please, have a seat," Mr. Richmond said. "My wife will be along in a moment. Checking on details; you know how fussy women are." He motioned for Charles and Dora to take the burgundy settee pulled across from his chair. Dora took a place beside him and recognized it as the one Mrs. Tillday had occupied at the meeting. Many of the chairs and tables had been repositioned from her last visit. With fewer occupants, the room looked even larger and grander than before.

"I wonder if you've had a chance to think any more about that importing business?" Charles asked, setting his half-finished glass on the mahogany tray table beside him.

"Charlie, Charlie," Mr. Richmond said, sitting back in the same wingback chair he'd been in when they arrived. "Let's set aside work for one night and enjoy ourselves and our wonderful wives. Take it from a man who knows: You should appreciate your wife while she is young and beautiful." He smiled at Dora and lifted his glass to her before drinking again.

The gallery's door rolled open again, and Mrs. Richmond entered. Her hair had been swept up into a pompadour with a silk lily pinned to the side of her bun in the same mauve shade as her taffeta skirt and bodice.

Dora's stomach seized. Had the apology note been enough? She searched for signs of Mrs. Richmond's disposition.

"There she is, the love of my life," Mr. Richmond said when she neared.

Mrs. Richmond dipped her head bashfully. "I apologize for my delay. Just checking on dinner. I hope roasted goose is to your liking. The cook is terribly proud of the one she found at the market today. Says it's the finest bird she's seen in a season."

"Sounds delicious," Dora offered, waiting anxiously for Mrs. Richmond's response.

The woman smiled quickly at Dora, then turned to Charles and held out her hand.

He took it and kissed it politely.

"It is so good to see you again, Mr. Chambers. It's been ages. I can't remember the last time . . . Oh, yes, the memorial service for Mr. Forrest." Her smile diminished and her eyebrows pinched. Then her brow smoothed and her smile returned. "But so much has happened since then, hasn't it? Like your wedding, which has brought this lovely lady to our midst." The flat tone of her voice didn't match her words.

Something was wrong. What she said was pleasant enough, but the way she said it made Dora's heart pound, and the woman would not make eye contact.

"Mr. Richmond just scolded Charles for talking business," Dora said, "but I hope he'll indulge me in sharing a bit of good news with you." She glanced over at Mr. Richmond, who threw up his hands in playful resignation.

"Never mind him," Mrs. Richmond said. "What is it, dear?"

"Mrs. Tillday and I had a productive visit with the belly dancers yesterday. They've agreed to all your recommendations and more. I don't think the Fair is going to have any more trouble with them." She watched the woman's face for any sign of a thaw.

Mrs. Richmond wagged a finger at her. "Don't you be fooled by them. They'll say one thing and do another. They cannot be trusted."

"They seem quite willing to make the adjustments," Dora said. She bit her tongue to keep from saying more.

"You're young," Mrs. Richmond added, "but I don't think you are naïve. We'll see if you prove me right. On the whole, though, I'd say that is excellent news."

"All right, all right, enough with this talk of the dancers," said Mr. Richmond, trying his best to look stern. "Can we get back to serious matters now? Like when is that dinner going to be ready? I'm starving."

Mrs. Richmond went to her husband and kissed his cheek. "Yes, dear, let me check on that for you."

She excused herself and a moment later returned to announce that the meal was ready. "It's such a lovely night, I've asked the staff to set up in the conservatory. So if you'll follow me . . ." She led them down a hallway to a glassed-in botanical room. Beds of colorful orchids and leafy palms encircled a central fountain, and beside the fountain a table for four was set with white linen and fine porcelain.

Mr. Richmond pulled out Dora's chair, then his wife's, and then he and Charles sat. The butler filled wineglasses while four other servers appeared at each diner's shoulder. With a nod from the butler, the servers presented each bowl and set it before a diner at exactly the same moment. The meal began with a beef consommé, followed by a duck sausage cassoulet, and finally the roasted goose. Each served in succession and each with the same precision. The food itself was beyond anything Dora had ever seen. She marveled at the grand arrangement on the plate, and the way Charles relished each bite. She knew it was something special, and she chewed slowly, languorously, searching for the flavor. But there was none. It was all so terribly, utterly bland. Instead, she listened as the others chatted. She nodded at intervals and smiled. She spoke little. The night was going well enough; she didn't want to spoil it with a poorly chosen word.

Mr. Richmond made sure there was never a lull. Though he directed most of his commentary toward Dora, he didn't require her participation to keep the conversation going. "So you've visited the Exposition, I understand," he said in that smooth timbre of a voice that reminded her of the glowing embers of a warm hearth on a cool evening.

"Absolutely," Charles answered for her. "I took her the first week. She's been back, of course, with the Lady Managers."

"This is a very exciting time for Chicago, young lady." Mr. Richmond grinned beneath his bushy mustache. "I can remember when we first arrived, the missus and me. Came from New York City, just a year after the Great Fire burned most of this city to the ground." He lifted his glance to the ceiling glass panels and gazed on the Braille of lights in the night sky. "Could it already be twenty-one years? So it has. I'll bet you hadn't even entered this world yet. Am I right?" His face held a grandfather's tenderness, but there was something sad in the way the creases pulled at the corners of his eyes.

"What made you come after the fire?" Charles asked. "Hadn't you heard of the devastation?"

"Not heard? Of course we'd heard. It was the very thing that compelled me to come. Don't look surprised. That fire was a blessing." Mr. Richmond's voice gained vigor. "It purged the city of everything old and worn out. It blessed us with the opportunity to rebuild, better and stronger."

He studied Dora for a moment, then said, "Think of it, dear, a century ago Chicago was nothing. A trading post, no more. But as the country marched west, it flourished into a vital transportation artery supplying goods and men to the cause. The city grew, and it grew fast. But that growth followed the old ways."

"I'm sure they've heard all this, dear." Mrs. Richmond twitched a finger toward Cecil, who stood rigid and silent off in a corner. "Would anyone like another glass of claret?"

Dora shook her head; Charles nodded.

"I'm quite enjoying it, actually," Charles said, urging Mr. Richmond on.

"Thank you, my good man. But Aggie's right. I do get carried away. The point is that we have entered a new age. The Industrial Age. The old rules are obsolete; the old ways of thinking wiped off the map. A clean canvas. Because of the fire, the city could modernize." He intoned the word like a prayer. "Every new building became a testament to advanced architecture and civil engineering. The streets were improved. The railroads integrated into the new design." He looked to Dora for a response.

"I had no idea" was all she could manage.

"It was the very thing that is making Chicago the economic center of this great land. New York City? It's rotting beneath the weight of its own filth. No, my dear, Chicago has all the advantages now, and the Fair is showing the world every gleaming one of them."

"All right now, Archibald. I'm sure that's enough," Mrs. Richmond said. She motioned again to Cecil.

He came at once to clear the goose away. A final course of cheese followed: soft brie, blue-veined Stilton, a crumbly mimolette.

"I can't eat another morsel," Mrs. Richmond said.

"I couldn't agree more," Dora said. "But everything was simply delicious, and your cook was absolutely correct. A superb goose. The best I've had in a long time." Ever, really, but there was no point in disclosing that.

"Charlie, how about taking a port with me in the study?"

"Splendid idea, Archibald. It'll give Mrs. Chambers and me a chance to chat," Mrs. Richmond said.

Dora shot a glance at Charles. What did he want her to do? She waited for an indication. He pulled his napkin up from his lap, dabbed the corners of his mouth, and folded it into a square beside his plate. He nodded to Mr. Richmond. "Yes, I'd enjoy a port."

The men pulled away from the table and walked off toward the study.

Mrs. Richmond leaned toward Dora. "Now that they're gone, there's a question I've been dying to ask."

Fear struck Dora.

Mrs. Richmond glanced over her shoulder, making sure the men were gone. She lowered her voice, and asked, "How are you getting on with Mrs. Tillday? I felt terrible making that match, but honestly I don't know what to do with her. She's such a timid mouse of a thing. No one can get a peep out of her. I thought you being new, she might open up."

"Mrs. Tillday?" Dora blurted out in surprise. What a relief that her fears were unfounded; she was not the source of Mrs. Richmond's concern! Quickly, she recovered her composure. "Interesting that you ask. When you introduced us—that day for which I am again so very sorry for my hasty departure"—Mrs. Richmond waved off the reminder as if it was of no consequence—"she hardly said a word. But she was a different person when we visited the Fair. Talkative, opinionated . . . there was quite a change in her."

Mrs. Richmond sat back in her chair, an approving look on her face. "You see, I was right. The company we keep makes all the difference."

The rest of the conversation concentrated on the weather: dissecting the vagaries of the climate, the day's unusual dampness, and the more common dry and sunny days of June in Chicago, as well as the humid, tropical air of New Orleans. They talked of the advantages and mostly disadvantages of each, comparing and contrasting them in great detail.

Dora could hardly recall a word of the chatter when they rose from the table, but she couldn't remember ever being so exhilarated by an exchange. It was a conversation Mrs. Richmond might have had with any lady of her rank. If only Charles could have witnessed it. He would have been so proud of her.

Mrs. Richmond reached over to extinguish the candles, and tipped a goblet by mistake. A few dribbles of red wine tricked onto her skirt. She jumped up. "I must get some water on this before it sets," Mrs. Richmond said, madly dabbing at the spot with her napkin. "But you go on ahead. The men will be deep into business talk and they'll need a diversion. Perhaps you can take the cheese platter with you. I'll be right behind."

*R*ichmond opened the mahogany cabinet and pulled out a bottle and two glasses. He unstopped the bottle, poured the tawny liquid into a glass, and handed it to Charles.

Charles sipped. If his instincts were right, he needed the fortification. He settled on the leather chair and waited.

Richmond took his time pouring his own, then worked the cork back into the bottle and set it back in the cabinet. He took the seat beside Charles and stared into his glass.

Charles had played the game all through dinner, acting as if the invitation were a simple social occasion. But he knew better. "So is it the directors? Have they rejected my proposal?"

Richmond shook his head, still staring into his glass. "I haven't talked to all of them yet, but the few I've told like the idea. You probably have a very good chance at that vice president spot if it goes forward."

Charles sank back. "That's stellar news. You don't know how much I appreciate—"

"It's not exactly what I wanted to talk to you about."

"I don't understand."

"I want to know if you've ended it with Geraldine Forrest."

Charles sat forward, his voice lowered. "Of course I have. I told you."

"I know what you told me, and I know I still see her coming around the bank. Not a day goes by that she doesn't make some excuse to show up."

"She's asked me to help her with an inheritance matter. That's all. It's completely innocent." He brought the glass to his lips and drank.

"Why you, Charlie? She could've gone to anyone."

"The woman has a mind of her own. She's a major investor. Why shouldn't she be allowed to come to the bank as she pleases?"

"Because you're a married man. Because the directors are watching. But that's not the only reason I asked you here tonight."

Charles braced himself.

Richmond took his time. When he spoke, he seemed to choose his words carefully. "I wanted to see if your wife was the sort who could keep you faithful."

"I really don't think it's your place—" The drink was affecting him, giving him courage. His fear of Richmond was giving way to anger.

"It absolutely is my place. If I go out on a limb to recommend you and you fail, that makes it my failure, too. And trust me, I don't like to fail."

If Richmond didn't pull for him, no one would. "I am faithful." The words tore through him. That last time was a mistake. He'd meant to tell her to stop coming around, to accept that he was married now. He hadn't meant for things to get carried away as they had. But he'd never be weak like that again. He'd be a better husband.

"That's what I want to hear. The directors don't like trouble, and they won't bring you on if they think you'll be trouble."

Charles nodded.

"Geraldine Forrest was out of your league then, and she'll always be out of your league. Be happy for what you have. Your wife is a good, sweet, beautiful girl, Charlie. Don't ruin your marriage over some pointless infatuation."

Charles took a long drink. Richmond was right. She was a good, sweet, beautiful girl. She was. Why wasn't that enough?

A crashing sound startled Charles. He shot a glance at the open doorway. It sounded so close, but he saw only blackness in the hall.

"It's all right; it didn't break." It was Dora's voice, but she was a good distance away. Not close, certainly not close enough to hear.

*D*ora came back from the end of the hall where she'd been when she'd called out to the men, and collected the bits of cheese scattered on the floor. She worked quickly, hiding the evidence of where she'd stood. She couldn't let them discover she'd been eavesdropping. At least the platter hadn't shattered, but it was still a disaster. She couldn't feel her limbs; she couldn't feel anything, not after Mr. Richmond had said that hateful name: Geraldine Forrest. Charles and Mrs. Forrest had been lovers? It was too awful to consider; it made her head throb.

She heard movements in the study.

She grabbed the platter with the cheese she had and rushed back to the conservatory.

Mrs. Richmond intercepted her in the hall. "Are you all right, dear? I thought I heard something."

Dora wanted to cry, she wanted to scream. She held up the platter. "I'm so sorry." She bit into her lip to force back the tears.

Mrs. Richmond took the wooden tray. "No harm done, dear." She set the serving dish on the table and moved closer to Dora, placing a hand around her shoulders.

"Is everything all right out here?" Mr. Richmond emerged from the doorway. Charles followed behind him.

"Everything's fine. Just clearing the table. Isn't that right?" Mrs. Richmond gave Dora a reassuring look.

Dora mouthed a silent "thank you" that was met with a pat on the arm.

"It's getting late. Dora, we should be getting home," Charles said. He approached Mrs. Richmond and extended his hand. "Thank you for the wonderful dinner. Everything was delicious."

"I'd like you to stop by my office in the morning, Charlie." Mr. Richmond came up beside his wife.

Dora saw Charles's face turn white. Mr. Richmond seemed to notice it, too.

"We have more to discuss about your proposal before next week's board meeting," he continued.

"Yes, of course." Charles looked relieved. "First thing." He edged his way toward the door.

Dora followed him at a distance. She watched his feet; she couldn't look at his face. She forced herself through the motions of the farewell.

"Get some rest, dear," Mrs. Richmond whispered when they kissed cheeks.

"Did you enjoy yourself?" Charles asked when they were in the carriage, the mare guiding them through the inky darkness toward home.

She wanted to scream that she'd heard him, that she knew his secret. Why had he married her when he loved Geraldine Forrest? The words clamored to be released. Instead, she smiled meekly, and said, "Of course. They're lovely people."

He nodded and stared straight ahead. "And they seem to have grown quite fond of you."

That was something, wasn't it? She told herself that it was, and she pretended not to notice how his lips curled in distaste when he said it.

When they were inside the house, Dora pulled the long pin from her hat and lifted it from her head, trying not to snag the lace veil. She held it, plucking dust from the lavender silk tiger lilies as Charles deposited his hat and overcoat on the rack in the foyer. Without a word, he went to his study.

"You aren't going to work this late, are you?" She kept any hint of recrimination out of her voice; she couldn't risk triggering his anger.

"Having a Scotch, if you must know."

She set her hat upon the rack and went after him. "Would you pour me a pinch?"

He had already poured himself two fingers' worth. He tipped the bottle again and added a third before sliding over a second glass. He tipped, then pulled it back. "Have you ever had Scotch?"

She leaned against the wood paneling and shrugged. "Tonight seems a good night to give it a try." How many times had she seen it soften him, drain his anger, put a lazy grin on his face? If ever she needed that kind of magic, it was tonight.

He tipped the decanter and let the liquid splash into the tumbler.

She moved closer to him, trailing her fingers along the cool polish of his desk. She watched how intently he poured, how his jaw set in that hard angle of concentration. "Did you have a good time tonight?" she asked.

His forehead wrinkled. "Of course. It was a pleasant enough evening. I was hoping Richmond would have more to say about my business proposal, but I suppose that can wait until the morning." He offered her the glass, hardly a finger's worth of the amber liquid.

She took a sip. The pungent vapors filled her nostrils, and a burning followed the Scotch's trail down her throat. She coughed.

"Too strong?" He looked amused.

"Just right." She took another sip to prove it. The burning transformed into a gentle warmth that comforted her. The muscles in her limbs loosened, her thoughts calmed. It was like slipping into a warm bed, soft and snug. "Did I make you proud tonight?"

He took a swallow, but she'd already seen the turn of his smile. "Of course you did. Why would you ask?"

"I want to know I make you happy," she said. She wasn't going to let her husband slip into another woman's arms. Not Geraldine Forrest's, not anyone's. She knew what she had to do. She took another sip and set down the glass. She walked behind him and wrapped her arms around his shoulders. "Let me take your jacket."

He said nothing but allowed her to slide off one tweed sleeve and then the other. She laid the garment across the back of his desk chair, careful to keep it smooth. She could feel his eyes on her, waiting. She hesitated. What was she supposed to do next? She wanted to please him, to give herself to him the way he wanted. But she couldn't make her body move. She didn't know what to do.

"Is something wrong?"

His voice was curt, annoyed. This wasn't how it was supposed to be. She wanted to feel herself in his arms, to lose herself in his kisses. But she stood paralyzed.

"Dora?" There was a hard edge to the word.

This was the moment. She had to act. She turned and pressed herself against him. Her arms flung around his neck, she raised her chin, closed her eyes, and offered him her lips. "Kiss me, Charles," she said breathlessly, and waited.

She felt his body stiffen; his hands moved to her waist. The tips of his fingers curled into her.

"Kiss me," she said again.

He leaned closer. She smelled the sweet liquor on his breath, the hair pomade. His lips brushed hers, then he pushed her back. He stormed by her to the door, his hand raking through his hair. "It's late; I've got to get to the bank early tomorrow. Good night."

He was gone.

She listened to the knock of his boots against each step of the staircase, and heard the sound diminish when he made his way along the hall. The door to his chamber opened and closed.

She was alone; only the weight of his rejection remained. She expected tears, but they didn't come. There had been so many tears. Maybe too many. She felt nothing. There was nothing more to do. She had failed.

*   *   *

*C*harles went to his dresser, opened the door, and slid his hand along jacket pockets until he found it, the locket containing Geraldine's likeness. He gripped it hard before opening it, looking again at those enticing blue eyes, that ravishing blond hair. Geraldine stared out from the golden frame with such a knowing look. So confident. Why did she have such power over him?

The soft click of Dora's slippers coming up the staircase stopped him. He froze, waiting until he heard her door open and then close. How perplexing she was. Always so timid and unsure of herself. But tonight he'd seen something else beneath that shy facade. A woman. Her brazen advance had surprised him. Isn't that what he wanted? No, it was too bold, too aggressive. He wanted her to receive his advances, not to pursue him with her own. That was why it had grated on him. He wanted a willing wife, not a harlot. It was all wrong.

He set the locket on the dresser, gazed again at that placid, porcelain face, and knew he'd just told himself a lie. The flaw was not Dora's. Even Mr. Richmond could see it. Tonight he'd lied to that man just as he was lying to himself. He wanted to believe the fault was in Dora. But the fault was in him. He couldn't be a proper husband because he couldn't betray the one he loved, the woman who had taken his heart and never given it back.

Six

*D*ora collected her parasol and hurried out the front door when she heard Mrs. Tillday's carriage arrive.

"Is everything all right, dear? You don't look well," Mrs. Tillday said when Dora settled in beside her. With the carriage's black accordion canopy pulled back, the morning sunlight hit Mrs. Tillday's blue taffeta dress in a shimmer of greens and yellows.

"I hardly slept. I might be coming down with something." She wasn't about to say she'd spent the night feeling sorry for herself. The thought of Charles and Mrs. Forrest being lovers did make her sick. That she'd been so stupid as to try to throw herself at him made her feel even worse.

But when the dawn broke and the sky turned from black to gray, she knew she had to try to set things right. She resolved to ignore Mrs. Forrest. She would act as though last night had never happened. Whatever Charles and Mrs. Forrest had between them, it was over now. Charles had chosen her to be his wife. She would have to be content with that.

"Spring fevers can be such a nuisance," Mrs. Tillday said. "I discovered this at the apothecary." She produced a brown medicine bottle from her purse. "Just two sips when weariness or anxiety overtakes me."

"Fresh air is all I need," Dora demurred. "I already feel better."

"As you wish." Her partner tipped the bottle and sipped, then tucked it back in her purse. "I need a little myself before we set foot in that belly dance theater."

When they arrived at the Midway gate beside Cairo Street, an early crowd was already queued to buy admission tickets. Businessmen in bowlers and tweed suits, men from the stockyards in dungarees and caps, wives in fine lace, and working women in cotton blouses and black skirts. Up and down the line, children in sailor suits or flour sack garments flitted around their mothers. Dora and Mrs. Tillday passed them all, and the ticket taker waved them through the gate.

At the Egyptian Theatre, an audience was filing in and a turbaned boy at the door admitted them. They took seats along an aisle and watched the rest of the hall fill quickly. On the stage, the musicians huddled together but the dancers were nowhere to be seen.

"What are you looking for?" Mrs. Tillday whispered.

"I was just—" She stopped. Hossam Farouk emerged from the side room. Their eyes met; Dora glanced away.

"That manager," Mrs. Tillday whispered. "In an odd way, he's rather handsome, isn't he?"

"Absolutely not," Dora hissed.

"It was just an observation."

Neither said more because the man was approaching. They stood; he bowed. "Good morning, ladies. What a pleasure to see you again." He took Mrs. Tillday's hand, kissed it lightly, then reached for Dora's. She felt her cheeks burn.

Mrs. Tillday returned his greeting, but Dora said nothing.

"Please let me know if I can do anything to make your visit more enjoyable," he said, and then he was gone, striding toward the doorway.

The audience was still filing in, filling the last of the seats and then the standing room gallery in the back.

Mrs. Tillday craned her neck to see the men around her.

"Who are you looking for?" Dora asked.

"Husbands. Some ladies have noticed unexplained absences by their men. Some suspect they're stealing away to see these shows. Does that look like Mr. Sheffield to you?" Mrs. Tillday pointed to an older, portly gentleman in a black derby coming through the door.

"I've never met the man. But stop—we're not spies," Dora hissed.

Mrs. Tillday continued her search.

Dora focused on the stage, where the musicians were taking up their instruments. The horn player initiated a slow melody. Then the performers' room door opened and six dancers emerged. Dora nudged Mrs. Tillday. Each dancer wore a veil draped across her face, revealing only dark, kohl-rimmed eyes and eyebrows, and instead of skirts, each wore voluminous jewel-toned pantaloons— in vermilion, emerald, fuchsia, azure, teal, and marigold. Over the pantaloons, they wore long, multicolored coats that fit snugly across the torso and flared from the hips to the knees. Amina Mahomet had kept her bargain.

"They're wearing the veils; they've covered everything," Dora gushed.

"That's what you told them to do."

"But they're actually doing it."

The delight in her voice was lost in the drummer's *doom doom tekka tek doom tekka tek*. Then the oud player joined the melody, and the Egyptian women took the stage. They arranged themselves on the open bench, except for the one who sashayed to the center and began to dance.

The costumes, Dora noted, were not the only change. The shimmies were restrained, and the movements involved more wrist flourishes and writhing arms than jiggling bosoms. The dancers had listened to her; they'd made every change she requested.

Because of the veils, it was impossible to identify the dancers—except one. The dancer who had kept her promise. Dora recognized Amina, despite her crimson veil, because she stood a good head shorter than the others. She was the final dancer to take the stage. As Dora watched, she noticed there was something different about the way she moved; it was more languorous than the others, less jerky or forced. And the way her stomach could roll!

Dora could see more grace in the way Amina moved. When the tempo quickened, and Amina's torso twisted and turned, and her feet stomped in a way that made her hips shake and her shoulders shimmy, Dora felt the music pulse through her like lightning beneath her skin. It started in her arms, and they twitched at her sides. Her wrists tried to mimic the dancer's flutter, but her parasol and satchel slid to her wrist with a thump and brought her back from her distraction.

Dora checked that no one had caught her lapse. She needn't have bothered; every set of eyes, even Mrs. Tillday's, looked to the stage. The men still appeared mesmerized, yet there were fewer hoots, rib nudges, and back slaps. They had made progress, and it made her smile.

As if on cue, Amina struck her final pose as the musicians hit the final note. The dancers formed a line along the stage, linked hands, and bowed. The crowd rose to their feet and applauded, but there was none of the wild "huzzahs" and "bravos" as before. Dora added her own clapping until Mrs. Tillday stopped her hands and shook her head.

Dora accepted the correction, clasped her hands in front of her, and watched the dancers shuffle off and vanish behind the performers' room door. The women sat again until the crush of bodies had thinned, then they made their way toward the exit.

Dora waited for Mrs. Tillday to praise the dancers. When she did not, Dora asked, "Wasn't that grand? We really couldn't have asked for anything better, could we?"

"I suppose."

Dora wanted to argue the point, but a tap on her back interrupted her. She turned to find a young Egyptian boy, the end of his long tunic nearly brushing the floor. "Come with me?" he asked in halting English.

"I beg your pardon?"

He repeated himself and pointed to the performers' room. Dora could see the door cracked open and the outline of a small body in the gap. A bronze arm slipped through and waved her closer.

Dora turned to Mrs. Tillday. "Should we say a few words?"

"Is it necessary?"

"We should tell them we appreciate their efforts."

"Why?"

Why was Mrs. Tillday being difficult? "You needn't come if you prefer not to," she said, a bit flustered. "I'll tell them."

"If you must." Mrs. Tillday sat back down in her chair, her arms crossed in front of her.

The woman could be exasperating, but something had to be said. Dora set off toward the side room with the boy.

When she neared, the door opened wider and she could see, as she'd suspected, Amina standing inside. She'd unhinged one side of her crimson veil and let it drape along the side of one cheek. Behind her the musicians and dancers were scattered about the room, talking and eating from platters of vegetables and roasted meats laid out on small tables. A midday meal, Dora guessed, which would explain why a new audience wasn't yet being seated.

"Did we pass inspection?" Amina asked, her eyes glinting with amusement.

"Absolutely. Well-done. The costumes are superb, and the dancing is much better."

Amina glanced back over her shoulder and said something in Arabic to the others. The gap-toothed woman and some of the others giggled.

"What did you say?" Dora asked.

"I told them you approve, of course, so we are no longer in your debt. Your doctor came by yesterday."

Dora glanced back at Mrs. Tillday. She stood by the door now, gazing out into the square. She couldn't overhear, but still Dora lowered her voice. "What did he say?"

"He saw Maryeta. He said she should not move from her bed while the heat on her forehead is greater than the heat of my hand. He gave us a powder to mix with her tea to help her sleep, and last night she did sleep through the night for the first time in six days. This morning she had color in her cheeks, and she asked for food. Good signs, I think."

"Thank goodness Dr. Bostwick could help."

"Thank you, Mrs. Chambers. You did us a great service." Amina reached out and squeezed Dora's hands.

"You have more than repaid me." Dora squeezed Amina's hand in return.

When Dora went back to Mrs. Tillday, she was watching a

camel pass through the square outside. The animal was led by a boy in a marigold turban and vest and wide indigo pantaloons. But the animal's costume was even more colorful. A rainbow of thick tassels draped along the harness across its head and back, and where the camel's hump should be, there rose a small scarlet tent trimmed with golden embroidery that rocked uneasily with the camel's lurching gait.

"Can you imagine having to get around in something as ridiculous as that?" Mrs. Tillday asked.

"I suppose it wouldn't be so bad if it's what you're accustomed to."

The look Mrs. Tillday gave her said she must be joking. "Have you noticed how little difference there is between the odor of the animals and the odor of these people? They must share the same quarters. It's quite disgusting."

Had Mrs. Tillday really said such a horrible thing? But already her partner was out of the theater and striding through the square on her way to the main Midway avenue.

"I'm sure they do their best with what they have," Dora muttered as she maneuvered her parasol open to shield her from the sunlight breaking through the clouds.

"Oh, dear, look who just spotted us." Mrs. Tillday winced.

Dora looked in the direction Mrs. Tillday had been looking and her heart sank. Mrs. Forrest and another Lady Manager she recognized from the meeting strode toward them.

"This is a surprise," Mrs. Forrest said when she neared. "We're going to visit the Egyptian Theatre to see how you've been faring with those poor belly dancers."

Mrs. Tillday twirled a ringlet like a schoolgirl. "Hello, Mrs. Forrest, Mrs. Loomis. How good to see you. We're faring as well as can be expected, thank you. How is Mrs. Sheffield? Is she enjoying her holiday?"

"I haven't heard from her yet, but I expect to any day." Mrs. Forrest hardly took her eyes off Dora. "We're so lucky these days. A person can send a message across the country in just a few days. Isn't it a wonder?"

"Absolutely," Mrs. Tillday gushed again.

Dora stared in amazement at Mrs. Tillday. Who was this woman?

"I hope you're right about the theater. I know Bertha's patience is running thin," Mrs. Forrest said. "Of course, there probably is only so much these creatures are capable of learning. I can only imagine the difficulty you must be having."

Dora knew she was being goaded. What could Charles have ever seen in this hateful woman? "On the contrary, we aren't finding the job difficult at all, are we?" She waited for her partner to concur.

Mrs. Tillday hesitated; finally she managed to shake her head.

"I'm sure you're doing your best," Mrs. Forrest said. "If everything is going as well as you say, you have nothing to worry about. We should be getting on our way, Mildred." She smiled at Dora in a way that made Dora's toes clench inside her black silk stockings. "Mrs. Tillday, I suppose we'll be seeing each other later this evening, at the Gilmores' dinner party."

Mrs. Tillday shook her head. "I believe that's tomorrow night."

A blush of a smile came over Mrs. Forrest's face. "She rescheduled. Didn't you receive her note? You see, I have an unexpected obligation that prevents me from attending tomorrow. The dear woman insisted on accommodating me. I hope it doesn't inconvenience you."

"Not at all," Mrs. Tillday stammered. "Tonight works very well, in fact. Thank you for looking in on us; it's very kind of you."

Dora's stomach twisted. Where was the woman who said people tolerated Mrs. Forrest only for her money? "Yes, it was good of you. I'm glad you'll be able to tell Mrs. Richmond how much the belly dancers have improved."

Mrs. Forrest laughed. "You can be sure of that. I'm quite looking forward to telling her what I think." She and Mrs. Loomis said their good-byes and made their way toward the theater.

Dora and Mrs. Tillday walked to the carriage in silence.

When they began the ride home, Mrs. Tillday turned to her, fuming. "You really shouldn't be so disagreeable with Mrs. Forrest."

Dora wanted to snap back. Instead, she forced a calm reply. "Why are you being so agreeable? You said people only fawn over Mrs. Forrest because of her money. Why must we do the same?"

"Why? Because you can never win against her. You don't have to like her, but you don't have to let her know it. You must stop aggravating her."

"Me?"

"I'm trying to help you. If you don't want to alienate everyone in town, you cannot allow yourself to become Mrs. Forrest's enemy."

They rode the rest of the way without speaking. At Dora's house, she asked Mrs. Tillday if she'd like to come in for a cup of tea or a bite to eat.

"I really can't. If we're dining at the Gilmores' tonight, I must get a suit prepared for Henry. And what will I wear? There's so much to do."

"Of course," Dora said. "I'll see you tomorrow, then." She thought of Charles; she had preparations of her own.

* * *

When Charles walked through the front door shortly after six o'clock, Dora was in the foyer to greet him.

"Hello, dear, let me help you with that." She guided him out of his coat and draped it on the rack. "I hope you're hungry. Bonmarie is working on your favorite, crown roast and potatoes lyonnaise."

"Why?"

"Why not? She just wanted to do something nice for you. We both did."

He scratched the back of his neck and his scowl deepened. "I'll have to take the meal in my study. I've quite a bit of work this evening."

He went into his room, and Dora felt the rejection like a slap. He was still angry. It wasn't going to be so easy to redeem herself. She found him already sitting behind his desk, searching in a drawer. "Shall I start a fire? The evening's developing a bit of a chill."

"Don't bother. Hazel will be along in a moment. She always does it." He turned to the cabinet behind him and searched there.

"I'll go and tell Bonmarie you'd prefer your meal in here, then." She waited for a reply, but he continued opening drawers and cabinet doors. He didn't even seem to notice she was in the room.

She walked out slowly, waiting, hoping he might say something to keep her. When she reached the hallway, she paused; his back was still to her. Perhaps it was still too soon. Perhaps tomorrow he would forgive her.

She left the door open behind her and went to deliver his request to Bonmarie.

*   *   *

*T*he next day Dora rushed Mrs. Tillday through their visit to the Egyptian Theatre. Again the costumes were in order, the veils in place, and the dancing restrained. Dora didn't speak to the dancers, but she caught Amina's eye and smiled when the dancer delivered her final bow. She saw Amina's eyes crinkle beneath her crimson shade.

By noon, she was back home again. A message from Charles waited for her on the silver tray in the foyer. She tore into it.

Dora,

Something unexpected has come up at work that requires immediate attention. Don't expect me for dinner. I may be very late—no need to wait up.

Charles

She crumpled the paper and left it on the tray.

Bonmarie came through the swinging kitchen door, wiping her hands with a dish towel. "I thought I heard you in here. A message came for you. I left it there." She nudged her elbow toward the tray.

"I found it."

"Not good news?"

Dora shook her head.

"I'm sorry, *ma chere*. Anything I can do?"

"No," Dora said. "Maybe. Have you started dinner yet?"

"Just a stock with roast bones for a stew."

"Do we have anything for a picnic?"

Bonmarie considered it. "We have fixings. Bit late in the day to be planning something like that, though."

"I was thinking of a supper picnic, and for my sake, I hope it isn't too late."

Together they went into the kitchen and worked out a meal of sliced roast beef, new potatoes and carrots, a freshly baked loaf, butter, and a cherry tart.

"I know Charles has a weakness for your cherry tarts. It'll be perfect," Dora said. "Even if he has to work, he still needs to eat. Think how delighted he'll be when I show up with dinner all ready for him."

"I hope that man knows how lucky he is."

Dora went to the bowl of pitted cherries on the counter, took one, and ate it. "If he doesn't, maybe this will remind him."

"Mr. Chambers has the carriage. Shall I tell Harold to arrange a hansom cab?"

"No, I have an idea."

She went out to the horse stable and found the bicycles where Harold had stored them, leaning side by side against an inside wall. She wheeled hers out and into the carriage grooves where the bare earth was hard, brushed off the dust, and lifted herself onto the seat. Carefully, she set one foot on a pedal and pushed forward with the other. The bicycle wobbled and she had to drop her feet to the ground a few times before she could keep the handlebars straight. She worked her way to the street, where the macadam made the process easier. She kept at it until she could pedal without losing her balance. Back and forth she traversed, and the faster she went, the easier it was.

When she turned back into the carriage drive, she slid off the seat to walk the bicycle up to the stable.

"Looks like you've mastered that contraption."

Dr. Bostwick was standing on his porch, a pipe in one hand, the other on the railing.

"It was a shaky start, but I think I have it now." She tried to pretend she wasn't embarrassed that he had seen that awkward beginning.

"Your bougainvillea seems to be doing better."

Dora looked over at her bush. "The leaves appear much healthier. I'd say you're to thank for that. And speaking of thanks . . . " She stopped. She couldn't very well holler that across the yard. "I understand thanks are in order on another score as well."

He smiled, understanding her meaning. "I believe all will be well. Just needs a bit of time. I was glad to be of service."

"It's very much appreciated. I'd like to stay and chat, but I must get downtown."

Dr. Bostwick lifted his pipe. "I won't keep you, then." He studied the sunlight breaking through the scattered patchwork of clouds. "I must say, though, you've inspired me to enjoy some physical exercise myself. I think I'll take a stroll down to the shore." He bade her good afternoon, stepped off his porch, and walked off in the direction of the lake.

Dora spent the rest of the afternoon in her room. She bathed herself in milk and rose water, brushed her hair until it shined, and picked a dress she knew Charles favored. Bonmarie helped her fix her curls and laced her into her corset. When evening neared, Dora stepped into her new knee-high riding boots and laced them. She wiggled her toes and rotated the ankle of one foot and then the other. The leather rubbed no matter how much powder she applied, but it was still a reasonable compromise.

She went down to check on dinner, but even before she reached the kitchen, she could smell the fresh bread, the pastry crust, and sweet and tangy cherries. Bonmarie was wrapping the tart when Dora walked in.

"It's absolutely perfect," she said when she saw the basket lined with linen.

"It should be. I spent the whole afternoon on it. Best meal I ever put in a basket. Seems a shame to hide it all away like this."

"But you're wrong," Dora said, delving through the basket's carefully wrapped jars and tins. "Charles will love it."

"There should be more than enough for the two of you. I figured he might not be working alone so you'd want some to share."

"I hadn't thought of that. Thank you." She kissed Bonmarie on the cheek and gave her a quick squeeze around the shoulders.

"That's the last of it," Bonmarie said when she finished wrapping the tart and set it in the basket. "I put in plates, napkins, and utensils on the bottom. Did I forget anything?"

"It's better than I could have hoped."

"Let's hope that man thinks so, too."

Dora checked the window. The sky was turning a deep shade of amber. "I should go. He'll be getting hungry by now." She threw a cloak around her shoulders and carried the picnic basket to the bicycle, wedged it into the bicycle's basket, and used a cord to strap it in.

Bonmarie followed her outside. "You mean to ride that thing all the way to Mr. Chambers's bank?"

"Of course."

"A lady shouldn't be out there all by herself. You need a cab. Just wait, I'll get Harold."

"No, I'm taking the bicycle."

Bonmarie stopped and stared at Dora. "What on earth for?"

"Charles gave it to me. He'll know how much I appreciate it if he sees me using it."

"What if you hurt yourself?"

"I'll be careful."

Bonmarie clasped her hands in worried prayer. "You be careful. Stay away from the industry, and the red lights, and the poorhouses." Bonmarie looked like she was trying to remember anything else to add.

Dora waved and wheeled the bicycle to the road. She slid onto the seat and pushed off. Bonmarie didn't need to worry. She'd seen enough of Chicago to know which neighborhoods to avoid, especially after dark. She'd take a route through the better residential neighborhoods, with a few lanes of merchant shops until she reached the financial district. Bonmarie had nothing to fear.

With every revolution of her wheels, Dora's excitement grew. She envisioned how happy Charles would be when he saw the meal she brought. How thoughtful he would think she was. How easily he would forgive her.

When she arrived at the bank, an imposing gray building that looked like a Grecian temple, she left the bicycle against the stoop and walked up the flight of steps to the main doors. They were locked, as she'd expected. She balanced the basket in one arm and pressed the night bell. With her face pressed up against the door's glass, she could see the dimly lit lobby and vacant teller windows. She waited, then pressed the bell again. Finally a guard emerged from a side corridor leading to a stairway and the upper offices. Her heart quickened.

The guard yanked a circle of keys from his pants pocket and flipped through them until he settled on one that he used to unlock the doors. "Bank's closed, ma'am. You'll have to come back in the morning."

She smiled. "I'm Mrs. Charles Chambers. I've brought my husband dinner; he's working late."

The guard rubbed the unshaved stubble on his cheeks. "Mr. Chambers isn't here, ma'am. Everyone's gone for the night."

Dora didn't want to argue, but the man was wrong. In her sweetest voice, she said, "He said he would be here. I have his dinner." She held it up as if that was the proof he needed to set him straight.

"Mr. Chambers left about half past four. Wished me a good evening."

Half past four? It was nearly half past seven. Could she have passed him on the road? No, he would've been home by five. Half past four was so early. His usual quitting time was half past five or six, sometimes later.

"Are you sure?" Dora resented the look of pity she saw in the man's eyes.

"I'm sure, ma'am."

She backed away from the doors. The man put the key back in and locked them. He gave her a final nod behind the glass before turning and walking back the way he'd come.

Dora sat on a step, the basket in her lap. Where could Charles have gone? She thought of Mr. Richmond. Of course. Perhaps he's visiting Mr. Richmond. They're probably talking about that proposal of his. But why wouldn't he tell her that in the note? Why would he say he would be at the office and not be there?

A terrible, evil thought struck her. Her stomach twisted. Charles wouldn't be with Mrs. Forrest. He couldn't be. He'd said so to Mr. Richmond. He'd said it was over.

But was it?

There was one way to find out, and then she could put her mind to ease.

She rose from the step and went to her bicycle, strapped the basket back in, and pushed off from the pavement.

The moon hovered above her in the darkening sky. Windows shrouded with thin curtains glowed with yellow light, and the gas streetlamps cast halos on the sidewalks where evening strollers walked in twos and threes. A Victoria carriage passed and Dora heard the trill of a woman's laughter over the clopping of the horses' hooves. She focused on her path. In the darkness, the streets looked different; she had to concentrate to stay on course. She passed the dressmaker's shop and the tailor's, a barrister's and a barber's. First came the town houses and then the mansions. The pedals grew heavier with each revolution. When she turned onto Mrs. Forrest's lane, the bicycle moved so slowly it wobbled. Like the street, the mansion appeared more daunting in the night. Dark and brooding. A monstrosity of a thing with two lighted windows on the second floor like eyes that watched Dora. She forced the bicycle forward. The street appeared empty. No strollers, no carriages. At least there were no witnesses to her silly delusion.

She was feeling silly. And relieved. She saw no sign of a visitor, no carriage in sight. With a lighter heart she rode up along the side of the house. Silence, except for the breeze through the linden leaves and a horse's hooves in the far distance. She was glad for the bicycle's soundless movement. Nothing announced her arrival.

Then she saw it. The carriage. Pulled up close to a back stable. The sound of a horse's breath. Dora slid off her seat and leaned the bicycle against a tree. She stepped carefully, avoiding the twigs and dried leaves on the ground as best she could. The carriage looked similar, too similar to Charles's, but she couldn't be sure without a closer look. At her approach, the horse shifted and whinnied quietly. When Dora reached the horse's shoulders, it swung its head and then she was sure. It was Delilah. The mare held her gaze, watching her. Dora reached out and ran her hand along the white patch on her nose. The horse whinnied quietly again.

Dora shushed her. Delilah dipped her head and nuzzled

it against Dora's shoulder. She patted her one more time, then turned to the house.

The windows were mostly dark and too high to see inside. She walked around the perimeter and saw no signs of movement inside. Then a light illuminated the front room overlooking the street. Her heart pounded in her ears. Dora checked the street again. Still empty. She tiptoed up to the veranda nearer the window and stopped on the shadowed side of a pillar. Only a thin sheer curtain covered the window, and she could see two figures in the room. She recognized Mrs. Forrest standing over a table, pouring tea from a pot that she then carried across the room. Dora leaned forward and saw a man sitting in a chair. That mustache, that beard, that charcoal coat. She knew he would be there, but still the sight made her knees nearly buckle. She held tightly to the pillar.

Paralyzed, she watched Mrs. Forrest hand Charles a cup and saucer. He accepted it and she walked behind him to rest her hands on his shoulders. He balanced the saucer on the chair's arm and lolled his head, encouraging the woman's caresses. Dora could see the smile on his face, and she could feel a scream building in her chest. Charles rose from his chair and went around to Mrs. Forrest. Dora moved to see them. She watched her husband press up against the woman and wrap his arms around her. Mrs. Forrest leaned into him, and their lips met. Dora turned; it was too much. She wanted to run, to bang her fists on the window, to make them stop.

But she couldn't move.

She watched Mrs. Forrest's hands do something frantic at Charles's throat. His bow tie fell to the floor. Then Mrs. Forrest's hands were at his shirt buttons, working them the same way. They flung open, one by one. Charles's hands were around her hips and pulling her closer, bunching her skirt into a rumpled mess. When Mrs. Forrest finished with the shirt buttons, her hands went to his trousers. Charles pressed her toward the settee against the wall. Dora stepped forward to keep her view and a wood plank groaned beneath her weight. Charles pulled back from Mrs. Forrest and stared at the window. Dora stumbled back. He rose and came toward the window. Dora pressed herself against the wall, her pulse racing.

"I'm sure I heard something" she heard him say, then something more from Mrs. Forrest she couldn't make out. He pulled a heavier drapery over the window and eclipsed the light that had streamed through the sheers onto the veranda. Dora rushed down the steps and into the shadow of a tree across the carriage drive. She heard the front door open and saw Charles's silhouette appear on the veranda. He was buttoning his shirt, but his shirttails still hung over his pants. He leaned out over the railing. She stood like a stone beside the tree, not moving, not making a sound. The moonlight gave the white bicycle an eerie glow where it leaned against the red-brick wall. If he came down, he'd see it plainly. He'd know what she'd done. She held her breath.

He gave the yard and street a final look and walked back into the house. The door closed; she heard the lock catch. She breathed.

She'd been lucky. Only it didn't feel like luck. She felt sick. She went to the bicycle and propped it up, the picnic meal for Charles sitting tall in the bicycle's basket.

*T*he house was quiet when Dora returned. She stowed the bicycle in the empty stable, left the picnic basket on the kitchen table, and went to her room without seeing a soul. She was happy for the solitude. The ache inside wasn't the kind to improve with conversation. She didn't want to be consoled; she didn't want to speak of it. Ever. She couldn't even tell Bonmarie. The woman would never forgive Charles if she knew, and then there'd never be peace in the house.

Keeping it secret meant it wasn't real, no more than a bad dream that disappeared in the daylight. It changed nothing. All that mattered was that she was Mrs. Charles Chambers. She comforted herself with that thought and told herself everything would be better in the morning. She pulled off her town dress, slid out of her petticoats, and crawled into bed. But every time she closed her eyes, the hazy image of Charles embracing Mrs. Forrest came back to her.

What hurt most was that none of it made sense. Why didn't Mrs. Forrest's advances repulse him? He should want a proper lady companion. Hadn't she, Dora, molded herself into the perfect wife? Pretty, courteous, virtuous? But while Dora was holding herself to high standards to please him, he was cavorting with a woman who conducted herself in a way completely unbefitting a lady, especially a lady of rank.

She rose, positioned a chair in front of the street window, and watched for her husband. Sleep would not come easily tonight.

Sitting there in the darkness, Dora thought of something else: the way Charles looked at Mrs. Forrest with such ardent, unabashed desire. She'd seen that look before. Her heart clenched. The men in the Egyptian Theatre looked at the belly dancers that way, with longing gazes, hopeful stares. There was fire in their eyes, just as there was fire in Charles's. She'd been naïve to think it was enough to earn her husband's approval, his acceptance, to make him proud. She wanted to see that fire when he looked at her, to feel that burning gaze brush over her. She needed it, or she'd lose him. Tonight was evidence enough of that. But there was something else she wanted, too. Something more. She wanted that passion. Seeing him take Mrs. Forrest in those hungry embraces had awakened her. She wanted him to kiss her so hard she couldn't breathe. And she wanted it more than she'd ever wanted anything.

The realization came as a surprise, and thinking of it gave her an unexpected thrill. She knew how to win Charles back. She knew *exactly* what she had to do.

The moon was in view now, peeking out above the elm tree's leafy canopy. A crescent of gray in the dark sky smiling down, as if the heavens themselves would console her. It was a new moon, a new beginning.

Seven

Dora awakened to sunlight and a pain shooting through her neck. She didn't remember falling asleep, but there she was, still sitting in front of the window in her nightdress. Her head bent to her shoulder, she rubbed at the sore muscles below her ear and nudged herself upright.

It took a moment to piece together the night before. The picnic, the guard, Charles, Mrs. Forrest; yes, it all came back. She had wanted to see Charles come home, if he had come home, but sleep had overtaken her as she plotted how to win back his affection. By the look of the sun through the window—more gray than gold—it was early. Good. She had much to do.

She reached for a sheet of stationery and a pen. Getting a message to Mrs. Tillday topped her list. She dashed off the note, rose from the chair, and felt another stab through her neck. There wasn't time for this. Standing, she forced her neck straight and stretched it on both sides, enduring the agony until the pain subsided. She lolled her head until the muscles calmed. She went to her wardrobe, selected a tea gown, and pulled it on. From her door, she looked over to Charles's room. The door was closed. He was there. She breathed easier and checked the grandfather clock. Seven in the morning. Plenty of time to get word to Mrs. Tillday.

She rushed downstairs and found Bonmarie in the kitchen, sitting with her coffee and a slice of bread slathered in butter. She rose when Dora entered.

"Where can I find Harold? He needs to deliver a message." Dora noticed the picnic basket on the counter where she'd left it.

"Feeding the mare," Bonmarie said after swallowing a bite of bread.

Dora went to the back door.

"Now, you just wait," Bonmarie scolded. "You can't go out like that. Catch your death of cold. Give me that. I'll tell him what you need." Bonmarie snatched the envelope. Dora stood at the threshold, watching her cross the yard to where Harold sat on a stool by the stable tooling a horse rein. He accepted the envelope and slid it into the front pocket of his overalls without looking up. A moment later Bonmarie was back in the kitchen.

"Is he going to go now? He must hurry, before—"

"He knows," Bonmarie snapped. "He's just finishing up."

Dora pulled back the curtain over the door's window. Harold was carrying the stool back into the stable.

"See there?" Bonmarie said. "No need to work yourself up."

Dora kept her eye on the man.

"Why's this basket still full, anyway?" Bonmarie was lifting the lid and looking inside. "Nothing's touched, I see. Wasn't it good enough for that man?"

The kitchen door swung open and there stood Charles, still in his bedclothes and yawning. "Am I the man in question?"

"We were talking about Harold," Dora answered.

"Harold? Why did he require a picnic?"

He was chipper this morning, more chipper than he'd been in days. Dora thought again of him with Mrs. Forrest, that tormenting display. *Stop it*, she told herself. It was going to be all right. Everything would work out, because she had a plan. "I left it for him," she said, "as a thank-you for errands he ran for me. But I was careless and didn't put it where he would find it. That's why he hasn't touched it, Bonmarie." She caught Bonmarie's glance and held it, her eyes wide with silent meaning.

"Doesn't look like any harm came to it," Bonmarie said, pulling the items out one by one.

"I came down for a glass of milk. Has the delivery come yet?"

"It came," Bonmarie said, setting down the last of the picnic items and going to a cupboard to retrieve a glass.

"Is that a cherry tart I see?" Charles asked, pulling the dish closer. "You know I love those cherry tarts. Do you think I might . . . ?"

Bonmarie set a glass of milk in front of him and went for a plate and a knife. She cut him a large piece and dropped it on the plate.

"The perfect breakfast," he said, taking up the plate, a fork, and his glass of milk.

The sound of the carriage leaving the stable caught his attention and drew him to the window. "Where's he off to?"

"Delivering a message to Mrs. Tillday for me," Dora said. "Lady Manager business, nothing important."

Charles's eyebrows squeezed. "I don't mind you giving him things to do, but don't send him off in the carriage when you know I need to get to work," he said, but not as sternly as he might have.

"Of course. I wasn't thinking. I'm sure he'll be back quickly. The Tilldays live only a few streets away."

"Yes, well, keep it in mind for the future." He took his tart and milk and pushed through the door.

Yes, she would keep it in mind for the future. She had many things in mind for the future.

Dora slipped out, too. She walked quietly by the study so as not to disturb Charles and went to wait in her room until he was gone.

By eight o'clock, he was climbing into the carriage beside Harold and on his way to the bank. A few minutes later, Dora, fully dressed and wearing her knee-high riding boots, skipped down the stairs, said a quick good-bye to Bonmarie, and pretended not to hear her inquire about her destination. She didn't have to explain herself, and Bonmarie must have sensed it because, Dora noted with a secret smile, the woman didn't follow or demand an answer.

Eagerly, Dora dropped her satchel and her parasol in the bicycle's basket, climbed on the seat, and settled in for the trip to the fairgrounds. The sun was working its way out of the clouds, so she turned toward the shore. Although the route was longer, the lake's ripples would be dancing with shimmering light, and there was always a breeze about this time that pushed back the sour reek of the stockyards and railcars, the horse droppings and rotting trash. She breathed the fresher air and pedaled to the rhythm of waves lapping against the concrete slope.

When she reached the Exposition, Dora parked her bicycle beside others stored near the Fifty-ninth Street gate, near the grounds of the University of Chicago's cathedral-like Assembly Hall. It was still too early for ticket sellers to be at their posts, so she approached the guard on duty, a man in denim overalls who stood hunched with his back against the towering wood plank wall that hugged the Midway Plaisance's perimeter, separating it from the surrounding neighborhood. His tweed cap dipped low over his brow and hid his eyes. When she reached him, she pulled back her shoulders and waited to be acknowledged.

"Fair's not open yet, miss," he drawled without looking up. A waft of whiskey breath touched her nose when he spoke.

In her most authoritative voice, she said, "It's missus, thank you, and I have business here. I'm a Lady Manager."

The man tipped up his cap with the flick of a dirty finger. "Is that right?" He rubbed his nose and left a dark smudge across the tip. "All right, then." He plunged a hand into a front pocket and pulled out a key on a long chain. He inserted it into the gate's rusty padlock.

She took her time opening her parasol to avoid his oily glare. The man looked like he might've been handsome once, but time had chiseled it away from his tawny face, one craggy crevice at a time.

"You take care, then, ma'am." He gave her a long look and a smile that might have been a sneer. Then, so low she could barely hear, he muttered, "A lady out alone should always take care."

He pulled the gate open, and she hurried by. Everyone in this city was so concerned about women out alone. In the French Quarter, no one minded, and it was never as if you were really alone anyway. Everybody knew everybody, and if anything happened they'd likely know of it back home before you ever reached the door. But not here. Chicago was a city bursting at the seams with strangers. Immigrants arrived by land and sea from every country you could name, and just as many folks, like her, had come from other parts of the nation. Wealthy people, poor people, workers, layabouts, con artists, all of them converging on Chicago. Just three years ago, the

1890 census had counted more than a million people living in the city, and more were coming every day. Maybe it was a risk to go out alone, but it was a risk she had to take.

At least it was still early. Only a few Fair workers were about. Two women in kimonos shuffled along the avenue ahead, and in front of her, a man in full Bedouin garb walked alongside his horse, on his way to the Turkish Village. The village usually bustled with visitors who gazed on the mock nomad encampment, toured the elaborately domed mosque, shopped for souvenirs in the Grand Bazaar, and watched stage productions at the Odeon, with the help of an English lecturer who explained the action as it unfolded. But the village was silent this morning, and she reached Cairo Street easily.

Entering the makeshift Egyptian village was like entering another world, one she was beginning to know as much by its smells as its sights and sounds. The hay and sour earth odor of the camels and donkeys greeted her first, then the spicy scents in the incense smoke that floated through the air, and the savory aroma of the cooking fires that signaled a morning meal was under way.

The place was stirring to life just as she imagined a real Egyptian village might be. Shopkeepers in long cotton tunics and peg leg trousers cleaned the awning-covered windows of the shops filling the ground floors of the smooth plaster buildings, which rose two and three stories over the street. On the upper floors, women wrapped in shawls wiped down the wood-framed balconies that jutted away from the building. Boys in short vests and billowing pantaloons raced through the street carrying pails of water or sacks of rice or flour.

Dora walked by the obelisks in front of the Luxor Temple replica, passing three women carrying bundles of clothing to the pump to get an early start on the day's washing.

When she neared the Egyptian Theatre, she saw the camel with the red tent on its back and tassels draping from its harness. A boy in a turban and vest was trying to coax it forward, but the camel refused to move. When the boy tugged harder, the animal bellowed. Dora giggled, and the boy glowered at her.

"Pardon me," she said. "I didn't mean to laugh."

He stared but said nothing.

She approached the beast. At its haunches it was taller than she was and its head moved about like a periscope. "Perhaps she doesn't like carrying such a heavy load," she suggested.

"She is willful." He spit the words. "Makes up her own mind what she wants to do; listens to no one else."

Dora guessed him to be no more than ten or eleven, and his English was better than she would have guessed. "You seem to know her quite well."

He puffed out his chest like a soldier. "She is my camel. I am her keeper."

"Then I do see your dilemma. May I touch her?"

He nodded, but gathered the camel's leather reins more tightly in his fists.

Dora slid off her lace glove and ran her fingers gently over the animal's ginger hair; its coarseness tickled her skin. "She is a beautiful creature. What's her name?"

"We call her Little Egypt."

"Hello, Little Egypt. It is my pleasure to make your acquaintance."

The boy shifted, his shoulders softened. "She is very smart, very good with the tourists. Always a smooth ride, even for the fat ones."

The camel swung her head around, and Dora could see her own image reflected in the animal's dark, placid orbs. "I'm sure that is because you are a kind and capable keeper."

Little Egypt extended her neck back toward the boy, nudged his hand, and grunted. The boy whispered in the creature's ear and passed his hand lovingly across her neck. The camel grunted again and nosed the boy's palm. He pulled a carrot from a pocket hidden in the folds of his pantaloons. "You see? I can hide nothing from her."

The boy's pride was obvious as he stroked the animal again, then his face rearranged into concern. "Are you the Lady Boss who is spying on us?" he asked.

It took a moment to absorb his question. The child's face held a defiance that reminded her of Amina. "I'm a Lady Manager," she said carefully, "but I'm not spying."

"Then why do you come?" How bold this boy was, with his upturned chin and his narrowed eyes.

The question made Dora pause. What was her purpose? To appease the Lady Managers? To earn their favor. Yes, it was that, but now it was also something more. "I'd like to think I'm helping your friends avoid some unpleasant business." She was helping, wasn't she? She felt surer of it as she spoke. "There are people in the city who believe Egyptian dancing is not an appropriate entertainment for the Fair. These people would prefer to shut the theater down, but I believe I'm helping your people and mine reach a compromise." She searched his face for understanding. Could he understand? Did she? "I'd like to think I'm doing some good," she added, almost apologetically.

He nodded solemnly. With a sidelong glance, he said, "I hope you will not make trouble for us. We have enough already."

"That certainly isn't my intention," she said.

He gathered the reins more tightly and tugged the camel forward. "Little Egypt must eat before your people come."

Dora shrank back but stopped herself. She wasn't going to let herself be intimidated by a boy. She was a Lady Manager. She pulled her glove back on and corrected herself. Perhaps other days she was a Lady Manager, but not today. She wasn't here on official business. She needed to find Amina before the Fair opened, and judging by the shopkeepers propping up their awnings, she didn't have much time.

"I'd like to speak to the dancer called Amina. Amina Mahomet. Do you know her?"

The boy turned back. His brows angled in worry. "She is in her room," he said, then proceeded down the cobblestone street with the camel in tow.

"Thank you," she called after him. *I really am trying to help,* she wanted to add, but he was already moving away, oblivious to her as he patted and whispered to his animal.

She faced the theater. He'd said Amina was in her room, but where were the dancers' rooms? The front of the theater was vacant. She went to the arched doorway and pulled the heavy drape aside. She leaned in and called out. No response. She followed the building around to the side and found a narrow alley that separated the theater from the adjacent rug shop. She saw a door leading into the back of the theater halfway down the alley. It opened and two women appeared, their heads bent together in quiet conversation. She backed away from the alley's opening. A Lady Manager couldn't be seen sneaking around like a thief. She hurried away, then turned back and strolled as if she'd only just arrived. She'd taken just a few steps when the women emerged from the alley into the square.

"Excuse me," she called to them, and waved. "Hello, yes, hello."

The women turned. They must've been dancers, because they were dressed in costumes like the ones she'd noticed on her first visits. Short velvet vests—one in scarlet, the other in violet—fitted over snug pink shirts that were so thin they were almost translucent and midnight blue skirts that brushed the women's ankles. The women looked at each other and then back at her.

She approached. "I'm looking for Amina Mahomet. Do you know where I might find her?"

"Why?"

Dora recognized one of the women from the stage. She was older and thicker around the middle than the others. "I'd like to speak with her."

The woman sized her up. "In there," she snapped, and glanced back over her shoulder, jutting her chin toward the door she'd just exited. "Third door."

Dora extended her hand. "Thank you. It's very kind . . . "

The woman looked at her hand like it was a strange, foreign thing. Dora retracted it self-consciously.

The older woman took her companion by the arm and led her by Dora, keeping a suspicious eye on her until she was well past. Dora watched them until they were across the square, then she approached the door. There was no knob, just an iron handle. She paused, listened for movement inside. Nothing. She took a handkerchief from her purse and used it to protect her gloves from the grime clinging to the handle when she pushed the door open.

The hallway inside was bare and damp, and it smelled of mildew. She covered her nose with her palm, stepped across the threshold, and the door swung closed behind her. From the paltry light trickling in from two slits in the wall high in the eaves, she could see a row of rough-hewn doors along the corridor, spaced a few yards apart. At the second one, a young goat lay curled into a nap, and it didn't stir when she stepped around. Dora stopped in front of the third door. This was the right thing to do, she reminded herself. It was the only thing to do, or she would lose her husband. She straightened to her full height and knocked.

No sound came from inside.

She rapped again.

A muted shuffling came from behind the fourth door and then it cracked open. A figure stood there, obscured in the shadow. A woman said something in a language Dora didn't understand.

Dora swallowed hard. "I'm looking for Amina Mahomet. I was told this was her room."

"Who told you?"

Moisture had gathered where her hat banded around her forehead. She ran two fingers under the edge to relieve the itching she knew would come next, then pointed to the door that led back to the square. "There was a boy. With a camel. It had a tent, I mean a—"

The figure stepped forward into the corridor.

"But it's you," Dora said, half relieved, half confused.

"Is there a problem?" Amina looked suspicious.

"No problem. I came to—" The words stalled in her throat. "I came to see about the sick dancer."

Amina's face softened into a smile. "Maryeta is much improved. She is sleeping, but you can see her if you'd like." She motioned Dora to the door where she was standing.

"I don't want to bother her. I'm glad to know she is recovering." She shifted uneasily.

Amina gazed into the room. "She is much better than before." She turned to Dora. "Are you sure you don't want to see?"

Dora shook her head, then hesitated. She looked around the corridor, taking in the walls that had once been white but were now colored by layers of dirty smudges and handprints, the wood floor built so haphazardly she could see gaps big enough for a finger to fit between the slats.

"I was going to have some tea. Perhaps you would join me?" Amina suggested.

"That would be lovely." She had answered too eagerly. She clenched her jaw shut to keep from saying more.

Amina, who appeared bewildered, approached and turned the knob on her own door. "This is my room. Make yourself comfortable while I get water for the tea."

"Thank you," Dora said, and stepped inside. "I hope it's no trouble."

"No trouble," Amina said, then disappeared down the hall.

Everything about the room took Dora by surprise. Nothing of the hallway's dreariness existed here. Bright golden sunlight filtered in from a window that filled much of the far wall, and a light breeze lifted its sheer white curtains. Beyond the window stood the wooden barrier that encircled the Midway. The room itself surged with color. Long cotton drapes in magenta, tangerine, and eggplant hung from the ceiling, covering most of the white walls. The fabric ends hid behind carved wooden trunks with hammered iron hinges set against the wall. Worn Oriental rugs spread over the wood plank floor. Beside the door, a long cushion wrapped in shimmering turquoise fabric was shrouded by a canopy made of the same creamy sheers covering the window and appeared to be the bed. In the corner, a profusion of garments in every color draped over a dressing screen, and all around the floor lay short, octagonal tables and large pillows covered in silky red, marigold, and shades of blue, some embroidered, others set with tiny mirrors stitched into a pattern. A sweet, pungent scent replaced the sour earth smell outside.

She heard footsteps in the hallway and then Amina was back in the room, carrying a kettle. She went to a corner where a tall, bronze teapot sat on a table beside four glass cups. Dora caught a mint aroma as Amina set the kettle on a woven trivet.

"You are the first visitor we have had away from the theater," Amina said, pouring the steaming water into the teapot.

Farther down the hall, Dora heard a door open and close, then footsteps. Someone passed the room but didn't notice Dora. She reached out to the door. "May I close it? I'd like to speak to you about a private matter."

It seemed an eternity for Amina to nod.

Dora pressed the door until she heard it latch. She turned back to Amina.

"Would you like to sit?" Amina asked.

"I prefer to stand." She walked to the window, then turned back toward the door. Perhaps this was all wrong. Maybe this wasn't the way. But there was nothing else to do. Without Amina's help, she had no hope of winning back Charles. "I'm not exactly sure how to say this."

"You may speak directly." Amina worried the beads of one of the many necklaces draped around her neck.

"I'd like to ask for your help."

"We already made our bargain. We dance in different clothes; we wear veils."

"That's not what I mean. My request is of a more personal nature." Goodness, how was she going to say this? How could she even ask? She breathed deep and resisted the urge to flee the room. "I've seen how the men look at you when you dance, at all of you. The way you move, the way you look . . . I don't know exactly what it is, but that's what I want to find out. That's why I'm here."

"I do not understand."

Dora rubbed at her brow. Frustration and shame ate at her. She clenched her eyes shut, and declared, "I want my husband to look at me that way." There, she'd said it. It was out and she couldn't take it back. A weight lifted from her.

"You want to dance?"

Her eyes shot open. "Yes, well, no, not exactly, maybe. Is that necessary?"

"We need the tea." Amina busied herself with pouring the brew into two cups and a new wave of the mint scent wafted through the room. She handed a cup to Dora. "I want to sit," Amina announced. "You may sit on a trunk if you prefer." She indicated any of the trunks in the room before dropping into a pile of jewel colored pillows.

Dora set her cup down at the edge of the closest trunk, along with her satchel and parasol, and smoothed her heavy skirts to sit as well.

"You want to know how to seduce a man?"

The bluntness of the question made Dora's cheeks burn. "That's not how I would describe it."

Amina cocked her head. "What is a better description?"

Dora's head felt woozy. No proper lady would be so vulgar as to blurt it outright. Seduction. That was it, wasn't it? That was exactly it. She grimaced, and said, "I'd like to know how you appeal to them, how you stir their interest."

"Not their passion?"

"All right, yes. Their passion." Dora hid herself behind a long sip of tea.

"Good. You must be honest. If you cannot tell yourself what you want, you will never get it. Do you have a particular man in mind?"

Dora flushed again, but the fire of her shame was burning itself out, leaving behind a single, purified purpose. "Yes. My husband."

Amina shook her head and smiled gently.

"Don't you have a husband?" Dora asked with a cock of her head.

"They are too much trouble."

Dora gaped. How could a woman not want to marry? What else was one to do? Even women who took up causes instead of husbands, crusading women like Susan B. Anthony and Jane Addams, were considered something less than fully realized for choosing a spinster's life.

"Other Egyptian women must marry, but a Ghawazee dancer is different," Amina continued. "We can marry if we choose, but it is not necessary. At least if a dancer takes a husband, she is the earner so she does not need to beg for money from her man." She took a sip. "I do not marry because husbands want to own their wives; I prefer my freedom."

"My husband doesn't own me," Dora countered. Marriage—a good marriage—*was* freedom: She was free to leave the hotel, free not to wait on others, free to do what she pleased.

She paused. Charles did make his demands, and the Lady Managers made theirs, so was that true? No, that was an entirely different thing. She lifted her tea and sipped again.

"Perhaps," Amina said thoughtfully, then returned to the matter at hand. "How do you know your husband does not desire you now?"

Dora glanced away. "I know. It's my own fault. I pushed him away."

Amina waited to meet Dora's gaze and held it. "If he is a man, you can get him back. I know this."

"I hope so."

"When did he last bed you?"

Dora bristled at the question but persevered. "About two

months ago. Our wedding night." It shamed her to remember her failure.

Amina leaned back and pondered Dora's answer. "That was the first time?"

"Yes."

"Was it good?"

"Not quite."

"Not quite? Or not at all?"

"I suppose you could say not at all," she answered without looking at Amina. She prayed for the end of the interrogation.

"Unfortunate. When was the last time he tried?"

"A few days ago."

"Then he is still trying. That is good."

"I don't think he will try again."

"We will make sure he tries again."

Dora glanced up, hopeful. "How?"

"Why do you think men watch us dance?"

"I don't know."

Amina rose to her feet. She shimmied her shoulders and then twisted her hips. She danced around the room like it was the stage. "Now what do you think?"

"They like to see how you move?" She thought again how parts of the dancing had reminded her of coupling, the ebbing and flowing of movements, one into another. A new wave of embarrassment washed over her.

"Not exactly. Get up and try to move the way I did. Come, you will get nowhere just sitting there."

Grudgingly, Dora relented. She removed her hat, set it carefully on the trunk, then held out her arms and moved her shoulders, forcing herself to mimic Amina. This was for Charles, she reminded herself. This was for her marriage.

"Move your hips."

Dora tried, but stopped when a corset stay poked her flesh.

"You see?" Amina was pointing at Dora. "All that clothing holds you like a cage; you can hardly move. But it is more than that. Watch me again." She flitted around the room, shaking her shoulders and bouncing her hips. She pointed to her face, to the playful grin and eyelids rising and falling, as if even that was part of the dance. "You see?"

"You're smiling, is that what you mean?"

"Yes, I am enjoying the dance. I am enjoying myself, my body. The way my limbs move, the way they feel as they move. It does not matter if anyone is watching, I dance for myself. Try again."

Dora held out her arms and shook her shoulders. She forced a broad, fake smile.

Amina waved her hands to stop. "That is not what I mean. Forget the dance, the dancing is not important. Maybe just walk, but walk like you are enjoying your walk. Like you are feeling every step, every twist of your hip, and enjoy these feelings."

Dora strutted across the floor, each foot landing hard on the rug below. She walked to the far wall and back.

"Try it again, more slowly. Feel each movement, sink into each step."

How was walking across a floor going to help her win back her husband? But Dora did as she was told.

She was halfway across the floor when Amina interrupted her. "I see the problem," she said, and moved closer. "It's all this," and she motioned around Dora's leg of mutton sleeves. "The waist, the hips, the legs, everything is so encumbered, all the way down to the feet. Your kind of women try to change the shape of their bodies with corsets, and you hide beneath so much clothing so nobody can see anything of your natural shape. You look like you are in a cage, so you move like you are in a cage. Perhaps that is why, when men see us dancing and enjoying our bodies, it makes them hungry for a woman who is not afraid of herself."

"I'm hardly afraid of myself," Dora retorted, and looked down at her dress, her leather boots.

"Why do you wear all this?"

"It's the fashion."

Amina rolled her eyes.

"So what you're wearing is so monumentally better?"

"Maybe, maybe not," Amina said. "But a man likes what he sees. Women like to hear pretty words, they like to feel soft touches. A man wants to see a woman. He makes love to her first with his eyes. What does he see when he sees you? When you want to stir your husband's passion, don't wear something like this. Let him see you; his imagination will do the rest."

The sound of footsteps in the hall stopped her. A knock sounded on the door and it opened. Another dancer poked in her head; an alarmed look flitted across her face when she saw Dora. She uttered something in Arabic to Amina, then closed the door again.

"The theater will open soon," Amina said, slipping behind the dressing screen beside her bed. "The others are gathering. You may join us if you like."

"I can't stay," she said, watching a vest fling over the screen and then a skirt. "I appreciate your help, though, with my . . . problem." And she was surprised to realize she meant it, despite the embarrassment, despite the discomfort, despite all of it.

Amina emerged wearing her dancing costume of a coat and pantaloons, her veil in her hands. "Your husband needs a nudge. That is all."

"I hope you're right." She bent to pick up her hat and used the hatpin to secure it on her head.

Amina reached for her hands and looked her in the eye. "I am sure I'm right," she said, and went to the door.

Dora picked up her purse and parasol.

Amina paused. "Is something wrong?"

"I'm just not sure how it will look if I come strolling out of your room. Is there any other way to leave?"

Amina tapped her lip. "If you go down to the other end of the hall, there is a door. It opens to the back. That is where the cooking is done. If you follow the path behind the buildings, you will see alleys leading back to Cairo Street. If you do not take an alley, you will end up at the Sudanese camp. It is more open there." She waited for Dora to say something. When she didn't, she nodded as though she understood. "You may leave whenever you are ready. Everyone will be in the theater in a moment." Then Amina smiled, said good-bye, and closed the door behind her.

Dora listened to the floor rattle with the belly dancer's footsteps, then more knocking on doors and the murmur of Arabic words. She heard the procession of several pairs of feet, and then silence. She waited, counted to a hundred, and checked the hall. Empty. She hurried past two doors, three, then four. At the last, she stopped and listened. Quiet. She opened it.

It led outside, just as Amina had said. Three boys in dirty tunics tended a trio of campfires, and an older woman in an apron and a shawl over her head kneaded dough at a table pressed against the back of the theater.

Dora crossed the clearing quickly but smiled to the cooks as if her presence there was the most natural thing in the world. She went to the narrow space between the buildings and the perimeter

wall. At the first alley, she saw a sliver of a Cairo Street building with a balcony on the second level. She passed another and
another until she reached the path's end near the Sudanese huts.
At the edge of the clearing, she saw visitors strolling through the
camp, and a group of black Sudanese men dressed in white togas
seated in a circle and singing. Then she saw Hossam Farouk.

He stood at the edge of the camp talking to a wizened Sudanese man who clutched a walking stick in one hand and an alu-
minum pail in the other. At their feet, a young goat nibbled at
a clump of weeds. While she watched, the old man struggled
to bend to a water pump beside them. Mr. Farouk must have
seen it, too, because he clasped his hand over the man's shoulders and deftly relieved the man of his pail, held it to the spigot,
and pumped water while he talked to the old man. When the pail
was full, Mr. Farouk returned it, waved farewell to the man, and
turned in Dora's direction.

She panicked and pressed herself against the wall, hoping to
hide. When it was clear she had nowhere to escape, she stepped
forward.

His gaze remained on the ground until he was almost upon
her.

"Good morning, Mr. Farouk."

His head shot up, and he stumbled backward a step.

"I didn't mean to startle you," she said, amused to see him so
flustered.

"Why are you back here?" he demanded.

"I might ask you the same thing." It was a baseless thing to say,
but she didn't appreciate his tone.

"I am returning to my theater." The tilt of his head made it
clear it was her turn to answer.

"I was visiting Miss Mahomet, if you must know." He had such remarkable eyes, so dark the pupil blurred into the iris, creating a solid black pool that held her in its gaze. But his arrogance grated on her. The way he crossed his arms and squared his shoulders. The way he shook his hair off his face. The way his glance dared her to continue.

"The theater has been closed."

"I saw her in her room." Now she had said too much. She glanced from him to a couple strolling by and caught the woman, a rotund matron with a face like an Easter ham, whispering something in the ear of her gray-whiskered sliver of a husband. The woman's deepening frown had one clear implication: What was a woman like Dora doing speaking with a man like Mr. Farouk?

"I must be going," Dora blurted. She grabbed her skirts in her fists and rushed off toward the gate. When she thought she was far enough away, she slowed and glanced back over her shoulder. He was still there, standing where she'd left him, watching her. She turned back and didn't stop until she was through the gate and out of the Midway.

*T*hat woman was trouble. He'd sensed it the first time he'd met her, walking through the theater with that older one like it was a dirty place unfit for their pristine Fair. Look how she ran from him. Rushing away as though he carried a disease she might contract. Would it have anything to do with why he'd been summoned to the Administration Building to account again for rumors? Quite likely. She might look guileless, so innocent with her wide eyes that had sized him up and found him wanting.

When she finally disappeared through the gate, he followed the path back to the theater's back door, but he couldn't shake her from his thoughts. She was beautiful, yes. And he might have been taken in by the curve of her smooth cheek and the delicately angled chin, but it was the upturn of her slender little nose that exasperated him. He knew what those Lady Managers were up to. They said they wanted to stop the complaints, to stop the storm of protests brewing against his theater, but they were the ones behind the complaints; he was sure of it. He could see it in their eyes. The disapproval, the recrimination, the self-righteousness. They were the threat against his people.

But he could play the Lady Managers' game. Pretend to accept their help. Amina and the others had fallen for the ruse. They'd changed their costumes and their dance. And for what? So a doctor would tend to Maryeta? Perhaps they'd been right to do it, but now they were in this woman's debt. Was that part of the Lady Managers' plan? He could think of no other reason why his own pleas on Maryeta's behalf had gone unheeded. And now to catch this Mrs. Chambers sneaking away from the theater by the back way. What was she up to?

Cook was spicing a leg of lamb for the fire when he entered the clearing. The old woman waved when he greeted her. "Another delicious meal in the making, I see," he said when he approached to check on the preparations. Bowls held quarters of onion and tomatoes and parsley leaves. Another held the milky white water of soaking rice.

The old woman's face crinkled into a web of creases and wrinkles when she smiled. "It's always a joy to prepare a meal for an appreciative tongue," she said.

"The true joy is ours, Sahra." He bent and kissed her forehead.

In the theater, the show was already in progress. He took his usual spot in the back, watching, waiting. When it finished, when Amina had taken her bow, he didn't wait for the theater to empty.

He'd waited long enough. He motioned her to join him in the performers' room, and he closed the door behind her. "Why was that Lady Manager here?"

"What do you mean?" Her face went blank like it did when she was hiding something.

"I saw her leave. I know she was here."

"It is a private matter."

He tolerated a lot from her, but not this. "If you are talking about this troupe, the people who put their trust in me—"

"Not private for me. Private for her."

Private for her? Perhaps he had underestimated how devious these Lady Managers could be.

"Her visit had nothing to do with us or anyone here."

He looked for the deception in her eyes, in the twitch of her lips. He saw nothing. He couldn't get anywhere with her when she was like this. "The Fair's Midway Commission summoned me this morning."

She paused, then kicked off her slippers and paced, wringing her hands like they were wrestling squirrels.

"They say they are losing money because of the rumors and protests. They say the scandal is hurting their profit."

"They have said this before."

"They say they will be forced into action if we do not resolve the problem."

"We have done what the Lady Managers have asked of us."

"They say they will reduce our wages."

"The theater is full. How can they say they are losing money when every day we sell out at least two shows?"

He shook his head; he knew the argument well. He'd made it himself only an hour before. "They say costs are high. They suggest adding additional shows."

"There are no more hours in the day. Should we never stop to eat?"

"We have another option." He braced himself, waiting for the tirade that had come the last time he'd mentioned the offer.

"We cannot go to New York. It is out of the question."

"I am assured the theater is very nice. We would be treated well. We would not have to travel to the other theaters as other vaudeville acts do. You would perform at just the one theater."

"That is what they say now. We could get there and find an entirely different arrangement waiting for us, just like we did here."

He shrugged. It was not a concern he could dispute.

"But we cannot allow them to cut our wages," Amina said. "We have already had to pay the doctor for Maryeta's care. If we lose any more, we will return home empty-handed. Or worse, we won't even be able to pay for everyone's passage home. What then?"

He knew the repercussions. He'd pondered them many times. "So far, they are only threats."

"Tell them again we are cooperating, that we do not want trouble."

"I will tell them, but at least consider New York."

Eight

Dora returned home on her bicycle to find Dr. Bostwick tending his rosebushes along the front of his house, a farmer's hat pulled low on his neck. He waved. "Your new mode of transportation suits you, Mrs. Chambers," he hollered.

She left her bicycle beside the bougainvillea and walked over to him. "I'm quite enjoying it, even more than I thought would," she said, still winded from the ride.

"I can see it. Your cheeks have quite a glow." He dropped a pruned branch onto his pile of cuttings.

She felt her cheeks with her hands. Had her hat not protected her? She was careful to wear her widest brimmed hats and to keep the sleeves pulled well over her wrists. Had it not been enough?

"It was meant to be a compliment."

She pulled her hands to her sides. "A woman can just never be too careful about the sun."

He made a look like he understood, but Dora doubted he did. Men never understood such things. "I wanted to thank you again.

I saw the Egyptians this morning, and I understand your patient is mending well. I wish you would allow me to give you something for your trouble." She lifted the purse that hung from her wrist and pulled the cord to open it.

Dr. Bostwick stopped her hand, but pulled it away quickly when he saw the dirt on his work gloves rubbing off on her silk ones. "Now look what I've done. I do apologize." He brushed his hands on the legs of his denim overalls. "You can see I'm quite a disaster when it comes to these sorts of things."

"It's all right," she said, brushing away what she could of the soil with her other hand.

"But please, payment is hardly necessary. I'm glad to help where I can."

"Protecting my bougainvillea, helping an ill stranger—I'm lucky to have such a charitable neighbor."

He pulled a linen handkerchief from his back pocket and rubbed at the dark marks. "It's nothing, I assure you. Happy to be of service."

"Then I look forward to the opportunity to repay your kindness," she said.

"As will I," he said, still rubbing, though it seemed to have no effect. Finally he gave up and reached around to tuck the handkerchief back into his pocket. "Perhaps we should keep these favors between ourselves, don't you think?"

Such an odd thing to say, but his eyes twinkled. "If you think so," she said.

"Can't have all my patients expecting complimentary house calls, you know. Bad for business."

"Yes, of course."

They parted and Dora walked her bicycle up to the stable.

At the kitchen door, she heard cabinet doors slamming and

pots crashing. She thought back over the day. Had she done something to trigger Bonmarie's temper? Nothing came to mind, but she'd been caught by surprise before.

When Dora latched the door behind her, Bonmarie's rage hit her like an open flame. "Something smells delicious," Dora said in her kindest, sweetest voice. "What's for dinner?"

Bonmarie didn't look up from the celery stalks that were losing their heads beneath her cleaver. "Don't try buttering me up. I know what you're up to. If you want to play games like that, you go outside and play them with that mean-as-a-kicked-dog driver man."

So it was Harold.

"Why would I want anything to do with him? He's no friend to me."

"I don't blame you. He's nothing but trouble. Do you know what he did today? I heard him yapping on the doorstep with Hazel that—" She stopped. "Well, it doesn't deserve repeating. He's a spiteful old coot and he needs to learn his place."

"What did he say?"

Bonmarie's face went blank. Dora thought she knew why. She had been the topic of his yapping. Bonmarie was free with her criticism, but she never tolerated a negative word about Dora from anybody else. "Where'd you run off to so early?" She scooped up the celery slivers and dropped them into a bowl.

Dora gave up. Bonmarie never said more than she intended to say. "The Fair. Lady Manager business."

"Why'd you take the bicycle instead of the carriage?" Bonmarie asked.

That had been Harold's complaint. She answered with care. "Charles might think I don't appreciate the gift if I don't use it. I can't leave it in the stable to rust because he's too busy to ride."

"I hope you were careful." Bonmarie cut into an onion,

releasing its odor into the room. "I've seen some of those riders take nasty spills. It's not dignified, especially for a lady."

"I was careful."

Bonmarie nodded with the rhythm of her chopping.

Dora resisted the urge to say more. She had better things to do than justify herself to Bonmarie or Harold or any of them. She had to find something to wear. Something to tempt Charles. In her room, she pulled the mauve taffeta dress with the bustle skirt and puffed sleeves from her wardrobe. Absolutely not. She tossed it on the bed. The chocolate evening dress with the drape sleeves? Maybe. It showed a good bit of décolletage, but a gown would be too much for a dinner at home. She threw it on the bed, too. The coral town dress? High collar, flounced skirt. No. One by one she worked through her choices, until she'd ruled out every dress she owned.

She closed the wardrobe door and examined herself in the mirror's reflection. The high, ruffled collar of her shirtwaist, the waist cinched to a perfect sixteen inches, the skirt that draped in deep folds. Except for her head and hands, no part of her natural body was evident, and even her hands were usually hidden beneath gloves. She unbuttoned her bodice and removed it. Unbuttoned her blouse and removed it. Unlaced her boots, unfastened her overskirt and underskirt, and removed them all. She shed her clothing until she stood before the mirror in just her chemise. She grabbed the white linen at the small of her back. It was still moist from where it swaddled her beneath the corset. She studied herself in the glass. Was there anything alluring in this plain form?

Charles had found her pleasing. He had hungered for her when she took it for granted, before she knew she could lose it. But had she done the right thing by going to that belly dancer? If anyone could help her, Amina Mahomet could. That woman inspired passion in men every day, every time she performed. What must that feel like, to look out from that stage and see such hunger in every man's eyes?

The strains of the Middle Eastern music filled her mind, the horn and the drum echoing through her like a heartbeat. *Doom doom tekka tek doom tekka tek.* She could hear it flowing through her. She recalled the way Amina's hips rolled, creating the illusion that she walked though she didn't move forward an inch. A simple movement, yet so mesmerizing. Dora rolled her own hips. She checked the mirror, but what she saw resembled nothing of the dancer's graceful gyrations. Instead of a rhythmic glide, her own hips lurched and twitched. She tried smoothing the motion, but still her torso jerked and far too many other parts moved. She tried but could not make that middle area move without her shoulders and knees and everything else moving, too.

She didn't care. She turned away from the mirror and mimicked the moves as she remembered them. The flourishing sweeps of her arm, the pepper-mill twists of her shoulders, the bounces and sways of her hips. She closed her eyes and in her mind could see out into that sea of masculine faces. They all looked back at her; they all desired her. She tried to feel each stretch and movement. She tried to enjoy each feeling.

Who knew hips could move like that, or that wrists tingled when rotated in just such a way?

A knocking at the front door made her stop. She heard the door open and then heard Bonmarie's voice. It closed with a thud and the stairs rattled with Bonmarie's steps.

She entered holding a white envelope when Dora invited her in. "It's from Mr. Chambers."

Dora took it. Bank stationery. She tore it open, pulled out the card. *Working late. Will not be home for dinner.*

Eight simple words, but enough to ruin an evening. No

greeting, no apology, no sentiment at all. "Thank you, Bonmarie. Mr. Chambers won't be needing dinner tonight." The words scraped through her, clawing her with the agony of the truth. If she were to check on him later, she knew she would not find him at the bank. He'd be in that woman's home again, pressing his affections on her and accepting those she pressed on him.

She turned away from the look of pity she saw on Bonmarie's face. "I'll have my dinner on a tray in my room. I'm feeling a little tired."

"Seven o'clock?"

By the slant of sun through the window, it couldn't have been more than midafternoon. Seven felt like an eternity. "Seven will be fine."

"I'll heat up water for a bath. That'll do you good."

It would take much more than a bath to do that, but she put on a grateful face anyway. "You always know just the thing."

In the downstairs bathroom, she soaked herself until the water that had scalded her turned cold enough to make her shiver. Even then she remained immersed, slipping down into the tub so her chin rested just above the waterline. She breathed in the rose petal aroma of the scented oil Bonmarie had mixed with the water and blew ripples into the surface. It seemed fitting for her body to be concealed by the water the same way it was concealed by her clothing. Only her head remained, as if it were a separate thing. It was the only part that didn't bring her shame or cause her worry. The only part she understood. There were no rules when it came to the head, beyond the need for a hat every now and then. Not like everything else, which had to be shrouded and hidden away.

A head was easier to understand in other ways, too. It was the center of the senses. The eyes saw, the mouth tasted, the nose smelled, the ears heard. No mystery, no confusion. Not like the stirrings that came from elsewhere, the sensations with no clear purpose or need.

Life had been much simpler as a girl, before a woman's rules applied. Dora's knees could peek beneath the hem of her short dress and no one scowled. She could push her sleeves above her elbow and no one grimaced. She could touch herself in the place between her legs when she was alone in her bed, at least before she knew it was wrong. The morning Mama walked in, caught her in the act, and slapped her hard across the face, she'd never dared to touch herself that way again.

She knew it was wrong to pleasure herself that way, wrong and improper, but thinking of it brought back the memory of that tingling between her legs. Mama wasn't here; Bonmarie was in the kitchen. Charles wouldn't be home for hours. She slid two fingers down over the tuft of hair between her legs and felt for the place where the flesh changed, the cleft where the slightest touch sent pleasure through her whole body. She rubbed the hard knot, sending wave after wave of shivers through her. She pressed her fingers harder, pressed her legs closer together, made the rubbing quicker and more urgent until the sensation grew into a volcano of feeling that finally erupted and made her shudder. She gasped, her heart racing, as she pressed her fingers to the throbbing flesh. She checked the door, listened for footsteps. Nothing, but still the voice in her head was reminding her she should be ashamed. She was a woman of rank, the voice said; she knew better. She couldn't let herself be weak like that again.

She lifted herself out of the tub and wiped down with the clean towel Bonmarie had left for her. She dragged a fresh chemise over her head and was tying back her wet hair when Bonmarie knocked.

"I put your dinner in your room," she said through the door.

The shame followed her upstairs, but the meal set out on the tray made her forget everything else. Red beans and sausage rounds in gravy over rice, and a good, hearty portion of it.

Dora settled in, took up the fork, and scooped a mouthful of rice dripping with the rich, red gravy. She chewed slowly, relishing every bit of the savory sausage, the gentle give in the beans, the hint of pepper, and the plump, firm rice.

Back home, Mondays were washing days at the hotel, and that meant Bonmarie's red beans and rice. It required the least amount of kitchen time to prepare, but it was Dora's favorite.

She saw Bonmarie standing in the door.

Bonmarie winked. "Not the sort of meal Mr. Chambers would like, but since he's not around, we should spoil ourselves a bit, don't you think?"

Dora ate two bowlfuls before giving up and pushing away the tray.

"I could eat a third, but I'm afraid my stomach will burst," she said when she delivered her tray to the kitchen.

Bonmarie was scrubbing the last of the cooking pans. "You didn't need to bring that down."

"I know. I just wanted to thank you again for it. After all of Charles's bland pot roasts and potatoes, I'd almost forgotten how good food can taste."

"I do make a good pot of red beans and rice, if I do say so myself," Bonmarie said.

Back in her room, where the dinner smells lingered, Dora settled in for the night. The clock struck half past eight. She looked at the window. She wasn't going to wait for Charles tonight. She could watch for the carriage, maybe even talk to him when he came through the door. But this wasn't the night for that. She needed to make things right with him, but she couldn't do it after he'd been with Mrs. Forrest.

She crawled into bed and sank into her pillow. She let go of her thoughts of Charles and that woman, she let go of her shame, she even let go of her enjoyment of the red beans and rice. How wonderful it felt to slip away from it all, to separate herself as if those images held no power over her at all. The Egyptian drumbeat came back to her. *Doom doom tekka tek doom tekka tek.* She could see herself moving through the dance steps. She was wearing a pair of the silky pantaloons and a filmy blouse with a tight crimson vest pulled across her chest. She dreamed of beaded necklaces draped around her neck, and fringed scarves and belts of coins wrapped around her hips. She saw herself with her hair down around her shoulders and the dark kohl paint around her eyes, and she drifted into the twilight before sleep.

In that half-awake state she was in an antechamber of a desert palace, where there were pillars with drapes billowing between them. There was incense and pillows, and she was dancing for Charles like a harem girl, danced for the man perched like a sultan on a throne of cushions. She undulated, moving in that serpentine way that was Amina's specialty. When she turned again to Charles, he was different. The soft, hazel gaze and muttonchops had been replaced by pitch-black eyes and long wisps of hair like polished onyx. Still she danced, and her skin tingled with the thrill of entertaining a man whose name came to her like a whisper over Saharan dunes. She said it to herself: Hossam Farouk.

*D*ora rose early the next morning. The images of that Egyptian man had been so vivid, so real. They'd made it impossible to drift back into sleep after the first flutter of awareness disturbed her dream. Desert palaces, Saharan dunes . . . Good heavens, where had those ridiculous thoughts come from? As if her shame in the bath the night before hadn't been bad enough.

Her mind was retaliating against Charles's infidelity, she decided. Or was it a test of faith in her marriage? She knew one thing: She was not attracted to that Egyptian man. He was awful. He made her anxious every time she saw him, and it didn't matter that he was handsome. He was cocky and condescending.

Why was she even thinking about this? It was a dream; she'd forget it by breakfast. She dressed quickly and went downstairs to the kitchen to find Bonmarie at the stove, stirring a pot of simmering apples and oatmeal.

"Has Mr. Chambers left the house yet?" she asked, as the kitchen door swung behind her.

"He left early." Bonmarie kept stirring without turning around.

"Do you know what time he came home last night?" She worked at a bit of dirt beneath a fingernail.

"No. Went to bed early myself."

"Harold will know; he must've readied the carriage for him this morning." She went to the door.

"Harold's gone. Took off downtown to get something or other. I'm sure everything's fine with Mr. Chambers."

Through the sheer curtain over the door's window, she could see Harold carrying Delilah's saddle into the barn. "He's right there."

"Don't ask him about Mr. Chambers," Bonmarie blurted when Dora turned the doorknob. "Just leave it alone."

The earth sank beneath her feet, ready to swallow her. She could see it in the unhappy lines pulling at Bonmarie's eyes.

"Mr. Chambers did not come home last night," Bonmarie whispered, nearly choking on the words.

Dora's hand dropped from the door. She wanted to sink into

the nothingness, but she couldn't surrender here, not in front of Bonmarie. She forced herself to stand tall. Then she willed her legs to move without crumpling to the floor. She made it to the door, then to the stairs, then at last to her bedroom.

She closed her door behind herself and fell against it. But there was still more to do. At the dressing table, she dashed off a note to Mrs. Tillday. *Feeling ill. Cannot make it to the Fair. My apologies.* She signed it, sealed it in an envelope, and left it beside her door.

Bonmarie's knock came moments later, just as she'd expected. Dora was already under the covers, the lip of her bedsheet pulled up tight against her chin, when the woman entered.

"I am so sorry, *ma chere*."

Dora turned away. "The note there is for Mrs. Tillday. Please see that she gets it this morning."

"I didn't want to hurt—"

"I'd like to be left alone. Please."

She heard shuffling and then the quiet closing of the door.

Did not come home last night. The words reverberated through her. They rattled and bounced and seeped into every corner of her thoughts. One more disappointment, one more failure. How could she make amends when he didn't give her a chance? Or had she already squandered her only opportunity?

No, she couldn't give up. When the time came, she had to be ready. Until then, she would wait.

The rest of the day passed in a haze of sleep and dreams. She dreamed of her father, of Mama at the hotel, then of the Egyptian Theatre with the belly dancers and the musicians and Hossam Farouk. And again she dreamed of herself among them. Those were the dreams that calmed her and eased her mind. Inside that make-believe world, her worries faded and her disappointments vanished. In her dancing dreams, she thrilled to the sultry music that moved through her body and made it respond with shakes and shimmies. The packed house audience adored her, but she sought out the one who thrilled her most. The one with black hair and penetrating eyes who stood at the far corner of the room.

When the dreams continued into that half-awake state, she knew she should have put them on a course more fitting for a proper married woman. But it was just a dream that meant nothing. It wasn't as if she'd spent the night in his arms.

Bonmarie interrupted the dreams twice, once with news that the message to Mrs. Tillday had been delivered and condolences had been returned, and again with a plea to eat something so the sickness wasn't worsened by hunger. Dora acknowledged both with nods and nothing more, but when she heard the front door slam with a masculine force, she rose and hurried to her wardrobe mirror.

She looked a fright, with her hair flattened on one side and wild on the other. She plucked out the pins, bent over her knees, and shook out the mass of curls. She flipped them back and patted them into place. Then she pulled a tea gown from a drawer and covered her creased chemise, tying the gown at the collar. But the image looking back from the mirror was all wrong. She looked like a tent of frills and lace with just her head popping out on top. Not the sort of image to inspire desire in Charles, was it?

She loosened the ties and let the gown fall open to reveal the linen of her chemise inside. No, still too much. She slid off the tea gown, removed the chemise, pulled on a lace camisole, and donned the tea gown over it. Now when the sides fell open, they revealed the curve of her neck and even a shadow of her bosom.

Dora emerged from her room and went in search of Charles. His hat and coat hung from the rack; the door of his study stood open. She padded to the room, knocked, and entered to find him sitting behind his desk, the evening paper spread before him. He looked like it might be any other day, as if nothing important had transpired at all. It gave her hope.

She glided to the desk, accentuating the twist of her hips, and leaned down just enough to make the sides of her tea gown gape open. "You've been working so hard, dear, perhaps you can take a break and spend some time with me in the sitting room." She rubbed her bare neck in an absentminded way.

"Why are you dressed like that in the middle of the day?"

"What, this?" She fingered the loose tie that hung over her chest. "I wasn't feeling well earlier. I've been resting." She slid her hip up on the desk and leaned toward him a little more.

He snapped the newspaper up again. "How nice for you. I hope you aren't neglecting the Lady Managers."

"But my health?"

He dipped the paper again, one eyebrow rose. "You look healthy enough to me. Do you want me to have Bostwick look in on you?"

"No, I don't need Dr. Bostwick. But you might show some degree of concern."

He slammed the paper on the desk. "It's not enough that I work all day to provide you with a place to live and food to eat, not to mention the clothes you wear and everything else? Instead of lounging about all day, it would be nice if you could take your role with the Lady Managers a little more seriously. Or perhaps it hasn't occurred to you that a man's place in business can be helped—or hurt—by his wife's social efforts. If you'll excuse me, I have some work to do. Please have Bonmarie bring my meal here. As for whatever it is ailing you, I do hope it will be cleared up by the morning."

He picked up the paper and hid his face behind it. She wavered for a moment, but there was nothing more to say or do, only deliver Charles's request to Bonmarie and tie the laces of her tea gown.

Nine

The next day, Dora changed into her bicycle riding boots and grabbed a carrot from the kitchen for Delilah. In the stable, she gave the mare her treat, rubbed her nose, and retrieved the bicycle from where it leaned against Charles's under a set of reins hanging on the wall.

Already the day was off to a good start. She'd been trying to devise a way to speak to the belly dancer alone when a message arrived from Mrs. Tillday telling her an errand would delay her until noon. It gave Dora the opportunity to suggest they meet at the Fair instead and provided her the window she needed to find Amina. Pedaling to the Fair, Dora rehearsed what she would say. But that would be the easy part. It would be more difficult to get Amina alone.

When she reached the Cairo Street gate, Dora parked her bike with the others. Inside, she hurried to the Egyptian Theatre, pulling the brim of her hat low to hide from anyone who might take too much interest in a woman out alone.

She arrived to find a line of men standing in front of the theater's ticket window, waiting to pay admission to the next show. Inside, a performance was already under way. Dora went to the curtained doorway, poked in her head. Though she could see little of the stage, she recognized the tune that marked Amina's final dance.

Dora worked her way through the full standing room gallery and searched for a spot with a view. It wasn't until she was nearly to the far wall that she could finally see the dancer, yet even with the veil and heavy clothing, she knew it wasn't Amina. The woman was taller and thinner, and her dancing lacked the same grace. Dora stretched to see the seated dancers along the bench on the stage, but none appeared to be the one she sought.

When the dance ended, the audience clapped and began moving toward the door. The dancers remained on the bench, waiting for the next audience to file in. When Dora approached the stage, the Egyptian women eyed her with suspicion.

"Where might I find Amina Mahomet?" she asked.

Two turned to each other and giggled.

Dora waited, her arms clasped over her chest. When an answer did not come, she tried again. "I'd like to speak to her, if that's possible."

The heaviest one, the woman who looked older than the others, said, "She cannot speak."

The woman's English labored under her accent. Dora shook her head, signaling her confusion.

"What she means is that Amina cannot speak with you at this moment."

Dora spun around. Mr. Farouk strode toward her, his hands behind his back, his dark eyes narrowed on her. She thought of the visions of him in her dreams and a hot flush rose from her collar.

"She has a guest, but if you would care to wait, I'm sure she will not be long."

Dora's gaze darted from his. She stared at the crisp whiteness of his tunic instead of his face. "That will be fine. Where may I wait?"

He grinned as if amused. "You are a Lady Manager; you may wait anywhere you like."

He was patronizing her. She held her parasol tightly under her elbow and straightened herself, trying to look more dignified than she felt. "I will wait outside, then. If you'll be so kind as to let her know where she can find me."

The belly dancers looked confused, but Hossam seemed to enjoy the exchange.

Dora marched from the theater, dodging the men filing in to fill the seats.

Outside, the midday sun beat hard on the stone-paved square and left no shady nook against the theater wall. Dora opened her parasol and hid beneath it, as much to shield her identity from unfriendly eyes as to protect her complexion.

"I fear I have offended you."

She lifted her parasol to her other shoulder and saw that Hossam Farouk had followed her.

"I don't know what you're talking about." She grimaced. How petty and childish the words sounded.

He ran his hand through his hair and turned as if he'd walk away, then pivoted back. "Whatever I say seems to irritate you, when it is not my intention to do so."

She watched him shift where he stood, moving from one foot to the other, putting a hand first on his hip and then running it again through his hair. He looked nervous. But why? A man like this certainly had no reason to be uneasy around a woman like her. He began to pace, anxiously watching her with his onyx eyes. There was no denying his apprehension, but surely she wasn't the cause.

"I'm not irritated," she said plainly.

"Yes, I suppose I have imagined those sharp looks."

Sharp looks from her could rankle this man? It hardly seemed plausible. Then it occurred to her. It wasn't her at all that caused his discomfort. It was her position. He would flail under the glance of any Lady Manager. She straightened. "I must learn to keep my expressions under better control. But you needn't worry. No irritation on my part will affect what I report."

"Yes, the Lady Manager reports. That is not my concern."

"What exactly is your concern, Mr. Farouk?"

The way he stopped dead and stared at her told her more than words could convey. There was something strange and new in his eyes. How vulnerable he looked now with his eyes twitching with frustration, his hands jumping from his chest to his sides. Perhaps Charles no longer found her pleasing, but it appeared this man did. She stifled a smile, then said slowly, "Do you find me attractive, Mr. Farouk?"

"I'm not sure I know what you mean, Mrs. Chambers." He emphasized the word "missus."

"I suppose it's not the sort of question a lady should ask. You must pardon me. I haven't been myself lately. You see, it's just that I've recently discovered that I do not please my husband, and I wondered if it is because my appearance is not pleasing. I'm looking for a purely objective opinion, of course." How exciting it was to feel this power over him.

"It would not be my place to offer an opinion," he said carefully.

She looked around to be sure no one was looking their way,

then stepped forward so they were close enough to touch. The nearness of him enlivened every part of her. In a lowered voice, she said, "Perhaps you can tell me this then: What ignites a man's passion for a woman? Is it her face? The line of her nose or the color of her eyes? Is it her hair or her waist or her bosom? Or is it something else entirely, like her voice or her sense of humor? I'm only curious."

How agonized he looked.

"Mrs. Chambers," he said, again emphasizing her title, "the answer would be different for every man, so you should take care whose opinion you seek."

A woman's laughter interrupted them. Amina emerged from the alley separating the theater from the rug shop next door. She was accompanied by a young man Dora had seen selling brass oil lanterns in a shop across the square. Amina's arm threaded through his and he gazed down on her with unguarded admiration. She spoke to him in Arabic. When she saw Dora and Hossam in the square, she turned to her young man, kissed him long on the mouth, and, when he reached to enfold her in his arms, she pulled away and waved good-bye. He touched his lips and stumbled back.

Amina approached Dora and Hossam with a grin spread wide across her face.

"I'm glad to see you," Dora said quickly, stepping back from Hossam. "I've been waiting for you."

Amina turned to Hossam as if to say, *And you?*

He clasped his hands behind himself and pulled back his shoulders. "I was just amusing Mrs. Chambers while she waited." He faced Dora as if he would say something but instead dipped into a low and formal bow. "I will look forward to our next meeting."

She curtsied back, and said, "As will I."

Then he was gone, bridging the distance to the theater door in long, lean strides, the ends of his white tunic fluttering in the breeze. The line of patrons waiting there parted to let him pass.

"Another visit so soon? You must have come to thank me." Amina wiggled her eyebrows as though they shared a secret understanding.

"That's not the reason, I'm afraid. The situation is worse than I expected."

"You did what I said?"

"I did."

"Come to my room. We can talk there."

*A*mina went around the room picking up discarded garments and arranging pillows while Dora set down her parasol and purse. The room looked much as it had on her first visit, except for the bed, which looked rumpled and recently used. Dora thought of the young man. "Your visitor, is he your beau?"

Amina tossed garments that had been on the floor over the dressing screen. She tilted her head. "Beau?"

"A gentleman caller? Suitor?"

Amina shook her head. "But he is handsome, isn't he? Strong arms and happy eyes—I like that. And he loves me all night, again and again."

Dora turned away to hide her blush. "I thought you didn't like that sort of thing."

"I do not want to marry, but I still like to touch a man. If it brings us pleasure, who does it harm?"

Dora pulled her skirts smooth to sit on a wooden chest. "I suppose I've always believed a woman should be intimate only with her husband."

"Those are your rules, not mine."

"Then what is to keep you together after you are intimate?"

"What if I don't want to be together after we are intimate?"

"What if he finds someone new?"

"What if I find someone new?" Amina laughed, enjoying the game.

"But aren't you afraid you'll end up alone?"

"No."

So much confidence in that single word. "Why not?"

Amina sat back on three cushions and stretched her legs out in front of herself. "I have my dancing sisters, my tribe. I will always have them; that is how we live. I can have a man any time."

"But what if you wanted just one man and he didn't want you?"

"Then he is not worth my time." Amina looked as if she immediately regretted the flip comment. She moved closer to Dora and took her hand. "Then I would not give up."

"He hardly looks at me."

Amina leaned back, crossed her arms. She tapped her lip. "There are other ways to get a man's attention." She rose, paced the room. Finally, she turned to Dora. "This is what you want?"

"More than anything."

*T*hat woman infuriated him, toying with him that way. *Do you find me attractive, Mr. Farouk?* She would not have asked if she had not noticed the way he looked at her. He couldn't deny he wanted to wrap his hands around her waist, press her against him, stop her mouth with his own. But she was another man's wife. Nothing would change that.

He went to the back of the ticket booth and pulled aside the curtain that cordoned off the ticket seller from the rest of the theater. He waited for the boy to finish a transaction with a white man in a top hat. "Yes, boss?" the boy asked in Arabic after handing the man his ticket and a few coins in change.

"What is today's take?"

The boy checked a sheet with tick marks, then rose from his stool and peered out his window. "Five hundred, and the line is still long for this show."

"Maybe six hundred dollars by midday, then. Eight or eight fifty when we close. Not bad for a day." Hossam nodded, shut the curtain, and kept his disappointment to himself. He walked to his usual corner. How were they going to get back to a thousand a day as the Midway Commission wanted? Add another show?

It was the costumes. A thousand a day had been easy before they changed. The veils and coats didn't pull in the audience like the other costume had. But Amina was stubborn. She said she had made the promise to Mrs. Chambers to get Maryeta's doctor, and she would not break that promise. But they had paid the doctor handsomely. Was that not enough?

And why could he not get that Mrs. Chambers out of his thoughts? He could have any dancer, from his own troupe or any on the Midway. This morning an Ouled Nail woman in ornamented veils and jewelry had watched him walk past the Algerian Theatre, and a pretty Syrian dancer had fluttered her eyes when she offered him a sip of her Turkish coffee. He had turned away from them both. Why? Why could he only think of that Lady Manager? He found himself sticking close to the premises for the chance to glimpse her.

But today he had gone too far and given himself away. Now she flaunted herself, daring him to admit what she already knew. He should have been repelled by the boldness of her questions.

He had never expected anything like those words to come from a woman like a Lady Manager. What other surprises might she hold?

He scolded himself for letting ridiculous notions get the better of him. He had to focus on the act. He observed the musicians and the dancers, he watched the audience for signs of trouble. He did his job and cursed his weakness for that infuriating woman.

*W*hen your gazes meet, don't look away. Like this." From where she sat on her cushions, Amina tilted her head and looked at Dora from the corners of her eyes. She fluttered her lashes slowly without breaking the connection.

A shudder ran through Dora that made her wiggle where she sat.

"You see? The eyes have power. They communicate more than you say, so hold the look as long as you can. If he holds it, too, you will have him because you will know he wants you."

"What if he looks away?" If Charles wouldn't look at her nearly naked body, why would he look at her eyes?

Amina shook her finger. "Do not give up the first time. Keep trying, keep talking. If his eyes dart off in another direction, follow them, try to bring them back. When he does look at you, tease him. Give him a little smile, lift your shoulder or dip your eyelashes as though you are shy. Like this." She demonstrated a sort of dreamy half smile, then a subtle rise of her shoulder, a dip of her lashes.

Watching Amina, Dora could see how a man could be aroused. She shifted and prepared herself for the smile. She lifted a corner of her lips, held it.

"That's good, but relax your cheek. Think of the wonderful way it will feel when he touches you."

Dora bent her head and laughed.

"You cannot laugh. If you laugh when you are with him, he will think you are laughing *at* him. That will ruin the moment."

"Sorry. How about this?" Dora tried the smile again. This time it came more easily.

"Now the shoulder."

Dora twisted slightly to one side, lifted the forward shoulder.

"Yes, yes. Now the eyelashes."

After several tries, she finally earned Amina's praise.

Her elation passed quickly into doubt. Her biggest failure had been when he made love to her. She had lain stiff and unmoving, so afraid of doing the wrong thing she had done nothing at all. "What is a woman supposed to do when she's in bed with a man?" She covered her face with her hands and waited for Amina to answer.

Small fingers pried away Dora's fingers. Amina knelt in front of her. "Are you afraid of the question, or the answer?"

"Both, I suppose. I don't know what to do with any of it."

"Do you think you could do this to him?" She kept hold of Dora's hands with one of her own and ran a finger of the other along Dora's forearm.

Dora nodded.

"Do it to me."

Dora recoiled. "What do you mean?"

"You will see that you can do it; then it will not frighten you."

Dora hesitated.

"I will not move. I promise."

"Will you laugh?"

Amina stifled a smile. "I will not laugh."

Dora bit her bottom lip, reached out, and dragged a finger along Amina's bare arm, making her profusion of bracelets jangle when she reached her wrist.

"Good, but now do it slower. Close your eyes, pretend I am your husband. Touch his arm like you never want to stop."

Dora closed her eyes and reached out again. She trailed her fingertip over the skin lightly, feeling gooseflesh form where she touched. She pulled away when she reached the bracelets and opened her eyes.

"Yes, exactly. Try this." Amina brushed the back of her fingers over Dora's cheek.

Dora mimicked the movement.

"Good. Can you do that to your husband?"

"I think so."

"When you touch him, you do not have to touch only his arm or his face. He will want to feel your fingers everywhere—his chest, his back, his limbs, his . . . " Amina made an up-and-down movement with her eyebrows and looked down at her lap.

"I can't do that," Dora said flatly.

"Why not? It is part of his body."

"Because. It's . . . " *It's what?* she wondered. *Improper? Embarrassing?*

"How is it different from his hand or his foot?"

"It just is."

Amina paused. "You are right, it is. It is far more important than a hand or a foot. That is why you must touch him there."

"But I can't do it. What if I danced for him instead?" she blurted. "What if you taught me how to move like you do? Maybe that would make him look at me the way men look at you."

"That is absurd."

"Why?"

"You are not a dancer. You are not even Egyptian."

Dora drew circles with her fingertip in the chest's wood. "Maybe I could dance if you showed me."

Amina paced. "What do you think you could ~~you~~ learn?"

Dora thought of the movement that always intrigued her. "The way you make it roll here?" She placed her hand on her midsection.

"Too difficult. Something else."

"Anything. You can teach me anything."

Amina paced again.

Dora waited.

Amina spun around, and said, "Let me see how you move. Stand up."

Dora obeyed.

Amina took one arm in each of her own and pulled them out from Dora's sides. "Straighten them."

Dora locked her elbows in place and ignored the tug in the seams of her sleeves.

Amina tapped Dora's hip. "Move here."

Dora tried. Amina frowned.

"Just your hips, not your whole body."

Dora tried again.

The frown deepened.

"I'm trying." Maybe this was a mistake.

"The clothes, you cannot move in those clothes." She went to her dressing screen, pulled down a mound of garments, and sorted through them. She tossed a pair of silky emerald pantaloons over her arm, then a forest green velvet vest and a white gossamer top with lacy sleeves. She shoved the pile toward Dora. "Put these on."

Dora accepted the bundle. What was she supposed to do with all of this? Amina's face told her she could not refuse. She disappeared behind the dressing screen and slipped off her gloves. Was she really doing this? She unbuttoned her boots, her blouse, her skirt. She unlaced her corset and petticoats. The cool air on her bare skin made her shiver.

She lifted the filmy white stocking shirt first and dragged it over her head. She put on the vest, which didn't cover enough no matter how much she tugged. She picked up the voluminous trousers and hesitated.

She'd never worn trousers. Ever.

"Are you ready?"

"Nearly." She couldn't wear trousers. But then who would ever see? No one but Amina. It would be their secret. Slowly she stepped into the baggy legs and pulled them over her linen bloomers.

Dora emerged from the screen.

"Better. Stand here."

Dora stood in front of Amina. The pillows that had been on the floor before she changed were thrown onto the bed, and the small tables were pushed to the wall, making a wide-open space on the floor.

Amina crossed her arms over her chest and rested a thumb on her chin. "Let me see you dance."

"There's no music."

"Pretend there is music."

She couldn't dance without music. She wanted to run back behind the screen. But then she would lose Charles for good. This was what she wanted. She closed her eyes and conjured the Egyptian drumbeat in her mind. *Doom doom tekka tek doom tekka tek.* She played it in her mind and began to move, first in a simple sidestep, and then adding hand flourishes and a shoulder sway.

"Stop."

Dora's eyes flew open.

"Stop," Amina said again. "The dancing is too much in your feet. Do not think of them. Think here." She touched her midsection and swirled it like she was drawing a circle. "Move from here."

Dora recalled the music again, and her feet moved. She stopped. She started again, forcing her feet to keep still. She concentrated on her stomach.

"No, no. Stop."

Dora steeled herself for more reproach.

"Perhaps I did not explain correctly." Amina moved closer and placed her palm on Dora's abdomen. "I did not mean you should stick the belly out, only to let your movements start from here."

Dora felt like a fool. She couldn't learn this Egyptian dancing. Her body couldn't obey these strange commands. It was never going to work.

Amina came up behind her and placed both hands around her middle. Dora straightened at her touch.

"I will tell you what my *usta*, my teacher, told me," Amina said. "To dance, you must know that movement is feeling, and that all feeling comes from here, your belly. It is where our nourishment goes when we eat, it is where a mother's womb creates life. Think of it as the place where you give life to your dance. Do not stick it out; hold it in, protect it."

Dora rearranged her posture.

"Good. Slide your chest forward like this." Amina's hands moved to the sides of Dora's chest. Gently she pushed her bosom forward and pulled back her shoulders.

Dora felt like a soldier standing at attention.

"Drop your chin lower, move your legs a little more apart, and let your knees remain soft. Do not hold them rigid. Now tilt your hips inward to straighten your back. How does that feel?"

"Unnatural. How is anyone supposed to move like this?"

"You are too accustomed to that"—Amina pointed to the corset flung over the dressing screen—"holding your posture for you. The dance will help you regain your own strength." Amina stepped forward with her back toward Dora. "Now watch me; follow what I do."

The dancer inhaled and assumed the dance posture. Her hips moved as though tracing an outline of a large circle on the floor.

Dora mimicked the move.

Amina turned and watched. "That is good. Now be at ease, feel the music, don't think about the movement. Try this." She made a smaller circle with her hips on her right side and then one on the left; the beads and coins hanging from her scarf and vest jingled each time. She turned back to Dora and nodded when she did it adequately.

With Amina's help, Dora swayed easily from the circle on the right into the circle on the left.

"Now change the direction." Amina stopped her own movement and walked around Dora, watching her from the side and behind.

The scrutiny would have made Dora nervous if not for the hint of approval in Amina's look. Dora stopped and began again in the reverse. She stumbled twice, but then found the right groove. She wished the room had a mirror like hers; she wanted to see if she looked as wonderful as she felt.

"Do not stop; keep moving. Try to hold your chest higher and lower your shoulders from your ears. Think of your hips. Hold everything else still. Close your eyes, if it is easier. Concentrate."

A rap sounded on the door and Amina hurried to open it, holding it only slightly ajar so the visitor could not see Dora. Dora heard a woman's voice say something in Arabic. Amina said something in return, then closed the door. "I must get back to the theater, but you can leave whenever you are ready."

"I must be going as well. Oh no, what time is it?" She had forgotten her meeting with Mrs. Tillday. She scrambled for her timepiece in her purse. A quarter past noon. She was already late. "You must help me with my corset before you go. Please."

She grabbed it from the dressing screen, and its laces spread out like wild tentacles. She slipped off Amina's garments and held it in place with her back to Amina.

"Must you wear it?"

"I must, and I must go quickly. Please, I don't have time to do it myself."

Amina inched toward her. She took the laces up and stared at them. Reluctantly, she threaded them through the grommets, tugging, lacing, tugging.

Dora held her waist. When the size diminished to an adequate degree, she took the laces and tied them. "Thank you."

Amina gave the corset a last look. "Don't ask me to do it again," she said, then disappeared behind the dressing screen. When she emerged, she was dressed in her performance costume. "Practice what I taught you, the dancing and the touching."

Dora nodded and Amina closed the door behind her.

A few moments later Dora, fully dressed, peeked into the hallway. She listened. No voices or footsteps. She made her way to the back door so she could work her way around the theater and approach Mrs. Tillday as though she had just arrived. The door opened before she reached it and a young woman entered.

The Egyptian woman started when she saw Dora, and dropped a small bunch of purple grapes. She was dressed as a belly dancer, but she wasn't one Dora had seen before.

"Excuse me," Dora said, and dropped to help the young dancer retrieve the fruit rolling along the floor.

"You are the Lady Manager, no?"

Dora hesitated. "Yes, I'm a Lady Manager." The woman appeared dazed. Dora laid her parasol down to gather the grapes, then handed the fruit back to the woman.

"You are the Lady Manager who helped me. You sent the doctor."

So this was Maryeta. Dora saw shadows beneath the young woman's eyes and hollows in her cheeks. "Shouldn't you be resting?"

"I wanted something to eat." She swayed a bit where she stood, as if the ground tilted beneath her.

"You shouldn't eat these." Dora grabbed back the dirty fruit, went to the door, and tossed it out into the clearing. "Get back into bed; I'll get you fresh ones."

Maryeta pressed her palm to her forehead. "I suppose I am feeling a bit tired," she said.

Dora steadied the woman and led her to the room she knew was hers. She led Maryeta to the bed, and whispered, "I'll be right back."

She opened the door to the back clearing. The sun shined impossibly bright, making her squint and shield her eyes. She spotted the old woman cutting vegetables at the table and went to her. "May I get more grapes for Maryeta?"

The woman gave her a blank stare.

"Grapes? For Maryeta?"

Still blank.

Dora looked over the mounds of onions and potatoes and sacks of rice on the table until she found a bunch of grapes in a bowl. She grabbed a handful and held them up. "For Maryeta?"

The old woman flipped her hand at Dora and turned back to her cutting. Dora didn't hesitate. She was already wasting time. She took the grapes back to the woman's room. She found her with her eyes closed, her breathing steady. "Here are your grapes." A soft snore rose from the woman. Dora placed the grapes beside the bed where Maryeta would see them when she woke, then quietly left the room.

She picked up her parasol in the hall and opened it when she emerged from the building. The cook was still chopping vegetables. A helper was stirring a pot simmering over a fire and another sat beside the young goat Dora had noticed before in the hallway.

The cook watched her cross the clearing but said nothing as she passed. Dora moved quickly, making her way around Cairo Street's back alley, looping around when she emerged at the Sudanese huts and working her way back to the front of the theater. She found Mrs. Tillday standing in front of the rug shop, pretending not to hear the seller's calls to come inside and peruse the merchandise.

"I'm so sorry for keeping you waiting. Time got away from me," Dora said when she reached her partner. She closed her parasol when she reached the shady patch and fidgeted with the folds of her skirt.

"I was starting to worry. I thought something must be wrong. Nothing *is* wrong, is it?"

"No, I just misjudged the time. I didn't expect such a crowd at the gate."

"Which gate did you use?" Mrs. Tillday asked in a suspicious tone. "The one at Cairo Street was hardly busy at all."

Dora pretended to be interested in something across the square. "Quite hot today, isn't it? She felt perspiration pooling beneath her bodice. "We should probably get inside or we'll have to wait for the next performance. Shall we?"

She threaded her arm through Mrs. Tillday's and acted as though she didn't notice her partner's suspicion. The boy watching the door let them pass. To Dora's surprise, there were still open seats and no one stood in the standing room gallery. They took two seats along the back row.

Dora recognized Amina by her crimson veil. She sat among the dancers onstage, while another performed in a violet veil. Dora watched closely. When the dancer's arms fluttered over her head, Dora felt it in her own limbs. She felt the stretch when the woman bent into a deep backbend, and her hips felt the sway of the dancer's undulations.

When Amina took the stage, Dora could hardly sit still.

"Is something wrong?" Mrs. Tillday looked concerned.

"No, I'm fine."

"Why are you fidgeting so?"

"It was just an itch." Dora turned back to the stage to hide the lie. Amina fluttered her stomach and rolled it in a wavelike motion. "Isn't it remarkable how she moves?" she whispered.

Mrs. Tillday snickered as though the comment was meant to be sarcastic.

Dora said nothing more until the music faded and the dancers bowed to the crowd's applause. People rose from their seats and pressed toward the exit.

"Should we stay for another show?" Mrs. Tillday asked.

Dora could feel the music still coursing through her like lightning in her limbs. It was all she could do to sit still. She wanted to get home, to get to her room where she could practice the movements before her memory of them grew stale. "I think we've seen enough for one day. The performance was acceptable, don't you agree?"

"Certainly not as bad as it was before," Mrs. Tillday said, "but I wouldn't call it acceptable."

"How can you say so? The dancers have done everything we've asked of them."

"Are you defending them?"

"I'm not *defending* them . . . "

"It's outrageous how they convey such a corrupted view of feminine nature."

Dora sat too stunned to speak. *You're wrong,* she wanted to say. She wanted to scream it, to shake Mrs. Tillday from this error in judgment. But she said nothing. Already she could see more suspicion gathering on her partner's face. It was as if she could see the thoughts unfolding behind those gentle blue eyes: *We are not the same, you and I.* "I'm not defending them," Dora repeated, "and of course, you're right. I just think they've made progress. That's all."

"I'll give them that." And as quickly as Mrs. Tillday's suspicion had set in, it vanished. The mistrust in her expression shrank away.

Dora wanted to get away from the theater, and away from Mrs. Tillday. "I don't see what good it will do to stay for another show, do you?"

"No, they've seen us." Mrs. Tillday's attention was on the stage. "They know we're watching. I suppose that's enough for now to keep them from slipping back into their old bad habits."

Dora felt a tearing inside herself. She wanted to be a good Lady Manager, but Amina and the other dancers didn't deserve such scorn.

The men who had been lined up out front were filing in and taking seats for the next show. Dora stood up and avoided looking at the stage. "We should go."

They left without saying another word. Outside, Dora hid from the bright sunlight beneath her parasol. A sick feeling churned within her as she walked beside Mrs. Tillday. Her partner paid no attention; she chatted about the warm weather, the size of the crowd gathered around Sitting Bull's cabin, the pungent smell of the Texan stew called chili con carne sold from a passing cart.

Dora nodded or smiled as they walked, and occasionally injected a simple "Oh, yes" or "You don't say." Finally they reached the Cairo Street gate and stopped to part ways. "Didn't you say you came in by another gate?"

Dora thought back. What had she said? She couldn't remember. She smiled. "No, you must've misunderstood."

A troubled look flitted across Mrs. Tillday's face.

"My bicycle is over there with the others," Dora said quickly, hoping to change the subject. "Charles bought us a matching pair."

"A bicycle? Aren't you the adventuress!"

Dora wished she had said something else. "Not really, but it is quite a thrill," she said, and fidgeted again with a skirt fold. She glanced back over her shoulder and spied her white model wedged in with the others. "You should try it; you can't imagine how wonderful it is."

Mrs. Tillday glanced at the bicycles; a shadow of a frown darkened her eyes. "Yes, I suppose I can't."

Dora stepped away. "I should be getting home. Shall I see you tomorrow, then?"

Mrs. Tillday cocked her head to one side. For a long moment, she looked at Dora as if seeing her for the first time. "No, not tomorrow. Mr. Tillday will want me home for the weekend. Let's say Monday." She air-kissed Dora and turned to her carriage.

Pedaling home, Dora worried about the coolness of her partner's farewell. Mrs. Tillday might be a weak Lady Manager, but she was a Lady Manager all the same. That made her dangerous. She couldn't afford to let the woman's doubts fester. She might already be questioning Dora's fitness to be a member of the board, and Dora needed an ally. When they saw each other again, she would make it right.

Tonight she had more pressing matters. She thought back over her morning with Amina. The way Amina had touched her, the way she had touched Amina, and the dancing. Oh, the dancing. That had been a surprise. Feeling the pull in her limbs, the thrust of her hips, the undulating arms. Who knew a body could move with such freedom? Or that it all would feel so wonderful?

But anything that feels that wonderful surely would have consequences.

Doubt seeped in. Would Charles be entranced or horrified by what she'd done?

The images came back to her of him and Geraldine Forrest tearing at each other. He hadn't been horrified by that woman's aggression. Instead, it had appeared to stoke his fervor. Her own propriety had only driven him away. Mama's warnings had helped her win Charles, but to keep him, she would have to ignore them.

At home, she found Bonmarie in the kitchen as usual.

"Any messages from Mr. Chambers?" She tugged off her gloves and tried to look nonchalant.

Bonmarie stood at a tub of soapy water scrubbing a soup pot. "No message." She immersed the pot in rinse water before setting it on a towel spread across the counter. "What's that smile for, *ma chere*?"

"Can't I just be happy?" Dora went to the icebox and pulled out the milk bottle. Charles would be home tonight, and this was her chance.

Bonmarie dried her hands and handed Dora a drinking glass. She took it and filled it.

"Of course you can." Bonmarie returned to her soapy water and dirty pans, and watched Dora. "Any particular reason?"

"Actually, there is." She was grinning like a madwoman; she could feel it. "I've been naïve, Bonmarie. I've been a silly, frigid girl, but not anymore. I know how to make Mr. Chambers happy; I know how to make him love me again. Don't look like that. It's all right. Do you think you could make something special for dinner? Something he likes? Duck or veal medallions? You know how he loves the veal medallions with applesauce. That would make everything perfect."

On her way up the stairs, her tongue tapped the Middle Eastern drumbeat. *Doom doom tekka tek doom tekka tek.*

*L*ord, what was that girl up to? What was her sweet baby Dora up to now? Everything's going to be all right, she says. I know how to make Mr. Charles happy, she says. I know how to make him love me again, she says.

Bonmarie grabbed a fry pan encrusted with remnants of the morning's eggs, and plunged it in the warm, soapy water. She scrubbed and scrubbed with the pot scraper, releasing the scorched bits and making them float to the top, where they mingled with the soapy bubbles.

Was it wrong not to tell her girl what she'd heard? But it was only gossip, silly gossip from the flappy jaws of a good-for-nothing housemaid who lived in one of those rich ladies' houses. Dora probably didn't even know that Mrs. Formish or Forrest or Forrish or whoever it was that sad example of a housemaid said employed her. The terrible things that housemaid said were lies. Servants lied all the time. Made visits to the market more interesting if they could boast and swap secrets about their employers. No one cared if what was said was true, just that it made a good yarn.

And that fat old woman's tale had made quite a yarn. She'd

been in Harris's Produce that morning, parked up right against the applecart with four, maybe five twittering women, servant dresses with those awful pinafores on the lot of them. Bonmarie had stuck around near the pears, waiting for them to leave so she could grab herself a few apples, otherwise she never would have heard the awful lies that came out of that woman's mouth.

Said her mistress had a new paramour, that's how it started. Said her mistress's paramour was a newly married man. That's when those other nitwit maids started clucking. Who is it? they wanted to know. How do they keep it secret? they asked. What if his wife learns of it? they pressed.

"The wife won't find out. Mrs. Formish"—or Forrest or Forrish, or whatever it was—"is a lady of discretion," that woman intoned, and the rest all clucked and murmured around her. "He comes at night when no one's around. You see, they've been lovers before." Oh, how that had enthralled her listeners. "Before he married, so he knows his way around, shall we say."

"What about his wife? Doesn't she suspect?" How they salivated at the taste of scandal.

"The wife?" the woman said with a laugh. "His wife"—such scorn filled the word, as if this poor, innocent creature bore the blame for the whole affair—"is young and stupid, and she isn't even from Chicago." A round of gasps. "Came from New Orleans or some other godforsaken outpost of civilization. Mr. Chambers— Oh my, did I let his name slip?"

That was all Bonmarie could bear; it was all she needed to know the whole thing was just one hateful lie. She decided to forgo the apples, paid for her pears, and walked home in a daze.

She held up the pan she'd been scrubbing and saw the worn place she'd worked into the cast iron. She dipped it twice, three times in the rinse water, and leaned it against the others on the towel to dry.

She'd meant to tell Dora when she came home. Even if it was a lie, the girl should know what was being said. The taller the tale, the more scandalous the story, the more likely it was a housemaid would share what she'd heard with her mistress. Who knew who those clucking wrens worked for? Who knew how far the story would travel? Gossip between servants spread faster than anything printed in a newspaper, and true or not, Dora should be prepared.

But her girl had been so happy today, happier than she'd seen her in a long time. She couldn't ruin it with dreadful gossip. She'd tell her tomorrow, or the day after. For now she'd fix a nice supper like she'd been asked to do. Duck or veal medallion with applesauce? She only had pears, so it would have to be the duck, perhaps a nice side of creamed spinach.

Funny how creamed spinach came to mind. She thought of the story about creamed spinach that she'd heard as a girl. The story about the voodoo woman who lived in the swamps of Lake Pontchartrain and how she'd wiped out a whole plantation family with a potion of snake venom sneaked into a batch of creamed spinach.

But where could Bonmarie get snake venom anyway? And it was only a story.

*I*n her room, Dora changed into her thinnest chemise, the one with the linen weave so transparent it lay on her skin like nothing more than cool breath on a winter morning. She wrapped her tea gown with the puffed sleeves around her and checked herself in the mirror. Pretty, but not enough. Too little chemise showed. She unfastened more buttons at her chest to expose the loose Irish lace across her décolletage. She smoothed the fabric against herself and felt the roughness of the lace, its whiteness contrasting against the darker contours of her breast. Better. Let him see what the corset usually hid.

The trick would not be how to draw his eyes to her, though. It would be how to demonstrate her new skills without sending him into a convulsive fit of laughter. Did the movements look as good as they had felt? Standing at the mirror, she practiced what the belly dancer had taught her. She drew imaginary circles on the floor with her hips, then drew them on the wall. She winced at her reflection. She looked nothing like the dancer. Amina's instructions echoed within her: "Be at ease, feel the music, don't think about the movement."

Dora heard the music in her head. She pulled her shoulders down from her ears and jutted her chest as she'd been told. She pulled her arms up at her sides into a gently dipping arc at the elbows and rotated her hips. Simple and slow, and then growing into more robust circles. In Amina's room she had felt the movement, and it was strange and wonderful. Now she could see herself in the mirror, and she knew she was doing it right. She was dancing.

The tune played in her head, and she embellished the movements, picturing Amina's dance, adding a bounce with her hips, or a deep dip from the torso and a flip of her hair. She lifted her arms at her sides in that snakelike way, and tried drawing circles with her chest.

The mirror reflected jerky movements that lacked Amina's skill, but still she was dancing. Charles would find it pleasing, wouldn't he? She imagined him watching her in the hungry way the men in the theater looked at Amina. If she could evoke that kind of desire in Charles, he would forget Geraldine Forrest.

She tried every move she could remember until her arms felt too heavy to lift and the sun sank in the afternoon sky, its light falling through the window at low angles. Perspiration soaked her chemise. Charles would be home soon. She needed everything to be perfect. Quickly she pulled off her garments and hung them over her dress form to cool and dry. She draped rose petal sachets over them, then went to her washbasin, drenched a towel, wrung it damp, and wiped the moisture off her skin. She worked fast, rubbing at her limbs and across her midsection, down her back and around her neck. The wetness on her skin made her shiver even in the still air of her boudoir. She wrapped herself in a negligee and padded down to the kitchen to check on dinner. The silver tray in the foyer was still empty. No messages; no excuses from Charles. She smiled.

Even before she reached the kitchen door, she could smell the duck roasting, the aroma mingling with the scent of butter, herbs, and onions. Her stomach panged for the meal that would still be hours away. Bonmarie leaned over a stockpot, stirring the contents with a ladle, when she entered.

"You've outdone yourself," Dora said, taking another deep breath. "Mr. Chambers will be so pleased." She approached Bonmarie to peek into the pot.

Bonmarie batted her away. "Leave the cooking to me, *ma chere.*"

"No one can do up a dinner like you can when you set your mind to it." She tried to angle around Bonmarie, but the woman hovered over her pot like a mother hen over freshly laid eggs. Dora gave up and went to the counter. She grabbed a slice of bread and slathered it with butter.

"Now, don't go ruining your appetite. I'm not working in here so all this fine food can go to waste."

"It's just one slice. You don't want the bread to go to waste, do you?"

Bonmarie turned back to the stove and shook her head, but from the door Dora could see the tug of a smile on the woman's cheek.

Back in her room, Dora brushed her hair, pinned it into a loosely sweeping twist, applied her face cream, pinched her cheeks for color. She spritzed herself with rose water and donned her chemise and tea gown. She applied more face cream and worked some of it into her palms to make them soft. When she'd done everything she could think of to ready herself for her husband's arrival, she turned her chair to the window, watched the street from behind the gauzy sheers, and waited.

The amber glow of the afternoon gave way to dusky streaks of raspberry and tangerine on the horizon, and then from lavender to violet to indigo. He must be working late. Probably working so hard he'd lost all sense of time.

She went down to the kitchen again. Bonmarie was sitting on her stool by the stove and working at her embroidery ring while she watched over her lidded pots.

"He'll be home any moment."

Bonmarie nodded and stabbed a yellow thread through the cotton.

"No later than nine, I'm sure."

Still Bonmarie said nothing.

"So there's been no word? No message?"

Bonmarie glanced up then back down at her embroidery. She shook her head and stabbed again with her needle.

Why didn't the woman say anything? Her silence was almost more than Dora could bear. A weariness came upon her. She shouldn't have exerted herself with the dancing. She'd pushed too hard. She wanted to slip off into sleep right where she stood. "Do you have anything in the kettle? A cup of tea would be lovely." That would revive her. She needed to freshen herself because it was becoming so difficult to speak, even to keep her eyes open.

"You go on upstairs. I'll bring you a fresh pot."

The words soothed her, like melted chocolate, thick and comforting. Bonmarie slipped off the stool, set down her hoop, and shooed Dora toward the door. "Go on now. Rest yourself before that man gets home. I'll be up in a minute."

Dora did as she was told. The stairs left her winded. She settled into her settee, leaned back in the cushion, and closed her eyes.

A moment later, Bonmarie was at the door carrying a tray with a teapot, a teacup and saucer, a small pitcher of cream, and sugar cubes. She set it on a table and picked up the teapot to pour.

"It's a special brew, *ma chere*. Drink as much as you can. You'll feel better." She added a lump of sugar, a dollop of cream, and stirred, then handed it to Dora.

The warmth of it tickled her nose. She sipped, and sipped again. "Is it a Darjeeling? No, not Darjeeling. Ceylon? What is it?"

"A special blend my mama taught me. Do you like it?"

Dora took another drink. "It's nice. Quite unusual."

"It's only for special occasions. You drink it now; I'll keep an eye on dinner."

Bonmarie went back downstairs and Dora drank down her first cup, then poured a second. She went back to her chair beside the window. The streetlamps were lighted now—she'd missed the lamplighter. How could she have missed the lamplighter? She so enjoyed watching that old man illuminate each lamp with his long torch pole. Bringing light to a dark world. She'd never cared before, but now she felt the loss, such a deep, aching loss, she thought she might cry. Nothing had gone right today, nothing. And now she'd even missed the lamplighter. She finished her cup, rose, and poured a third. She stumbled a bit on the way back to her chair, sloshing a bit of the tea onto the carpet. She held the cup more tightly; she had to be more careful. She took another sip and nearly spilled again. She giggled. What was wrong with her? Oh, but it didn't matter. She was too tired to care. She'd think about it tomorrow. Everything would be better tomorrow. What she needed was sleep. She set down her teacup and made her way to her bed. It took all her concentration to cross those three steps, but finally her head was on her pillow. Oh, she loved her pillow. So soft, so perfect. She hugged it to herself and drifted off to sleep.

Ten

The clanging of the grandfather clock awakened her. One pounding clang, two pounding clangs. Dora pulled the pillow over her head to muffle the racket. Three, four, five, six, seven pounding clangs—then silence. Oh, blessed silence. But the pounding in her head persisted. She pulled her pillow aside and squinted into the half-light of the room. She was still in her tea gown and chemise. What had happened? She noticed her chair pulled up to the window. The draperies had not been closed properly. Only the sheers protected her from the breaking light of day. Then it came back: She'd been waiting for Charles. She'd been waiting with their special dinner, and to show him her special new skills. Everything she'd been planning. But she'd fallen asleep. She sat up and nearly fell back down. She grabbed her head. Why was her head pounding? Oh, and now her stomach was protesting, too. She saw the teacup on her dressing table, and she knew. Bonmarie.

Her anger pushed her through the pain. How dare that woman

ruin everything. How dare she sabotage her only chance of winning back her husband's affection. Bonmarie might not like Charles, but this was too much. She struggled to her feet and waited for the pounding to subside.

She checked herself in the mirror. Her gown was a spiderweb of creases and her hair twist angled off center. She pressed the hair into place, tucked and maneuvered some hairpins, and tried to smooth her gown. She still looked a wreck, but it would have to do.

She went to the door and stopped when she saw Charles's door still closed. He was inside, but he should be off to the bank. She remembered more of the night before. He'd been late, she'd been waiting. What time had he returned?

She found Bonmarie in the kitchen, boiling eggs at the stove. She spoke only when she was near enough to whisper. "What did you do to me?" Her anger made the words rough and hoarse.

"A little bourbon in your tea. Just to help you sleep."

"Your mama's special blend?"

Bonmarie shrugged.

Maybe it was the unrepentant attitude that made her anger worse.

"But I had wanted to see Mr. Chambers when he got home."

"I know, *ma chere*." Bonmarie turned, her expression solemn. "I would have woken you up. It just didn't seem . . . "

"It didn't seem what?"

Bonmarie turned back to the pan. With a towel on the handle she pulled it off the stove and set it on a trivet on the counter.

"It didn't seem what, Bonmarie? What time did Mr. Chambers get home?"

The clearing of a throat behind her froze her where she stood. "I think it was about midnight or so."

Dora spun around. Charles stood in the doorway.

"Midnight? You didn't mention you would be delayed. Bonmarie prepared something special for you last night because you were working so hard." She forced her voice to be light.

"I do apologize for that, Bonmarie," he said, and yawned. "I hope you didn't go to much trouble. Is there coffee? Normal coffee, not that horrible chicory blend."

"Can have some ready in a wink." Bonmarie's head was stuck suspiciously far into a cupboard.

"I'll take it in the dining room, then."

Dora followed him and took a seat across the giant rosewood table. "It must have been something terribly important to detain you to such an hour."

"Actually, it was." He took his head in his hands and rubbed his cheeks and brow. He looked older in the morning light.

Her stomach churned with dread, intensifying the already ill effects of the bourbon-laced tea.

"Mr. Richmond invited me to dine with him and a couple of other fellows from the bank. I couldn't very well say, 'Sorry, gentlemen. I know you are considering whether to invest thousands of dollars into my venture, but I must get home to my wife.'"

He had been with Mr. Richmond? The menacing weight lifted. "I only worry that you are pushing yourself too hard, dear."

Bonmarie entered with the coffee and set the tray down between them. Dora reached over to pour for them both, and he took his up immediately. She added cream and sugar to hers and tasted. Still so bitter. She set it down.

He reached over and laid his hand atop hers. "Let's not speak any more of this, shall we?" He pushed his chair back and rose, picked up his cup, and went to the door. "I'll be getting to the office soon, but we'll see each other tonight, hm?"

Everything was going to be fine. "Yes, darling," she said with a tremulous smile. "Tonight, then."

e'd been right, of course: The brisk morning air was the perfect thing for clearing the head. Charles tapped his walking stick on the paved path and breathed deeply, filling his lungs with cool, fresh air and delighting in the subtle smell of the distant factories and stockyards, the mills and slaughterhouses. The scent of business and industry wafted in Chicago's air, a constant reminder the city was a living, breathing engine of progress. If you didn't move forward with it, you were bound to be plowed under by it.

He would not be one to be plowed under, not by a long shot. But he did need to sort out this muddle of his.

He checked his pocket watch. Ten minutes to the Division Street trolley pickup, another ten to Michigan Avenue, and then five before he was at the bank's door. He'd arrive in plenty of time for the meeting Richmond called for half past eight, and it should give him plenty of time to figure out what to do about Geraldine.

He'd been weak, yes; that was true. He'd given in where he should not have given in. It might have been fine if it had been that single time, or even a couple of times, a sort of final farewell. That's what he had intended it to be anyway. But she'd been getting entirely the wrong idea. Talking about the future as though they had one. She'd started planning a grand tour of Europe for next year; she wanted to go west, too, to see San Francisco.

He let her play with the ideas at first because they seemed harmless enough. It was a fantasy world they entered when they were alone together. There was no Randolph and no Dora. There were no parents, no directors, no Richmonds. There was only the two of them, and it had been thrilling to pretend. In that pretend world she was everything he had ever dreamed a woman could be. She let him touch her, watch her, taste her. There were no rules with Geraldine, his sweet, fearless Geraldine. Only a woman with the power she had could so easily flout the usual games women played.

A clanging bell signaled the trolley's approach and interrupted his thoughts. He stepped into the line of boarding businessmen, paid the conductor, grabbed the brass bar running along the ceiling, and held on when the trolley lurched forward.

He stared at the passing row of factory worker houses, the market street, and the financial district buildings, but it was the creamy whiteness of Geraldine's neck he saw, her shoulders, her arms, and her lower limbs as well. He pictured her at her most beautiful, wrapped only in bedsheets. She was a stunning woman, and one who enjoyed every advantage of wealth and status. Of course, that added to her allure, but it was also her bold spirit and—he was being honest, so he must face this as well— her sexual nature that made his need for her burn so deeply.

Perhaps it was even this nature that had saved him. Dora was a beautiful, wonderful girl, but that posed its own problems, didn't it? She was still a girl in so many ways. Some men, he knew a few, preferred women to be girlish, submissive, wide-eyed creatures to be led any which way. Not him. He needed a partner in bed, not a motionless thing to suffer through his affections. He needed the thrill of pleasing, as well as being pleased, of giving and taking.

To his credit, he hadn't known this about himself before his marriage. Or at least he hadn't known that all women didn't come alive in the bedroom as Geraldine did. That first night with Dora had been a shock for them both. And he'd been patient; he'd waited for her to overcome her inhibitions. Only when it was clear she would not, or could not, had he allowed himself to return to Geraldine's bed.

He had hoped that this solace would be a temporary diversion to give Dora the time to come to him when she was ready. But now he knew it had given Geraldine the wrong impression. He hadn't expected her to believe anything had changed; to think he didn't still need Dora, for her chameleon-like ability to fit into social situations and even more for her ignorance of his greatest shame, his transgression with a friend's wife. And who else but Dora could he look upon and see a beauty that stirred his desire without reminding him of Geraldine?

Yes, he still very much needed Dora, so there was only one thing to do. He would have to break it off with Geraldine once and for all. No more half measures, no more hesitation.

He hopped off the trolley at Michigan Avenue with a lighter heart. He knew how to sort out this muddle. He would explain it to Geraldine and she would see the sense of it, she would understand. She was a reasonable woman, after all. He would tell her today, perhaps over tea in a tearoom. Some public place where they could discuss the matter dispassionately, and it would appear a completely innocent meeting because it would be.

He skipped up the steps to the National Bank of Chicago's front doors, tipped his hat to the guard, and whistled down the hall toward his office door.

"Mr. Chambers, sir." It was Harvey, a nervous young clerk who sat outside Charles's door. "This came for you."

Charles took the envelope thrust in his direction. He recognized Geraldine's penmanship. "Do you know the sender?"

Harvey shook his head. "A delivery boy brought it, sir."

Charles nodded and took the sealed envelope to his office. He closed the door behind him before opening it.

Please come for dinner. Something awful has happened. I must speak with you.

Such a desperate message, quite unlike her. Was it bank business? Her inheritance? Had someone seen them together? He shouldn't go. No, he must. He would go to talk, nothing more. He would help her if he could, then explain that they couldn't continue. He would be gentle, and he would be quick. He owed Geraldine that much.

He wrote out a note, sealed it, and opened the door. "Harvey, see that this is delivered as quickly as possible to my wife."

*A*fter the note arrived, Dora went to her room and folded away the negligee she had planned to wear for the evening, then went to the kitchen to inform Bonmarie that Mr. Chambers would not be home for dinner. She'd tried to keep the disappointment out of her voice, but the woman knew something was wrong. She always knew. She'd looked at Dora again with pity in her eyes.

"Don't, Bonmarie" was all she could say before the sobs clutched at her throat. She choked them back and went to the upholstered chair at the sitting room window to watch for Mrs. Tillday. She kept her mind blank and stared at the maple trees, the carriages, the streaks of white clouds against the blue sky. Like the tears, she choked back each terrible thought of Charles and Mrs. Forrest. She watched the window and felt nothing. Green grass and yellow daffodils across the street. Purple and orange gladiolus. White shutters and red-brick walls. Dr. Bostwick leaving in his carriage. The pounding in her chest eased, the tension in her limbs lessened. Finches flittering from one branch to another. A couple strolling down the street.

Charles's note was still in her lap when Mrs. Tillday's carriage arrived. Dora tossed the note in the room's brazier and watched the flames lick the edges, then rose to collect her shawl and hat. She opened the door and was surprised to find Mrs. Tillday standing there instead of waiting, as she usually did, in the carriage.

"I apologize for the late notice," Mrs. Tillday said, "but I cannot accompany you to the Fair today. Mr. Tillday asked me to place an order for him with his tailor. He only just sent word as I was leaving. Oh, don't look so disappointed. I'm sure Mrs. Richmond won't mind terribly if we skip a day." She reached out and squeezed Dora's hand.

"Yes, I'm sure you're right." Dora struggled with the words, trying to hold back the swell of emotion in her throat. "Of course you're right."

"I know you're worried about making a good impression. I'm sure everyone is very happy with the progress, though. It's certainly more than I would have predicted."

Dora smiled, pretending that was her only concern. She squeezed Mrs. Tillday's hand back and bade her farewell. She waved until she could no longer see the woman's carriage making its way down the street.

She went back into the sitting room. She couldn't bear the thought of sulking there all day with nothing to keep her company but her doubts. She couldn't bear the thought of waiting for another evening when Charles pretended to be working late. She wouldn't bear it. She would go to the Fair herself. She didn't need Mrs. Tillday. She didn't need anybody.

She'd take her bicycle and she could leave now. She lifted the hem of her wool skirt and examined her ivory walking boots. These would be just fine; she didn't need the riding boots. She pulled her shawl around her shoulders, put on her hat, grabbed her purse and parasol, hollered to Bonmarie that she was leaving, and slipped out the door.

A few moments later she was on her bicycle and on her way. With the wind brushing against her, she almost felt like she could fly, like she could go anywhere, as far as her legs and her imagination could carry her. And it was a beautiful day to be outdoors. She lifted her face to the sun and let it warm her cheeks, her chin, her eyelids. The blue sky brightened the springtime colors in the trees and flowers along the street, making the greens greener, the yellows yellower, the reds redder.

When she reached the Cairo Street gate, she paused. She could go directly to the Egyptian Theatre, but why? She had all the time in the world, and she could go anywhere. She pressed on. With no one to answer to and no one to please, she set her course for the White City. She parked and made her way to the concrete rail that hugged the lagoon, where she could watch the gondoliers and gaze on the elegant white giants filled with their modern wonders. She watched the sun tickle the water and make it shimmer, and waited for that magical feeling, the one that always comforted her when she was in the White City, the one that whispered its promise of transformation.

But the familiar feeling didn't come.

It wasn't the grandeur she noticed; it was the people. The men and women in twos or threes, and whole families moving mechanically from one exhibition hall to the next. They hardly talked, or if they did, it was in hushed tones, as if they walked through a cathedral. No laughter, no camaraderie, nothing like the boisterous and congenial scenes along the Midway's amusement district.

She missed it.

She left the lagoon with its Wooded Island and gondolas, she left the white palaces and modern wonders, and worked her way to the Midway. The sweet smell coming from a vendor selling bags of candied popcorn and peanuts made her stomach grumble and reminded her she hadn't eaten breakfast. She took a place at the back of the line and was so focused on her hunger that it wasn't until Mrs. Richmond was behind her, tapping her shoulder, that Dora realized she had company.

"Mrs. Chambers?" Mrs. Richmond declared. "Where is your partner, where is Mrs. Tillday?"

At Mrs. Richmond's side stood a handsome but imposing woman wearing a finely tailored aubergine silk dress that complemented her silver upswept hair. She was not as tall as Mrs. Richmond, but her stance conveyed authority. She did not smile.

"You see, I was just . . . I mean, I could not—"

The woman in aubergine interrupted her with a forced cough.

"Oh, pardon me, Mrs. Palmer, you have not had the opportunity of meeting Mrs. Charles Chambers; she is the Lady Manager we've spoken about."

Dora curtsied and tried not to lose her balance in front of the most powerful woman in Chicago. If she had a mind to, Mrs. Bertha Honoré Palmer could banish her to the hinterlands of society with a simple word. "It is an honor to make your acquaintance, ma'am."

The woman acknowledged her with a regal nod. "I understood that Mrs. Tillday was working with you. May I inquire why you are out without your partner?"

The woman's hooded eyes bored into Dora, making her shift uneasily.

"Mrs. Tillday could not accompany me today," she sputtered. "She had an unexpected obligation. I wanted to make our visit to the Egyptian Theatre anyway, to be sure everything was in order." It was a weak excuse but close enough to the truth.

"I see," Mrs. Palmer said. "And you are not concerned about being out alone?"

There had to be a right way to answer that question, if only she knew what it was. She searched Mrs. Palmer's expression for some clue but came up with nothing. Mrs. Richmond's offered no help, either.

"Of course, you're right," Dora said at last. "I should be more sensitive to how such behavior could be perceived. It just didn't seem right to neglect our duty, and I have always felt completely safe here at the Fair."

"Our Lady Managers are to thank for that, Agnes," Mrs. Palmer said. "The Fair directors may question what women can do, but you see here, this young lady feels safe because Lady Managers have ensured this is a hospitable environment for all visitors. We haven't let the wrong sort get a foothold, you see."

"Yes, our ladies are doing a wonderful job," Mrs. Richmond said, looking as relieved as Dora felt. "And it is a testament to your leadership, if I may say so."

Mrs. Palmer turned again to Dora. "I like your dedication, young lady. Mrs. Chambers, is it?"

Dora nodded.

"I appreciate a woman who isn't afraid of a little hard work, someone willing to dig in and do what must be done, appearances be damned. Keep it up." With a twitch of her parasol, she motioned to Mrs. Richmond that it was time to proceed.

"Thank you, Mrs. Chambers," Mrs. Richmond said as she turned to leave. "Please give Mr. Chambers my regards."

That triggered another thought. "Mrs. Richmond?"

The woman glanced back, waiting.

She had to ask. She had to know the truth.

"Yes, dear, what is it?" Her cheerfulness gave way to slight impatience.

"I was wondering . . . I was wondering if Mr. Richmond had any trouble getting home last night. Charles said the trolleys were in such a state."

Mrs. Richmond laughed and shook her head. "Mr. Richmond takes his own carriage so he doesn't fuss with that business. He was home quite on time, five on the nose, if I recall. But thank you for your concern, dear," she said, and set off with Mrs. Palmer.

When Dora reached the theater, her thoughts were still centered on Charles. His deception overshadowed even Mrs. Palmer's compliment. How many lies had he told?

Inside, the belly dance performance was under way, and nearly concluded, by the look of it. A dancer in an emerald veil finished her dance and turned the stage over to another. Dora recognized the crimson veil. The musicians quickened their tempo and Amina began to shake. She shimmied. She swayed and sashayed.

When it was done, Dora didn't file out with the rest of the audience.

"Nicely done," she said when she approached the dancers.

"I'm glad you liked it," Amina said through her veil. She turned to the dancers and said something in Arabic that made them hurry off to the performers' room. She turned back to Dora. "We were just going to sit down for tea. Would you like to join us?"

"I shouldn't impose," she said, but realized she didn't want to leave, either. "I do have a question for you," she blurted.

"Have tea with us, then ask."

Dora pretended to hesitate.

Amina rose. "We would enjoy the company."

Some of the dancers had already removed their veils and lowered themselves onto thick cushions around a table with a tall brass teapot. One poured and handed glass cups to the musicians, who sat cross-legged on the floor.

Dora had second thoughts. "Are you sure I'm not intruding?"

"Come in." It was no longer a question; Amina took Dora's elbow and led her inside.

When she entered, the banter between the musicians and dancers stopped. A dozen sets of eyes turned her way. Amina dropped her veil on one of the low tables and muttered something quickly in Arabic. In English, she added, "Mrs. Chambers, I believe you have already met Maryeta."

Dora nodded to the young woman she now recognized from their hallway encounter. The dark circles under her eyes were gone and she had a healthier color.

"This is Fatma Houri"—the thick-waisted woman nodded and smiled—"and Hosna, Farida, Saida, and Zakia." Each woman greeted Dora in turn. "And of course Hakim, Ali, and Aziz." The musicians nodded.

"Hello," Dora said, as she nodded and smiled at her new companions. She took a seat on a bench and Amina handed her a cup of the hot mint tea. She sipped and waited for someone else to speak.

"Tell me your question," Amina said.

"That can wait. We needn't discuss it now." She had no question; she had just wanted to stay.

"They will not mind." Amina swept a glance around the room. Blank faces stared back.

"It's a silly thing. Hardly worth talking about, really." Her mind raced for something. There was something she had wondered about . . . But, no, she couldn't ask that. Not in front of strangers. In fact, this was all a mistake. What was she doing socializing with belly dancers? It certainly wasn't a proper Lady Manager thing to do.

But what did it matter? Her husband had already turned his back on her. He wasn't even going to care about the encounter with Mrs. Palmer.

"Is it the performances?" Amina pressed. "More complaints?"

Dora shook her head and tried to ignore the sick feeling in her stomach. "No, not that. Really, it's nothing. I'm embarrassed to have brought it up." Dora set down her cup and stood to leave.

"If it isn't the performances, is it about your dancing lesson?"

The tea rose in Dora's throat. How could she announce such a thing?

The others turned, eyebrows raised. She could see the glimmer of understanding in every brown eye. They already knew.

Dora swallowed hard. What more did she have to lose? She would only compound the problem by dodging it. "I was practicing the hip circles last night, and I couldn't get them quite right. I was hoping you could tell me where I'm going wrong."

"You were practicing?" Amina looked genuinely surprised.

The reaction emboldened her. "Yes, of course. At home. Perhaps after tea you might show me again."

"Why wait? We have plenty of room here."

Dora's courage faltered. "Not here. I couldn't possibly."

But smiling faces all around her were nodding that, yes, she could.

Amina reached out for her hand. "Don't be worried. Americans worry too much. Stand up. We'll help you."

Dora glanced at the door. Those devious musicians now sat in front of it. She couldn't get past them. Amina was still coaxing

Dora to her feet. Beside her, Maryeta and Fatma motioned for her to get up, too.

So this was a joke for everyone? They wouldn't release her until they'd had their fun.

The drummer grabbed his instrument. He tapped out a beat. Amina moved in front of her and turned her back. She lifted her hips in a vertical circle with the beat. Once, twice, three times, before looking over her shoulder. "Are you doing it with me? Let me watch you."

It was impossible to protest. They expected her to dance.

She lifted her hips. The corset stay pinched, but she moved through the pain.

"You are not moving with the music," Amina said. "You must follow its lead. Let your circle be at its lowest point with the strongest drumbeat. Like this." She quickened her own circle and made an exaggerated pause on the beat. She did it twice, then turned back to Dora. "You try."

How could she move with so many eyes upon her? She repeated the move. A quick swing up and around, a slow dip down with a pause at the beat.

"Yes, like that. Keep doing it. It will become smoother."

Despite the corset, Dora felt the difference. She let the music pace her body.

Maryeta and Fatma set down their cups, rose, and tossed aside pillows. They moved closer to Dora and circled their hips, too. The others pulled back to the walls, watched, and played the tiny cymbals on their fingertips.

When the drummer changed the tempo, the horn and oud curled a melody around the beat.

Dora concentrated on her circles. Amina turned to face Maryeta and shimmied her shoulders. The younger dancer followed the lead. Fatma moved toward Maryeta and Amina, and began to move her shoulders, too. Amina clapped to the beat and then stepped, swung her hip, and stepped around the room. Fatma and Maryeta followed. So did Dora.

They danced that way until Amina took Dora's and Fatma's hands and formed a circle with Maryeta. Each facing center, they shimmied their shoulders until Amina moved into the circle's center.

The music slowed. She reached out her arms and made them writhe in that serpentine way. She moved out of the circle, and Fatma moved in. The rounder woman made her belly roll from top to bottom, then flutter in and out in quick succession.

The dancers were so different in this room, so changed from their more serious manner onstage. Their eyes crinkled with laughter. Dora let their joy fill her, too.

Fatma moved to face Dora. They shimmied together, and then the older woman nudged Dora out of her place at the circle's edge. Dora found herself forced into the center. All right. She would play their game. She rotated her hips, the only move she knew. She let the music pace each drop. When the rhythm changed, she stilled her hips and let her arms move out from her sides, mimicking Amina's snaky arm movements. The corset bit, but she wouldn't stop.

Before Dora could step toward Maryeta to pass the lead, Amina grabbed her arm. "All that modesty. Look at what you did! It was as if you had danced a hundred times before."

The other dancers broke away from the circle, too. They patted Dora's arms and cooed encouragement.

Dora blushed, but it thrilled her, too. All this attention. The giddiness overtook her and she felt the ground begin to sway. She sank onto the bench before light-headedness overtook her, but still the room seemed to tilt. She dropped her head into her hands.

"Are you all right?" Amina's hand was at her shoulder.

Dora lifted her head; it felt so impossibly heavy. "Catching my breath."

"You need to eat," Amina said. "Come to my room."

"I'm fine, really. Just winded."

"The color is gone from your face. You need to eat. Come." Amina's hand was outstretched, expecting to be grasped.

Dora allowed herself to be helped to her feet. Standing was trickier than she'd expected. "Perhaps I will have some water."

Amina maneuvered Dora out of the performers' room and then the empty theater. She led her to the door to the back rooms. Amina's room felt almost familiar now. She let Amina guide her to the bed cushion.

"I'll lie down for just a moment." She sank into the pillows, the turquoise silk cool and soft against her cheek.

"Eat some bread."

Dora took a torn piece of flatbread from Amina's hand and nibbled the edge. When it was gone, Amina thrust another at her with a dollop of yellowish paste she'd scooped into it.

"What is this?" Dora asked.

"Hummus."

"But what is it?"

"You have never tried Egyptian food?"

Dora shook her head.

"Ground chickpea and sesame paste, oil, a little garlic, a little lemon. Try it."

Dora took a bite and her tongue played against the creamy texture. Like savory cake batter but thicker, a bit grittier. Nutty and tangy. She took another bite.

"I knew you would like it."

Dora nodded, her mouth full. She couldn't resist; suddenly her stomach ached with hunger.

Amina set the platter of flatbread and hummus on the floor beside Dora. "Eat as much as you like." She pulled up cushions beside Dora and grabbed a smoking contraption like the one she'd used before.

Dora took another piece of bread and dipped it in the hummus. She watched Amina take one long tube between her lips, put a flame to the metal bowl holding the tobacco, and breathe in deeply. She held the smoke in her lungs before exhaling.

"I've been meaning to ask you about your English," Dora said, rearranging herself into a sitting position on the bed.

"Is it not good?" Amina looked alarmed.

"No, it's very good. That's why I've wondered. Did you learn it here?"

Amina took another long breath on her tube. She held the smoke in her lungs and turned to the window as if she were looking at something more interesting than the sheer curtains that obscured the view of the bare wood wall outside.

The silence stretched. When it seemed Amina would not answer, Dora said, "I hope it wasn't inappropriate to ask. I'm sorry if I've—"

"I learned in Cairo," Amina said finally. "My brother taught me. He learned from British men who visit coffeehouses near our home. He wanted me to know their language so I could protect myself."

The answer raised so many more questions. Where was her brother now? Why did she require protection? What was Cairo like? Dora held her tongue. She'd already been too bold.

Amina took another inhalation. "I would like you to know something: I want to tell you why we are dancers."

"You don't have to explain anything to me."

"But I want you to understand. We know people say awful things, but we do not mean any harm."

"I know." Dora thought of Mrs. Richmond's harsh words that

first day. Of course, Amina would believe all Lady Managers shared that view. And in truth Dora had, in the beginning. But it was different now.

"I want you to know what our dancing means to us," Amina said, then paused as if searching for the right words. "It is not like the dancing in your country."

Dora shifted, trying to mask her discomfort.

"For people in Egypt," Amina continued, "dancing is how we express our happiness, our joy; it is how we celebrate life." Her eyes glazed into that distant look. "It is part of every important occasion: the weddings, the saints' days, any kind of festivity. And it is part of our daily life."

Her words came more quickly.

"And for me, and for all dancers who are Ghawazee, dancing means even more. We are different even in our own country because Ghawazee dancers and musicians receive money to dance at celebrations. Dancing is our joy, but it is also how we make our living. People disrespect us for this. It was not always that way, not in my grandmother's time, and not always in my mother's time. But it is how it is for us."

Dora saw pain gathering at the edges of Amina's expression. She sat quietly, taking in what the dancer said, unsure how to respond.

Amina straightened and took another breath from her tube. "A man visited us in Egypt and asked us to go to the Paris Exposition to dance. We were glad for the chance to put our difficulties behind us. Another man in Paris asked us to come to America, and we thought it would be the same." Amina smirked and shook her head as if she saw the folly in that now. "As you can see, we have many more difficulties here. We are treated even worse than we were in Egypt. If we had known this, we would never have come." She settled back in her pillows. "But now it is too late."

Amina was studying her now, waiting for a response.

"I sympathize with you," Dora stammered. It was the proper thing to say under the circumstances, and even as she said it, she realized it was true. She thought of her two months in Chicago. Hadn't they fallen far short of her expectations, too? Everything should have been perfect; Charles wasn't supposed to be in love with another woman, a woman who was not only beautiful, but powerful and wealthy in a way Dora had always hoped to be. It hurt to admit that. "How can I help?"

"You already have. You are the only person who does not look at us like we are the same as the camels and the donkeys. You are different; you are kind."

"It is you who have been kind to me."

"Helping you learn about men? Helping you learn to dance?" Amina shook her head. "Easy things."

"Not so easy for me." The pain and the doubt stabbed at her again.

Amina pulled back. "No, I saw you with my own eyes. You are a natural dancer."

"You're being kind."

Amina planted both hands on Dora's shoulders. "Did you not feel it?"

Dora grinned. It had felt like nothing she'd ever experienced before.

"Take off your clothes," Amina said. She went to the dressing screen and pulled down garments. "When you wear these, when your body can move as it should be able to move, then you will see."

Dora gaped at the garments in Amina's hands. "But the next performance. Don't you have to get back?"

"We have time. Change."

Dora accepted the pile. The cool silkiness of the violet pantaloons brushed over her skin, the warm velvet of the matching vest. She should refuse; that was the proper thing to do. It was the sensible thing to do. But how tempting these garments were. To feel that lush fabric against her limbs. She took the clothing behind the dressing screen and shed her hat, her skirts, the bodice, her petticoats and corset, all of it falling away from her like dead serpent skin.

She slipped the dancing costume on and emerged, anxious, ready.

"Yes, very good," Amina said. She turned her back to Dora and, without another word, swayed to imagined music, slowly lifting her arms and moving her fingers in waves. No other part of her body moved except her head. She watched her hands glide through the air, then motioned to Dora to mimic the moves.

Dora started with similar sweeps of her hand, flourishing with twists of her wrists as Amina did. She imagined herself looking like Amina, swaying her arms around herself as if she were dancing under water. Amina stepped to the side to observe. She whispered a correction: "Do as the music tells you. Do not do only what you see me do. Let it come from within yourself."

Dora focused on her imagined music. She tried to listen to her body, to hear what her limbs told her, how they wanted to move. She tried to turn off her mind and let the music guide her. Her left arm started to change the movement, but halted midway. None of it felt comfortable.

"Your mind is still getting in the way," Amina said. "Do not think; just do."

Impossible. But then her arms fell into a new movement: Her wrists moved over her head, sweeping like waves that flowed from side to side. Did she direct her arms to do that? She didn't remember. It felt natural. No force, no thought. She sank into the feeling and waited for what her body would do next.

The lesson progressed and Dora felt as if she could go on forever. No exhaustion, no breathlessness.

When Amina stopped, Dora collapsed on the bed. She closed her eyes, and when she reopened them Amina was at her feet, watching her. "You see? There is a dancer inside you."

"Then why am I so tired?"

"Your thoughts exhaust you, not the dance," Amina said, sitting beside the platter and taking up a piece of bread. "You're thinking too much about how your body moves and what to do next and how long to do it—that tires you. If the movements are slow and thoughts are quiet, the body can go on and on. When a dancer performs a fast dance, if she feels tired, she can slow it down. It will rest her."

Dora nodded, but something nagged at her. "How do you know if you are a dancer?"

Amina glanced at the ceiling, considering the question. "The feet know. The hands know. The body hears the music and longs to move with it. That is how a dancer knows."

A rap on the door interrupted them. The boy Dora had seen with the camel named Little Egypt opened it, his face etched with worry. He muttered something in Arabic, but footsteps echoing in the hallway stopped him. He stepped aside, and Hossam Farouk dipped his head to clear the doorway. The room shrank in his presence. He saw Dora and paused before saying to the boy, "Go see if they need you in the stable."

The boy rushed a bow and hurried down the hall.

Amina stood with her arms crossed, her lips pulled thin. She said something in Arabic. Dora rose behind her.

Hossam's gaze lingered on Dora before he turned his attention to Amina. "May I not visit my best dancer?"

Amina tensed.

Hossam turned to Dora and dipped into a bow that made his loose black tunic sweep across his knees. "Good afternoon, Mrs. Chambers," he said, and extended his hand. She met it with her own. He lifted it to his lips, as he had done with Mrs. Richmond, and the sight of her own naked fingers and wrist gave her a start. She didn't have her gloves. She was still in Amina's clothes.

"I see Amina is introducing you to Egyptian fashion. It becomes you."

Dora flushed. She choked out a "thank you" but kept her gaze on the ground.

"What do you want?" Amina's fingers tapped on her crossed arms.

Was this how Egyptian women spoke to men? Dora raised her glance. Charles would never tolerate that tone.

From the dark way Hossam looked at Amina now, Dora knew the dancer had crossed a line, though one she had likely crossed before.

"You know why I am here: I have just returned from meeting with the Fair Commissioners."

"We will speak of this later."

"We must reconsider the"—he glanced at Dora and back to Amina—"our other offer." He moved to leave but turned back. To Dora, he said, "I look forward to seeing you again, Mrs. Chambers."

He was gone before Dora could reply, but the image of him shaking his black hair back over his wide shoulders as he left stayed with her. Her heart raced, and the last of her energy drained from her, leaving a gentle, soothing ache.

"I should be getting back to the theater," Amina said.

Dora took the cue. "I'll change. It'll take just a moment."

"Are you in a hurry?"

"No, but you have to go."

Amina tilted her head, and with a half grin, said, "Go with me."

"I suppose I can stay for another show."

"That's not what I meant. Dance with us."

"I can't walk out of here wearing these." She fluttered her hand around the Egyptian garments.

"You could if you were onstage with us."

"Be serious."

"I am serious. You are a good dancer, and you should dance with us. Just a little, just in the circle, like you did with Fatma and Maryeta."

"But you don't dance that way onstage."

"We will."

It was out of the question. She couldn't possibly be so foolish. She wasn't even a real dancer.

"You can do it; I know you will enjoy it. The others have already seen what a good dancer you are."

The thought of it made her skin tingle. Her on the stage; she could see it perfectly in her mind. "Even if I wanted to, I couldn't. I would be recognized. What would people say?" Her heart fell a little and she stepped toward the dressing screen.

"Do not be so sure. I have an idea."

*W*ith a tap of his instrument, the drummer cued the other musicians to pick up the beat just as the ringing of the clock tower outside struck two. The show was getting under way in the Egyptian Theatre.

From the side of the stage where she stood with the other dancers, Dora gazed out at the audience. No familiar faces, only a massive blur of twill and tweed coats and denim overalls, and the occasional curious lady with a feathered hat. Her stomach prickled with nerves.

The musicians' improvised rhythm settled into a familiar beat and the dancers' finger cymbals clattered. Those attached to her own fingers and thumbs remained still. Anticipation and fear mingled within her. This was wrong. She was a Lady Manager, for goodness' sake.

Then the dancers moved forward. The thoughts of the crowd and the rules gave way; her mind emptied. She wasn't a Lady Manager anymore; she was a dancer.

The dancers paraded onto the stage and formed a half circle, a modification meant to give the audience a view of the central dancer. Dora searched for and found Amina on the far side of the half circle, shimmying to the music. She saw the hint of a smile beneath the slip of the crimson veil draped below Amina's eyes— the same kind of veil Amina had attached to Dora.

In the mirror, dressed in Amina's clothes and behind the veil, Dora hardly recognized herself. Feeling the tickle of the fabric across her cheeks and nose, it was as if she were in another woman's skin, as if she were looking out from behind a mask.

Amina took the first turn as the central dancer. She spun into the open space and stopped sharply. With a single, graceful motion, she lifted a saber Dora hadn't noticed on the floor. From another part of the half-moon formation, a long trill, a thrilling sound Amina called a *zaghareet*, issued from Fatma's lips as Amina twirled with the polished weapon over her head.

The dance entranced Dora. Amina raised the sword like an

offering to a god, circled it around herself, extending it and pulling it in close again. As she raised the weapon, her gossamer sleeves fell back to reveal her bronze arms, and she placed the saber atop her head. Her hands descended in floating circles to her waist and she balanced the saber. She undulated and lowered to her knees. The sword remained steady. Every eye in the room watched Amina as she swayed on the floor, leaning on one hand and undulating from her shoulders to her pointed toe. Only when she raised herself and removed the weapon from her head did the silence break. The gallery cheered and clapped. Dora could see Amina's smile beneath the cloth as the dancer shimmied toward her.

Dora realized she was being called out to dance. Horror struck, she shook her head, slightly yet emphatically, tried to scream with her eyes, *No! I cannot!*

Amina persisted. She nudged closer, working herself into Dora's place in the half circle and forcing Dora into the dance space.

"I can't do it!" Dora whispered through clenched teeth.

"Listen to the music. Close your eyes," Amina whispered from beneath the veil.

Dora knew she had no alternative. She shrank into a deep, hidden corner of her mind, far from the clumsy limbs that swayed and shimmied to the circle's center. As if ten thousand miles away, she heard Fatma trill another *zaghareet*; she saw the blur of faces staring back at her. The pounding in her chest drowned out the sound of the drum. Her hips fell out of time with the music. The dance lost its flow. She shut her eyes tight; thought only of the music. *Doom doom tekka tek doom tekka tek.*

The music quickened, and her hips marked the change by

bouncing to the side. She lifted her arms overhead, the way Amina did it. The tempo changed again, and she moved into a walking undulation. The audience cheered as if she'd performed an impressive feat. Still her heart pounded.

Another *zaghareet* behind her reminded her of the dancers. She turned to the half circle and shimmied toward Maryeta. They danced together, then swapped places. Maryeta went to the center, and Dora, adrenaline coursing through her, joined the half circle and tapped the rhythm with her finger cymbals with the others.

She watched Maryeta dance, and then another and another. Through the rest of the show, one thought gripped her, one desire: She wanted to dance like that again.

We must celebrate!" Amina declared, clutching Dora's arms after the show, a smile stretched wide across her face. "Stay and feast with us. We will have a *hafla*, or how do you call it?" Amina tapped her finger to her lips. "A party! Say you will."

Fatma and Maryeta and the others added their happy voices to the plea. Dora thought of the Lady Managers. What would they say? But just as quickly she knew it didn't matter; they'd never find out. And Charles? He wouldn't be home, and he certainly didn't care. If she declined, she'd have to spend the evening alone in the drawing room or in her boudoir with nothing but her regrets for company.

Here there was so much joy. Her heart raced. They were making such a fuss over her. Her. So tempting.

"Say you will, even for a little while."

But Amina's plea wasn't necessary. "I'll need a messenger," Dora said.

Before she could reconsider, a message was dashed off telling

Bonmarie that Lady Manager duties would delay her at the fairgrounds. When Amina recruited a merchant's son for the delivery,
there was no turning back.

*T*hey retreated back to Amina's room, and Dora sat on a cushion atop a wooden chest while the cooks fed the fire. The
smell of roasting lamb wafted in the window. At pauses in the
conversation, Dora listened to the snap and crackle of the flames
and the cook's orders shouted in Arabic. "Does this much effort
go into all your meals?"

The belly dancer was sitting on the floor, working a needle and
thread through the hem of a silky midnight blue skirt. She shook
her head, tied off the thread, and bit through to sever it. "Today is
special. You are our guest."

Dora went to the window. "Isn't it too much?"

"Any reason to celebrate is enough. It makes this place more"—
she paused—"tolerable." She smiled, and it was the kind of smile
that made her eyes crinkle and almost disappear behind the
mounds of her cheeks.

The realization of what she'd done weighed on her. How could
she have been so reckless?

"I know what will make you feel better," Amina said, perhaps
sensing her apprehension. She set aside her mending and pulled
her smoking contraption closer.

"I can't use that," Dora said.

"Of course you can. It is simple."

"No, I mean, it's hardly proper."

"You are among friends, so what is the harm?"

Dora shook her head, but Amina's words reverberated through
her. Was she among friends?

"Just try it."

She'd already done so much, perhaps too much. What would it matter adding one more transgression to the list? And she did wonder . . . "But I don't know how."

"Like this." Amina prepared the tobacco as Dora had seen her do it before. When it was ready, she motioned Dora to sit close enough to reach one of the tubes hanging limply from the water-filled chamber. "When I light it, inhale. Do it slowly or you will cough." She raised the flame to the bowl.

Dora put the tube between her lips and inhaled. She watched the chamber fill with smoke, and then she could feel the smoke in her lungs. It tasted of cool earth and spices. She breathed in deeper and deeper, then her chest felt like it was on fire. Coughs and smoke erupted from her.

Amina wiggled her finger. "Breathe slower. Like this." Amina breathed through the tube, held the smoke in her chest, then exhaled it toward the ceiling. "Try again."

Dora put the tube between her lips again and waited for the tobacco to be lit. She breathed in, as slowly as she could. When she felt her lungs fill, she pulled away and held the smoke inside. Again she tasted the spiciness, a bit of citrus, too, and something strong and sweet. She exhaled to the ceiling, mimicking Amina. Her head felt lighter. Not in the alarming way like after the dance, but in a happy way that made her smile without knowing why.

She took another inhalation and another. She settled back on the pillows and watched the designs in canopy fabric undulate, the contours suggesting faces, landscapes, animals. Amina settled back into cushions, too, and her eyelids drooped into sleep.

Dora watched the woman. How peaceful she looked stretched out like that, almost childlike. But this woman was no child. The way she spoke to Hossam, the way she spoke to Mrs. Richmond—

she could be fierce. She was strong in ways Dora had never seen a woman be strong. With her thoughts floating on soft, wispy clouds, she felt free to say anything. "You mentioned your brother before. Is he still in Egypt?"

Amina didn't answer right away. Dora wondered if she slept or simply refused to answer. But then she turned on her side to look at Dora. When she spoke, her voice was quiet, sad. "He is in Egypt; he is why I am here."

Dora wanted to ask about her mother, her father, other siblings. What kind of family did a woman like this have? What was her home like? Instead, she waited for Amina to continue.

"My brother cared for me after our mother died; I was still very young." Amina paused, as if remembering an old pain. "He worked in the Mohammed Ali Street cafés and saved everything to arrange a place for me in the house of the street's best dancer. Khalid—that is my brother's name—knew I would do well if she was my *usta*. I owe him everything. He would have his own café if not for me. That was his dream, and he gave it up for me."

"What about your father?"

Amina stared at the ground. "My father could not even help himself. He was a musician for my mother, and when she became sick, he left to find other work. We did not see him again."

"I'm sorry."

Amina shook her head. "That is how it is."

"Khalid must be a wonderful brother," Dora said. "You must be a good sister, too, for him to want to do so much for you. You are lucky to have each other."

"Do you have a brother?"

"No, no sister, either."

Amina tapped Dora's shoulder. "I will be your sister if you like. And you can be mine."

Dora flushed. It embarrassed her how much she wished that could be true.

Pots clanked outside and somebody was splitting wood to feed the fire.

"They really don't mind going to this trouble?" Dora asked.

Amina pulled together more pillows and nuzzled into them. She stretched out into a deep repose. "They do not mind. Stop worrying."

Dora pulled together more pillows, too. It felt wonderful to be out of her corset and petticoats.

"Have you really never danced before?"

Dora shook her head.

"Such progress is not common."

Dora thought back to the awkward lurching of those first tries. "Onstage, I couldn't move to the rhythm at first. Everything felt awkward and strange." She flailed her arms at her sides, like a clumsy marionette.

Amina laughed.

"But then I did what you said," Dora continued. "When I closed my eyes, I could feel the music." Dora tried recalling the feeling. "The music guided me, and the thinking stopped. Do you ever feel that way?"

There was a glint in Amina's eye. "It is a good beginning, Mrs. Chambers."

A loud knocking awakened Dora from her doze. Amina jumped up and opened the door. Dora could see only a silhouette of a figure in the hall. The dim afternoon light that had filled the room when she fell asleep was now the violet and blue of twilight.

"Everything is ready," Amina said when she closed the door.

Dora rose and went to the dressing screen. She couldn't help but feel a surge of excitement.

Amina grabbed her arm and turned her back. "I know what you are thinking, and no, you should not."

"What?"

Amina rolled her eyes. "You are thinking, 'If only I never had to wear that torture chamber of a corset again.'"

Dora giggled. "I do not mind it. Besides, I can't very well go out dressed like this. It would send the wrong message."

"To whom?"

"To the others. And what if someone else saw?"

"They are only clothes."

"What would your people say if you went out dressed in something they didn't expect, something they didn't approve of?" But Dora could already see that concern meant nothing to Amina.

"No one tells me what I can wear." Her tone was reflective, not chiding. She looked down at her snug-as-a-stocking blouse, the striped coat with the front buttons unfastened, the folds of her pantaloons. "The clothes I wear, I wear for myself. I enjoy them. I do not do it for anyone else."

Maybe the dancers were free to wear what they liked, but it wasn't that way for her. "It's different for me," she insisted. Behind the dressing screen's panels, she dropped the pantaloons to the floor and glanced up at the mound of her own clothes. On top sat the corset with its laces like fingers that gripped and squeezed. She dragged the chemise over her head and let it slide over her body. She picked up the harness and it felt heavier than before. Not a torture chamber exactly, but a nuisance, certainly. She did her best to tighten the laces, gulping her breath and pulling hard on the strings. She wound them into a knot, not as tight as Bonmarie's, but she couldn't ask Amina for help. It took three attempts to constrict it enough to fasten her skirt.

When Dora emerged from behind the screen, Amina was at the window, gazing at the darkening sliver of sky between the theater and the perimeter wall. Dora joined her.

"Can you see it?" Amina said, pointing. "The evening star. I loved searching for it when I was a girl. Even now it reminds me of home. We are so far away, but we are still under the same sky."

Dora recognized the tenor of homesickness in Amina's voice. Would anyone in New Orleans be watching that star? Mama would be busy feeding guests and setting up their rooms. She never had time to look at stars.

"We should join the others." Amina laid a hand on Dora's shoulder and pulled her back from her memories.

When they reached the entrance to the theater's main hall, a Closed sign hung from a rope barring the door. Amina unhooked the rope, swept aside the curtain, and ushered Dora through.

Inside, the space was transformed. The chairs for the audience were pushed to the walls, standing in stacks of three or four. Scattered about were tall, wrought-iron sconces, their candles making the room glimmer in a soft, amber glow. Oriental rugs covered the plank floor, along with low tables balancing broad brass platters. Brightly hued cushions surrounded the tables, and some were already being used as seats by Egyptians.

Fatma and Maryeta sat at one table with two other dancers. The musicians sat at another, and the boy with the camel sat with some of his fellow animal tenders. Dora recognized shopkeepers and washerwomen, even street entertainers scattered throughout the room.

Dora leaned in to Amina's ear. "All of Cairo Street must be

here." All but Hossam Farouk, but that didn't matter. She shouldn't think of him, and she definitely didn't want to see him.

"Not all," Amina whispered back, "but many. We can sit there." She indicated an empty table beside Fatma and Maryeta. She gave Dora a peculiar look, then raised a finger for her to wait.

Dora watched Amina go to the musicians' side of the stage and take a three-legged stool. She returned with it, set it beside the table, and dropped a sapphire colored pillow on top. "For you," she declared.

Dora took the seat and expressed her thanks as Amina settled onto a cushion on the floor. Around them, the din of conversation paused and all eyes turned to a procession of servers entering with platters perched atop their shoulders. Platters were set on each table, holding a bounty of food: hummus drizzled with oil, stacks of leaf-wrapped bundles, flatbread, skewered vegetables, and a giant mound of golden rice. In the middle were steaming slices of grilled lamb shank, crusty and sizzling at the edge, moist and pink in the center.

"This could feed an army," Dora said, taking in the savory assortment.

Amina tore off a piece of bread and held it out to Dora. "You have not seen us eat!" She tore bread for herself and used it to pick up a piece of lamb. She bit into it and groaned with delight.

Dora dipped the edge of her bread into the hummus and nibbled while Amina took a skewer of alternating chunks of red pepper and eggplant. She slid off a piece of eggplant and ate it. When she finished the skewer, she glanced at Dora, who was still working on her piece of bread. "Is that all you're going to eat? You must be starving."

Dora cringed to see others turn her way. "I'm a light eater," she mumbled.

Amina ripped off more bread, grabbed a section of meat with it, and scooped up a smidgeon of rice. "Here."

The patronizing tone reminded her of Charles. "I can feed myself, thank you." Dora snatched the bread and took a bite. No one was paying attention anymore, but Dora still bristled. Her companions were eating like they might never eat again, the women just as much as the men. She couldn't remember the last time she'd seen a lady consume more than a morsel in public. Well-bred girls learned early to eat before a social occasion.

Dora gave in and ate from the platter like the rest. She inquired about the foods she didn't recognize and reveled in all the different flavors: the rice-filled leaf packets of lemony tartness, the garlicky bite of the vegetables threaded onto skewers. When the servers came around with tin cups and wine jugs, she accepted their offering without a fuss. The more she chewed and drank, the easier it was to listen to the others. It didn't matter that she didn't understand the words; she felt as if she could follow a conversation by its tone, or by the way someone threw back her head and laughed, or leaned in to a neighbor. Dora was reminded of dinners with the servants in the kitchen at the Devereaux Hotel. Everyone was equal here; no one worried that she had to do the right thing.

When the platters were emptied and the chatter had quieted, the Egyptians stretched back onto their cushions, refilled their cups, and settled into comfortable repose. From somewhere in the room, a slow drumbeat emerged. After some rustling and shifting, another drumbeat followed, and then another. Then came the sultry whine of the horn that always made Dora's spine tingle.

The music came slowly, like a finger curling into a palm, enticing listeners to move in closer. Across the room, Dora spied the flash of a dancer's skirt.

"Watch Saida," Amina whispered in Dora's ear. "She joined us last year, after her husband died. She has a great talent."

The dancer stretched each undulation, each flourish, to fill the languid measures. She danced as if she were alone, as if none of these dozens of eyes gazed upon her. Her head bowed, and her arms hugged close around her middle, as if she held something precious and dear. With her chest, she drew circles in the air, and her arms reached out and pulled in again—a private dance for herself alone.

Amina gathered her knees to her own chest and watched. "Such a beautiful *taqsim*," Amina whispered. "It can be the most intimate of dances, when the dancer forgets everyone else and lets the music take her."

Then suddenly, as if she emerged from a trance, Saida's arms flew out to her sides and her eyes opened wide and met the gazes of the faces around her. The musicians quickened the beat, and the dancer strutted and bounced her hips around the room.

Amina leaned toward Dora again. "An exceptional dancer can perform for a crowd as easily as she can dance for herself."

Saida approached Amina then, shimmying and shaking in front of her. Instead of trilling encouragement to the dancer as the others had done, Amina rose, and they danced together. Then Amina reached for Dora's hand.

Dora smiled, but shook her head.

"You must dance."

Still Dora demurred.

Amina turned to the circle that now gathered around the dancers. "Would you like to see her dance?" With wide smiles, Saida, Fatma, and Maryeta clapped until everyone in the hall joined in.

Then she saw him. Hossam stood in the doorway as if he'd just arrived. He clapped, too.

Dora grabbed her wine and gulped it down.

"Just dance," Amina whispered in her ear. "I will dance with you." Loud trills came from two dancers in a corner and the clapping grew louder.

Dora knew she couldn't refuse. She let herself be pulled into the duet, making it a trio. Amina rotated her hips, Saida followed, and Dora managed as well as she could in her wide skirt, petticoats, and corset. When Amina wiggled her dark eyebrows at her, Dora knew it was her cue to initiate another movement. She moved her hips in figure eights, her favorite move despite the stabs from the corset. Amina and Saida took up the motion, until Saida began to slide her head from one shoulder to the other. Dora knew her jerking movement looked nothing like Amina's and Saida's, but no one seemed to care.

When the other dancers exchanged a glance and broke away from Dora, panic struck her. But they weren't forcing her to perform alone. With waving hands they motioned for the others to rise and join the dance. Soon everyone was dancing or holding an instrument and playing along.

Everyone but Hossam.

He had moved farther into the theater, but still remained apart, clapping, but not participating. She could see he watched her, and his gaze made her self-conscious. It was one thing to dance in front of a handful of Egyptians in a room, but to conduct herself this way before the whole of Cairo Street? She must look ridiculous to them. An American woman in a fine dress dancing around with Egyptian villagers. Pretending she was one of them.

The realization stopped her cold. She was always pretending, wasn't she? She'd been playing her new role every day since she'd arrived in Chicago. Little Dora Devereaux pretending to be the grand Mrs. Charles Chambers since that first day. No, even before that. All those afternoons in the hotel's parlor, watching and mimicking the fancy ladies. When had she not pretended?

She was letting her anger at Charles and Geraldine Forrest cloud her thoughts, or perhaps it was the wine. She slipped away from the dancing to find a pitcher of water. She filled a spare cup, settled into a chair to watch the others, and tried to compose herself.

But she couldn't; Hossam was approaching. When he was near enough, he lifted a chair off the stack beside her, turned it, and draped his arms across the chair's back. He watched the dancing without saying a word.

He was so close, she could reach out and touch his wrist, his shoulder, his face. The nearness of him shook her like a vibration. When he turned to her, she froze.

"You dance quite well for a Lady Manager," he said.

Dora studied the design in the lace of her gloves.

"Have you danced before?"

She forced a laugh. "I'm sure I've made a complete fool of myself."

He said nothing, only leaned back and swept his black hair back from his eyes. Was that a nod, or was his chin bobbing to the rhythm?

Amina was watching them, and now she rose from where she sat beside Maryeta. "Are you feeling unwell?" she asked Dora when she approached.

Dora shook her head.

"You said you would have an answer for me this evening." Hossam's manner didn't change, but his voice was lower, more serious.

Amina shifted and looked uneasy. "This is not the time to speak of that." Her glance slid over to Dora and Dora knew she was the reason for the hesitation.

She rose. "Please, don't let me intrude."

Hossam reached out his arm to stop her. "Perhaps you should know this as well."

"No, Hossam, she does not—"

"She is a Lady Manager. If she is truly here to help, she should know this."

"What's wrong?" Dora said. The creases etched into Amina's brow worried her. "What has happened?"

Amina's stare bored into Hossam like a dare.

"The troupe has an offer to perform in New York," he replied. "We could start immediately."

"But you cannot leave the Fair." The pleading tone in her voice made her wince.

Amina crossed her arms and jutted a hip to one side.

"We must leave if the Commissioners refuse to pay our wages," Hossam continued. "We will not even be able to pay for passage back to Egypt. The doctor you arranged took much of what little money we had, and he returned yesterday for even more. It would be foolish for us not to take this opportunity."

"I have told Hossam that nothing will change in New York, that we will face the same uncertainties," Amina said.

"What doctor?" Dora stammered. "Dr. Bostwick?"

Hossam and Amina nodded.

"He told me he would not charge."

"Perhaps he meant not his usual fee," Amina said sarcastically. "He tried to get his payment in another way, but I told him we did not settle our debts like that. Then he demanded money."

"Dr. Bostwick?" It had to be a mistake.

Amina nodded. "But he is not our concern. Hossam made sure he knows he cannot return."

"But he is all the more reason we should leave," Hossam pressed. "He could make more trouble."

Dora dropped into a chair. "How could he make more trouble?"

"He could go to the Commissioners. He could lie; they would believe him."

"But he would not. He's my neighbor." But he had already lied, hadn't he? "This is my responsibility. I will repay you. Whatever you gave him. Just tell me the sum." She looked around herself. Where did she leave her purse? Where was her parasol? Amina's room. Her things were there. "I don't have it all now, but I will get it."

Amina put her hand on Dora's shoulder. "It is our debt, not yours."

"The question is, what do we do now?" Hossam was looking at Amina, waiting for her answer.

"I do not think we should leave," the belly dancer said. "It will only be more of the same."

Hossam dropped his head back, his disappointment written clearly on his face.

Dora glanced at the door. "I should go. It's getting late."

"No, stay," Amina said. "There is more food, there will be more music and dancing. You do not need to leave."

Even after Dr. Bostwick's betrayal, they still wanted her company? "I do, but thank you. Thank you for all of it. I left some things in your room. I'll just get them, if that's all right."

She wanted to say farewell to Fatma and Maryeta and the others, but they were deep into conversations. She didn't want to disturb them. At the door, she glanced back at Hossam and Amina, offered a small wave, and let herself out.

The night air chilled her. Light, some electric, some from candles, spilled out windows, and cleaved the shadows. She wrapped her arms around herself and walked around to the dancers' rooms. She hurried in, found her parasol and purse by the moonlight filtering in through the open window, and stepped back into the hallway. A silhouette leaning in the doorway surprised her and made her heart pound. She recognized his outline. The hair that brushed his shoulders, the broad shoulders and slim waist.

"Hossam?" she whispered.

He watched her. "I am sorry if I have offended you. I did not mean to force you to leave."

She slid her purse onto her wrist and fidgeted with her parasol. Still he made her so nervous. "You didn't offend me. It's just that it's so . . . so late."

"It is late, and you should not be out alone. I will walk with you, to be sure you are safe." He stepped back from the door and made room for her to pass.

She'd never been to the fairgrounds this late, and she probably did need an escort. It was only a walk to the gate, she told herself. But standing this close to him, she could feel his presence like an electric current coursing through her.

All around them, windows glowed and people darted about in the shadows like apparitions.

"Which gate?" Hossam asked.

"Sixty-second Street," she said.

He turned toward the perimeter wall instead of the square. "This is a shorter way," he said to her over his shoulder when he noticed her falling behind. He led her to the back, to the walking space between the building and the wall. They passed a cook's helper poking the glowing embers of a dying fire, making them burst with tiny sparks like a small Fourth of July.

"This way," Hossam said, and pointed toward the narrow path lighted by the moon. The air was redolent with the aromas of so many nightly meals.

He walked slowly and didn't look at her, but then he spoke.

"Nighttime is the best time here, when the crowds are gone and the people are just living their lives. It is like any village then; it could be anywhere on earth."

"I've never been here this late," she said, hurrying to keep up with his long strides. "How late is it? It feels so empty."

"Not empty, not at all." He pointed to the cleared space between the Cairo Street buildings and the German Village. It was the Sudanese camp, with its ring of huts. She could see a dozen figures, maybe more, gathered around a campfire. But none of it registered. She only felt the shiver racing through her from where Hossam touched the small of her back as he pointed to the camp with his other hand. She tried to focus on the men who were sitting around the fire, passing a pipe as long as a sword. One took a puff, and then passed it to the next man. She was too far away to hear their words, but the tone was low. Something serious was under discussion.

Hossam urged her on, pressing her gently forward. "The Germans are always eating and singing. Look here." He led her to a window. Inside the alehouse, men and women sat at long trestle tables, sharing roasted meats and mountains of bread. In the corner, a man worked a small accordion.

She stepped back from the window. "I suppose people do the same things wherever they happen to be. I don't know why I thought it would be any different."

"You see, we are not so strange," he said gently, resuming his pace

I never said you were strange, Dora thought, but she said nothing.

Little light penetrated the path here along the Javanese encampment, and Dora stepped carefully to avoid the pebbles and marshy patches. At one place, Hossam stopped and reached for her hand to guide her across a puddle. Her hand slid into his, and his skin felt warm and rough. She could still feel the strength of his fingers closing around hers after their bodies parted.

"I wonder what you thought these people did after the tourists had gone," Hossam said as he walked. "Did you think their lives stopped? That they only exist to entertain?"

Dora's foot turned on a pebble and she stumbled. Before she recovered herself, Hossam was at her side. He took one of her hands in his and with the other held her back. "Careful there," he said. "I forget you do not know the terrain as well as I."

Dizziness overcame her. The musky scent of him was all around.

"Better now?"

He was looking down on her, the moonlight flashing in his black eyes. She felt his breath catch, then quicken. His fingers tightened and curled into her back.

"You are different from what I thought a local woman would be." His whisper was rough like gravel and hardly more than a breath in her ear. The hand on her back wrapped around her, cradling her close. His arms were so strong, like he could take her by force. The hand he held he placed on his chest, and then followed the line of her cheek with his finger.

She could feel the rise and fall of her chest.

"You are quite remarkable, Mrs. Chambers."

Hossam leaned in to her, his lips brushing her neck.

For the first time, she dreaded hearing those words. *Mrs. Chambers.* She was a belonging. *Mrs. Charles Chambers.* The name brought with it the memory of Charles with Mrs. Forrest. They'd been wrapped in each other's arms as she was now wrapped in Hossam's. Even now they were probably in just such an embrace.

She pulled away; the dizziness returned. Hossam reached out; she dodged his hand.

"I shouldn't be here," she said. "This is wrong. I must get home."

The look in his dark eyes made her pause. It was disappointment, but not the kind she brought to Charles's eyes. Hossam's held something else. Slowly he stepped back, prepared to let her go.

In that moment, she knew she would not leave. She didn't want to stop, and she didn't have to stop. She didn't belong to Charles. He didn't own her. She could do as she wanted—and this, here, under these stars and with this man—this was what she wanted. She reached for his hand.

He took it and pulled her close, lifting her hand to his lips, his hot breath on her fingers. When his eyes searched hers, she didn't look away. The strength behind his glance didn't frighten her anymore. She returned his gaze, opened herself to it. "I would like it if you called me Dora," she whispered.

He answered her with a kiss, cupping her in his hands, those strong, rough fingers playing gently along her neck, her cheeks, her ears. Then he took her, all of her, up into his arms and carried her back the way they'd come.

He took her back to the theater like that. She wrapped her arms around his neck, played with the black curl that brushed the side of his face, ran her finger along the sharp angle of his cheek. He grinned when it tickled and his eyes brightened with a boy's playfulness. How could she ever have been frightened by this man? When they approached the theater, he turned into the first alley instead of the one where the dancers' rooms were. Without putting her down, he opened a door and carried her inside. When he closed it, they were surrounded by darkness.

"I have a candle," he whispered, setting her down.

She stood where he left her, listening to him move about. A

moment later he returned with a wide cauldron of a lit candle atop a standing sconce, casting an orange glow on the room. It was a larger room than Amina's but more sparsely furnished. There were two steamer trunks, a table and pillows, and a large cushion with blankets that served as the bed. The air was filled with Hossam's musky scent, mingled with sandalwood and a bit of sweet citrus. No window, no other doors.

"It's not much, I know."

He was looking down at her, watching her take in the surroundings. A humble expression replaced his usual cocky look, as if he were nervous, too. He didn't take his eyes off of her.

"What do we do now?" she asked in a tremulous voice.

"Only what you want."

He was looking at her in that hungry way the men in the audience looked at the dancers, and it gave her a thrill that started in her toes and radiated out to every limb. Hossam watched her as if he could see through everything she wore: the bodice, the camisole, the chemise, the corset. She remembered Amina's lessons and held his gaze. When he moved toward her, she stepped back. She raised her fingers to the buttons of her bodice and worked them loose.

She unfastened each front button and then the buttons at her wrist before slipping off the garment, slowly and without looking away from him. She could feel his glance on her like the touch of his fingers, making her shudder with pleasure. She unfastened her skirt and let it fall to her feet, then the petticoat and the corset. He made no move forward, he never rushed, he only watched. She relished the moments when an article fell away and his lips twitched with a fresh smile. His arms crossed his chest and sometimes she noticed his fingers dig into his skin, as if stopping himself from lunging toward her.

Then she was in just her chemise, her nakedness hardly hidden beneath the thin weave. She pulled the pins from her hair, letting it drop like a dark waterfall over her shoulders, and she stepped toward him.

He enfolded her in his arms. She wrapped her own arms around his waist, grabbed the fabric of his white tunic, and lifted it. She worked it up and up and over his shoulders and his head, until she stood facing his bare, bronze skin. His chest was smooth but for a light sheen of silky black hairs gathered at the center, and the candlelight made his skin look so warm and soft, like coffee smoothed with just a dollop of cream. She pressed her cheek to his shoulder to feel the heat of him, like a hot summer's day in the French Quarter. It was strange and wonderful in a way she couldn't describe.

His hands roamed over her back and she could feel her heart pounding, but no, that was his heart pounding against her, and then she could feel the hardness of him pressing through the muslin of his pants and the linen of her chemise, searching for her.

She yearned to touch him, every part of him, and she yearned to be touched by him in return. What a remarkable feeling it was. There was no fear, no dread, not as there had been with Charles. No thought that this was another test she must pass. Her mother's words didn't echo within her because there was no place for them. This wasn't a trial; there was nothing to gain, thus nothing to lose. This was passion, and it was simple and pure. Hossam expected nothing from her that wasn't already standing in front of him. In his eyes, she could see his hunger, and she let him lead her down to his bed. He leaned over her and kissed her gently, tenderly. His eyes, black as pools, stared at her, memorized her. He kissed her mouth and her chin, her neck and her shoulder. He leaned her up and pulled off her chemise; she tugged at his trousers. When they'd shed the last of their garments, he tried to lay her back, but she slipped around so he lay back and she leaned over him. He smiled at her trick and she returned his kisses to his face, his chest. How savory he was, deliciously salty, like the sea.

That was how their passion was, like the sea—ebbing and flowing, first a torrent, then calm. She rode each wave of it, each rise and fall, each one wrapped in Hossam's strong embrace. When the need within her grew so strong she could no longer resist, she worked her contours against his, found all the places where their bodies fit together. When he entered her, her body seized. He held her still, until she began to rock, slowly at first and then with more vigor. Then he rocked with her, and they were two bodies moving in unison. He was the first to cry out, to gasp and to whisper her name—*Dora*—harshly into her ear. She smiled to hear the sound of it pass his lips, then the same seizure coursed through her, shooting through her like a lightning bolt, starting at the place where their bodies met and radiating out to every part of her. Her feet tingled, her hands, her lips. The feeling intensified, blocking out all other thought. There was only this, only her and Hossam, and then . . . and then . . . and then it was gone in a cascade of sensations that left her weak and gasping. She crumpled against him.

He held her without speaking, caressing her back, running his fingers through the long strands of her hair. When she'd caught her breath again, she raised herself to look at him. "What was that?"

He rolled her over onto her back and leaned on one arm. He smiled that same boyish smile as before. "You don't know?"

She shook her head.

He leaned down and kissed her again, a long, slow kiss that lasted several moments. When he pulled back, he held her gaze, and said, "I hope it was a beginning."

* * *

*H*e hadn't expected it to be so difficult to watch her walk through the gate to that lonely bicycle. Harder than leaving Egypt, harder than facing those Commissioners. He wanted to protect her, his Dora. He'd heard stories about the horrors in these American cities, especially this Chicago, with its thieves and cons, its pickpockets and prostitutes. He'd seen some of it at the Fair, a wallet or watch or some other treasure liberated from an unsuspecting owner. That kind of thing existed in Cairo, too, but it was different there. His were the people to watch, and he knew their games—it was nothing like the stories he'd heard here. Murders, vice, deception of every stripe. Horrors. And he was letting her ride off into that abyss. He'd nearly called out, begged her to come back.

Imagine, him, Hossam Farouk, chasing after a woman. An American woman at that. He rolled over on his bed, pulled another cushion under his head, and stared into the black room, the glow from the candle extinguished and only the silver moonlight penetrating the spaces around the door.

He'd liked the look of her from the start; that was true. The way her dark eyes flashed hot and cold. He could read her temperature with just a glance. The way her delicate chin lifted just so, like a dare. And there was that impossibly constructed form, that ample bosom that narrowed to a waist he could nearly hold between his fingers before widening again below those fussy skirts. So many nights he'd lain awake, wondering how that form appeared without all those extraneous ruffles and ties and padding. Now he knew. The memory of it filled him again.

Their coupling had been a surprise. Before tonight, he would never have pursued such a thing. He did not shrink from trouble, but he did not seek it out, either. Bedding a Lady Manager fit easily within that category. He had not done it for the thrill, though it certainly had been that. And it was not as if he had never bedded a married woman before. But this was different.

They had lain together after the lovemaking, their legs entwined and her finger drawing invisible patterns on his chest. He was nearly asleep when she had risen to dress and leave. When he told her it was too late for a woman to be out, especially alone, she had reminded him she had no choice. She had stabbed at the air playfully with her folded parasol then to make him laugh. And he *had* laughed. But the laughter only made him feel the loss of her more sharply. He did not want her to leave. He did not want to know she was going back to a house where a husband awaited.

But what could he do? He had risen, dressed, walked her to the edge of the dark, lifeless fairgrounds. She had smiled up at him with that bashful, sheepish smile, and said, "Please, let's say nothing of this. Let it be just between us." He should have protested, or even thrown her over his shoulder and carried her back to his room. But he had not. He had merely nodded and smiled, and she squeezed his hand, then turned and walked away. He watched her grow smaller in the distance, until the darkness swallowed the last of her. Then he had returned to his room, snuffed the candle, and lain down again on the bed. He gathered the blankets up around him and the pillows she had used, and he breathed in the sweet, floral smell of roses that had been in her hair and on her skin, letting the memory of her keep him company through the night.

Now that she was alone, pedaling her bicycle through the dark and empty streets, Dora waited for the remorse to set in. She expected it, braced for it, even resigned herself to it.

But how could she feel regret when this fire burned within her? Her heart still throbbed and her body still thrilled at the memory of those hours with Hossam. Yes, the feeling had frightened her at first, as if she had lost control of her own wits. She'd feared getting caught, but that quickly gave way to something much greater. Is it what people called desire, or passion? Those had been words she thought she understood, but how can you understand what you have never felt? How could someone understand the color blue without seeing it? Or the sweetness of an apple without tasting it, or the touch of water against your cheek without feeling it? Nothing had prepared her for the way that man made her feel. His touch and his kisses were such new experiences. Her body reacted through no will of her own. Like an instinct. Who could ever have known such wonderful sensations existed?

And he had been so charming and attentive, so unlike Charles. He was perfect, wasn't he? He had shown her those wonderful things that could be shared between a man and a woman in a bedroom. It didn't matter that she was surely no more to him than just one in a long line of conquests. Even that was a thrill. This man, who had certainly had more than his fair share of lovers, had not looked upon her with disappointment as Charles had. She had pleased him; she knew it. The way Hossam had looked at her, even when they parted at the gate, she knew he would have liked to have her again. Perhaps she had changed enough that Charles might look at her that way, too.

Dora rolled up the side of her home to find the carriage parked by the stable. Her heart jumped. How late was it? She fished her timepiece out of her purse. Half past one. But each window was dark—a good sign. Everyone inside must be asleep, including Charles. If he'd come home late, he'd have assumed she was asleep in her bed as well.

She slipped quietly into the stable to leave the bicycle and found Delilah motionless in her stall. Carefully she moved so as not to rouse her. When she slipped out again, she was relieved to see that the horse's breath still came in heavy, rhythmic intervals. She stepped just as silently to the back door, opened and closed it behind her gently, and tiptoed to the swinging door that led to the hall.

"Who's there?" Bonmarie barked from the corner of the room where a short corridor led to her room. The moonlight streaming in through the kitchen window created shadows that made it impossible to see where she stood.

"Shhh," Dora whispered harshly. "It's me."

She heard shuffling footsteps, then Bonmarie's form appeared in front of her. Her hair was wrapped in a swath of fabric that matched the floral print of her nightgown. "I thought you were Harold or Hazel rummaging through the icebox. What are you doing up this late?"

Dora started to answer but stopped. Who was the mistress here? She didn't have to explain herself. She straightened. "I was delayed. When did Mr. Chambers get home?" Bonmarie gave her a sidelong look. Evasive answers never sat well with her. "Rolled in about midnight, I guess it was. Went right to his room."

"Did he know I wasn't home?" She tried to sound cavalier.

Bonmarie's brows knitted. "Like I said, he went to his room. Didn't ask for anything; didn't say anything."

He would've made a fuss if he'd known, and he would've checked if he'd suspected. Dora breathed easier. "I see no point in mentioning it, then." She raised her eyebrows to complete her meaning.

Bonmarie shrugged and turned back to her room. Over her shoulder, she muttered, "No point whatsoever."

Eleven

"Are you still worried about Mrs. Forrest?"

Mrs. Tillday's question startled Dora. She'd been gazing out the window as the carriage rumbled toward the Richmonds' mansion and the Lady Managers' meeting. But she wasn't thinking about Mrs. Forrest. She was thinking about the day—and night—before. She hadn't wanted it to end.

She'd all but forgotten Mrs. Forrest.

"Don't antagonize her," her partner continued, pulling a folding mirror from her purse and checking her face. "She'll have to let go of this nonsense eventually, and then you won't hear another word from her."

When Dora offered no response, Mrs. Tillday tried again. "I should let this be a surprise, but maybe it'll cheer you up."

Dora turned. "What surprise?"

"Oh, I shouldn't have said anything. Please pay me no mind."

"You can't drop it. Tell me." Panic crept over her.

"Hm, should I? Or should I make you wait?" Mrs. Tillday slipped the mirror back into her satchel.

"Please!"

The woman laughed. "Fine, fine. I'll tell you part of it. It won't completely spoil the surprise. Mrs. Gilmore had tea with Mrs. Richmond yesterday, and she heard about your encounter with Mrs. Palmer. Apparently the woman was quite impressed with you and she wants to offer you a new assignment." Mrs. Tillday's eyes widened with delight. "But that's all I will say. I've already said too much, so act surprised."

Dora knew she should be pleased. With Mrs. Palmer's favor, her place in society was assured. Charles would have to be pleased. So why was there a lump in her throat?

When the carriage turned up the long drive to the Richmonds' front door, Dora had the urge to tell the driver to take her home. She didn't want to go. But that would be ridiculous. *Be happy,* she chided herself. *Yesterday meant nothing.*

The Richmond mansion stood before her. All the carriages assembled in front, all the Lady Managers waiting inside, and Charles—these were the only things that mattered.

Mrs. Richmond met Dora and Mrs. Tillday at the door, and Dora saw something different in the woman's face. She'd never smiled so widely at her before. But it was such a rushed welcome; maybe she'd imagined it. Their hostess ushered them into the gallery, and left to greet another set of Lady Managers coming up the walk.

When they entered the room, Dora felt Mrs. Tillday retreat into her shell. The woman called these Lady Managers her friends, Dora thought, but obviously they made her terribly uncomfortable.

Dora steered her partner to the buffet table, where they filled porcelain china dishes with glazed pastries and poured cupfuls of steaming tea. Mrs. Tillday insisted on the same settee where Dora had first discovered her. Now, just as then, it could not have been farther from the rest of the group.

Dora scanned the room for a more central seat and saw Mrs. Forrest enter, sweeping into the room in a wide butter-colored skirt and appearing unaware that conversations paused and eyes turned in her direction. Dora's teeth clenched.

Was it only that woman's wealth that made her so fascinating? Dora studied the onlookers. Was it respect in their eyes? Admiration? Envy?

Mrs. Forrest paused near a group that quickly rearranged to include her in the circle, but she turned as if she sensed Dora's attention. Their gazes locked. Dora turned away and leaned back into the settee beside Mrs. Tillday.

"What do you think of Mrs. Richmond's Impressionist paintings?" Dora hoped the topic would draw the woman out of her silence. "Isn't it a wonder how the artists capture the quality of light on a canvas?"

Before Mrs. Tillday could speak, Mrs. Richmond entered the room, her hands raised in a call for quiet. The crowd hushed.

The meeting opened with routine business: reports and praise from the Fair directors and commissions, an inventory of dignitaries to be honored with luncheons or special dinners in the coming weeks, an update on the Fair's attendance figures. "Now, ladies, there is news that it troubles me to share, but I must: The Midway continues to receive complaints, and the letters in the newspapers are not abating."

The news stunned Dora. How could there still be complaints?

"Excuse me, Agnes." Mrs. Forrest stepped forward from her

coterie. "Forgive me for saying so, but perhaps the supervision has not been sufficient?" She cast a long look at Dora then, and every eye in the room followed.

"No, my dear, it is Mrs. Palmer's view that no fault is to be placed on the quality of our supervision. Significant strides in the dancers' appearance and conduct have been noted." She smiled and nodded encouragingly at Dora and Mrs. Tillday. "It is rather, in her view, a matter of public perception, and there is nothing to do but return the matter to the Fair officials."

What did that mean? Dora's mind raced with options until she heard Mrs. Richmond say her name again.

"As our newest member, Mrs. Chambers has more than exceeded our expectations with the challenging assignment at the Egyptian Theatre." Mrs. Richmond was reading from a letter in her hands. "She spends more time than is required on her duties, and we offer our sincerest gratitude for her dedication and efforts. It is this kind of diligence and concern for quality that sets an example for all Lady Managers and which I am pleased to reward with the new assignment of Liaison to Visiting Dignitaries, under my own supervision. Signed with warmest regards, Mrs. Bertha Honoré Palmer."

Around the room, ladies smiled at Dora and politely clapped, except for Mrs. Forrest, who showed no expression at all. Mrs. Tillday beamed. Dora could hardly believe that she had heard correctly.

"Congratulations, Mrs. Chambers, on behalf of all of us," Mrs. Richmond said. "It is a well-deserved promotion, and I'm sure you'll not be sorry to leave the Egyptian Theatre behind. I feel it is safe to say that, under the circumstances, your transfer is effective immediately."

To Mrs. Tillday, Dora whispered, "I cannot abandon the theater."

Mrs. Tillday gave her a look like she'd lost her senses. "Don't you know what this means? It's socializing with kings and presidents. You'll be accompanying Mrs. Palmer to the best dinners and balls—even Mrs. Forrest will envy you."

"What about you? I can't just leave all the rest in your lap."

"You heard what she said about turning it over to the Fair officials. I doubt anything will be left in my lap. I'm happy for you. You deserve this."

Dora dropped the subject because they were no longer alone. First Mrs. Loomis approached, then Mrs. Gilmore, and another woman Dora didn't know. All the women were gathering around, laying their gloved hands on her and embracing her. Women she had never met crowded around like adoring, clucking hens.

She expressed her thanks softly and demurred at the compliments. Mrs. Tillday melted to the fringes, but Dora remained at the center, accepting the good wishes and the calling cards pressed into her hand with invitations to tea and dinner.

The attention baffled her, but invigorated her, too. When most of the women had drifted away, retrieving hats and coats and cloaks, the one she did not expect approached.

"Mrs. Chambers, what a remarkable honor this must be for you," Mrs. Forrest purred. "Even you must know what a tremendous duty this will be, quite an obligation. I must say, I'm surprised Bertha has enlisted someone so very new to our little group and someone so . . . "

Dora tensed.

"Well, I'm sure she sees something special in you, as we all do. Don't we, ladies?" She nodded with the other women who stood like drones around a queen bee.

Mrs. Forrest moved a step closer and put a protective hand on Dora's shoulder. "Let's take a turn in the garden, shall we? We can talk about all these new responsibilities, and perhaps I can help you decide if you're up to them."

Dora wanted to decline, but the crowd had already parted.

With Mrs. Forrest in the lead, they moved outside and onto the winding brick path leading away from the mansion's back steps. They walked side by side through a manicured rose garden, all sweet smiles and pleasant glances, as if this encounter were nothing more than two friends sharing a friendly chat.

"Dora, you must tell me: Were you as surprised as I when Mrs. Richmond announced this new assignment of yours? Imagine Bertha thinking that you of all people should be given this honor. It is quite astonishing."

What was the point of this? Dora murmured something affirmative, though her thoughts reeled with speculation.

"You know, I feel that I might even be responsible for it. I happened to visit Bertha yesterday on your behalf, you know." She met Dora's gaze. "Yes, I thought that would get your attention. But I'll be honest with you, this isn't at all what I had in mind. You see, I told her about all the time you've been spending at the Egyptian Theatre."

Dora couldn't believe what she was hearing.

"Oh, don't look surprised. I don't believe for a moment that you're there to be a good Lady Manager. In fact, when I dropped by yesterday, I saw you enter without your partner and in the company of that belly dancer. What's her name? It doesn't matter. I was quite surprised, you see, because the theater was closed. You can imagine my confusion. Now, why would she do that? I wondered. And, that wasn't even the first time I've spotted you there at odd times."

"I don't know what you're implying. I've been working with the dancers, advising them on their costumes, helping them modify their behavior and the like." Dora held her voice steady. She forced herself to keep walking, though her legs felt like dead sticks.

"I see."

Dora could hear in her tone that she didn't believe a word.

"Do you know what Bertha said when I told her what I'd seen? It really is a testament to her trusting nature, the dear woman. She actually seemed pleased that you had taken such an interest in the Egyptians. She seems to think it stems from a healthy concern for their rehabilitation." Mrs. Forrest paused, lingering beside a particularly prolific rosebush.

Dora didn't know what to say; she could hardly breathe. She stared at the edge of her skirt hem. There was a long silence as they approached the end of the garden, where the path widened and benches were set to overlook a koi pond and a moon bridge that rose among clusters of slender reeds.

Then it all made sense. All her fear was over nothing. Mrs. Forrest had nothing to hold over her. Emboldened, she turned to the woman. "So then your plan to ruin me has failed?" The words came out steady, but only by sheer force of will. She had to face up to Geraldine Forrest, now or never.

The woman's hand moved to her throat and smoothed her lace collar.

Dora straightened her spine, angled her chin. "You can't hurt me with your spying and your accusations." *And you'll fail with Charles,* she ached to add—and that would come; she was sure of it.

A red flush passed over Mrs. Forrest's neck and up into her cheeks.

All that was left was to walk away. To turn her back in victory.

But Mrs. Forrest's natural color returned. The anger slipped back behind her poised exterior like a wave pulled back into the sea. A grim smile curled at the edges of her lips.

Dora started back toward the house.

"But, Dora," Mrs. Forrest called out, "you haven't let me finish."

Dora halted. She glowered over her shoulder.

"I received a post from Mae Sheffield today," she began. "You did know she was traveling, didn't you? Visiting your hometown actually, New Orleans." She paused, letting the information sink in. "She says to tell you she can't imagine why you would leave. It's truly lovely this time of year, though a trifle warm for her taste."

Dora's breath caught in her throat.

"The train was tiresome, but she seems to be looking forward to taking in the sights. She'd been visiting with her husband's relatives along Lake Pontchartrain, but now they're staying in the quaintest little inn in the French Quarter. What was the name of it?" She tapped her finger to her lip. "Devereaux Hotel. Charles used to speak of it. You must know it."

Did Mrs. Forrest know her connection to the hotel? But no, Charles would never disclose such a thing.

"She's such a dear. Writes me every day, and I can't tell you how much I look forward to each letter. Perhaps when she returns, the two of you should get together. I'm sure she'll have some very interesting information to share."

The words fell on Dora like iron hammers. She couldn't move. How could she pretend she wasn't seeing the walls of her world cracking around her? She would not look defeated. No, she would not give Mrs. Forrest that satisfaction. Instead, she turned and left the woman where she stood, gazing at the orange and silver fish darting beneath the calm, glistening waters.

*T*he next morning Dora stowed her bicycle beside the Cairo Street gate and checked her timepiece. It was still early; the first performances at the Egyptian Theatre wouldn't start for at least an hour. She hurried to Amina's room, exchanging hellos and nods with the shopkeepers and Fair folks she had come to know on the way, but she didn't slow to chat. She didn't stop until she reached the door and knocked.

No response. She knocked again and called out, "Amina, it's me, Mrs. Chambers. Are you there?"

Still no response. She returned to the alley to see who else might be around. No one. She walked back to the square and saw Amina striding toward her, a troubled look on her face.

"You are here too early," Amina said. "The theater does not open for another hour." Her mouth pulled into a frown, and her eyes lacked their usual glimmer.

"I must talk with you."

"Can it wait? Now is not a good time." She had a faraway look, like she had not slept.

"Can we speak inside?"

Amina eyed her suspiciously. "What is this about?" She passed Dora at the threshold and moved toward her door. Dora followed.

Inside the room, she made no effort to clear the pillows strewn about the floor or the clothing scattered in untidy piles.

"Has something happened?" Dora asked.

Amina forced a laugh. She shook her head as if the question were ridiculous. "Don't be silly. Everything is fine. I was just speaking with Hossam. He can be such a worrier. Always expecting the worst."

Dora's heart clenched at Hossam's name. She couldn't think about him now. She focused on why she'd come. "I've heard some things you need to know." The words caught in her throat, and her fingers tugged at the folds of her skirt.

Amina faced her. She looked older, as if she'd aged years in the days since she'd last seen her. "What have you heard?"

"Complaints."

What little life remained in Amina's eyes vanished. "How can that be? We've done everything you asked."

"I don't understand it. I'm . . . I'm sorry."

Amina went to the window and stared out, her eyes lifted above the barrier wall to the blue sky. "What do your Lady Managers want us to do now?"

This was the news it pained her to deliver. "They're handing the matter over to the Commissioners."

Amina spun around, her eyes wide. "They cannot. Please, tell them they cannot."

"I have no say in it."

"You know what this means. They will take our wages."

A loud knocking sounded at the door and Hossam entered the room. The sight of him took her back to their night together. The long kisses and caresses; those thick, bronze arms wrapped around her waist; the feel of his hair brushing against her skin. Every touch, every sensation returned to her and made her stumble back.

Her motion caught his attention, and he stopped short. The strong set of his jaw weakened. "I did not know you had company," he said to Amina. "We can speak later." He turned to leave again, but Amina started after him.

"Wait, did you meet with the Commission?" she asked.

He turned back, shot a glance at Dora and then back to Amina. "Yes, but we should speak of this later."

Dora stepped forward. "I would like to know what was said."

He rubbed his chin. "It is not good. They say we have not cooperated with the Lady Managers. They say there will be consequences."

"I never told them you didn't cooperate. I've only ever commended you, all of you, to any of the Lady Managers."

"Of course. We don't think this has come from you. Do we, Hossam?" Amina gave him a forceful look.

"It is a convenient excuse for them," he said.

Why wouldn't he look at her? Perhaps he did blame her. But how could he? After everything, after that night.

"The troupe will discuss this when we eat. That is what I came to tell you." He backed up to the door, his head still low. "Good-bye, Dora," he said, and left, closing the door behind himself.

Dora watched him leave, then she looked at the empty space where he'd been.

"Why did he call you Dora?" Amina said, frowning.

Dora shrugged, as if the name didn't matter.

"Why would he call you by your given name?"

"He's upset; surely he wasn't thinking. If the Commission withholds your wages, will you change your mind about New York?" She needed to change the subject.

"I do not know. Perhaps it would be for the best." Amina dropped her head into her hands.

"I hope it doesn't come to that."

Amina lifted her head and studied Dora. Quickly and without warning, she embraced her. "You are a good friend. I know you will help us."

Slowly, gently, Dora embraced Amina back. "I promise I'll do what I can."

Dora left when it was time for Amina to prepare for the day's performances. It hadn't been easy keeping up a confident face, but she'd done it. Amina seemed heartened by her promise to help, but what help could she be? She'd thought their compromises would be enough to protect them, and they hadn't. She stepped out into the alley between the dancers' rooms and the rug shop next door and in her distraction nearly collided with Hossam.

He stumbled back, looking as stunned to see her as she was to see him. He brought his hand to his brow and rubbed his temples, eclipsing her view of most of his face. "Excuse me, Mrs. Chambers," he muttered. He turned and walked toward the back perimeter, avoiding her eyes.

"Please wait, Hossam." She closed the door behind her and went to him.

He'd stopped but had not turned around. Wearily, he dragged a hand through his hair.

She stopped just behind him. Standing so close, she couldn't help but notice the way his tunic lay taut over his shoulders like a second skin. She remembered running her fingers over those shoulders, kissing them . . . She dropped her gaze. "Have I done something to offend you?" Her voice cracked. This was more difficult than she'd anticipated.

He dropped his head back and gazed into the clouds.

His silence hurt worse than anything he could say. "Tell me if I've offended you so I can make amends."

"You have done no such thing," he said softly. "But you should go."

She took the last step that separated them. Her hand moved toward his back, but she stopped, pulled it back down beside her. "Then why won't you look at me?"

He turned, slowly, and gazed down on her, taking in her face, her hair, and then locking onto her eyes. She felt each sweep of his glance like an electric current pulsing through her. He moved as if he would reach for her, then backed away, darting his glance back to the sky. "I cannot look at you, I cannot even be near you, because I do not trust myself." He shook his head again as if she'd forced him to disclose a secret that shamed him. He glanced over his shoulder. He lowered his voice to a scratchy whisper, and said,

"If I thought you would let me, I would pick you up and carry you back to my room and never let you leave again."

She could feel the hot flush of her cheeks. All those feelings came rushing back and made her dizzy. She straightened, steeled herself against the temptation. In her own labored whisper, she said, "That would hardly be proper."

Sad resignation came over him. His lips twitched as if he might even smile. "No, Mrs. Chambers, there would be nothing proper about it." He bowed to her, formally, as he had that first day, and wished her a good day before striding off down the alley.

Dora watched him go, unable to move until he'd disappeared around the corner.

*D*ora was lifting the pewter knocker on the Richmond mansion before she was even sure what she meant to do. Cecil the butler opened the door and offered a formal greeting before inviting her into the foyer, where he left her to admire the towering rose bouquet on the center table as he went to inquire if his mistress was receiving callers.

He returned a moment later to say Mrs. Richmond was in the conservatory and would be delighted to see her. He ushered her through the corridor and Dora tried not to recall the last time she'd seen this part of the Richmond home, the night she'd first discovered Charles's infidelity. She focused straight ahead and smiled as sweetly as she could when Mrs. Richmond came into view.

The woman was dressed in a simple, fitted tea gown with pearl buttons down the front and a neckline bordered with silver velvet ribbon. She sat at a small table that had been set at the edge of the conservatory, overlooking the koi pond. A small teapot was at her elbow and a cup and saucer were in her hand. She set them down when she saw Dora and rose to welcome her.

"How nice to see you, dear. May I offer you tea?" She air-kissed Dora, gestured for her to take the seat across the table from her, and instructed Cecil to bring another cup and saucer. When he was nearly out of the room, she called him back and added another pot of tea to the order. Then she turned her attention to Dora. "What brings you to see me this morning?" she asked, settling back into her ivory upholstered chair.

Dora forced herself to meet Mrs. Richmond's gaze. She had to summon all of her courage. "I've been thinking about Mrs. Palmer's offer."

"Yes, that is something, isn't it? Quite an honor, you know."

"I can't help but feel I haven't earned it."

"Nonsense, Mrs. Palmer holds you in very high regard for all you've done with the Egyptian Theatre."

"That's just it. Perhaps I should have done more."

Mrs. Richmond waved away the concerns. "Sometimes there is just nothing one can do. You certainly did as much as anyone could expect."

"But I can do more."

"Now, dear, in your new assignment you won't have time to be dillydallying around with those Egyptians."

"But what if I remained in my current position?"

Mrs. Richmond's eyes widened.

She couldn't abandon the Egyptians, but even as she spoke, the lure of Mrs. Palmer's offer still tugged at her. And there was that other reason. Forfeiting the post might appease Mrs. Forrest enough to make her drop her vendetta. But the thought of giving in to that woman made Dora bristle. Handing Mrs. Forrest a victory was the last thing she wanted to do. But now that she was here, there was no going back. "I know I can help, but I don't want to appear ungrateful. That's why I've come to you. I know what faith Mrs. Palmer has in you. I'm hoping you can advise me on how best to persuade her."

Mrs. Richmond sat speechless.

"If I were to try even harder, do you think Mrs. Palmer would reconsider turning the matter over to the Commission?" She bit her lip.

Cecil entered carrying a tray laden with a teapot, an extra cup and saucer, and a plate of scones. He set the tray in front of Mrs. Richmond and poured a cupful for Dora. He handed it to her and removed an envelope from his coat pocket. He extended it to Mrs. Richmond. "This just arrived for you, madam. From the Forrest household."

Mrs. Richmond took the envelope, tore it open, and read the contents. Then she folded the letter, slid it back into its envelope, and tucked it between her skirt and the chair's arm. Her expression was strained.

"I hope everything is all right," Dora offered.

Mrs. Richmond glanced at her as though she had forgotten she was in the room. "Oh, fine, fine. Now, tell me again what you are asking?"

Dora tried again, making her plea as succinct as possible. "I'm afraid the Fair Commissioners will deal unfairly with the Egyptians. I'd like another chance to help."

Mrs. Richmond trained all her attention on Dora, as if the matter were a complex one that must be examined from every angle. Finally, she asked, "Even if it means giving up the position as Liaison to Visiting Dignitaries?"

Dora nodded.

As Mrs. Richmond contemplated this, her eyes darted from the letter to her guest.

"Will you help?"

Mrs. Richmond pulled back into the chair. "I will see what I can do, but I cannot make any promises. Mrs. Palmer can be adamant about getting what she wants."

"Yes, of course. Any help will be appreciated." From the way Mrs. Richmond regarded her, she knew the visit had come to its end. She rose, and Mrs. Richmond did the same. "I'm sure you have a full day ahead, so I won't keep you."

Mrs. Richmond smiled and nodded. "Cecil, Mrs. Chambers is leaving. Will you see her out?"

The butler, who appeared at the doorway, bowed, and waited for Dora to join him.

"I'll be in touch soon," Mrs. Richmond said before turning away.

On the bicycle ride home, Dora replayed the exchange in her mind.

What had Mrs. Forrest's note said? Had it conveyed bad news, or had Mrs. Richmond's reaction not pertained to the note at all? Perhaps it was simply a reaction to Dora's request. Mrs. Richmond had appeared flustered, annoyed, and stridently polite all at the same time.

Perhaps it was presumptuous to think the message could have anything to do with her. Still, as Dora pedaled down Lake Shore Drive, feeling the wind off the lake on her cheeks, the question troubled her.

When at last she turned up the carriage drive alongside the house, something else troubled her. Dr. Bostwick was leaning over her bougainvillea, examining the slender branches and the tiny green leaves, pinching them and turning them to look at their undersides as if he were examining a sick patient.

Dora stopped her bicycle beside him, and he turned with a start.

"So you've caught me," he said, chuckling, and then returned again to his examination.

"So I have." Yes, she'd caught him all right. Pretending to be good and kind while he extorted payment from the Egyptians.

"I'm concerned about this little fella." His fingers moved from one branch to another. "I don't like this spotting on the leaves. Not a good sign. You haven't been overwatering, have you?"

"I've been watering just as you said." She slid off her bike, leaned it against the wall, and looked over his shoulder. She'd noticed the bougainvillea hadn't sprouted new leaves in the last week, but she hadn't noticed the brown spots growing on the older leaves. She reached out and touched one. "What's causing it?"

"Not sure. Might be a parasite in the roots, might be watering, might just not like our harsh Chicago climate."

"What should I do?"

He let go of the plant and rubbed his hands together, wiping away the soil. "Just have to wait and see."

"Before you go, I must ask something."

"Is everything all right?"

Even now there was such kindness in his voice. Perhaps she had jumped to the wrong conclusion. Perhaps there was an explanation. Hope swelled within her that this had all been a mistake. "It's about the Egyptians, that woman you helped."

"The Egyptians? My dear, why would you let yourself get worked up over Egyptians?" He chuckled and shook his head.

Her jaw tightened. "They said you charged them. But you told me—"

"Now, now. You've seen how that theater fills up. I'm sure they could more than afford the modest stipend I requested." There was no guilt in his voice, no regret.

"But that was not what we agreed."

"Yes, but there's no reason to bother yourself about—"

"You made me into a liar."

His brows pinched. "I hardly see a reason for you to turn this into a capital crime."

"How much was it?"

"I don't think there's any need for—"

"How much did you take, Dr. Bostwick?"

"My usual house call charge only. Five dollars. Plus the Fair entrance fee, and some other incidental expenses."

"Seven dollars, then? Eight?"

He glanced away. "Twenty, I believe it was."

Rage roiled within her. "So you had quite a time of it at their expense, did you?" How could she have trusted him? Those shifty eyes, those thin, stingy lips, that straggly gray hair. What a devious lout he was.

"My dear, they're only Egyptians."

"I suppose that makes it all right?"

He shrugged his assent.

There was no use arguing. He would never see fault in what he'd done. The lesson here was hers, not his. "I will never forgive you for what you've done," she said, as she turned on her heel and left him shaking his head beside her wilting bougainvillea.

*S*he was still sulking in the sitting room, flipping through the newest issue of *Collier's*, when she heard Charles's footsteps scraping on the front step. She jumped up and tossed her magazine on the settee. As soon as he opened the door, she was there. "How was your day, dear? Can I help you with that? Here, let me take it for you." She reached around and took the coat from his shoulders, holding it as he shook his way out of the sleeves. The opportunity she'd been waiting for was finally here.

"Settle down, Dora. Just give me a moment." Still he let her take his bowler and place it on the rack as he brushed the remainder of the day from his suit.

While he was turned away, she slipped her hand up to where the tea gown tied at her throat and pulled the laces free. She pulled open the collar to reveal the thin chemise beneath.

Charles went to his study. "What can I expect for dinner this evening?" he asked over his shoulder.

She leaned against the door of his room and trailed her fingers down the front of her chemise. She'd practiced the move in front of the mirror, trying to make it look spontaneous. "Roasted lamb, can't you smell it?" She took pride in telling him one of his favorite meals was on its way. She'd begged Bonmarie to make it on the chance that he might dine at home. She'd held out hope, and now that hope was paying off.

Charles finished pouring himself a Scotch, but he didn't answer. He patted his cravat as if preparing to say something, but then only raised his glass and took another swallow.

"How was your day?" she asked. That always got him talking. She waited for a dissertation on the current state of business at the bank.

"Nothing special." He sank into the chair behind his desk and took up the newspaper Hazel had left there. He opened it and hid behind the headlines of the latest treaties and trials. She glanced away, not wanting to glimpse any more bad news about the belly dancers.

"You must be tired." She walked behind him and laid her hands on his shoulders. She felt them relax at her touch. She worked her fingers, rubbing at the base of his neck and up over his collar. She thought she heard a bit of a moan and she knew it was working.

"What were you up to today?"

His question surprised her. He so rarely asked these days, and there was so much that she couldn't tell him. "The usual," she said. His neck twitched beneath her. He strained to turn his head to see her. She thought quickly. "Dr. Bostwick," she blurted. "I saw Dr. Bostwick today."

"Oh? And how is he?"

He's a rotten snake, but she couldn't say that. "How well do you know him?"

Charles lolled his head, relishing the massage. "Pretty well, as far as neighbors go. He was a good friend to my father."

"I don't like him." There, she'd said it, and it felt good. She felt Charles chuckle.

"What has the poor old man done?"

"He practically swindled the Egyptians."

"Swindled?" Even Charles liked good gossip.

"Yes, swindled. I asked if he might look in on one of the dancers who had taken ill. I offered to pay him but he assured me he would take no payment. Then he turned around and overcharged them. Can you believe it?"

Dora expected commiseration, even patronizing commiseration. Instead, he laughed.

"Why is that funny?"

"I'm sorry. It's not. But everyone is entitled to make a profit, aren't they? Prices are determined by what the market will bear. It's just business."

"Charles!"

"Fine, you're right. He shouldn't have done it. Were they very angry with you?"

"No, not with me, but they need their money. You don't know what it's like for them."

"So they paid him and they weren't angry with you. I'm sorry, but I don't exactly see a problem."

"The problem is he took advantage of them." It was all she could do not to throttle his neck. How could he be so callous?

He laughed again and swiveled his chair around to face her. He took her waist between his hands, and she thought she could see a glimmer in his eye when he felt that she wasn't wearing her corset. His fingers roamed over her hips and her thighs.

It was the effect she had wanted, so why did she want to pull away?

There was a hunger in his eyes when he said, "My dear, you are too kindhearted for your own good. They're only Egyptians. Have you done something different with your hair?"

"I saw it in a magazine ad. Do you like it?" She did pull away then, and turned so he could see the loose waves she'd assembled into a knot at her neck. She pretended to be flattered, not dwelling on the heartless thing he'd said about the Egyptians.

"I do like it. Very becoming."

He looked as if he would reach out for her and pull her toward him again. She stepped to the door, just out of his reach. "I'll go look in on dinner," she said, forcing a smile. She closed the door with more force than she intended and sent a shudder through the walls.

Later, at dinner, she avoided his glance. When he came to the table, she could see the drink had softened him. He took his place, and she felt his gaze linger on her. He savored his meal, and even complimented Bonmarie when she cleared away the plates. He was in a more jovial mood than she'd seen him in weeks, and she knew tonight was her chance to make amends. More than a few times over the course of the meal, she'd noticed him looking at her. Not at her face, but lower. It was the kind of look she'd yearned for all these weeks, yet it gave her no satisfaction. When he was finished eating, he folded his napkin, came around behind her, and leaned into her ear. "Come to my study to say good night before you go up to bed."

"Of course, dear," she said, spearing another bite of potato. She knew what it meant, and it should have made her push away from her plate and throw herself into his arms. But she didn't. The thought of lying beside him now, let alone beneath him, revolted her.

He bent and kissed her cheek; his lips were cold and soft where they touched her skin, his breath still heavy and sweet with Scotch. She heard him walk down the hall and go into his study. There was a clink of crystal as he poured another glass from the decanter.

She waited another few moments, finished the last bites on her plate, and pulled off her slippers. She held them by the nubs of the heels as she padded quietly, so quietly, by his door and up the stairs and into her room. She closed the door and lowered the latch so it didn't make a sound.

When she crawled into bed, she hoped sleep would come quickly.

But it didn't.

She lay in the dark, wondering what Charles would do when he realized she hadn't fetched him to bed, or if he would believe it when she told him it had simply slipped her mind.

Later, she wondered why she felt nothing when she heard the front door open and close and then the carriage take off down the street, knowing exactly where it was Charles intended to go.

And why had Hossam's kisses burned, but Charles's had left her cold?

Twelve

Dora was sitting at her dressing table, preparing to face the day, when Bonmarie rapped on the door. "Come in," she said, pulling up another curl and securing it with a hairpin.

Bonmarie came up beside her and held out a letter. "This came for you."

Dora set down her pin and took it. "Who's it from?"

Bonmarie shrugged.

Dora ran her pewter letter opener across it, pulled out the folded sheet, and read:

Please come to my home at noon.

It was signed by Mrs. Richmond. Her heart leaped. The woman must have already talked to Mrs. Palmer!

At noon precisely, Dora approached the Richmonds' door and knocked. Cecil greeted her and led her through a set of double doors off the foyer. Dora entered to find a library that smelled of stale cigar smoke, and heavy wood paneling made it dark, though the sun shone brightly outside. Mrs. Richmond was sitting on a settee in front of a grandly carved desk and pouring herself a cup of tea from a pot perched on a silver cart.

But any hope that this would be a happy occasion disappeared when Dora saw Mrs. Richmond was not alone. In a wingback chair beside her was Mrs. Forrest, smiling as if this were a friendly visit. Dora struggled to maintain her composure.

"I am happy you've made it on time," Mrs. Richmond said, her voice more somber than usual. "Please sit down. There." She indicated a hard wooden chair.

Dora moved to it and smoothed her skirts to sit.

"Mrs. Tillday, I would have you sit as well." Mrs. Richmond looked toward the window behind the desk.

Dora's partner appeared there, as if she had been conjured from thin air. Dora sought a glance from her friend, something to give her a clue as to what this was about, but she could read nothing in the woman's face.

Mrs. Richmond took a sip from her cup, then said, "Mrs. Chambers, information has come to light that calls into question your fitness to be a member of the Board of Lady Managers."

Dora didn't move; she could hardly breathe.

"I cannot pretend to know the reasons why you would purposely deceive us," Mrs. Richmond continued, "and frankly I don't care to know. But this deception constitutes a breach of conduct that cannot be condoned." For a moment she hesitated, as if overcome. Mrs. Tillday still had not moved from the window. "After conferring with Mrs. Palmer, we have decided that your membership on the board must be terminated."

"I don't understand," Dora blurted.

Mrs. Richmond stopped her with a raised hand. "This is not a negotiation."

"Listen," Mrs. Forrest began. "We know it's not your fault, not really. Mae found out so many interesting things about your family, Dora Devereaux."

Hearing her given name hit Dora like a thunderclap. How did they know?

A hint of malice passed over Mrs. Forrest's expression. "Seems your mother kept you as separated from public life as she possibly could, and she did have her reasons, didn't she? I'm sure you know this kind of information, if it were to spread, could damage not just you, but those around you. I can only speak for myself, but I would hate to see that happen. Perhaps you'll want to take the opportunity to consider whether Chicago really suits you."

"Please, Mrs. Forrest. I really must insist." Mrs. Richmond turned to Dora again. "Unless there's anything more, our business is concluded. You may go."

Dora rose and went to the door, holding back her tears until she cleared the room. Then the dam broke, and they flooded over her cheeks. Mama, the hotel, the shame. They knew all of it. She pulled the front door closed behind herself.

Her head pounded with the sound of her own footsteps and sobs. Then there were more footsteps. Someone was following her down the cobblestone path. She wiped her gloved fingers over her cheeks to dry them.

"Wait."

It was Mrs. Tillday. Dora stopped.

Her partner—her former partner—came around to face her. Her lips twitched and tears welled. "Honestly, I didn't know they planned to do this. You know how Mrs. Forrest can be. Your family doesn't matter to me. I'm so sorry."

It was probably true. And it wasn't Mrs. Tillday's fault; it wasn't anyone's fault but her own.

Dora took Mrs. Tillday's hands. "I don't blame you. I tried to be grand, but the truth is I'm not. I'm just the daughter of a widow who runs a hotel in the French Quarter. I thought none of it would matter here; I thought I could be somebody different. But you all saw through me. It must have been so obvious."

Mrs. Tillday's tears stopped. "But this isn't because of your mother."

"Then what? There's nothing else."

Mrs. Tillday glanced away.

"What?" Dora pressed. "You must tell me."

"It's your father." Still she refused to meet Dora's eyes.

"My father died before I was born. I've never even known him. I told you that. I told Mrs. Richmond that."

Mrs. Tillday stiffened.

"What aren't you telling me?"

Finally Mrs. Tillday looked at her but for only a moment. She stared into the lace under Dora's chin. "Mrs. Sheffield found someone in New Orleans who knew your father, or at least had heard stories about your father."

"So?"

"When the rumors began, they said he quit his job with your grandfather and went to Baton Rouge and took your mother with him. They figured the rumors had to be true to make him leave like that."

"What rumors?"

Mrs. Tillday closed her eyes. "That his mother had been a slave. An African slave."

It was absurd. It was a ridiculous, absurd lie. So why was Mrs. Tillday looking at her with such pity? Surely she could see it was nonsense. Just more of Mrs. Forrest's malice. "It isn't true," she snapped. "That woman invented this awful, stupid lie. You must tell them." Still, Mrs. Tillday looked at her as if she were a cripple or a beggar.

So this was Mrs. Forrest's new game. It was a clever lie. She had to give her that. No one would speak of it openly. It was the kind of accusation relegated to whispers and sidelong glances.

"Yes, you're right," Mrs. Tillday said. "Of course it isn't true. I don't know why I believed it. But you'll have to convince Mrs. Richmond."

So there was still hope. "I can, I know I can. Tell her this is slander, tell her it's a ridiculous claim. But tell her when she is alone. Let Mrs. Forrest think she's won for now. It will keep her from doing any more harm, at least."

"But what will you do?"

"I have to find a way to prove the truth."

*O*n the way home, Dora racked her brain for a way around the obvious course. Getting proof from Mama would be the simplest way to go, but Mama was the last person she wanted to ask for help. She couldn't admit what a mess she'd made of things in Chicago. And for twenty years the woman had refused to answer Dora's questions about her father. "Don't mind about the past," she'd say. "Keep your mind on the future; he has nothing to do with your future."

But right now that past had everything to do with her future.

Once Dora had returned home, she pulled her stationery from the dressing table drawer and picked up her pen. *Dear Mother.* She stopped. She set down the pen and paced the floor. She could already see the disappointed look on Mama's face. "This is your time, Dora. Everything we ever wanted is going to happen for you in Chicago. I know it." Mama's words shortly before her departure from New Orleans had given her such hope.

The letter would tell Mama how much she had failed. She cursed her dark hair and eyes, the skin that browned too easily in the sun. These stupid claims would never even be considered if she'd inherited Mama's blond hair and pale skin.

But she had to swallow her pride. Birth certificate. School records. Mama would have to send anything she could.

She raised the pen and began to write. She was just about to explain the allegation when she heard Bonmarie on the stairs.

The pen stopped moving. She had overlooked one very important person. She hurried down the stairs and threw herself through the kitchen's swinging doorway.

"*Chere,* you nearly scared me to death," Bonmarie heaved, clutching at the kitchen counter to steady herself. "There's no reason for a lady to run through a house—"

"I need your help."

The woman ignored the urgency in Dora's voice. "What are you talking about?" She grabbed a kitchen towel and tucked it beneath her apron strings. "If this is about the other night, you needn't worry. I won't say anything."

"I'm not talking about that." She slid onto a stool at the counter. "You've said my father was already gone when you came to work for my mother, but you must know something about him."

Bonmarie turned from Dora and pulled a bowl from the cupboard. She set it near an open flour bag on the counter and measured out a cupful. "Your father?"

"I need to know whatever you know. A woman is spreading the most horrible lies." She hesitated a moment, then added, "I need to find some documentation about my father's family. The Devereauxs."

"What are the lies?"

"They say he had African blood."

Bonmarie stared at the flour.

Shame came over Dora. "You know how those women are. They say they believe in tolerance, but this woman spreading the lies knows I will never be accepted if people thought . . ."

Bonmarie turned back to the cupboard and rifled for another bowl.

"You know it makes no difference to me."

Bonmarie spun around, her eyes ablaze. "But it does. It makes so much difference you can't think of anything but proving it false. What if your father did have African blood?"

Dora said nothing.

The woman turned back to the cupboard. "Don't ask questions you don't want answers to."

"You won't help me?" Of course she wouldn't. She could be so stubborn. Mama was her only hope. She went to the door. She turned back to Bonmarie. "Why did you even come to Chicago? Just to watch me fail?"

Bonmarie's shoulders drooped.

"Won't you please help me?"

"I can do nothing, *ma chere.*"

*D*ora needed to think. She pulled her dressing table chair to the window and her fingers played along the filmy shade that let in the sunlight. Rain clouds gathered in the distance, erasing the colors of the landscape, leaving only gradations of gray. In the window's reflection, she saw she wasn't alone. Bonmarie had followed her. She was standing at the door. Dora turned. "Did you come to gloat about the mess I've made?"

She regretted her spiteful words as soon as they were out of her mouth.

Bonmarie's frown deepened. "I won't lie to you, *chere*. Not anymore."

A shiver ran through Dora. "Will you tell me about my father?"

Bonmarie went to the edge of the bed and sat. "Yes, *chere*, I'm going to tell you about your father. He was my brother."

The words that followed passed over Dora like hurricane winds, twisting and tangling the past she thought she knew into something unrecognizable, something unthinkable. The syllables stabbed and hurt more than anything Mrs. Forrest had ever hurled at her. And now that Bonmarie laid it out, it made so much sense. It was why Bonmarie had stayed with Mama for so many years, and it was the truth that had made Mama so desperate. Dora sat numb, feeling nothing as the words spilled out.

Bonmarie told Dora how Charlotte Benoit had fallen in love with a man who worked for her father. He was darkly handsome, and she assumed his French accent was proof enough of a European heritage. "You see, our mother had taken up with a wealthy French landowner in Baton Rouge," Bonmarie said. "My father made sure our mama and us kids were educated and free.

"When my brother fell in love with your mother, he didn't dare tell his secret until after they were married and she was with child. They were so much in love; you never saw two people more devoted to each other. He believed that, as his wife, she would forgive him anything. But he was wrong. She lived with him in Baton Rouge during the pregnancy, but planned to leave him— and leave the baby, too. But when it came time, when she saw her beautiful newborn girl, who looked for all the world like a perfectly white infant, she couldn't leave you. She fled back to her parents with you in her arms."

As the story unfolded, it filled the holes of Dora's childhood, bridging the parts that had never made sense.

"Your mother, she began her life again with her parents and with you, and she got along just fine. I imagine she's the kind who would always do fine. Her parents were already struggling when she returned to them. Through all those troubles, she still might've been happy—except she missed your father. As time went on, she realized she felt more love for him than shame. She sent a letter to him in Baton Rouge, where she'd left him. But there was no answer. And none to the letters she sent after it. It was only near your third birthday, I guess it was, that I wrote back to tell her he was gone. He had left a few weeks after she'd returned to New Orleans, hired by her own father to work a ship headed to the Mediterranean Sea. Some said he'd taken pity on his son-in-law; others said he just wanted to get him farther away. Either way, your grandfather had hoped that ship would restore the family's fortune, but I suppose you know the rest."

It was the vessel that was lost at sea. All the family's wealth, all the family's hopes, everything. At least that part of Mama's story had been true.

Dora asked the question Mama would never answer. "What was my father like?"

Bonmarie sighed. "His name wasn't Devereaux. Your Mama made that part up to hide what she'd done. My brother's name was Sebastian Marcel Beauprix." When she spoke his name, Bonmarie slumped forward and sobbed. As great heaves came from her, Dora wound her arm around Bonmarie's warm, soft shoulders and buried her face in the woman's collar and cried, too.

They sat for some time, silent until Dora couldn't stand the silence any longer. There was still something she didn't understand. "Why did you come to live with us if your family is free?"

Bonmarie lifted her head and smiled as if amused and embarrassed at the same time. "As you can see, I was not blessed with my father's light skin, as my brother was. Our father had another family, a white family, and he stopped visiting my mother when we were still young. He left her a tobacco farm and that was all. We lived well while the farm did well, but after my brother left for the last time, we struggled, too. The crops dried up. Mama had just died when I wrote to your mother, and I told her of it. Out of pity, I guess, she offered me a job at her hotel."

"My mother turned you into a servant? How could you do it?" Tears welled again in Dora's eyes.

"Freedom doesn't taste so good when you're starving, *ma chere*. I could have become a white man's mistress, maybe, like my mother did, or I could do this."

It still didn't make sense to Dora.

"I guess that's what I told myself, anyway. Maybe it wasn't the only reason." She smoothed away a tendril of hair that had fallen over Dora's eye. "I missed my brother; he was the last part of my family. You were all that was left of him, and the only part of our family that would go on."

New tears came to Dora's eyes; she realized that she had never loved anyone more than she loved Bonmarie. There were no memories before Bonmarie. It comforted her to know that more than chance had brought them together. They were family. They were blood.

They sat together at the edge of the bed, and Dora reached out to be enfolded by Bonmarie's arms. She gave in to the sobs that welled within her. Bonmarie rocked her gently and whispered loving words into her ear.

When the tears stopped, Dora fell into a restful doze. And when she awoke, Bonmarie was still beside her. Her friend, her aunt. She was still caressing the length of Dora's arms and humming a hymn softly to herself. Dora felt as if she had awakened from a long sleep.

She pulled herself up and kissed Bonmarie's cheek.

Bonmarie smiled.

"Thank you for staying with me," Dora whispered.

Dora saw Bonmarie stiffen and shift. "Didn't want you to be alone, *chere*. I shouldn't have said what I said. You were better off not knowing. I'm so sorry."

Dora took Bonmarie's hands and felt their warmth. "Don't ever be sorry about that. I want to know. I thought the hole in my life was missing my father. But it was so much more. Everything was a lie until now. I never questioned the things I suspected. I should have. You've given me the truth."

The sound of the front door opening stopped her. Charles called out. "Dora, are you home?"

Dora clutched Bonmarie's hands tighter. The afternoon sun still shone through the windows. "How can I tell him?"

Bonmarie shook her head. "You can't, and you won't. No one ever needs to know."

Dora rose and smoothed her clothes. She moved toward the door and called out. "I'm here, Charles."

He was standing in the foyer. His gaze passed over her at the top of the staircase. "May I have a moment with you in my study?"

"Of course, dear." He was angry, and there was no telling how much angrier he was going to be when he heard what she had to say.

He motioned for her to enter in front of him. As she moved into his room, she saw his gaze rise to the top of the stairs. Bonmarie was there, blank-faced and imposing.

Charles took his chair behind the desk and fumbled through the drawers for something. He produced a cigar and a match, and began the ritual of preparing to smoke.

"You're home early. Is everything all right at the bank?"

"Yes, everything is fine at the bank. There's something I need to discuss with you. Some information shared with me about your family. Very troubling information."

So he already knew.

"Geraldine Forrest?" she asked.

"The source doesn't matter. But there is a distressing rumor about your parentage." He stopped, swallowed hard. "That your father was not a white man. I'm sorry to be so blunt. I know it's a preposterous notion; but we may be obliged to prove it false nonetheless."

He didn't think it was true. He only wanted her word that it was a lie. Poor Charles. Couldn't he see the truth of it on her face? No, he wasn't looking at her. Not now, maybe not ever. The truth would be whatever he wanted it to be. A hope came to her that they would be able to put this behind them. Somehow Charles could make it all go away. There was a chance to start again.

But it would only be more lies.

"It's true, Charles."

She watched him wither at her words. He slumped like a leaf dying on the branch. He stayed like that for several moments. When he finally raised himself, he murmured, "How could you do this to me?"

How old he looked, how pathetic.

"I'm doing everything I can to be a good and decent husband to you, but you are making this difficult." Such pleading in his voice, such pain.

All of her remorse washed away. The image returned of him

with Mrs. Forrest behind that curtain. The way he looked at that woman, the way he touched her. A searing pain surged through Dora, disappointment and shame alchemized into white-hot anger. She looked directly at this man, who was her husband yet felt more like a stranger. "Tried to be a good and decent husband? Does that include your visits to Mrs. Forrest's house?"

His face lost all color.

"Was it part of the plan all along, to marry some naïve girl who would be too stupid to catch on to what you're really up to? Or did you think I would simply be too intimidated to demand that it stop?"

A red flush came over him. "Dora, I must insist—"

"Insist on what? That I continue to pretend my husband is not sleeping with another woman? Or that she makes it her sole mission to cause me misery at every turn? I'll bet you didn't even know that, until today, I presumed it was my own fault because I could not please you. I can hardly believe it now myself."

"Why are you doing this?"

"Because it's become so clear to me now. If anyone has lied, it's you. You didn't marry me because you loved me; you wanted to appear to be something you're not so the bank directors might give you that precious promotion. It didn't have to be me; it might have been anyone. It was just that my mother and I made it so easy for you. I admit I'm not proud of that, and I was naïve enough to think it would all turn out for the best."

Charles straightened. His lips pursed. "Don't say something you'll regret."

"Believe me, there's already too much I regret. I regret thinking fine dresses and a beautiful house would make me happy. I regret wishing I could please you and thinking everything would be perfect if only you loved me the way a husband should love his wife." She saw hardness in his eyes. She wanted to say more—she had so much more to say—yet something inside her made her stop. Perhaps she had said too much.

He ran his palms over his face. "It's been a difficult day for both of us. I'm going to go up to my room and rest a bit. I suggest you do the same. We can discuss how to resolve this over dinner."

She watched him reach out for the banister and go up the stairs, then turn toward his room. He didn't look back at her, not once.

Dora found no comfort in her room. The tears came with a deep ache in her chest. Her future was unraveling. The walls around her no longer embraced her. The settee felt hard beneath her, and the pillows propped against it offered no consolation. This was not her sanctuary anymore.

When the tears finished and a weary calm settled in, she went downstairs. She went out the front door and closed it quietly behind her. The sun hung low in the sky, casting long shadows across the street. From the portico, she looked out over her Gold Coast neighborhood. The grand houses all in a row, their perfect faces lined up side by side. This was no longer her home; perhaps it never had been. Charles would ask her to leave; she felt sure of it. It was simply a matter of time. Pretending she had come from a well-to-do family was one thing, but now everyone who mattered knew the truth, or would know it soon enough. People would say she had deceived him; Mrs. Forrest would see to that.

She walked down the pathway, listening to her heels scrape against the brick pavers, the birds chirping in the elm trees. A cold breeze touched her cheek. It was summer, yet the air chilled her. In New Orleans, it would be moist and warm. Mama would be putting ice in the rooms for the guests to refresh themselves. When she went back, Mama wouldn't have to protect her anymore. There was no more reason to hide behind the hotel's walls.

She turned up the carriage drive and hardly recognized her bougainvillea. New brown spots dotted what had been the few unblemished leaves, and the already afflicted branches had shriveled into dry twigs and lifeless leaves. She searched the stem for green growth, but there was none. The patient had succumbed. A new round of tears worked their way up into her throat.

She yanked the dismal bush from the ground and threw it across the lawn. The bougainvillea didn't belong here any more than she did. She didn't belong in Chicago, but she didn't want to go back to New Orleans, either. She lifted her face to the last ray of sunlight. Twilight was settling in fast. Toward Lake Michigan, she could see the streaks of coral and pink darkening into violet and blue. Above the stretched swirl of color, a star shone bright, a pinprick of light against the dark. The evening star. She wondered if Amina was looking at it, or Hossam. "We're still under the same sky," Amina had said that day in her room. That wonderful, perfect day she had spent with the Egyptians.

*L*ess than an hour later, Dora was pedaling toward the fairgrounds. Except for the carpetbag resting in her basket, it might have been a visit like any other day. She wrapped her fingers around the handlebars. Had she ever been more grateful for a gift than she was for this bicycle? She would be sad to leave it behind.

And Bonmarie would be angry at first when she found the note on the kitchen counter, but she would understand. She would know Dora intended to keep her promise to call for her as soon as it was settled.

She rode on, and the farther she rode, the further away she felt from that image she had imagined for herself. That fashionable lady of society. It had only been a vision, a dream. Nothing real.

Dora tried to conjure a new image, but nothing came. It was too soon for that. She felt free; that was enough. For the first time she didn't have a plan for her future; she didn't know what tomorrow held. A wonderful feeling rose up in her and made her laugh into the cold evening air.

When she walked up to the Cairo Street gate, the man at the ticket booth recognized her as a Lady Manager and waved her through. She swaggered a bit, enjoying this last opportunity to enjoy the privilege. She walked through the crowd with her head high, impervious to the glares from the matrons and older gentlemen who silently chastised her for walking alone.

It took only a few minutes to get to the Egyptian Theatre. When she reached it, a stream of men was filing out. A performance had just concluded, and another line stood by, ready to enter. She wasn't too late. They hadn't fled to New York, at least not yet.

She intended to find Amina first, but when she saw Hossam beside the ticket window talking to the boy inside, she stopped. She watched him laugh and gesture toward something at the rug store.

She froze. Maybe she couldn't do this after all.

Someone nudged her shoulder. Startled, she turned to see a camel behind her. A boy giggled behind his fist. She opened her mouth to scold him, but his laughter was infectious. "She remembers you. She wanted to say hello," the boy said between giggles.

Dora looked again at the animal and noticed the familiar tassels along the harness and those wide black eyes with the impossibly long lashes. It was Little Egypt. Dora dropped her bag and held out her hand so the animal could brush her nose against it.

"You're teasing, aren't you?" she said to the boy. "She couldn't possibly remember me."

"Quite the contrary."

The voice made her spin back around again. Hossam was behind her.

He stroked Little Egypt's neck. "Camels are very intelligent creatures. More so than many people I know."

Dora felt the heat rise in her face. Was he talking about her?

"I am glad you've come back," he said. "I wanted to apologize—"

"No, I should apologize," she interrupted.

He flicked his hand at the boy, a signal to take Little Egypt and move on. He looked to the passersby and back at Dora. "Perhaps we should go somewhere else to continue this conversation."

Around them ladies in fine feathered hats and men in twill suits paraded through the square. There were shopkeepers and performers and barkers. "I have nothing to hide. Do you?"

"No, but there is the possibility—"

She reached up and covered his mouth with her fingers.

He looked confused, but he didn't pull back.

Dora pulled her fingers away and wrapped both arms up around his neck. He glanced around nervously.

"You once said to me, 'If I thought you would let me, I would pick you up and carry you back to my room and never let you leave again.' Does that offer still stand?"

"Are you playing a game, Mrs. Chambers?"

"No, I'm not playing, and I'm not Mrs. Chambers. At least, I don't expect to be for long."

His eyes scanned her eyes, her cheeks, her lips, as if unsure she was really there, standing in his arms. "I think I'd like to kiss you." His voice was hoarse and heavy with emotion.

Instead of letting her answer, he bent over her, pulling her hard against him and wrapping himself around her. Their lips met and that familiar fire coursed through her, making her body tingle from the tops of her ears to the tips of her toes.

From inside the theater, she heard the beginning of the next performance. The slow whine of the horn, the steady beat of the drum. *Doom doom tekka tek doom tekka tek*. Her future would be like the dance now. She would surrender to the music, and follow it wherever it led.

Epilogue

*D*ora leaned close to the massive mirror along the backstage dressing table and carefully followed the rim of her
eyes with the stick of black kohl.

Amina stood by, watching like an anxious mother. "Draw the line
out, beyond the eyelid. Like this." Amina used her finger to show
her meaning. "No, use the darker powder. With the stage lights,
the makeup must be heavy or you will look too white."

Dora saw Amina stiffen.

"I mean you will look pale under the lights."

"I know what you meant. It might be the only time someone
could accuse me of looking too white." She pulled her silky robe
tighter around herself and smiled to let Amina know the words
didn't sting.

When she had left Charles, the Lady Managers, and all
the trouble in Chicago behind her, all the pain seemed to stay
there, too.

That first day, Hossam had taken her and her carpetbag back

to Amina's room, and Amina didn't ask a single question, just took the luggage, put it behind the dressing screen, and forced a plate of hummus and bread on Dora.

Later she learned that when Amina and Hossam had stepped out, they'd agreed they would book passage for one more to New York. Even now, Dora wondered how they had been so sure of her intentions before she had fully realized them herself. She'd left Charles's house thinking she would hide out with the Egyptians long enough to let him think she'd returned to New Orleans. Then she could go anywhere: San Francisco, St. Louis, even New York, if she wanted. But the more time she spent with the Egyptians, the more she wanted to stay with them.

Two weeks later, they were in New York, the middle act on the theater's bill. Two weeks after that, they were the top act. In a month, the troupe had pulled in twice what it had been promised for the full run of the Fair.

And everything would have been perfect if Amina hadn't announced on that first payday that she intended to return to Egypt. "I want to see my brother," she announced to everyone one night over the evening meal. "I have saved enough for him to finally open his café."

There was no arguing with her once she'd made a decision. Fatma and Maryeta and the others were already treating Dora like one of their own, so she couldn't complain that she was being abandoned. She was even picking up some Arabic.

Amina had packed and bought third-class passage on a ship setting sail the next day, and Dora was already feeling the loss.

Yet it was difficult to be sad when the thought of returning to Egypt was making Amina happier than Dora had ever seen her. Even now, as she hovered over her with the black kohl stick, she beamed.

"I'll look like a clown if you make me put any more of that on my face."

"No, no. You look very beautiful. Very exotic," Amina said playfully. "The audience will think they are looking on an Egyptian queen, maybe Isis herself. With the right costume, the right makeup, you can be whoever you want to be on the stage."

Dora thought of the Lady Managers and how much she had wished to be like them. "I'll settle for being myself for now."

"Yes, be yourself," Amina said. "You are exceptional, even if you don't know it yet. An exceptional dancer. I can leave because I know you can take my place with the troupe."

"I don't want to take your place. I'd just like to contribute, and I still want to pay back what Dr. Bostwick took."

"No paying back. Maryeta is well, and now we have you."

A knock at the door interrupted them. Bonmarie poked her head inside. "*Ma chere*, you have a visitor." Her expression held a warning.

"Who?"

Bonmarie stood aside and a man entered, fumbling with the rim of his bowler hat.

"Charles?"

Amina gave Dora's shoulder a squeeze and excused herself from the room behind Bonmarie.

"Thank you, Bonmarie," Charles stammered after her. He was dressed for the autumn temperatures outside, with a thick gray overcoat, wool scarf, and gloves. "You look like you've just seen a ghost, my dear. Am I as bad as all that?"

Dora hesitated, trying to regain her composure. "Not at all. I'm just surprised to see you."

He forced a grin. "It's taken me some time to work up the courage to visit. I heard from your mother, actually; she told me you were here. She begged me to fetch you. I didn't know what to tell her."

"Of course. Mama." Dora didn't know how to interpret his reticence. "I'm sorry if she caused you any trouble. I thought I'd made the situation clear to her."

"That's why I'm here, Dora. I'd like you to make the situation clear to me."

"I explained it in the letter," she countered.

"Yes, the letter." He fumbled inside his jacket and pulled a crumpled and worn bit of paper from his breast pocket. He began to read:

Dear Charles,

I know I've caused you a great deal of trouble and I'm sorry for it. I know you might not believe that now, but I hope in time you will see it is the truth. You see, when you asked me to be your wife, I believed nothing could make me happier. I wanted to be everything you wanted me to be; I wanted to be a woman you could love. Please know that I never hid my father's past from you. My mother kept this secret from me, yet I accept full responsibility for it. I relieve you of your marital vows, and I wish you every future success. This letter should be enough to secure a divorce. I'm truly sorry for all of it.

Dora

"I thought that made my case clear," she whispered.

"It's plain enough, but you gave me no opportunity to respond, no chance for rebuttal." His voice rose with frustration.

"I didn't think you would rebut."

"You didn't think I would fight to keep my wife? Did you really think I would be happy to see you go?"

"Yes, I did. I still think so." His argument was making her dizzy; had she been wrong?

"So what do I tell people? That my wife just left when I wasn't looking?" His voice cracked.

"Tell people the truth: I was more trouble than I was worth, and you're glad I'm gone."

Charles flinched. He fell forward, down on one knee so that his face was nearly at hers. Any stranger walking in might think he was proposing marriage, not pleading to save one. "How can you say that I'm glad you're gone? You can't believe that."

"I can say it, and I do believe it." She had gone over it in her mind so many times. "Have you stopped seeing Geraldine Forrest since I left?" She searched his eyes for the truth.

"She has only sought to console me during this difficult time." His hands had taken hers in his now, and he was clutching them hard.

"How do you think you would fare with a wife on your arm who was always the subject of whispers and innuendo?"

"Stop talking nonsense. Just say you'll come home with me. You don't know how it tortures me to know that my weakness has brought us to this point."

She could see the pleading in his eyes. This was his last stand. She thought of how it would be to go back to the way it was in those first weeks in Chicago when there was so much hope. "It will never be like it was, and I don't want the life that awaits me there. Long days alone in the house because no one will be seen with me, no letters, no invitations." She stopped. That was not the true reason. Not since Hossam. He had never asked her to pretend to be something she was not. He loved her for herself, with all the flaws and imperfections. Dora put her hand on his shoulder. "Go back to Chicago. My place is here."

Charles stood and ran his fingers around the rim of his hat again. "So this is how it is?"

Dora nodded.

He slipped his hand into his jacket pocket and produced another sheet of folded paper. Slowly he opened it and handed it to her. "I was afraid that was how you might feel. I wish things could be different, but if they cannot, I must ask you to sign this."

Dora took the paper. Across the top it read "Dissolution of Marriage."

"Geraldine thinks your note alone will not be enough to secure a divorce."

"Geraldine Forrest? She has a part in this?"

"She's only looking out for my interests."

Of course, Geraldine Forrest would always be involved. "I'll sign this, and you will be free. And there's one more thing I'd like to say to put your mind at ease: Do not berate yourself too harshly about your weakness. You see, you weren't the only one who strayed." She glanced up and noted his incredulous expression. "Let's just say good-bye and put it behind us."

"I wish it had turned out differently."

His words were barely out when the dressing room door opened again. Bonmarie was there. "*Chere*, it's time."

Dora stood and checked herself quickly in the mirror. "That's my cue. I must go."

He took a deep breath and nodded. "I'll see myself out."

Dora extended a hand formally and he took it. Words died in her throat. When she let go, she could not look at him, just went to the door. She untied the sash holding her robe in place and let it slip down to the floor. She imagined she could hear Charles gasp at what he saw: Dora garbed in a wide sapphire silk skirt, and snug stocking shirt, a velvet vest trimmed in shimmering golden fringe, beads and baubles hanging around her neck, bangles on her wrists.

She left the room and passed Hossam standing in the wings. He held her gaze for a long moment, and she felt suddenly lighter, freer, than even that day so long ago when she'd danced in Congo Square. Quickly she kissed him. "Wish me luck, my love," she said.

He grabbed her around the waist. "Are you sure you want to do this?"

She kissed him again. His lips held hers and he pulled her close.

"This is what I want," she whispered into his ear. "You and this, all of it. This is where I belong."

The music cued and he released her slowly. She moved to her place behind the stage curtain, waiting for the master of ceremonies' introduction: "Ladies and gentlemen, with a glance she can entrance; with the sweep of her hand she lifts mortals to the heavens. Sheiks and kings and maharajas fall under her spell. All the way from the streets of Cairo, we bring you the Midway Plaisance sensation, Little Egypt!"

The drummer tapped a slow beat to set the mood.

The theater owner hadn't cared that Dora wasn't an Egyptian, only that she could dance like one. When he'd pressed her for a name, something to splash across the marquee, Dora Chambers wouldn't do, and even Dora Devereaux no longer felt right. In a rush, she'd thought of that remarkable camel, that creature who wasn't born in Egypt but whom the Egyptians had accepted as one of their own.

The horn began to weave a melody around the drummer's beat. She adjusted her finger cymbals and let the music seep inside her. Then she worked the small brass discs, creating the rapid brass percussion, and strutted confidently onto the stage. The belly dancer had arrived.

Acknowledgments

Writing is a funny thing. People call it a lonely business because an author's work is generally done by oneself, sequestered in a room with one's thoughts and either a computer keyboard or a notebook and a pen.

But the truth is, authors don't do it alone. I have been privileged to have had help and guidance from many people along the way, and to each of them I owe a hefty debt of gratitude.

First and foremost, I would like to thank my amazing agent, Ellen Pepus. Her vision and enthusiasm transformed my slush-pile submission into the book it is today.

And I would be nowhere without my extraordinary editor, Jackie Cantor. She is a dynamo and a delight who has taught me so much through this process. I will be forever in her debt.

I am also deeply thankful for the exceptional artwork created by artistic director Judith Lagerman and illustrator Alan Ayers for the book's cover. It astounds me still that they captured the mood of the story and the beauty of belly dance so perfectly in a single image.

I would also like to acknowledge my parents—all four of them—and my brother, who've always told me I could accomplish whatever I set out to do, and have made me want to prove them right.

I have also had the support of many dear friends—Alane, Catherine, Diane, and Tina in particular—who encouraged me and helped me believe anything was possible. My writing group buddies Claudia, Diane, and Kathy offered invaluable insight and kind words during early drafts of this novel.

In my writing, I am inspired by many instructors and mentors, including Lynette Brasfield, Phyllis Gebauer, Lisa Glatt, Caroline Leavitt, Lou Nelson, and Lisa Teasley. Many other teachers and mentors, particularly Angelika Nemeth, inspired my love for the art and history of belly dance.

I am also deeply thankful to authors Wendy Buonoventura and Karin Nieuwkerk for their examination of the history of belly dance, and especially to Donna Carlton for her investigation into the identity of belly-dancing legend Little Egypt.

Finally, I would like to thank my husband, Austin, for bringing so much joy into my life. He makes me the luckiest woman in the world.

Historical Note

This story is inspired by the legend of Little Egypt, a turn-of-the-last-century dancer who has become one of the most well-known and enduring figures in the world of belly dance. While it is a work of fiction and the main characters are purely inventions of my imagination, the truth is that the identity of the original Little Egypt is still a source of debate among historians.

Many women over the years have claimed to be the original Little Egypt, and a widely accepted theory is that Little Egypt was a Middle Eastern woman who danced at the Street in Cairo exhibit on the Midway Plaisance of the 1893 Chicago World's Fair. Some, such as author and history professor Robert Muccigrosso, identify her as a Syrian dancer named Fahreda Mahzar—often billed as Fatima—who performed, as he writes in *Celebrating the New World: Chicago's Columbian Exposition of 1893*, "the genuine native muscle dance" from the Nile region, and who acquired the "Little Egypt" moniker as her backstage nickname.

Extensive research done by author and dancer Donna Carlton offers another explanation. Carlton spent years poring over records, photographs, and other documents, and never found concrete evidence that a dancer ever performed on the Midway under the name Little Egypt. That name, she argues in *Looking for Little Egypt*, didn't become well-known until a few years after the World's Fair closed, when Ashea Wabe, a dancer in New York who went by the stage name Little Egypt, became the focus of a notorious police investigation detailed at the time in the *New York Times* and in other newspapers around the country. In that investigation, Police Captain George S. Chapman was charged with improperly raiding a dinner held December 19, 1896, by Herbert Barnum Seeley for his brother, Clinton Barnum Seeley, and other prominent men—an incident that came to be known as the "Awful Seeley Dinner"—where Wabe and other dancers had been hired to perform indecent dances.

Carlton's theory also supports what Sol Bloom, the entertainment entrepreneur largely responsible for the Midway Plaisance, states in his 1948 autobiography. He writes, "I most emphatically deny that I had anything whatever to do with a female entertainer known professionally as Little Egypt. At no time during the Chicago fair did this character appear on the Midway."

As I've said, my characterization of Little Egypt is purely fictional, but the camel she meets, which leads to her choice of stage name, was inspired by something Sol Bloom purportedly said decades after the Fair while he served in the U.S. House of Representatives. A newspaper clipping held in the Chicago Historical Society Library's collection shows that he told a reporter, via his secretary, that no dancer performed as Little Egypt on the Midway, but that it had been the name of one of the Street in Cairo riding camels. Bloom never implied the connection that I have made in the novel, but I found the comment to be compelling nonetheless.

In addition to Bloom, other historical figures who play important roles in this story are Potter Palmer and his wife, Bertha Honoré Palmer, as well as Eadweard Muybridge. I have done my best to portray them accurately within the story's framework, and incorporated documented facts about their lives, such as Potter Palmer's precedent-setting move to the Gold Coast, Bertha Honoré Palmer's leadership of the Fair's Board of Lady Managers, and Muybridge's passion for his moving-picture invention housed in the Fair's Zoopraxographical Hall.

For further reading about the 1893 Chicago World's Fair, I recommend:

The Autobiography of Sol Bloom (G. P. Putnam's Sons, 1948), by Sol Bloom.

Celebrating the New World: Chicago's Columbian Exposition of 1893 (Ivan R. Dee, 1993), by Robert Muccigrosso.

The Chicago World's Fair of 1893: A Photographic Record (Dover Publications, Inc., 1980), text by Stanley Appelbaum.

The Devil in the White City: Murder, Magic, and Madness at the Fair That Changed America (Crown, 2003), by Erik Larson.

Looking for Little Egypt (IDD Books, 1994), by Donna Carlton.